SEALed
WITH
A KISS

MARY MARGRET
DAUGHTRIDGE

SOURCEBOOKS CASABLANCA™
AN IMPRINT OF SOURCEBOOKS, INC.®
NAPERVILLE, ILLINOIS

Sourcebooks and the colophon are registered trademarks of Sourcebooks, Inc.

Published by Sourcebooks, Inc.
P.O. Box 4410, Naperville, Illinois 60567-4410
(630) 961-3900
FAX: (630) 961-2168
www.sourcebooks.com

Library of Congress Cataloging-in-Publication Data
ISBN-13: 978-1-4022-1118-8
ISBN-10: 1-4022-1118-X

Printed and bound in the United States of America
10 9 8 7 6 5 4 3 2 1

DEDICATION

To my mother, Besse Holloman, who taught me to love words,

To my tenth-grade English teacher, Dorothy Powell, who taught me to craft with those words,

And

To Diane Spitler, an extraordinary friend who, even from the Other Side, made me write a book.

ACKNOWLEDGMENT

Working on book isn't a realistic thing to do. It's an act of faith. Without faith in a book's possibility, contributed by many people other than the writer, a book doesn't come into existence.

Elsa McKeithan kept the faith through my ups and downs of writer-angst while I chiseled characters from the bedrock of my unconscious. Katherine Highfill held out the carrot of Starbuck's once a week, if I'd show up with a rewritten chapter. MariBeth Graham could discuss theme, premise and plot, could cut a synopsis to the bone, and knew when Mercury was retrograde.

Yvonne Harris, Jennifer Loman, and Amy Padgett ignored their own writing many times to squeeze me under deadlines. Nancy Yow proofread the manuscript on her vacation, and Ben Wilson rescued lost files.

All credit for insider feel goes to two former SEALs, John Carl Roat, and Martin Strong. They not only answered hundreds of emails, they exemplify the generosity, humor, and perseverance of the men who put the "special" in Special Operations. Lt. Josh Wilson provided modern navy background. Any errors are my own.

Sensitive to the nuances of character-based plot, Stephanie Evans, agent extraordinaire, and Deb Werksman of Sourcebooks, suggested changes, subtle yet powerful, that brought the book to its final form.

Finally, when talking about faith, I must mention Pat Moore, Glenda Gayle Sink, and Alma Pendergast who had the fortitude to read rough drafts and still believe the book was publishable, and my family—Daughtridges, Greens, and Hollomans—for contributing their faith by believing in me.

ONE

LITTLE CREEK, VIRGINIA

Sometimes, even the most dedicated worka-
holic needs to unwind in a low class dive,
Jax Graham mused with self-deprecating
humor. He signaled the bar girl to bring him and
Do-Lord two more beers. The Sea Shanty, as neon
grunge on the inside as it was dilapidated on the
outside, always lived down to its name. A smart
man would be grateful darkness hid the dirt, and
the odors of beer and ancient cigarette smoke
obliterated smells even less savory. Nobody who
gave a damn would see him, a lieutenant, having a
drink with his best friend, Caleb "Do-Lord"
Dulaude, a Chief Petty Officer.

The beer joint would fill up later with a
volatile mix of bikers, SEALs, and Marines, but
it was early now. Only a few tables were occupied.

In one corner a couple of SEAL groupies used
a lazy game of pool to offer generous displays of

tits and ass, occasionally casting acquisitive eyes in Jax and Do-Lord's direction.

The tall blonde wasn't bad, Jax mused in unconscious, automatic assessment, but neither girl was anything special. Still neither one would leave alone at closing time—not that he'd be here to see it.

Picking up groupies or closing down bars wasn't something he did much anymore. He'd done plenty of both five years ago after Danielle left him, taking his baby son. But it didn't take him long to learn all he got out of it was hangovers. Hard work and dedication turned out to be more effective for blotting out the pain. And it paid off in advancement of his career. Since his latest deployment to Afghanistan his superiors had recommended him for early promotion to Lt. Commander.

Ironic. Danielle left him because being a SEAL claimed most of his time. But after she took Tyler the only thing that eased his grief was spending even more time at work. Danielle's death last month wouldn't really impact the life he lived now at all. It gave him a hollow feeling, but it was the truth.

"You haven't said much." Do-Lord's soft Alabama drawl slid easily through the happy hour chatter. "You worried about Commander Kohn chewing you out?" That his friend knew what had taken place behind closed doors between him and his mentor didn't surprise Jax. Chiefs knew everything.

"Nah," Jax used the bottom of his beer mug to press interlocking rings of condensation on the table top until he made an Olympic symbol. "It's not a problem."

Do-Lord made a dubious rumbling sound, and raised one reddish eyebrow.

"Okay, yeah, I was ticked. Kohn questions whether I really know what I'm doing about my son. He kept asking how often I see Tyler. Shit. How much does any SEAL see his kids? And because Danielle and I were divorced, I saw him even less."

"He thinks you should bring Tyler to live with you?"

"No, he didn't tell me what to do, except to make sure I spent some time with Tyler—more than a couple of days—before I made up my mind." Jax scrubbed at his hairline with a fist, a habit when he was frustrated—a habit he thought he'd broken. "But here's the deal. Sure, custody reverted to me at Danielle's death, but I know what it's like to be raised by housekeepers and babysitters. Screw 'im. I'm doing what I think is right."

Jax could feel Do-Lord listening, though he said nothing. Jax went on, a little calmer, "Giving custody of Tyler to his grandmother is the only plan that makes any sense. I'm not palming him off. She wants him. I don't like her but Lauren loves Tyler and he's already living with her."

Do-Lord's sympathetic smile said he understood the bad blood that existed between Jax and his ex-mother-in-law. But his raw-boned face immediately turned serious again. "Maybe you ought to be worried, though." Do-Lord's light green eyes leveled a look at Jax. "Face it man, it ain't natural for commanders to chew out lieutenants over filling out child care forms. He coulda and he shoulda passed that duty down the chain of command. Kohn could have you discharged if he's not happy with the provisions you make for Tyler. And I think he'd do it."

Jax grinned inwardly. Do-Lord's homespun manner fooled a lot of people. Like his sandy red hair and slow speech, it made effective camouflage for his incisive intelligence. But he was taking Kohn's threats too seriously.

Jax shook his head. "You know how Kohn is when he gets the family responsibility bug up his ass. Tyler's already lost his mother. Why should he be ripped from the one person he really knows? Tyler's going to be taken care of. It's essentially the same custody agreement I had with Danielle. Now, it's just a matter of signing the papers."

Do-Lord tilted his head and looked at Jax through narrowed eyes. "You really think it will be that easy?" he inquired softly.

Do-Lord's question fell into one of those conversational lulls. For a moment the bar was so quiet Jax could hear the click of billiard balls in the corner. "My lawyer's ex-Navy. He'll make sure everything is regulation," he said, but he knew that wasn't what his friend was asking. Finally he said the thing he hadn't said to Kohn, or even to himself. "It's like this, I don't see that I'm losing anything I ever had."

Uncomfortable at revealing so much, Jax pressed a wet circle on the battered table top, then bisected it with another circle.

Do-Lord pointed to the wet circles. "You made a vessica piscis."

Good friend that he was, Do-Lord was offering a change of subject. Jax canted a humorous eyebrow. "You know the damnedest things." It was a mark of the trust between them that Do-Lord would reveal what an information-sponge his brain was. "What the hell is a...a whatever you said?"

"It's a symbol meaning enlightenment through union with the Divine Feminine principle. See?" Do-Lord pointed to the lens shape formed where the two circles intersected. "It looks sort of like," Do-Lord's eyes twinkled with deadpan humor, "the feminine portal."

"Feminine portal!" Jax hooted. "You know what, you've been talking funny ever since you read all those romance novels while we were in Afghanistan." Jax laughed again then tilted his head one way and then the other to peer at the shape he'd made. "Well, damn! It sort of does. Okay, you're the guy with the psych degree, how do you interpret my spontaneous Rorschach?"

Do-Lord took a swig of beer. "I think it means you need to get laid."

Both men chuckled and settled deeper into the scarred wooden armchairs. After a moment Jax broke the easy silence.

"I was just thinking about something the Commander said...Do you think a lot of men wonder if their children are really theirs?" Do-Lord had never been married and had no children, but there wasn't another man on earth Jax would have shared his musings with.

Do-Lord scratched his upper lip with a knuckle. "I don't know. I guess the question has got to enter your mind sometimes. Specially considering how much we're away." Do-Lord straightened abruptly in his chair. "Hey man, you don't wonder about Tyler, do you? His latest picture looks just like you. He even stands like you."

Jax grinned at his friend's earnest reassurances. "I don't wonder now. But I did." He leaned forward resting his forearms on the table. "You know when they're born—they're so little it scares the hell out of you, and they're all red and mashed-looking? They don't look like you."

He let out a soft, humorous snort, "They don't even exactly look human. And then, they put him in my hands…" He spread his fingers to show how Tyler had fit.

Jax found he had to clear his throat of a sticky feeling, and stare at the ceiling until a hot sensation in his eyes passed, "and I felt so…umhmm."

Jax covered the suspicious crack in his voice with another bout of throat clearing, and began again. "The point is, I knew I would gladly die for him. I didn't care whose son he was. From that moment on he was mine."

Five days later: Topsail Island, North Carolina

Heat, built up through the day, blasted Pickett as soon as she opened the door to the unoccupied beach house. She was going to sweat through her silk blouse and shantung slacks, which would mean a dry cleaning bill. She considered putting off preparing the elderly couple's cottage for a hurricane until morning.

No, her mother would be on the phone tonight wanting to know if it was done.

Pickett had to quell a surge of resentment. Her mother had a tendency to use Pickett's time as if it were her own. It was easy for her to tell Mrs. Howell, "Pickett lives at the beach now. She'll just be glad to shut off everything and close the storm shutters."

Well, 'Pickett' didn't live on the beach! she fumed. She lived 30 minutes away in Snead's Ferry, where over her mother's and sisters' protests, Pickett was restoring the family home-place. You'd think, having spent childhood summers in the house Pickett now occupied, her mother would be able to tell the difference between a house on the beach and one on the sound!

Pickett let out a huff of exasperation with herself. If it was pointless to argue with her mother face to face, it was truly futile to argue with her in her mind.

Besides her mother was right, partly. The kindly couple who were her mother's next-door neighbors were getting frail. They still clung to the beach cottage they loved, but a frantic two-hour trip from Goldsboro to batten down the hatches would be hard on them.

So it was Pickett's own fault if her therapist attire got ruined. Nobody made her come straight from her job at Camp Le Jeune instead of stopping at home to change into shorts.

Leaving the door open, she crossed the expanse of the great room and opened the ocean-side door. Instantly a strong cross breeze began to pull through the house, but even so, the cottage wouldn't cool off before she was done.

Battling the roller-shade style storm shutters took the longest time. Not designed for someone 5'3" to operate, even on tiptoe the catches were almost beyond her reach. Like most island cottages, the Howell's was built on pilings.

Theoretically it was only one story, but, in fact, if she fell out the window from which she leaned precariously, it was a two-story drop.

Her stomach quivered every time she looked down. Sometimes, like now, she hated that she was such a wimp. It only made doing what you had to do harder.

Kind of like getting married. Not that she had to, but she wanted to. Sometimes when playing with a client's child, her arms ached to hold babies of her own. Her mom said she was too choosy, there ought to be one marriageable man among the hundreds she saw everyday at LeJeune. But Pickett knew exactly the kind of man she needed to complete her dream of a stable, secure marriage, and it wasn't a military one. She'd seen way too much of how the stresses of military life caused marriages to fail.

Sweat prickled at her hairline and made her silk shirt cling damply to her shoulders by the time Pickett stepped onto the deck of the cottage. It was hot out here too, in the afternoon sunlight, too sultry feeling for October. But after the stifling heat inside the cottage, the wind that lifted her golden curls felt wonderful.

Pickett loosened another button of her barn-red shirt to allow the breeze to reach her breasts. She ran her eyes over the long flight of weathered steps that crossed over the dune and led down to the beach. If the hurricane lurking off the coast struck, they'd probably be torn away.

Already the surf had taken on that odd, booming sound that heralded a storm at sea. Tides were running above normal, nibbling at the base of the dunes in some places, pushing the threat of the ocean closer. But as long as the dune held, the cottage would be okay.

Unless the hurricane strengthened.

Up and down the shoreline, gold and blue in the afternoon sun, the broad expanse of sand was almost deserted. No gulls swooped. No sand pipers played tag with the ocean's advancing and retreating edge. Already they were seeking shelter in the deep marshes and protected coves of the sound. Pickett murmured a little prayer for the safety of all wild things.

It seemed the only creatures left on the beach were herself and a man and a little boy sitting in the soft sand in front of the cottage next door.

The man, muscular brown arms clasped around raised knees, sat looking out to sea. The little boy dressed in coordinating red striped shirt and red shorts, half-squatted, half-knelt outside the reach of the man, playing joylessly with toy trucks. He kept his face averted, shoulders hunched.

Hmm. This didn't look right. Subtle signals passed between people who were emotionally close, even if separated by a crowded room: the set of a shoulder, matching tilt of a head, unconscious synchronization of hand movements. If she had to guess she'd say this pair were keenly aware of— yet pretending to ignore—each other. Rather like two shy strangers. But from their matching seal-brown hair, Pickett presumed they were related.

Therapist instincts aroused, Pickett went down the steps to the first landing to see them better.

The man picked up a blue and yellow kite and said something over his shoulder to the child. The little boy's shoulders hunched tighter and he shook his head. The man said something else and got the same response.

So. The man was trying to interact, and judging from the restless movement of his powerful shoulders was losing patience.

He probably thought the child who looked four, maybe five was being sulky, peevish. He probably didn't know the little boy's defensive crouch was typical for an insecure child who was afraid of doing the wrong thing, and so wouldn't do anything.

The sun was bright, the ocean dark blue and sparkling, with only a few more white caps than usual. A day to rejoice in, but they looked so lonely. It broke Pickett's heart.

They wanted to be together yet neither one knew how.

It would be so simple, a piece of cake, really, to show them how to get into rapport. The thought lured her like the scent of chocolate.

Pickett squeezed her eyes closed so she wouldn't see them and be tempted. Uh-uh. No. No. No. They weren't her clients, and it wasn't any of her business.

Taking herself metaphorically by the scruff of the neck, she turned back to the task of closing the shutters on the ocean side of the cottage. Thank goodness she could stand on the deck to reach them.

As the shutter clanked into place, Pickett felt herself light up. There was another way to look at it! From his superb physical condition he could be a Marine from nearby Camp LeJeune. If he was, then her part-time job with family services there could make it her business.

Pickett squashed the thought. She was a soft touch and she knew it, but no matter how much she wanted to rescue, she had no right to intervene unless asked.

She snapped the shutter into its slot, then, still drawn by the puzzle of the pair on the beach, moved to the rail to peer down at them.

As if he had felt her eyes on him, the man's head smoothly swiveled like a lion's surveying his territory. His own eyes were hidden by aviator sunglasses, and yet a jolt that sprinkled goose flesh up her arms told Pickett the instant he spotted her.

Embarrassed to be caught staring she gave a little wave and almost turned away, but hesitated when the man's rather forbidding expression gave way to a smile of great charm.

Just like that, Pickett made up her mind. If there was any place on earth it was acceptable for a stranger to casually walk up and start talking, it was on a beach.

Quickly, she stepped out of her low-heeled pumps, stripped off her stockings and started down the steps.

Maybe this day was looking up, Jax thought, watching the shapely woman skip down the steps of the cottage next door. Unless the hurricane struck ahead of schedule, it sure couldn't get much worse.

Monumentally bored with inactivity, more frustrated by Tyler's refusal to play than he cared to admit, he'd watched her watching them from the deck of the cottage next door. He couldn't help but grin at the still intensity with which she studied them. It said she was interested. Very interested.

It wasn't a novel experience for Lt. Jackson Graham, US Navy SEAL, to catch the eye of a pretty woman, though if he met one on the beach, he'd prefer she was in a bikini. He watched her however because right now any distraction, even a fully dressed one, from the hopeless task of doing quality time with Tyler was welcome.

When she reached the base of the steps, she waved and turned his way. His lungs expanded with what felt like the first satisfaction in days. He tilted his head, riding a wave of masculine calculation. O-o-o-h yeah. She was going to come to him.

Pickett might dither, but once she made up her mind, she didn't look back.

It would be child's play—literally!—for her to get rapport with the boy herself, but that wasn't what she wanted. How to get him into rapport with his father without seeming to, that was the question.

The soft sand near the dunes was warm on top, cool underneath, a sensation Pickett relished with her bare feet. The breeze, stronger near the water, snatched locks of gold hair from the clasp at the nape of her neck, and caused the legs of her beige slacks to snap and flutter. She let her mind turn over strategies for approaching the pair.

The little boy's body language said he felt something was wrong, something he was helpless to fix. Okay. She would confirm for him that something was wrong, but make it completely external to him. Then she would offer him some action to take to make it right. Boys his age were still engaging in parallel, rather than interactive play, one reason the kite and ball hadn't worked well, so if she had to, she would just plain tell the father to play beside him.

The man rose from the sand in one smooth motion. His welcoming smile was confident, bordering on arrogant, and just for a second Pickett wondered what on earth she had gotten herself into.

Only of average height or maybe a little above, he nevertheless seemed to command the entire beach as if it, or maybe the whole world, was his.

Suddenly she could feel the heaviness of her breasts, and the way the wind pressed the red silk of her blouse against them. The heavier silk of her slacks, moved in a sensuous slide, outlining then fluttering around her legs.

The salt breeze carried the scent of his sun-warmed skin overlaid with coconut oil sunscreen, and she inhaled reflexively. She ignored the way her heart was beating much too hard and told herself to get a grip. Working at a Marine base Pickett dealt with well-built, thoroughly masculine men all the time. How different could this one be? Resolutely she held her hair out of her eyes with her left hand, and thrust out her right.

"Hey." She infused her tone with a combination of friendliness and authority. "I'm Pickett

Sessoms. I noticed y'all from the deck of the Howell's cottage. I thought I should warn you two that both of you are wasting that sand over there," she indicated the strip of firm sand beyond the reach of the breakers, "and that's wrong. In fact, it's a crime."

Jax's smile broadened at her cheerfully imperious tone. As a pick up line, it was a little thin, but he'd give her points for originality. He still wished for the bikini, but he would settle for shorts. Nobody needed to be that formally dressed on a beach.

Her hand in his was slightly cool, tiny, and soft. So soft. She was tiny all over. He wondered if she was this soft all over.

"I'm Jax Graham. This is my son, Tyler. Stand up, son," he added in gentle command. "You don't sit when a lady is standing."

Tyler scrambled to his feet grudgingly, then stood head down, rolling a car up and down his chest. Typical. Would a good father prompt him to speak? How the hell was he supposed to know?

The woman was tugging on her hand. He released her and slid off his sunglasses so he could look directly into her eyes. "We've been committing a crime, huh? Are you going to arrest us?"

"Nope," a tiny dimple dotted the corner of her mouth though she continued to pretend to look stern. "I'm going to let you off with a warning this time."

Pickett bent down to look in Tyler's face, not easy, as he kept his head down. "Besides," she added with soft compassion, "you didn't mean to do anything wrong, did you?" Tyler shook his head and sidled closer to his father. "That's okay then."

Still speaking to the child, she went on. "If you and your daddy work together, there'll be time before the tide comes back in to build a sand castle, and then you wouldn't be wasting the beach. Have you ever built a castle in the sand?"

Tyler shrugged, then as he realized she was going to wait for a reply, raised grey crystal eyes so like his father's to her face. "Maybe. When I was little."

Pickett straightened and transferred her attention to Jax. "How about you? Have you ever built a sand castle?"

Wow. A couple of sentences and she had the kid talking to her. Whatever she was doing worked. If she wanted to concentrate on charming Tyler, he'd play along. "Maybe," he drawled, loading his tone with innuendo. "When I was little."

"Good!" The perfect bow of her lips primmed in smile of officious satisfaction. "If the two of you get right to work, you can fix your problem with the sand."

Suddenly her mouth opened in an 'O' of horror. She smacked her forehead. "Oh no! What was I thinking? You can't build a sand castle! You don't have a dump truck."

"Nuh-uhn!" Tyler scooped a toy truck from the sand at his feet. "I have a dump truck! See?"

Pickett's huge sigh of relief made it clear they'd had an extremely narrow escape. "That is so lucky," she deadpanned. "I don't suppose you have a sand pail and shovel, though."

Tyler smiled. His too thin cheeks grew pink and his grey eyes glittered with little boy enthusiasm. "I do! Gan-gan got me one. I'll go get it." Heels flying he raced for the steps up to the cottage.

Deep inside Jax a knot, an agonizing twist he'd lived with so long it didn't feel like pain any more, loosened.

Stunned, not sure what he'd witnessed, Jax turned to the woman who had changed everything. Unaware of his scrutiny, she was watching his son climb as fast as his skinny little legs would carry him. Intelligence sparkled in her ocean colored eyes. Lips pursed, cheeks bunched, she looked like a woman delighted with a job well done.

Was he an ass or what? She hadn't come down those steps to flirt with him. At all. He registered the tiny prick to his ego, while a real regret that he might've met her at the wrong time and in the wrong place grew.

He had the oddest feeling that he was just now, for the first time, seeing what she really looked like.

She was more wholesome-looking than pretty, coral tinged cheeks free of make up. The wind, having freed her curls from the tortoiseshell clasp at her nape, was busy whipping them into a golden froth. Though a trained observer, like himself, wouldn't miss the tiny waist, or full breasts, in a flash of insight he saw that those too serious clothes had been chosen to conceal her charms more than complement them.

She turned to him now, one golden eyebrow lifted in a smile that invited him to share the triumph.

In a voice gone scratchy with wonder he said, "Who are you, lady? I've been trying for three days to get that kid to smile. What the hell did you just do?"

TWO

Tyler had withdrawn again by the time he returned, bumping the yellow plastic pail against his knee. "Now, you have to look for the perfect spot," Pickett told Tyler with calm, kind authority. "You need sand that's wet, but not too close to the breakers."

"Here?" Tyler asked with that little quaver in his voice that sliced off a piece of Jax's soul.

"I don't know." Pickett tapped her cheek with a forefinger. "Look around some more. You'll know it when you find it."

Tyler moved a few feet. "Here?"

Pickett waggled a hand. "Maybe. Does it look right to you?"

Tyler looked around. Really looked. Jax could almost see the shell Tyler had pulled around himself open to let the world in. "I see it! Over there!" Knees and arms flying, kicking up little spurts of sand, the little boy raced to another spot.

"All right," Pickett's coral lips moved in a secret smile, "if you're sure."

Tyler jerked his little chin. "Right here."

"In that case, you've got a castle to build. Get to work." Jax had been so engrossed watching her maneuver Tyler into claiming the project as his own, he was jolted to realize her gaze was fixed on him with a look in her ocean-colored eyes that read and this means you.

Then she knelt in front of Tyler and looked directly into his face. "You know that you are the king, don't you?"

Tyler shook his head and pointed at Jax.

"Uh-uh. On this castle, you're the king." With a conspiratorial jerk of her head she indicated Jax, "Can't you see how strong he is? On this castle" she gave a magic nose twitch, "he's the bulldozer."

Tyler ducked his head and giggled.

Pickett's expressive face lit with humor that a flick of her gold-flecked eyes invited Jax to share. Then lingered longer than it had to. A lot longer.

She inhaled sharply, then stood, slapping sand from her knees. "I think you two will do fine without me, now. I'd better get back to work closing up the cottage."

With polite "Nice to meet you" and a cheerful wave she was gone, striding with light grace across the slipping sand.

That poised grace was the first thing he had noticed about her, when he'd seen her standing on the deck of the cottage next door.

With the sun in his eyes she'd been only a feminine shape. But he knew, even then, no matter how she moved all parts would be in exquisite balance. She'd invested the simple act of standing with a regal air as if the flick of her finger would command him to come to her.

Jax added some arrow slits to the tower he was building. His eyes crinkled. Apparently, she was right. He was hers to command. He and Tyler were building a sand castle, weren't they?

But she was aware of him too. She might hold her head at that snooty angle and try to save all her warm smiles for Tyler, but sometimes she forgot. And then the heat that arched between them...yowsa.

"Dig over here," Tyler indicated a section of moat he wanted widened, and Jax obligingly moved beside him to begin scooping.

He could have her, he mused, pressing the sides of the moat. It would take some work...he crunched the thought like an empty beer can. Okay, he admitted he had a weakness for women like that, challenging women who turned on his hunting instincts, but he was a man who learned from his mistakes.

Women like Pickett were high-maintenance. They expected a lot. Too much. Marriage to Danielle had taught him all he wanted to know about high-maintenance women.

Now he looked for women who could be satisfied with what was left over from his SEAL career. Easy-going, good-natured women who knew the score. Those relationships didn't last either, but nobody got hurt. It was a price he paid.

The tide was coming in, filling the moat he and Tyler had dug, making Tyler crow with delight, but also sucking away some of the exterior fortifications. Deep blue shadows striped the beach as the sun sank into the sound behind the cottages.

Tyler's arms and legs were coated with sand. His hair stood up from his forehead where he had pushed it back with a sandy hand. His red striped shirt was wrinkled and his matching red shorts were wet up one leg and across the bottom. Those fancy designer clothes were fairly well wrecked. Jax grinned. At least he looked like a boy.

A retreating wave carved out a section of rampart Jax had just reinforced.

"That's it Tyler. It's time to go in."

"No. I don't want to." The whispered protest from the suddenly hunched over child was almost inaudible.

It wasn't often that anyone told Jax "No." He encouraged his men to disagree, to freely share their opinions about the best way to accomplish an objective, but once he told them to move, they moved.

"Now. Move it."

Short dark lashes screening his grey eyes, Tyler hunched even further, exposing the vulnerable nape of his neck that looked too slender to hold his head. "I don't want to," he mumbled even more softly.

Jax's lean jaw tightened in an all too familiar helpless frustration, then he shrugged. Tyler's refusal was progress, he supposed. Before they worked together on the sand castle, Tyler rarely spoke to him at all.

He tossed the toy trucks into the pail, then tucking the unresisting child against his hip, headed up the beach stairs.

On the deck, Tyler neither cooperated nor fought as he was peeled out of his sandy clothes and rinsed under the deck shower. Jax ignored Lauren's screech at the sight of the naked kid being thrust through the door. He wondered how she gave Tyler a bath without looking at him naked. Jax thought the little white buns disappearing into the back bedroom were kind of cute.

"Tyler," he called out on impulse. When the beautifully shaped little head snapped toward him, he grinned mischievously and gave a broad wink. Whatever response he hoped for was disappointed. Tyler went a little white and ducked into his room.

Jax faced the beach and gripped the weathered deck rail hard enough to crumble splinters from it. It wasn't as if he usually did the right thing where Tyler was concerned, but damn. He didn't know why the sight of that white face bothered him so much. He'd wanted the little guy to grin back and share a guy-moment, but it hadn't happened. So what?

Until the light was almost gone, Jax watched their castle melt in the oncoming breakers.

Through the sliding glass doors, Jax could see Tyler in dry shorts and shirt, playing with his trucks on the floor. Didn't the kid ever do anything but play with those trucks?

Tyler didn't scoot over when Jax opened the slider, so Jax stepped over him rather than edging around. It looked like the concord they had reached as they built ramps and molded turrets was over.

He was acting once again like his father was invisible—or like he wished he was.

Baffled, Jax wondered again if Lauren was right. Had he really seen Tyler so rarely in his short life that he didn't know what the kid was like?

But damn it, he'd seen him as often as he could, and if Danielle hadn't been such a bitch about visitation, he'd have seen him more. If he missed a visit because his leave was cancelled—all too likely—or because he was away on training, Danielle wouldn't allow him to make it up. He had to wait for the next scheduled visit, when the same thing could happen.

But the thing was, for a little while on the beach. Tyler had seemed more like the kid he remembered.

"Jax," Lauren stood at the cooktop in the kitchen area patting chicken pieces with a paper towel. Her glazed eyes indicated she'd already made inroads on the cocktail hour. "I've decided to make fresh corn salsa to go with the chicken, and I'll need cilantro. Would you go to the supermarket on the causeway and get some?"

Jax might think his ex-mother–in-law was a vain, silly, shallow woman, but she was a good cook, a hobby she indulged mostly at the beach. He'd rather take a shower, but it was a small enough thing to do for her.

"Sure," he said sliding into sandals and pulling a tee shirt on. He was reaching for wallet and keys when his cell phone beeped. He glanced at the caller ID. His lawyer.

"Okay, Mancini," he said without preamble, "why are you calling so late?"

"I wanted to tell you I'm faxing the custody papers with the changes Lauren has asked for. I gotta tell you, it looks to me like this woman is after money. Are you sure you want to give her permanent custody?"

Jax stepped through the sliders and pulled them closed behind him. The air on the deck seemed even warmer and more humid than before the sun had set. He hunkered down beside the hose, and turned on the water. Tucking the phone in the crook of his neck, he rinsed one arm, then the other. Had he been far enough from the spill of light from the great room, he would have stripped and stepped naked under the outdoor shower.

"We've been over this before. I paid Danielle alimony as well as child support. Why shouldn't I pay Lauren a living allowance? Anyway, I remain in control of Tyler's trust fund."

"So consider joint custody."

"Joint custody isn't feasible." What the hell. Jax whipped off his tee shirt and sluiced water over his chest, letting his shorts get wet. "I'm out of the country more than I'm in it. When I'm in the country, I work 36-hour days. Fixing things so that my signature is required will just result in delays and foul ups."

"Well, think it over one more time before you sign these papers. Tyler's too young to live with you now, but in a few years, he won't be. Once you give up custody of Tyler, it'll be hard to get back."

As Jax reached for the beach towel that hung over the deck rail, he looked through the glass doors at the child quietly crashing the toy blue Camaro off the sofa. He was already so different from the boisterous kid Jax remembered. In a few years, he wouldn't know him at all.

The pain that sliced through him took him totally by surprise. His own father hadn't known him. Ultimately had nothing to give him except money. Was that going to happen to him and Tyler? He pushed the thought away. He was nothing like his father. His father was a lawyer. He could have come home from his big time money-making whenever he wanted to.

"Jax, I'm talking to you like a friend here. I'm faxing the paper, but you don't have to sign it. We can at least come up with a visitation agreement that's fairer to you."

"It's essentially the same as the agreement I had with Danielle."

"Yeah. Well, it stank then and it stinks now."

Jax glanced at Tyler through the sliders. Why did he sit like that, crouched over his trucks? And why was he, Jax, arguing? Everything Mancini said was what he was just thinking a minute ago.

"You know what Mancini, you're right. Let me think it over and call you back tomorrow. In the mean time, go home to your kids."

Jax closed the phone and stepped back through the sliders.

"Tyler, do you want to ride to the grocery? We'll pick up some ice cream for dessert."

There was no answer from the small figure. "Tyler, you heard me. Do you want to go?" A tiny headshake was the only answer.

Okay, we were back to that. Jax let himself out the door.

As if she were the only woman in the place, he saw her almost as soon as he stepped into the brightly lit supermarket. For the space of a skipped heartbeat he thought his wish to see if he could coax a response from her had come true.

Even with her back turned, he'd know that queenly carriage anywhere. She looked all smooth and demure with her gold curls clasped once again at her nape. Expensive slacks, the color of vanilla ice cream and red silk blouse no longer fluttered in a stiff breeze but flowed from breast and hip.

She was deep in conversation with the deli clerk. Over and over, she would point to an item in the glass case, listen to the clerk's reply, then shake her head and point to another item.

Jax's fantasy of asking her for a date vanished with an almost audible pop. She was apparently going to make the clerk describe every single one of the prepared dishes before she made up her mind.

Oh, this lady with the superior attitude was high maintenance all right. This was one choosy woman. No wonder she reminded him of Danielle.

Nah. He might still have a knee jerk attraction to women like her, but he was older and wiser now. He didn't need the grief.

He turned toward the produce aisle.

Like prey that knows it has been spotted, Pickett felt the man's eyes on her. Jax. He was here. He was looking at her. Vital, and elemental from his sweat-dried hair to his strong brown feet, he seemed incongruous in the tameness of a grocery store. His face was impassive, his light grey eyes cold and remote. A small shiver chased over her scalp. This was a dangerous man. Not just military, he was a true warrior, a hunter.

He nodded almost imperceptibly and walked away.

Well. When somebody turns their back, literally, the body language is pretty clear. She'd already reminded herself a thousand times she was Not Interested, so she refused—she absolutely refused—to feel disappointment.

It took a minute for the deli clerk's impatient voice to shake her from her daze. "So have you decided, ma'am? Ma'am?"

THREE

Good old Hobo Joe, the three-legged German Shepard mix who lived on her porch when he felt like it, greeted Pickett when she pulled into her drive. He walked her to the kitchen door, but as always declined to come in. Behind the door, Patterson, part Lab, and Lucy, whose ancestry was undecipherable, snuffled and whined.

"Okay guys, let me in." You'd think the dogs would learn to stand back so she could get the door open, but they never seemed to. Instead, she had to push her way in, careful not to let doggie toes get pinched under the moving door. "Boy, the two of you make sure I don't come home to a silent house," Patterson used his superior height to try to sniff the deli bag. Pickett lifted it higher and tried not to step on Lucy who was snuffling her serviceable low-heeled pumps avidly.

"Where'd you go? Who'd you see? What did you bring me to eat?" Pickett spoke for Lucy. Dogs took in an amazing amount of information through smell. Maybe Lucy was extra curious because she smelled Jax. Setting the food on the counter, well away from the edge, Pickett kicked off her shoes.

The dogs, having sniffed and wagged to their satisfaction, ran to the back door and whined to be let out.

"Okay! Okay! Go on out and do your jobs, but come right back, because it's supper time." Pickett blessed the invisible fence that meant she no longer had to supervise potty time. She only wanted to get out of these clothes, and eat some supper.

She especially enjoyed the days she worked with her favorite project at Camp Lejeune—a group to overcome the social isolation of certain at-risk young mothers. But adding that group to the rest of her client load at the base made for a long day, and today she had made it even longer by stopping at the Howell's cottage.

And spending an hour or more with Jax and the little boy, Tyler.

Jax. Darn that man! He wouldn't get out of her mind. Pickett crossed the wide hall, stripping out of slacks and blouse even before she arrived at her bedroom. Pickett slipped the silk blouse onto a padded hanger. Had he followed her into the grocery? Surely not. The encounters must be random, and yet for a minute in the grocery, she had felt his gaze. And knew it was him even before she turned her head.

Sharp yips were coming from the back door. Pickett quickly pulled on an old pair of exercise shorts and tee shirt, both sizes too large, and hurried to let the dogs back in.

Dogs fed, she pulled the plastic container from the deli bag. She eyed the soggy artichoke salad with disfavor. This is what came of letting discipline slip in planning meals. And she'd been so rattled by Jax's sudden appearance she wasn't sure she'd asked about all the ingredients. She hesitated, sniffing the container carefully as she considered the possible consequences of eating unknown ingredients.

Oh well, a salad was unlikely to have hidden wheat in it. Wearily she dug a fork from the drawer and began to eat straight from the container, standing at the counter.

Jax. Her heart gave a funny little kick every time she thought of him. It was like he was determined to shoulder his way into her thoughts, no matter how she tried to push him out. Lack of closure, her therapist-self diagnosed, that was the problem.

Or, he must have some really potent pheromones.

Was this sense of magnetic pull, of attention being riveted on a person, what people meant when they talked about falling in love? She'd never been in love—a barrier sometimes to understanding what her clients were going through.

Pickett didn't believe in love.

Not the true-love stuff of romance novels. As a counselor she dealt with too many failed marriages, broken relationships to think that love was a strong enough glue to keep people together.

And in her experience, love certainly didn't make people happy. Respect, affection, shared humor, and values were more necessary than love to make a successful relationship.

And if that seemed a little dry, well that was life, folks.

If this was a romance novel, he really would have been following her in the grocery. He would have come up to her and said, "Did you think I would let you get away?" Then he would gently, oh so gently take her face in his slightly rough hands, gazing deep into her eyes. And he would say, "I have to do this," as his perfect lips came down on hers.

How absurd! Pickett softly mocked herself. This was real life of course, so what he had done was look at her as if he didn't like what he saw— at all—and walk away.

Pickett rinsed out the plastic container, debated briefly if it was worth saving, then tossed it in the recycling bin.

She was pathetic. Having Jax obviously see her and just as obviously walk away from her had been more of a blow to her self-esteem than she wanted to admit. No matter how many times she'd reminded herself to step back, to treat his behavior as a fact, not a judgment about her, his apparent rejection stung. She wasn't an over-weight nerd anymore, still, she had battled attack thoughts all the way home. She hadn't just found him incredibly male in a way that made her super aware of being female, she had liked him. She'd been exhilarated by his quickness to understand what she was doing and his complete willingness to follow her lead. She'd rarely felt such a sense of companionship with the person for whom she was demonstrating.

But the man had no interest in her, a fact she should have known from the second she saw him, and now she'd wasted 20 minutes thinking about him. Years of her own therapy made that easy enough to analyze. He was safe because he was remote. There would be no need to take a chance on real rejection from him. She could project on him any quality, without regard for whether he, or she, measured up to an a ideal.

She'd might as well call this what it was. Lust. She'd been startled, then a little flattered, to think he thought she was coming on to him. Pickett snickered. As if she would know how! It hadn't been precisely comfortable, but she'd liked the little hum of awareness that actually intensified after he went from flirting to paying her real attention.

She could really get into a fantasy of sweaty, rolling around sex with Jax. Pickett decided to ignore the caveat that she had never especially enjoyed sex before. This was fantasy. A lot safer than sex in the real world, and safer for her heart than dreams of love.

Lack of closure, her therapist mind labeled her unrest once again. Talking it over with her best friend would help, but Emmy was out of the country. An assistant professor at UNC-W, Emmy was in Ecuador for the semester with a group of students studying the rainforest. One of the attractions to Snead's Ferry had been living near enough to see Emmy weekly. Emmy would be back at Thanksgiving, and Pickett was counting the days.

The baby blue phone, a relict of the seventies hanging above the kitchen sink, rang.

"Where have you been, little sister?" Lyle's voice had lost a lot of it's southern essence from living in New York. Pickett was always startled to hear the sister she was closest to sound like a stranger. "I've been calling and calling."

With a guilty clutch, Pickett glanced into the darkened dining room she'd made into her home office and saw the red message light blinking on her answering machine. She'd been so bemused she hadn't checked her messages.

"Never mind," Lyle went on. "I'm in a rental car. I'm turning into your drive now. Be there in a sec."

Pickett flipped on the backyard spotlights and opened the door to let out the dogs who were already wiggling with excitement. She looked down at her faded shorts with their frayed cuffs. No time to change.

Lyle stepped onto the back porch, flanked by Patterson and Lucy. The dog's tails wagged wildly at the sight of their mistress but they didn't leave Lyle's side. Seeing her sister all city-chic in a black suit, no one would guess Lyle was a pied piper for dogs.

"I'm so happy to see you!—even though you've stolen my dogs again," Pickett moved into Lyle's arms. Closest in age to Pickett, the three years that separated them had seemed unbridgeable when Lyle had been a teenager, attempting to find herself as an artist while coming to grips with her sexual identity. Even so, she'd always shared Pickett's love of creatures.

Pickett had to step back to be able to look into Lyle's face. She was both the youngest and the smallest of her siblings, and Lyle was the tallest of the four Sessoms girls. All had blond hair but Lyle's had deepened to dark honey over the years. "But what are you doing here, Lyle? I wasn't expecting you until the weekend."

"The meeting with the client got moved up because of the hurricane. We flew into Wilmington this morning and we leave again tonight."

"You mean you're not going to stay? I'm so disappointed!"

"My boss has visions of being stranded in Wilmington the way people were in New Orleans. I keep trying to tell him a Category One hurricane is not the same thing at all. He's got a point though. They probably will start canceling flights if the weather service upgrades the Watch to a Warning. You almost missed me. I was going to leave you a note."

"I wanted us to have the whole weekend together," Pickett wailed. "I was late getting home because I had to close up the Howell's cottage for them." *And because I spent an extra hour interfering in the life of a stranger. Talking to a man who, now that he knows who I am, prefers to remain a stranger.*

Pickett wished she could tell Lyle about the encounter with Jax, not just the facts but the strange pull she'd felt, but…. All the reasons not to crowded into her brain. She and Lyle had never talked about what could euphemistically be called a love life. Pickett because she didn't have one, Lyle because she much preferred relationships with women. The habits of confiding in one another had never been formed. Maybe if Lyle was staying the weekend as planned she would have had time to lead up to it.

Lyle quirked a dubious eyebrow. "They asked you to help?"

For a second Pickett stared at Lyle, thinking she'd somehow read her mind. She felt her cheeks get hot and her heart thumped in embarrassment. Then who her sister meant clicked in. "The Howell's? No. Mother told them I would."

Lyle's mobile lips curled. "Sucker."

Lyle loved to play the hard ass. She didn't know what an idiot Pickett had been this afternoon, nevertheless, the sisterly jab stung. "Easy for you to say! You moved all the way to New York City to get outside Mom's reach. At least I had the nerve to try to live my life on my terms while still in the same state with her."

Lyle planted a fist on her hip. "Nerve, hell. You thought if you didn't rebel too much, she wouldn't disapprove too much."

"Hey, you're the rebel, not me," Pickett defended herself. "I'll grant you I'm a wimp, and I'm not following the family script of marrying locally and becoming a young society matron, but I honestly wanted the career I've chosen. I wanted the challenge of establishing my own practice. I love the work I do with children and families, and I'm good at it."

"Well I'm good at graphic design." Lyle snapped, honey dark brows drawing together.

"Yes, but you don't love it," Pickett snapped right back. "You should be painting full time and you know it. Landscape is your gift. But Mother would adore having a fine artist in the family—so of course you can't do that!"

In the profound silence that ensued, Pickett stared at the sight of her sister's shocked face. She never used her insightfulness as a weapon against people, but she'd just come alarmingly close. She felt as shocked as her sister looked. Lyle's reasons for her choice of career and place to live were complex, as well she knew. She shouldn't have lashed out just because her sister had stepped on her toes.

Pickett shook her head and threw up her hands. "Listen to us. We haven't been together ten minutes and already we're squabbling like…"

"Like sisters," finished Lyle. "But not like you. What's got you so riled up?"

I'm a day-dreaming idiot who needs to get her feet back on the ground. Jax, confident to the point of arrogance, a certified hero, represented everything that had never been part of her life and never would be. She was usually smart enough to back away from men like him.

"Nothing," she said. She pushed away the wistfulness that threatened to engulf her. Pickett had heard of friendships as close as sisters, but she didn't fully understand what that meant. She had a hard time imagining feeling as close to one of her sisters as to her college roommate, Emmy Caddington.

It was normal for the youngest sibling to form her most significant relationships outside the family. Still, she'd often wished for a sister who was as close as a friend. "You hit a nerve when you called me a sucker. I am a soft touch. I was blaming Mother but the truth is I probably would have gone to the Howell's cottage, even without Mother's interference." She opened the refrigerator. "How about some iced tea?"

"'The house wine of the South?'" chortled Lyle, quoting from Steel Magnolias. "Of course I'll have some. People in New York don't know how to make it." She leaned against the worn counter while Pickett ran water over the ancient ice trays.

"You have too big a heart, kid," Lyle said softly, returning to the previous subject. She gave Pickett a one-armed squeeze. "You know what? I've always been afraid that big heart of yours would lead you to marry some loser just because he needed you."

In other words, Lyle thought no man would ever want her for herself.

She thought Pickett was too stupid to avoid being manipulated.

Pickett kept her eyes on the ice cubes, making sure she put an equal number in each glass, until she had control of her hurt. She fell back on reflective listening. "You think I'm pretty pathetic, don't you? Feeble? Foolishly sentimental?"

"Feeble? Sentimental? No. But I do think you don't always stand up for yourself. You make sure the other person gets their needs met, and you ignore your own. I think you don't know your own strength or your own power. And unless it's for someone else, I don't think you ever do what you want. You deserve happiness too. That's what I meant."

"No need to worry about that," Pickett reached for the tea pitcher happy to have the conversation back on comfortable ground. "When it comes to marriage I know exactly what I want. I don't mean to sound arrogant but I do have a Ph.D. in the subject. There are well-documented factors that predict success. Furthermore, I know the qualities needed to make a good husband. Never fear I will plunge myself into an impossible situation for emotional reasons. I know a lot about the odds for success, and I intend to do everything I can to stack them in my favor"

"I guess that makes sense, but aren't you looking, first of all, for love? Some people defy the odds. Isn't it love that makes the difference?"

Pickett set down the heavy crockery pitcher, and turned to face her sister. "Sure, you can always find people who heroically overcome all odds, but make no mistake, commitment is what makes the difference. Plus stability and security. A year or two doing family therapy on a military base will destroy any romantic notions you ever had about the power of love. Trust me, love won't keep you together if the military is keeping you apart. I'm no hero. It would take more courage than I've got to go up against heavy odds." Pickett waved a dismissing hand, and picked up the pitcher again. "Enough about me, I want to hear about you."

"No it's not enough about you. You've told me all about what you think. You haven't said anything about how you feel."

Pickett paused in the act of pouring tea over ice. How very sensitive of Lyle! "Have you been taking counseling lessons?" she teased.

"No, you idiot. Unlike you, I don't give a damn about how most people feel, but I do care about you."

Pickett's head jerked back. For so many years she'd either felt invisible or wished she were invisible. It was still hard for her to reveal personal stuff about herself. Only to Emmy and a couple of her closest friends did she open up. Since she was a great listener, most people never noticed. Until this minute she hadn't known Lyle was one of the people who did.

Again the urge rose up to unburden herself to Lyle, and again she felt the wistful knowledge that she didn't quite dare. "I feel fine," Pickett said, handing one moisture-beaded glass to her sister and taking the other for herself. "Between seeing clients in my office here, working at the base, and working on the house, I'm busy and happy. And health-wise," she added, "I've never been better."

Lyle looked like she might have asked more, a small frown shadowing her light blue eyes. Then she nodded philosophically. "I'm glad. Now show me all you've done to the house since I was here last."

Not surprisingly, Lyle approved of Pickett's color scheme, since she herself had selected the Chinese red for the living room and dark spruce green for Pickett's bedroom. The carefully preserved window and door moldings were antique white. The intense colors acted as a unifying influence on the mishmash of family castoffs and the few true heirlooms with which the rooms were furnished. The twelve foot ceilings accommodated the exquisite, but immense, Federal period secretaire that had been in storage for years because no family member had a house large enough to accommodate it, but the sectional sofa upholstered in a print of huge red flowers had literally been snatched from the junk man.

She looked at Pickett's large pineapple post bed piled with pillows, and laughed in disbelief. "Good grief! Half the bed is taken up with pillows, Pickett. There's hardly room for you, much less someone else." She glanced at Pickett's face and lifted her palms in a hands-off gesture. "Hey, I'm not criticizing. Who am I to talk about empty," she laughed again, "or in your case, not-empty beds?" There's one thing about it, it means you'll really like the house-warming present I made you." She turned toward the door. "You wait here. I'll be right back." In a minute she returned and handed Pickett a large bag.

"You made me a needlepoint pillow!" Pickett exulted. "At last, I get one of my own." Lyle's pillows were works of art. She used both large and small stitches, sometimes working one stitch over another, creating shimmering color reminiscent of pointillism. They were, in fact, paintings rendered in wool, acting as the background for some wry saying. Pickett withdrew the intricately worked pillow from the bag, wordlessly exclaiming at its beauty. "Plus je vois…" Pickett read haltingly as she traced the stylized cream and white letters worked into a motif of leaves. "This is a totally new design, isn't it?"

Lyle nodded, managing to look both shyly pleased and mischievous.

"O-o-okay," Pickett narrowed her eyes in suspicion. "What does it say? You know I don't read French as well as you."

Lyle's grin widened. " 'The more I know about men…,'" she paused for dramatic effect, " 'the better I love my dogs!' "

FOUR

Jax stared at the fast moving clouds streaming toward the island and the ocean awash with foam from almost continuous breakers, and considered his options.

Since breakfast, Lauren had been scurrying around the cottage, bracelets jangling, Ferragamos clacking, packing to return to Raleigh now that evacuation of the beach had been ordered.

Tyler crouched on the floor in front of the sofa. He alternated beeping and grinding noises as he maneuvered the dump truck load of poker chips.

"Stop that noise Tyler. I don't know how I'm supposed to pack, if I can't even think." Lauren marched into the living room and plunked a designer bag down beside the door. "And I told you to pick up those cars and put them in your toy sack. When I'm ready to get in the car, anything you don't have with you will be left for the hurricane to get." Lauren pushed the hair back from her face with be-ringed hands that shook. "I'd have left yesterday if I'd had any sense. But no. Mr. Navy doesn't want to budge. Who knows what course the hurricane will take? he says. He'd rather stay here with Tyler. Mr. Navy can play better with Tyler here," she muttered not quite under her breath.

Jax heard her. She meant for him to. Her hands were shaking. He could see a fine tremor running under the shiny silvery fabric of her cropped pants. Was she that scared? or was she hung over? She was sloshed last night by the time she served dinner.

So, should he just let Tyler go with her? Call it? Tell Commander Kohn that his idea for 30 day's leave so that Jax could spend time with Tyler was a fiasco. A goatfuck from day one?

Oh yeah, like that was an option.

Kohn was a good commander, and Jax's mentor, but he had this slow cowboy drawl that told you you were so screwed. Jax could still feel his neck get hot when he remembered Kohn's dressing down, no less scathing for being delivered in that lazy, I don't give a damn voice.

And Kohn had this bug up his ass about family responsibilities. He said he didn't know how Tyler's old DOD 1332.30 had gotten on his desk. Bullshit. He probably had the thing flagged to his attention.

"How long has it been since you've seen your son, Graham?"

"I saw him at his mother's funeral a month ago."

"And before that when did you see him?"

"In April, six, no seven months ago."

Kohn had looked out the window a long time and when he looked back at Jax, his eyes were bright and hard. He let fall the thick manila folder containing a plan covering every contingency imaginable concerning Tyler's care as long as he was a dependent—Tyler's old 1332.30. It hit the shiny desk with a soft plop. The gesture was somehow more final than slamming it down would have been.

"My friend, if you're smart, you'll take the leave you should've asked for as soon as that boy's mother died.

"You go to North Carolina and you make sure that child is all right.

"And you come back here with a new 1332.30 that is so perfect in every detail it could have been written by God.

"I can promise I will review it. If I'm not completely stunned by its glory, I'll hate to lose you, but you're outta here. Your service to your country is valuable, but Congress has spoken: Your duty to your dependent child comes first."

Then Kohn said something strange. He said, "Your son, does he look like you?"

Jax glanced now from the window to the sofa where Tyler had made a sort of garage from piled up cushions. His hair grew from a double crown as Jax's did, and allowing for Jax's permanent sun streaks was the same color. His face still had too much baby softness to guess what his adult features would be, but the grey eyes with their straight brows were his.

No doubt about it. This was his son.

His son that he was screwing up with.

Even with his ass chewed, it had all looked so simple at the base in Little Creek, Va. As soon as he learned of Danielle's death, he'd known the best thing to do was give custody of Tyler to Lauren. If Kohn thought he should take 30 days leave just to get some papers signed, so be it.

Lauren would still have to take Tyler full time eventually.

But, it felt like quitting to let Tyler go to Lauren's house with Tyler still acting as if his father didn't exist.

He hated to quit.

And it felt like losing.

He hated to lose.

Hell, it couldn't get any worse, and maybe without Lauren grating on him, he would handle Tyler's silence better.

He walked into the kitchen where Lauren had a trash can pulled up to the refrigerator and was pitching out leftover food. "Lauren, if you're packed why don't you get on the road? I'll clean out the refrigerator and close up the cottage after you're gone."

"Oh Jax, would you?" To Jax's cynical amusement, the change in Lauren was astounding. The tightly down-turned lips turned up, and it almost looked like there were tears in her eyes. "I-40 is going to look like a parking lot with everybody trying to evacuate. The sooner I get on the road, the sooner I'll get home." She closed the refrigerator. "But, Jax I want you to know that you are welcome to come and stay at my house in Raleigh. Any time. I really mean it."

Now she was kicking into the Gracious Lady act. He'd be about as welcome as a case of head lice. "No, thank you. I'll stay here."

"Well," Lauren had the grace to try not to look delighted, "if you change your mind, Tyler and I—"

"Tyler is staying with me."

When they were twelve, his best friend Corey said a name like 'Jackson Graham the Third' sounded snooty, so he'd dubbed him 'Jax' because that sounded like a Jedi knight. But when he wanted to, Jax could keep his face so impassive that the new guys in the platoon sometimes called him Stonewall.

"What?" Lauren blinked her mascara-ed lashes and swiveled her gaze around the room as if she wondered who had spoken. "No. No, you idiot!"

Good bye Gracious, hello Nasty.

"I have to…I mean…What are you thinking? There's a hurricane! Tyler has to leave. I care about the welfare of this child even if you don't. I'm the closest thing to a mother he has. You can't take care of him. He has to go with me."

"I'm his father. He stays with me."

"Are you telling me you're not going to let me have custody?"

"No. Nothing has changed. Tyler will still need someone to care for him full time. But dammit, Lauren, this 30-day leave is the longest time I've ever had with Tyler, and the longest I'm likely to get. I'm not willing to cut it short for a storm that'll be gone in thirty-six hours."

"But where will you take him? You can't stay on the island."

"I'll find a hotel room in Wilmington."

"That's the stupidest thing I ever heard! There won't be a room to be had between here and Raleigh."

Lauren was way overreacting. Any hurricane had to be taken seriously, but a Category One was not a Katrina. Only the beaches and low-lying areas needed to be evacuated, and an hour's drive in any direction would take them out of all danger. He suspected she welcomed an excuse to take Tyler and return home to Raleigh. "I'll find something. We'll be okay. When it's over, we'll come back here."

"This is insane! You can't do this."

"I can."

"But I have to leave! I can't stay here." Lauren's drawl thickened as her voice rose in a hysterical wail. "I have to be home! Don't you care anything about my feelings? I'll be worried to death about Tyler. I'm terrified of storms. I have to get home!"

It wasn't any ground they hadn't already covered. Jax saw no need to answer.

"If you don't care anything about me, don't you care about your baby? How can you keep him where a hurricane's going to strike within 24 hours. You're putting that child in harm's way!" Lauren snatched up a makeup case and stalked to the door with quick, sharp taps of her sandals and flung it wide. "You're not going to get away with this."

Jax placed the last of Lauren's Louis Vuitton luggage the trunk of her silver Lexus and closed the hood. "I'll call you when I know where Tyler and I will be staying."

Lauren didn't answer. An improvement, Jax considered. It beat the hell out of the ranting that had gone on as he had carried her suitcases down.

Now she put her handbag in the car and held out her arms to Tyler.

"Come give Gan-gan a kiss."

Tyler went to her with slow steps, his head down.

She lifted his face in her hands. "You want to go to Gan-gan's house, don't you?" Tyler's eyes never met hers; his headshake was almost imperceptible.

Lauren made her eyes go big with horror. "You don't want to stay here and let the hurricane get you, do you?" Again a tiny shake. "Then you make your daddy bring you to Gan-gan's house. You'll be safe there."

"Gan-gan left me." Tyler gazed at the departing Lexus with a very old look on his smooth little face. This morning Lauren had dressed him in another of his coordinated outfits, a blue polo shirt with sailboat doo-dads embroidered on the collar and matching sailboats on the leg on the shorts. Under the blue shirt Tyler's shoulders lifted once, then fell.

Jax didn't know how to interpret Tyler's expression, still, seeing his son look like that caused something inside him to ache like an old wound.

"Come on inside," Jax held out his hand to Tyler. Tyler didn't take it, but followed obediently. "Let's finish packing up."

"Stay close to me Tyler," Jax snapped, even though Tyler wasn't doing anything wrong. Clutching his red toy sack, he obediently stood beside his father in the parking lot of the hotel. Jax squeezed his eyes shut in a fruitless effort to blot out his shame at snapping without reason. What the hell was the matter with him?

Jax had made quick work of closing up the cottage after Lauren left. He'd hoped with just the two of them, Tyler might be forced to deal with him and start talking more. It hadn't worked that way. Instead, without her jittering presence to distract them from each other, Tyler's silence went from uncommunicative to nerve-wracking. Impossible to penetrate, impossible to ignore.

Now that they were inland, the heat seemed twice what it had been on the beach; the supersaturated air and no hint of breeze made it impossible for sweat to evaporate. The overcast had thickened; the light was dull and shadowless. Elvira wasn't due to come ashore until the early hours of tomorrow morning, but a hurricane, even a small one like Elvira, was big.

Jax retrieved his duffle and Tyler's designer suitcase. Who knew there was designer luggage for kids? Jax expelled a pained laugh at himself. Now he was glomming onto insignificant details like suitcases and the quality of the light in order to distract himself, but it was way the hell better than snapping at Tyler.

Despite Lauren's predictions, a hotel room had been easy to come by, although the desk clerk warned him his reservation would be held only for an hour. Fortunately, the new Highway 17 bypass put him in the historic section of the Wilmington in half the time it used to take. Jax checked his watch. They'd made it in time.

Jax was proud of his choice of hotels. The hotel was adjacent to the historic Southern Railway terminal which had been rehabbed into a convention and expo center. Though it overlooked the Cape Fear river, folks back then had known how to build, but even more important, where to build. High water posed no threat to it.

Jax slung his duffle over his shoulder and tucked Tyler's suitcase under one arm. "Take my hand, Tyler."

Tyler hadn't let go of his sack of toys since his grandmother had left. He'd gone in the cottage, quietly collected all his cars and tucked them into the red drawstring sack. The sack was hard and lumpy and so heavy the strings gouged into the soft skin of his wrists, but he hadn't put it down, not once.

Now he tried to tuck it under one arm to give his father his hand, but it was too big and too heavy for one little arm. Tyler jerked his hand back to prevent the bag from slipping to the ground.

"Give me the sack," Jax said, "and take my hand."

Tyler shook his head emphatically, and pulled the sack closer to his chest.

"You can't carry it and walk. Come on, Tyler."

The hotel parking lot was crowded, and Tyler's head wasn't visible above the fenders of the cars. A driver would be right on him before he saw him. Jax believed in picking his battles, but now was the moment to enforce obedience. One flick and Jax would have the bag out of Tyler's arms and grab his hand.

As if Tyler divined his intention, he wheeled away and hunched his shoulders in a vain attempt to shield his sack with his body.

Tyler's protection of his toys was so desperate and so brave, respect and pride lumped together in Jax's throat.

"Okay, son," Jax soothed, "okay." He clasped Tyler by the shoulder, biting back a curse when he felt the tiny flinch. "Stay right with me, though."

In the paneled lobby, Tyler halted and looked around. He hefted his sack further up his chest. "What is this place?"

Jax nudged him toward the desk. "A hotel."

"Why did we come here?"

What kind of question was that? "To spend the night."

The lobby was crowded. People thronged at the desk two and three deep. An older man backed up without looking and stumbled over Tyler. He glanced down to see what he was tripping over and cursed, "Look out kid!"

Tyler yelped as he was knocked against his father. Jax stepped forward to protect Tyler with his legs, at the same time grabbing the man to keep him from falling. As soon as he regained his feet, the man jerked himself away. "You need to keep that kid out from under foot!" he snapped, red-faced and straightening his shirt.

Jax dropped the duffle and suitcase and picked up Tyler and his lumpy sack which he had held onto throughout the altercation. "You okay, buddy?"

Tyler was white around his lips but with a little shuddering breath, he nodded. "Why do we have to spend the night here?" He wiggled and pushed at Jax's shoulders

"Be still, Tyler." They had finally reached the front of the line. Jax shifted Tyler onto his hip to extract his wallet from his back pocket. To the desk clerk he said, "Reservation for Lt. Jackson Graham."

The clerk regarded him with the stony face of a woman who has already dealt with too many irate people to care about one more. "We stopped honoring reservations an hour ago,"

"I made the reservation less than an hour ago."

The clerk rolled her eyes. "Whatever. It's first come, first served now," she said, "and you're too late. We're full."

FIVE

J ax re-settled the squirming Tyler, and gave the clerk his most steely-eyed glare. "You mean you gave my reservation away? I drove past other hotels to get here."

"That's right..." the woman looked into his face and added, "sir."

"What's right?"

"You could have stopped somewhere else. It happens all the time. In the meantime I would have turned people away."

"So instead, you let me drive all the way over here, missing out on other rooms I could have had." Jax reined in his ire. "I don't care for myself, but I have a child with me."

The clerk's brown face softened with contrition. "Really, sir, I am sorry. The high-rise hotels, the big chains will be filling up, but the smaller, independent motels might still have rooms. We're full mainly because of hurricane parties."

She had to be kidding. "Hurricane parties?"

"Hurr'cane?" Tyler stiffened, suddenly paying attention to the exchange.

"Yeah, it's not supposed to get too bad. A lot of people are treating it like New Year's Eve. They come here so they can party and then sleep through it." Raucous laughter from the lounge area adjacent to the lobby lent credence to her explanation. The party apparently was already in full swing. "The smaller places don't have bars, room service and stuff."

They also didn't have interior corridors, game rooms, and continental breakfast. At a small motel, once the storm hit, he and Tyler would be trapped in one very small room until it blew itself out. He had some milk and cheese in the cooler, but he hadn't brought things like cereal thinking he'd return to the cottage in a day or two.

"Here's to Elvira," a voice shouted from the lounge.

"Yeah, bring that hurricane on."

Tyler's head jerked. "The hurr'cane's coming here?"

"If I was you," the desk clerk added, "I'd head inland. Two hours in any direction will get you all the rooms you want."

Tyler wiggled and patted his father's shoulder for attention. "The hurr'cane's coming here?"

"Hush Tyler. If I want to stay in Wilmington, what would you recommend?"

"The Bide-A-Wee on Independence Blvd. The rooms are clean, no hookers, and there won't be drug deals going down in the parking lot—the way I guarantee there are in the hotels over on the interstate. Hang on. I'll call them and see if they have anything."

Tyler bounced on Jax's hip. "I don't wanna stay here," Tyler whined.

"You get your wish, Tyler. We're not staying."

Tyler bounced again. "Gan-gan said we gotta leave."

"Yes sir." The clerk hung up the phone. "They have a room and they will save it for you. But I suggest you don't lose any time getting there." She pointed to Tyler. "Does he have to go to the bathroom?"

"Tyler, do you have to go to the bathroom?"

"No! I want to leave."

Jax shouldered the luggage. "Okay, we're going."

The Bide-A-Wee was as promised. The long, low cinderblock motel leftover from the fifties had recently been painted glistening white, the room doors dark green. Gay planters were spaced along the covered walkway that was all that separated the room doors from parking spaces.

In the office a grey-haired man got up from a recliner stationed in front of a large-screen TV. It was apparent that the space beyond the counter was more someone's living room than an office.

"Old Elvira's run you off the beach, has she?" The man ambled over to the counter. On the tube Hurricane Warning scrolled across the bottom of the screen, intermixed with lists of closings. "Twelve o'clock update says she might swing north a tad. We might not get more than a lot of rain. Just you and the boy?" He didn't wait for answer, but shoved a registration form in front of Jax. "I've got you a room with two double beds. That okay? The restaurant next door has good country food and they'll be open for supper. I figured we'd lock down about eight, so if there's anything you want, you tell us before then." He dropped an old-fashioned metal key with a large plastic number on the counter. "I've sent the maids home, but I'll get you towels and such like."

Jax pocketed the key with a nod of thanks. He placed his hand on Tyler's shoulder. "Let's go open the room and then I'll get the bags."

Tyler looked up at him, a frown between his brows. "Why did we come here?"

"Because the other place was full."

"No-o-o," Tyler fussed. "I mean, why are we here?"

"To spend the night, just like the other place."

"Why are we going to spend the night?"

The question made no sense. Tyler knew why you spend the night for cripes sake. Jax shoved the key into number fourteen. A blast of stale, super-moist air, hit them.

Tyler wrinkled his nose. "What's that smell?"

All the air freshener in the world wouldn't cover up the smell of cigarette smoke and accumulated mildew in a carpet that had to be twenty years old. However, the sheets were clean, the miniscule bathroom spotless.

Tyler halted on the threshold, a tiny figure silhouetted against the light. "I don't like it here. I want to leave."

Jax found the remote and flicked on the TV. "Sorry fellow, this is pretty much our last option. It's clean and we have to make the best of it until the hurricane passes."

Tyler rubbed one leg against the other. He'd done that several times now. His brows came together. "Is the hurr'cane coming here, too?"

"Yes, Tyler. A hurricane is big."

"I want to leave," Tyler's mouth turned down tragically. "I want to go home."

"Do you want me to take you to your grandmother's house?" Jax made up his mind he would take him, if that's what he wanted. Around his grandmother he'd seemed, if not happy exactly, content. Jax would somehow deal with Kohn's demand that he spend 30 days with Tyler. Kohn meant his threats and he had the power to carry them out, but Tyler's misery was unendurable.

Tyler blinked as if the question bewildered him. His lower lip quivered. "No."

"Well those are your choices. Stay with me or go to your grandmother's."

Tyler rubbed on leg against the other, and scrubbed with his fist at his hairline, a gesture Jax recognized as his own. The gesture gave Jax the oddest little kick right underneath his heart. Tyler hadn't been around him enough to be imitating him. He knew Tyler favored him, but Jax had never before seen himself in Tyler.

Jax felt like rubbing at his hairline himself. Tyler was finally talking but all he would say was he wanted to leave—wanted to leave any place they were. It didn't make any sense.

Tyler's chest heaved. "We got to leave! The hurr'cane will get my toys."

Lauren only said that to manipulate him. Jax didn't bother to contain his disgust. "The hurricane's not going to get your toys."

"You said the hurr'cane's coming here."

"Yes but we'll be fine here." Jax was out of patience. "Now come on in."

Tyler shook his head, a mulish expression twisting his lips. "It stinks in here."

"I'll leave the door open for a while to let it air out." Tyler tightened his hold on his sack, and stared in defiance. "Tyler," Jax used his command voice, "come in right now, or I will carry you in."

Slowly, sandaled toes dragging, Tyler moved past the threshold. Just.

"All the way in. I mean it." Tyler dragged himself to the center of the room, taking care to stay out of Jax's reach. Jax inhaled and counted to ten. "I'm going to bring our luggage in. You watch TV and I'll leave the door open."

Jax glanced back at the forlorn little figure sitting on the end of the bed. Twenty-five more days of this. Since he arrived, they'd had exactly one good hour together, and only because of that woman, Pickett. She seemed to be able to decipher Tyler, to understand what would make him happy without his saying a word—a feat Jax couldn't manage even if Tyler did talk.

The helpless knowledge he was screwing up and he had no idea how to fix it dragged at him like undertow. He wished Pickett was here right now. Maybe she could figure out what Tyler wanted. Maybe once the hurricane was past he'd call her. Pickett was a woman he needed to stay away from, but if it was for Tyler, that was different.

Looking back one more time to make sure Tyler was where he had left him, Jax pulled out his car keys. Too bad a pickup was parked in the space directly in front of their room. He pulled the luggage from the cargo compartment and headed back to the room. He'd need one more trip to carry in the cooler.

Tyler kept his eyes on the TV when his father came back into the room. The local stations had gone to an all-news format to cover the storm. And since there wasn't a lot to say after announcing shelters opening and reporting Lowe's had sold out of generators, they were filling the time between weather updates with inane chatter.

A perky blonde shuffled the papers in front of her. "Here's a piece of trivia. Did you know Elvira is the name of the Wicked Witch of the West in the Wizard of Oz?" she asked the jowly man to her left.

"I didn't know she had a name." The man turned a professional, and rather condescending, smile on his co-anchor.

"Technically, it's the name of the woman who turns into the witch once Dorothy is in Oz. Elvira Gulch is the woman riding the bicycle in the tornado."

A clip from the black and white portion of the movie showed the bad-tempered woman furiously pedaling through the tornado. Then a quick cut to the green-faced witch pointing a bony finger at Dorothy. "I'll get you, my pretty—and your little dog!" Terrified, Dorothy clutched Toto to her breast and the clip ended.

"Well, lets hope Elvira isn't going to 'get us' with any tornadoes in addition to high winds and flooding," the jowly man chuckled. "What do you think, Randi?"

The picture changed to a young woman in front of a weather map. She cheerfully assured her audience that thunderstorms and tornadoes were indeed a possibility.

"Shit," said Jax under his breath. The local station was clearly so delighted to have some news of their own, they'd go to any lengths to dramatize it. "Here," he handed Tyler the remote, "why don't you see if you can find some cartoons? I'm going to bring in the cooler. Be right back."

After only a few minutes sitting with the A/C off, the SUV was stifling inside. The ice in the cooler would melt rapidly. It had to be carried inside or there wasn't a chance the food inside wouldn't spoil.

He was halfway to the room door when the pickup in the slot in front of the door backed away.

Hot damn! He set down the cooler and raced back to the Cherokee. He could move his SUV before someone else took the space.

After parking and retrieving the cooler he hurried back to the motel room. The space on the end of the bed in front of the TV was empty. "Tyler," he called, "where are you?"

"Tyler!" he went to the tiny bathroom. "Are you in here?" His heart began to pound. He checked under the beds, jerked open the closet door. No Tyler.

He looked out the door. "Tyler!" The pickup pulling away. The driver could have looked right in and seen a child sitting alone. Could have taken Tyler. The thought froze his heart.

"Stop," Jax could hear Kraskow's laconic instructor-voice. "Assess the situation. If you don't have time to assess, you don't have time to do anything that's going to make any difference."

Tyler hadn't come by him. In the other direction, across a side street, was the restaurant the motel owner had mentioned. In front of the motel across a narrow parking lot was a six lane street on which cars moved bumper to bumper. Tyler was a city kid. Surely he had more sense than to attempt to cross it. That left the direction of the restaurant. Jax couldn't see him but as he'd already noted, he was too short to be visible behind a car.

And there were cars everywhere. The motel lot was full, the restaurant lot was full, and cars were parked all along the curb of the side street. He climbed the wrought iron supports of the walkway's cover as he would a ladder to the motel's roof to gain a higher vantage point.

A flash of blue caught his eye. How the hell had he gotten so far? He was on the other side of the restaurant's parking lot and getting ready to cross another side street. This one, unfortunately, was a major thoroughfare. Fortunately, the red toy sack, now being dragged behind him, was slowing him down.

Jax sprinted the length of the motel roof, keeping Tyler in sight. He let himself down by clinging to a gutter and dropping the rest of the way.

On the ground he could no longer see Tyler, he could only continue in the direction he'd last seen him. He vaulted a car parked at the curb. The shortest way to where he thought Tyler was, was through the bed of knobby purple cactus planted in front of the restaurant. He took it. Spines, long as toothpicks and sharp as needles, ripped his shorts.

He rounded the corner of the restaurant. There he was, on the curb, looking both ways. Thank god, someone had taught him that, but it hadn't been him. He wanted to yell for Tyler to stop, but the sickening truth was, Tyler was as likely to spook and dash into the traffic, as obey.

Jax added another burst of speed.

The light had changed and the street in front of Tyler was clearing. He looked both ways and stepped off the curb. Unfortunately he didn't know to watch for turning cars.

Jax saw the black Camry out of the corner of his eye.

Slow down, you idiot driver.

There's a kid in front of you.

Three more steps that's all he needed

And then everything happened at once. Breaks squealed, Jax swept up Tyler, his momentum carrying him into the next lane, the car stopped, horns blared.

"Keep your kid out of the street!" the Camry driver screamed at Jax, before angrily pealing rubber as she sped away.

He had him. In his arms. Safe. He had him.

He felt one second of jelly-kneed relief. Then, the blood pounding hot in his scalp, the breath he couldn't quite seem to catch, was all he knew.

He pushed his face up against Tyler's, determined to transmit his anger eyeball to eyeball. "What the hell were you doing? You were in the road! Shit! Were you fucking trying to get yourself fucking killed?"

Jax was crossing the restaurant parking lot when the meaning of Tyler's white, set face and dilated grey eyes penetrated his grinding fury. The narrow shoulders—the child's whole body was shaking.

Oh shit! A thousand pounds of self-reproach landed on Jax's chest. As if things weren't bad enough between them, now he'd made Tyler afraid of him by reacting as he would if one of his men had done something so dangerously foolhardy.

Maybe he should just put Tyler in the car and drive him to Raleigh. He hadn't had him by himself for three hours before he'd almost gotten him killed.

Warm, wetness spread across the Jax's arm supporting Tyler's butt.

Shit, shit, shit, shit, shit! Guilt rose up and grabbed him by the throat. He'd scared Tyler so bad he'd wet his pants.

He had to get inside and get a hold of himself. Jax forced himself to breathe slowly in time with his steps as he retraced the path back to the motel.

"Okay," Jax pushed the door to behind them and locked it. He set Tyler on the bathroom counter, so he could see his face. Tears spiked the thick lashes and ran down the red-blotched cheeks. Jax forced his voice decibels lower, but found he still had to clear his throat a couple of times before he could speak. "Let's start over. Where the h— Where were you going?"

"Gan-gan said the hurr'cane's gonna get us. She said it'll get us if we stay where it is. We got to run away. We got to hurry."

So the witch had scared Tyler first. There was some comfort in knowing he wasn't solely responsible for the tight shoulders and quivering lips. But he couldn't shift the blame to Lauren for screwing up with Tyler. If he'd let Tyler leave with her, this wouldn't have happened.

No. He'd screwed up all by himself—and his mistake almost got Tyler killed. Only though sheer dumb luck had he noticed Tyler was AWOL in time to avert disaster.

The sight of Tyler's terrified little face was like a knife twisting in his gut. He needed to reassure the child. He wasn't sure how. "It's all right," he patted the boy's narrow shoulder. "Don't worry about what your grandmother said. I'm going to take care of everything."

Inside his head the voice always evaluating whether he led well or poorly, sneered. Yeah, right.

Reacting would have to stop. What he needed was a plan.

A knock sounded at the door. He lifted Tyler down from the counter. "Find some dry shorts in your suitcase," he said, "I'll be right back."

The paunchy owner of the motel was at the door, a scowl on his grey-whiskered face. "You the fool that was running on the roof?" he demanded. "What the hell were you doing?"

Jax felt his face coloring. "My son ran away." Because I failed to anticipate him.

"And you thought he was on the dad-blamed roof?" the man bellowed.

"I needed a high vantage point to see which way he went."

"How the hell did he get away from you in the first place?"

I didn't understand what he meant when he kept saying he wanted to leave. "He was afraid of the hurricane. He got away when my back was turned."

"Got away!" The old man hauled his pants up over his paunch. "They said he was clear on the other side of Sal's before you caught him. He's in more danger from you than from a hurricane."

The old windbag was right. Jax deserved every bit of scorn the man could give him.

You didn't realize how upset Tyler was, he accused himself. You didn't anticipate he would leave the room by himself. You didn't keep up with where he was. You didn't lock the door between trips to the car. Excuses don't count. Results do.

"Yes sir," Jax met the motel owner's faded blue eyes without flinching. "It won't happen again."

"Damn right, it won't." The old man's mouth was a thin, angry line but after a moment his eyes slid away. With his gaze fixed on one of the planters, he continued, "Not enough sense to know you gotta watch kids. Running on the roof. I don't need this with a hurricane coming on. Get your stuff and get out. I'll tear up the charge slip. Just get out."

So that he wouldn't give into the urge to slam it, Jax closed the door very, very carefully after the departing owner. The man was a coward, unable to look at him while giving him the boot, but the responsibility for their predicament rested squarely on Jax's shoulders.

He was out of options for keeping Tyler with him. By now, there probably wasn't a hotel room to be found. If he was going to have to drive further inland he'd might as well take Tyler to his grandmother's house in Raleigh.

But damn! He wasn't ready to accept defeat. He wanted, needed, to keep trying. If he let things end like this between them, every bit of hope for him and Tyler was gone. From the day he arrived on Topsail Island, and found Tyler so cold, so changed from the child he remembered, he'd only been reacting to everything that happened, thinking maybe time would close the gap between him and Tyler. Thinking maybe it didn't matter if the gap didn't close, regardless of how it made him feel, because he'd shortly have to give up Tyler anyway.

Reacting, instead of thinking strategically, had gotten him here, fresh out of options.

What he needed was a plan, and he didn't have one.

He scrubbed at his forehead with a fist. He knew 86 ways to kill a man, how to make a bomb from ingredients found under a kitchen sink. He could hot wire a car, pick a lock, and start an IV. He spoke four languages, two fluently. SEALs, able to operate on the sea, in the air and on land, were the most highly trained warriors in the world. And a helluva lot of good that did him right this minute.

Tyler was where he had left him, sitting on the black and white tiles of the bathroom floor, still in his wet shorts.

First things first. He lifted Tyler to his feet. "Come on, buddy, let's get you some dry pants."

He pulled the wet shorts from the smooth little buns and his mind, still turning over his problem, slid on the crumbling-edge feeling of déjà vu.

Wet shorts. Tyler got his shorts wet when they built the sand castle. The hour or so they had spent digging and molding sand was the best time they'd had. They hadn't said much. Pickett had hung around making suggestions and chatting. Jax was amazed later when he realized how much information she had elicited without seeming to. Once Pickett left Tyler had acted a little shy again, but they'd done okay. Good really.

The corners of Jax's mouth kicked up. Pickett with the mischievous bright turquoise eyes and dancing golden curls—the sand castle was her idea.

She said she lived near Topsail Island, but on the mainland.

Tyler liked her. This was more than he could say for how Tyler felt about him. At last he could imagine something happening between him and Tyler that he wanted to happen.

It would take a lot of balls to call up a woman he hardly knew and ask for shelter from a hurricane, but hell, he was a SEAL. SEALs did things all the time other people didn't think was possible. And—he grinned at the thought—they showed up where they were least expected.

Pickett…what was her last name? — Sessoms! His even teeth gleamed white in a sharkish smile.

"Put these on." He tossed dry shorts to Tyler.

Jax flipped open his cell phone and reached for the phonebook. "I've got us a plan."

SIX

Hurricane Elvira, a Category One storm, packing winds of 82 miles per hour, is barreling down on the North Carolina coast, folks, and it's already bringing tides four feet above normal, with beach erosion as far north as Nags Head. Located 320 nautical miles—," Pickett cut the weather girl's relentlessly upbeat recital of the storm's current position. Someday she'd have to learn what a nautical mile was but today all she needed to know was that the storm would come ashore sometime early tomorrow morning. Neither did she need her ridiculously cheerful warnings about the dangers of storm surge, high winds and flooding.

Pickett made a face. The boring truth was that the worst danger she faced was loss of electricity, and that was pretty much sure thing. Her great-grandfather could be proud of the farmhouse he had built. In its hundred year history it had weathered worse hurricanes and despite being on the sound had never flooded.

But the amount of dirt and dog hair that would accumulate with two dogs in the house? Now that was scary. Not to mention the laundry that would pile up. And living without hot water.

The worst thing about no electricity though, was that she depended on a well. All she could do was fill plastic jugs and the bathtub. When that was gone she'd have to buy drinking water for herself and the dogs.

Lucy thrust her black muzzle with its white streak under Pickett's hand, and raised anxious eyes to Pickett's face. Patterson's radar instantly detected affection being handed out and lumbered over, leaning his big old yellow lab body against Pickett's other side.

Pickett knelt and put an arm around each dog's neck. "It's going to be okay, you guys. But let's go over the hurricane rules. One. No shedding. Two. No drinking from the toilets. Three. Try to convince your brother, Hobo Joe, it's safe for him to come in the house. He's lived here long enough to know this is his home now."

The two pairs of eyes fixed on her were earnest enough but Pickett didn't sense a lot of cooperation would be forthcoming.

She gave each dog a final pat and stood. "Okay, since we're going to end up with a mess, we'd better start this hurricane with a house as clean as I can make it." Pickett grabbed dish towels from the sink and headed for the mud room to start the washer. "But I do wish you'd talk to Hobo Joe."

Two hours later Pickett smoothed clean sheets onto her bed and pulled the comforter in its blue and white eyelet duvet into place. She surveyed the room with satisfaction. This room was the most recently finished in her on-going renovation of the old house.

Pickett's face softened with affection for her family as she looked about. Everywhere she looked she could see some family member's contribution.

The king size pineapple post bed came from her grandmother. She said she needed to get rid of it since she was going to convert the second bedroom to a studio for her painting hobby. The oriental rug in shades of green, rose, cream and blue, her aunt declared was a decorating mistake she never wanted to see again, and the exuberantly feminine duvet with its matching pillow shams and dust ruffle was a gift from her mother. A slipper chair and lamps came from her sisters Grace and Sarah Bea. And Lyle had been right. Painting the walls a deep green harmonized all the elements.

It was a shame she'd had to leave last night after less than an hour, but since it looked like this section of the North Carolina coast might take a direct hit, it was probably for the best.

Lyle was the only member of her family who wouldn't be calling to ask if Pickett planned to evacuate, for which favor Pickett was grateful. Her other sisters would be on her case as would her mother.

Pickett nudged Patterson from the nest he had made of the bed's pillows on the floor. "Get up, Patterson. I've got to put the pillows back on the bed."

The brown face looked at her accusingly. "I know you think it's my fault if you lie down on the pillows. You're saying 'Pillows on the floor are for dogs,' and I put them on the floor. However, I am the mama and you are the dog, so move!"

Patterson shambled his old bones into the hall where he hoped to find a place a dog could get some peace. It sounded like someone had dropped a sack of potatoes when he lay down. Pickett laughed in amused affection. Patterson wasn't going to be happy when she vacuumed in the hall, and that was going to happen next.

She giggled and tossed the new needlepoint pillow with it's cynical epigram high in the air. She didn't know all that much about men, but she did love her dogs! She set Lyle's gift on top of the other pillows in the very center of the bed.

The phone rang.

"Pickett, this is Jax Graham." His voice came to her warm and dark through the phone.

Pickett's heart changed gears without warning. Having a fantasy call, when you were expecting your mother to be on the line, did that.

He continued, "Have you heard the weather report? The hurricane has turned this way, and speeded up. They've ordered evacuation of the beaches from here to Nag's Head."

She Wasn't Interested in Lt. Jax Graham, US Navy SEAL, stationed in Little Creek, Virginia, visiting his rarely-seen son (and what did that tell you about his priorities?) with whom he was definitely out of his depth. She'd learned a lot about him as they talked—getting people to tell her a lot in a short time was her job—but that didn't mean she was Interested. Really she wasn't—fantasies last night notwithstanding. His behavior in the grocery store made it clear he wasn't interested either.

Professional sympathy, that's what she needed to respond to him with. "Too bad," she said. See? It wasn't too hard to stay cool. "This will really cut you vacation short."

"Yeah, well, that's what I wanted to talk to you about. Is your house safe or are you planning to leave too?"

Pickett gave a short laugh. "My house has withstood storms for nearly 100 years, and going to my mother's house with three dogs and a duck is more hazardous than facing a hurricane. And I will not leave my animals," she finished simply. "Why do you ask?"

"Actually, what I was wondering is…" Jax sounded oddly hesitant, not so cocky. "Look, the thing is," he started over, "I need to ask you for a favor."

A favor, not a date. Guessing the rest of what he wanted wasn't hard. "Does your mother-in law not have anywhere to go? Would you like to bring her and Tyler here?"

Whoa! What made her say that? Her heart gave a little lurch, whether of gladness that Jax hadn't disappeared from her life, or dismay that kindness might force her to sit out a hurricane with three relative strangers and no electricity, she didn't exactly know.

"That's the thing. Lauren is going to go to her home in Raleigh, but I was wondering if Tyler and I could camp with you for a couple of days. If it's not a bad blow, we'll just open the cottage back up tomorrow or the next day."

A family was one thing, but a man by himself was another. Did she really want to invite a man she hardly knew into her home? They wouldn't be alone together of course with Tyler there, but you couldn't expect a child to be much of a chaperone.

Jax realized that Pickett had been silent just a beat too long. "Look, Pickett, I'm sorry. I didn't mean to put you on the spot. Forget—"

"No, wait." Pickett interrupted again. "Forgive me if this is blunt, but why do you want to stay here? Why don't you just go to Raleigh with your mother in law?"

Jax took a deep breath. "It's a reasonable question. Look, you know I've pretty much made a mess of my relationship with my son, right? But I'm trying to see what can be pulled out of this screw up I've made. We don't exactly get along when we're here, but when we're at his grandmother's house in Raleigh, he just ignores me, like I'm not there. If we go back there now,

I'm afraid we'll lose every gain we've made. And by the time we get back here, my leave will be half over."

Pickett stepped out on the back porch. The sky, milky-looking earlier, was grayer, and the air was hotter and more humid, even since this morning. "What is it that you want to have happen with your son?"

"I don't know Pickett." Jax sounded sad and tired. " I guess I need to find out if he really is better off with his grandmother, if I should just leave him with her. But I need to find out too, whether he could be better off with me."

"Y'all come on here." Pickett's voice was so quiet, Jax almost wasn't sure he had heard her.

"You mean it?"

"Yes. Come on."

"I appreciate it."

Forty-five minutes later, Pickett had the flashlights and batteries organized, the spare battery pack for the cell phone charging, and the Coleman lantern located.

As soon as the phone rang again, Pickett knew who it was.

She considered answering "Yes Mother," but that pushed her mother's buttons. Since she was going to upset her mother anyway, there was no need to make it worse.

As usual her mother started in as soon as Pickett said hello.

"Did you know the hurricane is going to come ashore tonight?"

What did her mother think? They didn't have TV? Patience and the respectful manners drilled into her kept her tone even, but nothing, since her mother couldn't see her, kept her from rolling her eyes.

"Yes, I knew that."

"You're going to come here aren't you?"

"No, ma'am."

"They've ordered evacuations of the beaches!"

Pickett prayed for patience. "Mother, I don't live on the beach." Why should she have to say that? Her mother knew that. "I'm not in any danger."

"Well I'd feel better if you were here. What if your power goes out?"

Pickett took a deep breath. The power was sure to go out. So what? Did she really think Pickett couldn't light a candle? She tried reason. "The hurricane is as likely to hit Goldsboro as here. There's no reason to think I would escape it if I was with you. Besides, there's no way I'm leaving the dogs and you know you'd not be pleased to welcome them at your house."

Now that was an understatement. Pickett's mother did not share her love of creatures, and was particularly appalled that she had three large dogs and kept two of them in the house.

Oh no! Why had she mentioned the dogs? To her mother that would be just one more instance of Pickett's impracticality, her over-emotionalism. Proof that she couldn't take care of herself—anybody who would take in three strays had a few screws loose as far as her mother was concerned.

"Mom," Pickett took control of the conversation, "please don't worry. I'll batten down the hatches and I'll be fine."

"It's just that I hate to think of you being there alone." To hear her mother's nervous dithering, you'd never think she was head of one of the largest producing insurance agencies in the state.

Not for the first time Pickett reflected that being a family therapist didn't make the dynamics of one's own family any easier to deal with. What was she supposed to say?

Look mom, you did your best. When Daddy died you had to save the business from bankruptcy. And I got left to my big sisters to raise. At least I had them.

It wouldn't help.

They had done their best, but the nagging sense that Pickett was not quite up to the family standard had settled like a mildewed blanket on the very real love in their relationship.

Her mother felt guilty because she'd neglected Pickett, so now she tried to over-mother. Too bad knowing all that didn't make a bit of difference. Because it always felt like she never did anything in a way her mother could sincerely approve.

Pickett wondered what her mother would say if she knew Pickett would not be alone during the storm, but with a Navy SEAL whom she had just met yesterday? No, she knew what she would say and that's why she wasn't going to tell her. There was a lot to be said for living where one's family couldn't know what was happening on a daily basis.

She didn't need to listen to her mother's warnings and cries of doom.

"Look, mom. I need to get off the phone. Someone's coming soon." Her mother would assume she meant a client, and would accept that business came first. Pickett winced at the knowledge that she was being deliberately misleading. "I'll call you as soon as the hurricane passes, okay? And make sure you take care of yourself."

The air was like a moist blanket, hot, thick and eerily still. Between bursts of cicada whirring it was so quiet that she could actually hear waves hitting the beach over on the island in that odd booming cadence that heralds a storm.

A pot of lantana under one arm and a begonia under the other, Pickett struck out for the garage, crossing the drive just as Jax driving a Jeep Cherokee pulled up to the back door.

Her heart kicked against her breast bone. Oh lord, what had she done? How had she forgotten the moment she'd looked around in the deli and seen Jax watching her?

Her gut had told her in that very minute he was a dangerous man.

"Listen to your gut," she always advised her clients.

She had to tell him he couldn't stay, and do it right now. Pickett started across the drive.

SEVEN

J ax was out of the Cherokee, reaching through the rear door into the back seat.

Now. Before he got Tyler out of the car, she had to tell him he couldn't stay. Letting a chance-met stranger into her house was too dangerous. The rough clay of the flower pots dug into her palms. She set them at her feet. Now.

Childish wails, interspersed with hiccupping sobs issued from the car. The wails escalated to screams. "No! The hur'cane's going to get us! We have to run away! Let me go!"

Jax held the little flailing hands in one big hand, confining the squirming body in one muscular arm. The ease with which he held the child was apparent, as was the fact that he only used enough strength to confine, not overpower.

Jax's bronzed cheeks held extra ruddiness. "I'm sorry about this. His grandmother is the nervous sort. She really managed to scare him."

Unless Pickett missed her guess, what his grandmother was, was the idiotic sort, who was not happy that Jax was going to Pickett's and had attempted to manipulate the situation by getting Tyler upset. That was low.

Pickett made her decision.

"Tyler," Pickett used the voice a client once said was steel encased in goose down. "Tyler, look at me," Drowned grey eyes peered at her from the reddened, tear streaked face. "Now feel your Daddy's arms. Your daddy's arms are warm, aren't they? And you can feel how strong they are." The little body relaxed slightly, allowing the strength to hold him. "Your daddy will keep you safe. Your grandmother was scared of the hurricane and so she had to run away. But your daddy is not scared, he is strong and he can keep you safe. Now let's get your things in the house, because we have a lot to do."

In the house she introduced Tyler to Lucy and Patterson, and assured him that she really did have a duck. Quackers was nowhere to be seen but would show up at dinner time.

"I think I'll let the two of you share my room and I'll use the day bed in my office," she fore-stalled Jax's protest with a wave. "I'm afraid you'd be pretty miserable on the day bed and Tyler will be more secure in a strange place if you're with him. Anyway, it's only for one night."

Jax shouldered the luggage and followed Pickett down the cool, dim hall, admiring the view of Pickett's backside.

Who would have thought those classically restrained slacks and man tailored blouses concealed a lush, utterly feminine body? Full breasts tapered to tiny waist then flared again to rounded butt softly hugged by green running shorts.

Her legs were all shapely curves flowing from trim ankles to substantial thighs. He knew women worried about heavy thighs but personally he found that evidence of womanly strength erotic.

He jerked his mind from the implications of strong, yet soft thighs, and made himself take in the furnishings of the room.

The antique four poster was piled with the most pillows Jax had ever seen.

"Plus je vois les hommes, plus j'adore mes chiens." He read the saying on the pale green needlepoint pillow in the center.

"The more I know about men, the more I love my dogs," he translated. He gave a snort of laughter, and turned to Pickett. "I wouldn't have figured you for a misanthrope."

"That's a housewarming present made by my sister Lyle in New York. I think she meant it as a joke, although with Lyle you're never sure." She tilted her head. "You recognized the quote. Are you fluent in French?"

He nodded absently. "Why so many pillows?"

Was she blushing? What brought that on? Her eyes moved from the bed to him a couple of times. She shrugged. "I like pillows. But feel free to move any that you don't want." She put her hand on the doorknob. "I'll leave you to get settled. Be aware that this house was built long before central heat, so every room, including the bathroom, opens into the room adjoining as well as into the hall. For privacy, make sure you close both doors."

The latch clicked behind her. She liked pillows. Standard pillows, a long pillow that crossed the width of the bed, big pillows and small fluffy pillows. Pillows of plush velvet and pillows covered with crocheted lace. Jax felt his body tighten, again. He could imagine her naked, her peach skin bare against that white lacy cover-thing, as she curled amongst all those pillows.

Whoa. That was so not going to happen. There was no reason to pursue women who might have regrets afterward. That just led to messy complications.

There were too many women who were delighted to throw themselves into bed with any SEAL. Lately, though, the look of sexual calcula-tion he saw in women's eyes when they learned he was a SEAL had become a turn off.

It was best to go with women who no more wanted him to be there the morning after than he did. And yet being with some woman he wouldn't remember in a week or a month, no longer seemed worth doing. He'd found a few women whose company he enjoyed in addition to the sex. Women who could accept the very loose arrange-ments he was able to make, but even those never lasted long. How long had it been?

There was Joanie. The last time he called she mentioned she'd found someone who was around on a more regular basis. Six, seven months ago. Before Afghanistan.

Okay, so maybe he was horny. Maybe that's what was making Pickett look so good, in spite of the fact that she was exactly the kind of woman he stayed away from. It wasn't her full breasts that made his palm curl to think of testing their soft weight. It wasn't the way she seemed to be all soft curves, utterly feminine to his maleness. It wasn't the way her sparkling aqua eyes looked at him, guilelessly aware of the attraction, and yet, as if she saw him, not some SEAL stud package. He was just horny. Yeah. That was it.

Well, he liked sex as much as the next man, but he had never been the kind of man who allowed his hormones to control him.

And in spite of her patina of gracious hospitality he could tell she was still wary of him. Any move on his part could spook her, make her tell him to go, and he didn't want that to happen. Not while she could work what looked like magic with Tyler. She had calmed Tyler with just a couple of sentences, while nothing he had said in the thirty-five minute trip from Wilmington had had any effect on the screams issuing from the back seat.

It was ironic that while his SEAL buddies, strong and superbly competent men everyone, went with him into dangers unimaginable to most people, and trusted him with their lives, his small son only trusted him after a hundred pound woman told him to.

But maybe that was normal. How the hell was he supposed to know? He'd never been around little kids much, didn't remember a lot of his own childhood before he had met Corey. He wished Corey was here. Corey knew more about almost everything than most people, but more than that, he had a way of cutting through to what really mattered.

Back in Little Creek, his decision had looked so easy. Simple. Go to North Carolina and get the custody papers notarized. The only reason he'd come to North Carolina was Commander Kohn's insistence that he visit Tyler. Lauren's suggestion that they meet at her Topsail beach cottage, instead of her house in Raleigh seemed a little odd, but he had no objection.

Jax hadn't been around Lauren much, never for any extended time. Had Danielle ever told him her mother drank too much? He didn't think so, but she certainly did now. Too much, too often.

Still, he knew plenty of rock-solid, dependable men, women too, who hit the officers' or enlisted clubs the minute they were off-duty. Heavy drinking was a way of life for some in the Navy. As long as they did their jobs, he didn't begrudge them—or Lauren, who had just lost her daughter—whatever helped them make it through the night.

Until he realized hard work and long hours were more effective than scotch in blotting out his pain, in the months after Danielle left him, Jax had closed down a lot of bars himself.

From what Jax had seen, drinking didn't interfere with her care of Tyler. She bathed and fed and
clothed Tyler adequately. More than adequately if
he counted the number of new clothes and toys
she'd bought him.

Sober or loaded though, now that he had
gotten to know Lauren better, one thing was
clear: he couldn't stand her. But did that matter?
Jax wouldn't have to live her. Tyler would, but
he couldn't tell how Tyler felt about his grandmother. He couldn't tell how Tyler felt about
anything.

Tyler was not the boisterous little extravert Jax
remembered. The child who drifted, silently
absorbed in his cars along the edges of a room was
hardly recognizable. In a way Jax liked it better
when Tyler went ballistic. At least he felt like he
understood that child.

Jax didn't like mysteries. He preferred problems he could get his hands around. The uneasy
feeling that something important was happening
before his eyes and he was missing it crept
through his chest again.

Jax realized he had been standing in the open
closet door staring sightlessly at Pickett's clothes.
There were not many. A few pairs of slacks, some
blouses, that jacket he'd seen her in.

A couple of dresses wrapped in plastic were
pushed to the back. There was room to spare for
the hanging clothes he had brought. So different
from the overflowing closets he remembered
Danielle having.

The closet smelled like her. A subtle smell of lilies or something, and sunshine and softness and feminine essence. Just for a second he could imagine himself, naked, satisfied, replete with love-making, smelling that scent of her on his own skin. His lower body tightened. He glanced at the bed piled with seductive softness, but also with one small pillow in the very center that warned, "The more I know about men, the better I love my dogs."

Damn.

On a whim he picked up the pillow and sniffed it. It smelled like her too.

A night of smelling her without having her.

Damn.

EIGHT

They worked through the afternoon, clearing the yard of lawn chairs and other items that could become missiles once the wind started, ferrying hanging baskets of ferns and wandering jew to the garage. Tyler tagged after them for a while, asking questions, and manfully carrying small items. Once his interest in that flagged, Pickett showed him how to play fetch with Lucy.

Lucy, who adored fetch, was willing to agree that enthusiasm was as important as a strong pitching arm. The Frisbee wouldn't sail very well in the unpredictable gusts, but the fly ball proved to be a great success, as Tyler got the hang of making a toss that Lucy could grab out of the air.

"What's with your three-legged dog?" Jax indicated the large German Shepard mix with his head.

Pickett smiled. "He doesn't take his eyes off you does he? Truth is, he lives here, but I'm not sure he's my dog yet. I haven't had him long, and he won't come in the house. Sometimes he'll let me touch him, but he never asks for affection."

Jax noticed the wistfulness in her voice. That bothered her—that she had affection the dog wouldn't let her give. "How long have you had him?" Jax bent to pick up a large pot of pale purple flowers.

"Oh, don't bother with those petunias. The urn is too heavy to blow around and they'll die back soon anyway. I was just going to kiss them goodbye."

Jax hoisted the plant higher. "Show me where to put it."

"I guess we'll have to put it in the garage. The shed is pretty full."

Hobo Joe paced them, always outside arms' reach, always keeping them in sight. "So what about the dog?"

"I found him at the other end of Folkstone road. If I hadn't glanced right where he was lying I would never have seen him. His black and tan blended perfectly with the tall brush he was in. Actually, what I saw was the blood, something red in that brush and it just didn't look right." Pickett opened the garage door. "So I stopped the car, and went over to see what it was."

"He'd been hit by a car?"

Pickett shook her head. "The vet says he'd been shot." She pushed her shoulders back as if pushing away a thought. "Anyway, he was unconscious and the leg—it was this obscene-looking thing with the bone showing and sort of hanging." She shuddered, then looked up at Jax, her eyes troubled. "I'm going to tell you the truth: I wished with all my heart that I was the kind of person who could just walk away. I did not want to touch him."

"But you did touch him."

Pickett made a what was I going to do? face. "I had to, to find out it he had a heartbeat. And then it wasn't so bad. I had a bunch of clothes I was carrying to Goodwill, so I made a tourniquet. But then I had a problem. I knew I couldn't pick him up. I had an old rain coat I could put him on and drag him. So that's what I did."

Jax measured the dog, measured Pickett. He probably weighed 100 pounds, close to if not more than Pickett did. "You got him in the car by yourself?"

"You know that saying, 'coincidence is God's way of remaining anonymous?' Well, just as I got him on the raincoat, Isabel who runs a junk shop down on Highway 17 saw my car and stopped. We did it together." Pickett rolled her eyes. "Now I had a huge dog and a huge vet bill to go with him."

"You already had two rescued dogs and you brought home a third—just like that?"

"Makes me sound a little strange doesn't it?"

"Not strange. Caring. Courageous."

Pickett shook her head. "Don't give me too much credit. I wouldn't have touched Hobo if I'd seen another way."

Jax wandered over to a section of the garage behind where the cars were parked. All sorts of household detritus was crammed in, thick dust testifying to how long it had lain undisturbed.

Pickett saw his interest. "You're looking at something else I haven't wanted to touch. You should have seen what was crammed in the house. My great-uncle had the property and I don't think anything had been thrown away for fifty years."

Jax bent down to look under the pile. "You have a generator."

"I do?"

Jax pointed.

"Oh, that. I guess it's a generator. There's no telling when's the last time it worked."

"You have a generator. What are we doing standing here talking?" Jax handed her a card table, covered with spider webs, which instantly flopped a leg.

"Yechh! Spider webs! I hate spider webs."

"Sorry." Jax shifted and sorted old suitcases, a toaster with no cord, part of a plow, a chamber pot. "Hot damn!" He smeared the dust from the manufacturer's name. "The army still uses these. This is a workhorse."

The enthusiasm, not to say joy, in his voice was unmistakable. Pickett rubbed spiders' webs from her hands and shook her head. There was no accounting for tastes. The junk people paid Isabel good money for proved that...And Isabel did have a bed Pickett would be willing to take off her hands.

"Do you like it?" Pickett inquired politely. "If you want it, you can have it."

Jax stared at her blankly for a moment. "Pickett, you want it. It. Makes. Electricity," he softly emphasized each word.

"Yes. I. Know," Pickett matched his emphasis perfectly, the dimple appearing in the corner of her mouth. "It. Doesn't. Work."

Jax grinned. "It's going to."

Pickett stuffed the package of frozen hamburger Jax had brought from the cottage into the freezer compartment. He'd also an ice chest full of ice. Putting bags of ice into the refrigerator once the power went off would extend the life of her perishables. In fact, she should put some in now, so they'd stay frozen longer. To make room she pulled out the loaf of whole wheat bread she kept on hand for guests and set it on the counter to thaw. One good thing about having company for a hurricane: she had a better chance of using up her food before it went bad.

Pickett found gallon zip-locks and opened the ice chest. It was going to be a miracle if Jax could get the ancient generator running. She chuckled soundlessly. What was it about men and smelly mechanical things? You'd have thought he was a teenager handed some cherry bombs when he saw the grimy thing lurking among the cobwebs in the back of the garage. It was left from her great-uncle's tenure of the property, so there was no telling when was the last time it had worked.

She was only glad the man had something to do. Something that got him out of the house for a while until she could adjust to the fact that for the next day or two he was going to be in it. She was too aware when he was around. And he made her feel like she didn't fit inside her skin. Her breasts felt too large and seemed to press against her clothes. Her hips felt too loose, her eyes too hot.

The plastic bag she was scooping ice into slipped from her grasp and hit the floor, scattering ice cubes in all directions.

Oh, this had to stop! Now she was getting as bothered when she was just thinking about him as when he was in the room.

Abruptly she raised her head and listened. She could no longer hear sounds of play coming from the side yard. A quick look out the window showed a light rain being borne on fitful gusts, but no dogs or boy. She stepped outside. They were not on the porch that ran around three sides of the house.

Remembering the fun Tyler had jumping on the pile of cushions taken from the lawn chairs she peeped in the cobwebbed window of the shed where they had been piled. There he was.

She circled to the front of the garage. Jax squatted beside the generator. In the airless heat of the garage he had taken off his tee shirt and his broad shoulders gleamed with sweat in the dull light. His hands were dirty and a dark smudge traveled up one long forearm, skipped a space, then continued across defined pecs. He balanced on the balls of his feet, poised and motionless, as if he could remain in that position indefinitely, and yet he rose in one flowing movement when he heard her approach.

Pickett laid a finger against her lips. "You've got to see this." She motioned him to follow and led him back around the garage to the shed door. She opened it then stood aside so he could see.

On a haphazard pile of flowered cushions the little boy slept surrounded by dogs. Tyler lay on his back, one arm flung over his head, one grass-stained knee cocked. On either side of him, Patterson and Lucy also lay on their backs, their legs spread, paws in the air.

Only Hobo Joe was not asleep. He reclined at Tyler's feet, studying the intruders with level yellow gaze. He twitched his nose as if to test their intentions, then apparently satisfied, sighed and rested his square head on his paws.

It was a darling tableau. Too precious not to share, but a lot of men wouldn't let themselves react to something so frankly sentimental. She'd already observed how often the expression on his face hid as much as it revealed. Pickett tilted her head to catch Jax's reaction. His eyes were soft, blurred a little with unshed tears. Rosy color suffused his cheekbones and his lips were relaxed, turning up at each corner. She expected him to be amused by the scene, perhaps touched by its sweetness, but not this naked—what? Love? Tenderness? Longing? Carefully she laid her palm against his biceps.

She was so close he could smell her shampoo and the same scent he'd noticed in her bedroom. Her palm, warm, soft, rested lightly on his upper arm. She was looking at him, not the sleeping child, a bemused smile on her face, her eyes ocean-deep and liquid.

With a crooked little smile he tilted his head to the scene in the shed. She nodded.

And that's when it happened. He looked into her tilted eyes with the golden flecks, her lips open in a little smile and he just had to kiss her. She had so many smiles. Winsome, flirtatious, mischievous, humorous. This one was just...sweet. Precious. He just had to kiss it. He cupped her shoulder with one hand and bent toward her.

Her shoulder was soft, firm with feminine strength yet the bones oddly fragile feeling under his cupped palm. Slowly, he bent toward her, until their lips just touched.

NINE

Fuck. He'd kissed her. He promised himself he wasn't going to put any moves on her and then the first time she got inside arm's length he kissed her.

Hell, he was a guest in her home. He hadn't missed that wary look when he and Tyler drove up. Any woman would or should be wary in a situation like this. So he was going to do the respect bit all the way.

And then he kissed her. And the part that really twisted his tail was that it wasn't even about sex.

Not that he wouldn't like to have her naked under him, all soft sweet curves. He'd wanted her from the first time he saw her, all cool and prissy, with that you'll-never-fuck-me attitude.

A woman like that might tick him off, and God knows after Danielle he'd learned never to take one seriously, but they sure turned him on.

He'd wanted to muss her hair, and tease her by flicking open a couple of buttons of that cool silk. God, who would have known, when she took off those restrained silk shirts and rich girl slacks, she'd have a little body that was all curves? He felt his body tighten.

He hoped he hadn't scared her, or screwed everything up. Wouldn't you know that the time it's not about sex would be when he'd forget his good intentions?

She had touched him first. For most women that was a signal, a come on. But that was no excuse; she was a toucher. She seemed to always have her hand on something, soothing, smoothing, fingering. Her dogs, Tyler—she even petted her house plants.

When he'd set that big leaf thing down in the shed, she had stroked it and talked to it, reassured it that it would be safe from the hurricane. Then Tyler had leaned up against her, one arm wrapped around her creamy thigh, and questioned her about the safety of every item in the shed.

Tyler might be silent around his father and grandmother, but he had no trouble talking to Pickett. Yes, she had assured him with grave patience, the plants were safe, the chairs and the cushions were safe, the grill was safe, while she stroked his hair and traced the rim of his ear.

"And you, Tyler, are safe because your daddy has big strong arms, and he will keep you safe." Then Tyler did something strange. He leaned even closer and whispered "Is he going to stay here with us?"

"Yes, precious," she smoothed his hair back from his upturned face—touching was just her way—"he's going to stay in the house with us and we will all be safe."

So he knew it didn't mean anything if she touched him. But when he felt that soft palm against his arm, it was like a circuit opened between them and he knew she understood the aching sweetness that had almost blasted him away and even shared it. She had given it to him. Then for him to touch her, to kiss her and somehow complete the circuit was the most natural thing in the world. So he kissed her.

Oh well, it was done. She hadn't been so offended that she had thrown him and Tyler out. Her eyes had widened. A pulse was visible in her neck, but she only said, "It's starting to rain. You'd better carry him in the house."

He was on his guard and wouldn't let it happen again. He needed to let it go. Worrying about what had happened instead of what was happening could get a man killed.

Jax wiped his hands, and gave the generator a long look. Okay, he'd oiled this sucker, cleaned the spark plugs, and checked the carburetor. He added more gas, set the choke and hauled on the starter rope.

It started right up.

"Hey," said Jax from the doorway. He had pulled on shorts he had worn earlier and his chest and feet were bare. "Couldn't sleep?"

Pickett sat curled up on the flower-splashed sofa in a pool of yellow light, the light bringing out the golden highlights of her hair and peachy tones of her skin. Small round reading glasses perched on her nose, and the man's tee shirt, so large that it threatened to slip off one shoulder, made her look absurdly young.

The old yellow dog, Patterson slept stretched out on the floor beneath her. Placed in readiness on the low pine chest that served as a coffee table were flash light, candle and matches.

"I woke up about thirty minutes ago and couldn't go back to sleep. The noise of the wind makes me uneasy." Pickett shrugged as if she felt silly to make such an admission, causing the shirt to slip, further exposing the delicate hollows where collarbone and shoulder met. She centered the wandering neckline with a flustered twitch. "I thought coming in here to read would be better than lying in the dark listening to the wind. At least we haven't lost power yet."

"Are you scared?" He sat down on the opposite end of the sofa and turned to face her.

"No." He raised a dubious eyebrow. "I'm really not. Not rationally. I'm a little worried about Hobo Joe, because he wouldn't come inside. But I don't think we're in any real danger." She looked at the dark windows. "There's just something about the way the wind sounds. Do you hear it? It's not only that it's blowing hard. It's that long, slithery sound—it gives me a feeling of dread. I don't know why."

"It might be the low barometric pressure. Some people's emotions are affected by changes in atmospheric pressure."

"Might be," Pickett agreed so readily he was sure she was humoring him. "So what are you doing up?"

"I woke up too. I saw your light and wondered," the lights flickered, "if we could talk a minute."

Just then the lights went off and stayed off.

"Since it looks like I'm not going to read anymore, we'd might as well talk." Pickett fumbled on the chest for the flashlight. It proved to be just out of her reach, forcing her to put one foot down. That foot landed on Patterson who grumbled sleepily. "Excuse me, Patterson." The woman was so polite she apologized to a dog. "Actually, Jax," he could hear a wry smile in her voice, "I'm glad of the company."

Being able to visualize where things were, even in total darkness was a fundamental SEAL skill. Jax struck a match just as she found the flashlight and flicked it on. She lifted the hurricane chimney so that he could light the candle, then replaced it as he shook out the match then broke it. "Thanks."

"Your hands are shaking. The feeling of what did you call it, dread—is it very bad?"

"It's..." Pickett took a ragged breath, "manageable. Distraction helps. Talk to me. Tell me something."

"I didn't know you wear glasses..." That wasn't what he meant to say. But finding the way to start was harder than he'd thought it would be when he woke and saw the light under the living room door. She looked little and vulnerable, and so damned cute in a tee shirt that came to her knees and her hair coming down from its topknot.

"Only for reading, and only when I'm tired." She touched the frames and gave a little laugh. "I forgot I had them on." She took off the glasses and put them on the end table.

"This feeling of dread. Does it have anything to do with me?" he felt more than saw her stir at the other end of the couch, "because if it does," he hurried on, "I need you to know you're absolutely safe with me. I won't hurt you."

"Thanks," Pickett's voice was a little husky, "I knew that, but thanks for saying it."

"How did you know it? You don't know me. When I think of you letting another man in your house that way you did me, it scares me sh- to death."

"I have pretty reliable intuition, but in your case I had data as well." Data. Little round glasses and she talked like a textbook. It should have been a turn off, but somehow it wasn't working that way. "You didn't use your strength to overwhelm or subdue Tyler. Even if you didn't hit him or anything, it would have been so easy for you to hold him tight enough to make his struggles hurt. That's when I decided."

Jax thought back to the scene in the drive. Pickett holding a flower pot in each arm, looking so wary, then suddenly taking over.

"Yeah, I wanted to ask you about that. How did you know exactly what to say? I'd been telling him for twenty-five minutes that the hurricane wasn't really dangerous as long as we got off the beach."

"Did you explain all about storm surge and tornadoes and everything?" she inquired, eyes wide with fake innocense.

Jax chuckled, and let his head drop to the back of the couch. "No, I wasn't that idiotic. I do know he's a little kid. But I'm serious, how did you get him turned off in two seconds flat?"

"It's a technique. The problem is that the person, in this case the child, is totally referencing an internal state. You might say they're not in touch with reality. So you demand they focus externally, offer a reinterpretation of what's happening, with sensory corroboration, and then redirect to some action."

"Sensory corroboration. That's when you said 'feel his arms,' right?"

"Right." Pickett flashed a smile at his ready comprehension. "In this case it was easy because four-year-olds tend to see cause and effect as something being stronger than something else. For instance, they would say that an airplane can fly because it's stronger than air. So reinterpretation was a piece of cake. You are stronger than his grandmother, a fact he could check out for himself, ergo, you could keep him safe without needing to run away."

"And you could work out all this in a split second?"

A shrug sent the tee shirt sliding off the other shoulder. "Practice helps."

"I think you must be really good at what you do. Because, you said the right thing for me too."

Her eyes widened slightly and head tilted. It was like she opened a space as wide as hangar doors. He didn't have to steer his thoughts. He could go right through.

"When Danielle and I got married, I knew right away that it was a mistake, and I think she did too. She thought our marriage would be glamorous and exciting. Hobnobbing with admirals and hanging out at the pool at the officer's club. The reality is that I'm gone way more than I'm here, and most of what I do I can't talk about." He shifted forward to rest his forearms on his knees. "But just when I realized our marriage was all wrong, she got pregnant. We decided to stay together till after the baby was born.

"I didn't think about what I would do with a baby. I know it's stupid but the baby wasn't real to me. It just seemed like something Danielle was doing, and it didn't have much to do with me. I was focusing on being a SEAL and that's all I was focused on.

"Anyway, by sheer luck I was there when he was born. He was so little. He didn't even fill up my two hands." Jax spread his hands, remembering weighing the tiny creature in them. "I never expected to feel like that. That love. I just wanted to protect him and keep him safe. I knew I would die for him."

"My platoon left on assignment three weeks after he was born, and while we were gone Danielle took Tyler and moved back to Raleigh to her mother's house.

"I didn't fight for custody. Hell, she was more able to take care of him than I was. Any fool could see that."

Pickett hadn't said anything at all, mostly wasn't even looking at him. But her capacity to listen was like a vast force that floated him and drew him on.

"I haven't seen enough of him, I know. Even though I've tried to visit when I could, I'll bet we haven't spent a total of four months together since he was born.

"But today when he was so scared and he couldn't believe I would keep him safe…" Jax rubbed at his eyes and then his nose.

"That really hurt, hm?"

Hurt. Jax swallowed. Nodded. "The whole op was going to sh —excuse me. And you stood there looking like I was Godzilla."

"For the record, the image I had in mind was more Attila the Hun, than Godzilla."

Jax slanted her a glance. "That's supposed to make me feel better?"

"A military man—of a sort—rather than a monster? I think so." Her tone was judicious, but the tiny dimple that appeared in the corner of her mouth said she was twitting him. And enjoying it.

"Okay, you were looking at me like I was Attila and then suddenly you weren't.

"You believed I wouldn't hurt you and I would keep him safe." He swiveled to face her fully. "You believed in me."

She was regarding him with a tender little smile. She nodded. She had the shining-est eyes.

The force of the storm had steadily increased as they talked. The wind was a steady roar, interspersed with even stronger gusts that shook the house. Suddenly the old house creaked and shuddered as if it had been slapped by a giant hand. The windows and storm windows were closed, nevertheless the curtain moved from time to time.

Pickett let her breath out slowly.

Jax covered her slender foot with one brown hand. "How's the dread?"

"Not as bad. Thanks."

She was lying—he'd seen her holding her breath. But she was determined to be brave. "I told you something, now you tell me something." Her foot was so soft, the skin, even on the sole, smooth and moist. He massaged it, stroked it like some woodland creature to be tamed.

Pickett didn't know whether she wanted to pull her foot away, or put the other one where he could reach it. Well, she did know what she wanted, she just didn't know which one she should do. Pickett wasn't so naïve she didn't know what was happening. But she'd packed her fantasies away where they belonged when he'd unbuckled his screaming son from the car seat.

He's not a client, a voice constantly enticed. He's only here because he needs you, another voice warned sharply. You're not maintaining boundaries for his protection, as you would for a client. You're maintaining them for yourself.

The intimacy of the hour, the intimacy of the a soft pool of light cast by the candle on the coffee table, the rest of the room lost in shadow. Even the knowledge that, until the storm passed, fire-fighters, police etc., would not move from their stations, contributed to the intimacy. Until the storm passed they were as alone together as anyone in the modern world could be.

Intimacy could be a seduction in itself.

The house had grown warmer in the few minutes since the air conditioning went off with the power. She could smell his sweat, a whiff of motor oil he'd gotten on his shorts.

He kissed her this afternoon. Afterward, they'd both pretended it was a nothing, not a liberty—which it wasn't, and not an intimacy, which it was.

Pickett wasn't naïve. She knew where all this intimacy led.

His hand warm, companionable, utterly male, stroked her foot, while he let his head loll against the cushions of the sofa back. In the candle light the color of his eyes was lost. She could only see their glitter under lazy, half lowered lids.

All she had to do was put the other foot where he could reach it. Stretch her leg just a little to stroke his thigh with her toes. Everything was in place to live out her fantasy, including the fact that she really liked the man. Except, well, now that her wish was coming true, she couldn't be sure she'd enjoy her wish when she got it, because...

Jax jiggled her foot indicating he'd waited long enough for her answer, "Say something."

"I don't like sex," Pickett said.

The hand covering her toes stilled. Jax did a slow sideways take.

Pickett felt her face heat up, and her eyes widen in horror as she realized she'd spoken her thoughts aloud. "Oh God!" she clapped her hands over her mouth as if she could stuff the words back in. "I don't know why I said that! Blame it on...hurricane insanity." Hurricane insanity—now that sounded insane. "Just—just forget I said it, would you?"

Jax hooted, loud, masculine, confident, throwing back his head so the candlelight revealed the strong column of his neck. "No way!" He turned to her, eyes still gleaming with mirth. "Is it true?"

"Yes." She was frozen. Too shocked, too mortified to lie. How could she have let slip out what she had never told anyone—not even her therapist.

"So, you can't get off, or what?"

Somehow the very crudeness of the question punctured some of Pickett's ballooning embarrassment.

"That's not it. If you must know, I don't like it because it's embarrassing, and messy, but mostly I don't like it because it is so bor-ring!"

"Let me make sure I'm tracking this. You think sex is embarrassing and messy and boring and you get off?" Jax threw back his head and roared. "Jesus! Imagine what you could do if you liked it!" The image of what she could do, what he could do, flooded her face with heat.

Pickett snatched her foot away. She pulled both knees under the baggy tee shirt and smoothed the cotton over them.

"You could try for a little sensitivity, here, you know. And the correct term is orgasm." She added primly.

"I know what the fucking correct term is." Jax didn't really mind that she had taken her foot away. With her knees pulled up like that the tee shirt gaped at the neck. If he tilted his head only a very little he could see the tops of her breasts.

He tilted his head.

"But I don't see how talking about sex in Latin and Greek will clarify the subject." He smiled the smile of a bridge player laying down an unexpected trump card. "The words that were good enough for Chaucer are good enough for me."

Pickett's eyes widened at the accuracy of his riposte. Good. Let her find out right now that intellectual intimidation wouldn't work.

Intellectual intimidation wouldn't work on him but he bet it had worked plenty of times in the past to keep men at arm's length. It would take a guy with a lot of confidence, and a tough skin to get past her cool façade. But combining with her air of vulnerable femininity, it would act like an irresistible lure to guys who liked to score for the challenge of it. All right, he was one of those guys, but he damn well made sure that the woman knew it was a game. And liked to play it too. That way everybody won.

"Good sex is messy. But embarrassing and boring are pretty much the opposite of good sex. How much experience have you had?"

"Enough to know, all right?" Pickett snapped. "I really don't want to talk about this. I've never told anybody, not even my shrink how I feel."

"How much experience?"

"Twice. It didn't take three strikes before I realized I was out. I discovered I was being used..." Embarrassment wasn't even the right word, although there had been plenty of that. Humiliation was more accurate.

She had thought Doug liked her, and found her desirable. Taunts about being fat, about being nothing but a brain, and even, illogically, overheard remarks that she was stacked, had corroded her confidence in her attractiveness.

She thought he admired her mind, and he did. He wanted her to write his terms papers.

He had charmed her and curiosity, her besetting sin, had done the rest. She wanted to know what all the fuss over sex was about.

Pickett had been reluctant to let him see her body but he had kissed her softly as he unbuttoned her blouse, overcoming her doubts. He had aroused her skillfully, patiently, and the experience of losing her virginity hadn't been bad. The first time at least had novelty to keep it interesting.

The second time thoughts about a really good book she was only half way through and eager to finish kept intruding. She moved her hips to get him to pick up the pace. She'd forego an orgasm to get him to finish this. Though intellectually lazy, he was thorough in other ways, so he held back until he felt her contractions begin. She lay there with his sweaty body sticking to hers, and wondered how other people could think this was wonderful.

The next day studying at her favorite table tucked in the stacks, she saw one of Doug's fraternity brothers pass down the aisle. He didn't see her, and it was possible he wouldn't have recognized her even if he had. In a few minutes her study was disturbed by low male voices. One of the voices was Doug's.

"Whatcha doing in the stacks, man? I thought you had a way to ace that lit course without doing research papers."

"I do. But if I show up with the right books, it will be easier to convince her I really need her help."

Male laughter.

They were talking about her! Doug had said he would drop by the library today to pick up some books she'd recommended. Pickett felt her face grow hot. Her heart pounded, and her sweating palms left droplets on the oak table.

"So, is she easy?"

"You're wondering if you can get the same deal next semester." More male laughter. "She's easy for me. Who knows if the same would be true for you, my man."

"Just let me know when you're ready to move over. She's got great boobs and I could use an A."

"She's okay if you keep the lights off."

She's okay if you keep the lights off. Pickett could never remember afterward how she got back to her dorm room. All she could remember was that phrase that seemed to repeat over and over.

"Twice. With the same guy, right?" Jax's dark rumble broke into her memories. Pickett nodded. "Were you in love with the jerk?" Jax's voice called Pickett back to the present.

"No." She hadn't thought she was in love with Doug or vice versa. It was not her heart that got broken that day, but something much more fragile.

The thought of some man getting under her guard, of carelessly using that sweet little body with no appreciation for the jewel that she was, made his gut clench. One thing was clear: Pickett might say now that she hadn't been in love, but she wouldn't enter into sex lightly, and she wouldn't think sex was a game. Much as he might wish to run his hands across her soft curves, to touch her and taste her and sink himself into that soft awareness—he was half hard right now—it wasn't going to happen. But still he couldn't let it go.

"Let me get this straight. You had sex, all of twice, with a jerk, and on the basis of that vast experience, you decided you don't like sex? Forever?" Jax sounded angry, frustrated, as if something about his summation pushed him to the edge.

Pickett didn't feel able to pursue it. In spite of his sarcastic tone she had the feeling that he had said something really important. Something that made all the difference if only she knew exactly what.

The wind blew almost continuously now, and rain could be heard hitting the side of the house, even where it was protected by porches. Lucy woke up and stretched, yawning wide to reveal her pink tongue. With the air conditioning off the house was already becoming hot and humid.

Pickett used the flashlight to look at the little crystal battery driven clock. "It's quarter to six. There's no point in going back to bed. I am now officially declaring tonight over, and today to have begun. I'm going to take a shower while there's still hot water in the tank."

Jax rasped a hand over dark early morning stubble. He looked thoroughly rumpled and incredibly sexy. "Good idea. I'll start the generator. Save some hot water for me?"

TEN

"Is my mommy really dead, do you think," Tyler swung his legs, kicking the opposite chair with every other swing.

Pickett's hands paused in the act of cracking an egg against the counter edge. Okay, where had this come from? "What makes you ask?"

"You said Hobo Joe would get dead if he didn't come in from the hurr'cane."

"I know. I wish he would come inside." And let that be a lesson to me to watch what I say around this child. "But he's a smart dog and I'm sure he's safe, and so are you. Is that why you asked about your mother?"

"Well, they said she was lost and she wouldn't come back. But Hobo Joe runned away and then he came back, and I think Mommy will too."

Having no idea where this had come from or where it was going, Pickett fell back on the therapist hum.

"Hmm," she said, and waited to hear if he would elaborate.

The generator rumbled under the constant roar

of the wind. Pickett glanced out the window but could see nothing except the blowing, almost solid curtain of rain. The wind had been so steady for the last hour that she had grown accustomed to it. It was only when sudden heavier gusts struck the house that she heard it. Now what she heard was the intermittent slapping of sneaker on chair.

"What's this about your mom?" a dark voice asked from the door to the hall.

Pickett dropped the whisk she was using on the eggs and the dogs scrambled, scrabbling their nails on the smooth floor, vying to be first to lick up the puddle.

"Sorry," Jax muttered. He crossed the room in two strides, picked up the whisk, and rinsed it, before handing it to Pickett.

He was dressed this morning in a navy T-shirt that said "The only easy day was yesterday," and loose shorts. There must have been enough hot water left in the tank to shave and she caught a whiff of shaving lotion. As always, his sheer physical presence seemed to overwhelm whatever space he was in. Pickett stood her ground when he reached past her for the coffee pot, but only just.

"Stop kicking the chair, Tyler, and tell me what you were saying about your mom."

Two kicks. "Nothing."

"I said, stop kicking."

Two more kicks. Louder.

"Tyler," Pickett opened the silver drawer, "I need somebody to get out the knives and forks. Can you count? We'll need three forks."

The little boy slid from the chair, "And three knives? I can count. I'll get 'em."

"Great, now put them on the table next to the plates."

Tyler placed the flatware, near and sometimes on the plates, but not beside, and not with each place having one of each.

When Jax would have pointed out his errors, Pickett caught his eye and shook her head.

"Good setting the table, Tyler. Thank you. Now maybe you'd like to make the toast. But you'd better get your dad to help. The oven'll be hot."

"Okay!" the boy's face lit with eagerness that almost instantly changed to bewilderment. He glanced around the kitchen as if looking for something. "But how do you make toast?"

Pickett stirred the eggs, checked the home fries warming in the oven. "Jax," she said, "did they teach you to make toast in the Navy?"

The corner of his mouth kicked up. "Yes ma'am, they did."

"Excellent, " Pickett gestured regally with the spatula. "Then you may be the head toast maker this morning, and Tyler will be the chief assistant toast maker.

"I suggest that you" Pickett aimed the spatula at Jax, "cut the butter into pats. I'll bet, if you observe closely, you will see Tyler put the butter on the bread with remarkable dexterity." And if you don't see it, she telepathed, I will have your head.

The man might be entirely too good looking, but at least he wasn't dumb. He snagged a chair for the youngster to stand on, and in a moment two dark heads bent over the cookie sheet spread with slices of whole wheat bread.

Pickett set the eggs aside and picked up the paring knife. She visually measured the bowl of sliced bananas and pineapple, measured Jax and reached for another banana.

He was entirely too good looking, but not because he was handsome, exactly. His straight brows, high cheekbones, and long nose combined into something too sharp too qualify as handsome. And yet handing Tyler pats of butter, he was so beautiful he took her breath away. He could have posed for Michelangelo with that perfectly toned and balanced body, but even that wasn't it.

It was something about the man. The memory of his kiss yesterday body-slammed her. It had definitely been more than a peck. Sweeter. More real. His lips looked hard, but had been soft.

Pickett shook off the sudden hunger to put her lips against the strong column of his neck.

He hadn't meant anything by it. Of course not. He had looked at Tyler with such longing.

Was she interfering too much between him and Tyler? Probably. Nothing she could teach Jax in twenty-four hours was going to make much differ-ence. Ultimately, he and Tyler would have to work out their relationship for themselves.

How was he going to integrate the needs of a small child with the demands of the life of a SEAL? He was walking proof of the sacrifices families made to a service career. One thing was sure, he couldn't place any dependence on the help he would get from that ex-mother-in-law of his. She wouldn't help him maintain a relationship with his son.

As for herself, she would do well to remember they would be gone tomorrow.

Pickett flicked the oven controls to broil and poured the eggs into the pan when she heard Jax's "Good work, man. We're done."

Jax scraped the plates while Pickett wiped the stove and counters, and Lucy and Patterson snuffled under the table for crumbs. He saw now why she said not to worry about any food Tyler dropped. He suspected that most of Tyler's toast was being scarfed by the dogs.

Privately, Jax had agreed with Tyler when he said that whole wheat bread looked dirty and tasted like sawdust. Still, he thought he ought to apologize for his son's rudeness. Pickett had just laughed, though, unoffended. "I know what you mean," she'd giggled. "It takes a strong person to eat whole wheat toast!"

Jax had piled golden fig preserves on his and eaten it. He wasn't swayed by her remark, he just thought he should set a good example. Even Tyler had nibbled the buttery parts before it started "accidentally" falling to the floor. However, large scraps of toast lay on Pickett's plate. Mentally reassembling the pieces, he wondered if she had taken even a bite.

Jax scraped Pickett's toast into a plastic pail to be taken to the duck. "Tyler ate a little of his toast, but I guess you weren't feeling strong enough."

Pickett acknowledged his teasing with a sideways nod and a wry smile. "Guess not."

Jax admired her slender waist visible between the crop top and low-rider shorts. For all her curviness there wasn't an ounce of excess on her. He didn't see why she restricted herself so severely. But some women seemed positively afraid of food.

He could step up behind her, slide a hand across that bare midriff, and drop kisses into the hollows of her collarbones that seemed shaped just right for his mouth.

Too bad he'd decided she was off limits. "I'm going out to check on the generator."

He snagged the pail of scraps from the counter. "I'll feed the duck while I'm out."

"Fine," Pickett answered from the floor where she was sponging up spots from the heart pine. "And could you make sure Hobo Joe is all right?"

Jax doubted if the huge dog would let him come anywhere near, but in fact as soon as he stepped out on the porch, catching the screen door before the wildly gusting wind could tear it off, Hobo appeared around the west corner of the house. He was as rascally looking as ever and he swayed like a drunken reprobate as he fought to stand on three legs against the wind. But he wasn't as wet as he might have been. He'd obviously found shelter somewhere. When he saw Jax he stopped, keeping a careful six feet between them, and sniffed the air, waving his black snout from side to side.

"You don't trust me do you?" Jax kept his voice low. "Okay, I don't exactly trust you either. But maybe you'd better stay here and keep an eye on things until I get back." Jax pointed to the door. "Lie down, Hobo. Guard."

What do you know? The dog did it, lowering himself slowly till he lay across the threshold. Maybe there was more to the ugly stray than met the eye. He wouldn't have figured Pickett for the type to fill up her house and yard with strays. Although, come to think of it, he and Tyler had wandered into the yard and Pickett had taken them in. Should he wonder if he was as ugly and reprehensible-looking as Hobo, or hope he had as many redeeming qualities?

Then the full force of the sheets of rain blown by hurricane force winds hit him and he thought of nothing, but forcing his way across the yard, inches deep in water, to the garage doors.

Water had blown under the hanging doors and it looked like a leak had started in one corner. Nothing that looked serious. It was hot in the garage. The air was thick with moisture and the smell of earth and motor oil.

Jax pulled off the dripping nylon parka before running an inspection of the vehicles. Pickett's five year old Civic looked well maintained but it would be fairly useless if they had to evacuate. Jax was glad he had the Cherokee, with it's greater road clearance. It could be driven through water without swamping the engine. He inspected the tires, checked battery cables and fluid levels, even though he had done it the evening before. It wasn't likely they'd need to evacuate. Until the storm passed, they'd be safest to stay with the house no matter what happened. Years of training held sway, however, and no matter how unlikely, if he needed the Jeep, he wanted it to be ready.

Ready. He thought about the endless training and preparation that made up most of the life of a SEAL. Being ready, rehearsing, practicing to move instantly and correctly in any situation was the essence of SEAL training and philosophy.

Being ready. He hadn't been prepared to be a father when Tyler was born as Pickett had so gently pointed out last night. And he wasn't ready now. But he was sick of feeling like he'd just washed out. And he was tired of watching Pickett save his fumbles with Tyler, while he didn't even know what she had done.

Jax zipped himself back into the clinging, clammy parka, grabbed a can of gas, and headed back into the storm to refill the generator.

Pickett poured what was left of the coffee into a thermos. This would be a good time to check her email. She was through the connecting door to her office, which was set up in what would usually be the dining room, when she stopped. No computer. The generator wasn't strong enough to power more than the refrigerator and the well pump, and a few lights. For once, she was glad she hadn't had the money to replace the ancient gas kitchen stove. Cooking wouldn't be a problem. But it was funny how when the power went off, the only things you could think of to do required electricity.

Tyler played in a corner by the bookcases making truck noises. The outside door banged and a gust of moisture laden air swooshed into the room.

From her seat at the desk, Pickett could see Jax standing just inside the kitchen door. Dark hair was plastered against his head, and rivulets ran down the silky straight hair that covered the defined muscles of his legs. He toed off sodden sneakers without trying to unknot the wet laces. He used a dish towel left on the counter after breakfast, to dry his legs and feet, then swabbed the puddle he had left on the floor.

Time elongated while her awareness contracted to this one man. Masculine, elemental, coming in wet was so much part of his life that it required no thought. He could live in storm and wildness and wind and water, then methodically tame himself, stripping the wildness till he was once again a creature that could walk about in a house.

An illusive memory tickled the edge of her consciousness. There were myths about sea creatures, seals come to think of it, who from time to time would leave the sea and change into humans. Pickett smiled at the whimsy of the thought.

Jax looked up, caught her looking at him, smiled a smile of pure masculine satisfaction. He tossed the towel in the mudroom, and walked barefoot into the office.

Pickett reminded herself that those selkies, that's what those magic seals were called—liked to mate with humans, but they always wanted to return to the sea.

"How is it out there?"

"Wet. Not as bad as it could be, but you and Tyler don't go out until I give you the all clear."

Pickett tried not to snort. Like she needed him to tell her not to go outside in a hurricane. And if she did lose her mind and decide to go out, she didn't need his permission.

A heavy gust slapped rain against the house so hard it sounded like gravel.

She might not need his permission to go out, but she would need his help. She giggled. It would come down to the same thing. "Aye-aye, sir! Are Hobo and Quackers okay?"

"They're fine. Hobo is under the porch, and Quackers apparently has decided to sleep though it."

Tyler hadn't acknowledged his father's entry in any way. He merely continued to drive his toy cars along the window sills, making car noises, and when he drove them over the edge, appropriate crashing sounds. Jax's eyes rested briefly on his son, flickered with pain, then returned to

Pickett. Jax gestured with his head to the kitchen. "Are you busy? Can I talk to you for a second?"

"Sure." Pickett unfolded from the chair, and laying her book aside, walked toward him. "Would you like a cup of coffee? We can go in the kitchen."

Jax took the cup of coffee Pickett had poured him from the thermos and glanced at the door to the living room to make sure it was closed. He leaned against the counter. "I need some advice."

So often when people said they wanted advice, what they really meant was that they wanted someone to solve their problems for them. Pickett had plenty of experience with that, but her well honed intuition told her this man was unlikely to ask someone else to do what he perceived as his job. On the other hand her intuition also said this man wanted something from her.

Pickett pulled one of the ladder back chairs from the table and almost sat before she realized her mistake. It was necessary that she not subordinate herself to this man. His energy already dominated the room. If she sat, he would be in an even more dominating position. She kept one hand on her chair and gestured toward the chair opposite with her other hand. "About…?"

"You seem to know what to do with Tyler. How to talk to him. What to expect from him. How do you know these things?"

"Is that what you need advice about?"

"Yes. I've realized that the things that you know are the things I need to learn. I'm square in the middle of a goatfuck here."

"Goatfuck." Though acquainted earthy language the expression was new to her. She tried to keep her expression neutral, but could not suppress an inner spurt of humor. "Is that a technical term?"

Jax's lips twisted. "Sorry. It's what we call an operation where everything is going wrong. I'm messing up with Tyler. I want to be his father but I just don't know how. We don't know each other very well, and that's my fault, but I want to fix it. I thought I would just come down here and we would hang out together and get to know each other and then I would know what to do with him." Jax gave a snort full of self-disgust. "Pretty naïve, huh?" He looked down at the floor, and shoved his hands into the pockets of his khaki shorts. "What bothers me is that he's paying for the fact that I don't, I mean I really don't, know what to do with him. Not like you do." Jax looked up to meet Pickett's eyes. His own were level, intense with desire and determination. "You make it look easy. But I'm willing to learn. So how do I learn?"

Thoughts jostled and elbowed for space in Pickett's brain until she felt a little dizzy and battered. He stood there erect, broad shoulders squared, bare foot, his damp hair furrowed where he had pushed his hands through it, and the image she had was of a man, standing at attention, addressing his commanding officer, admitting to the failure of a mission. Unflinching. No excuses.

Somehow she bet this man had not often in his life had to admit he screwed up, and even more rarely was he forced to admit incompetence. Everything about him spoke of mastery and a self-assurance that bordered on arrogance. Her heart beat harder at the combination of courage and humility it took for him to ask for her help.

He did, indeed want something from her and a part of her was shocked that he would ask for it so directly. But in the face of such directness, her generous nature could not fail to respond. She couldn't keep her distance.

Pickett realized she had been silent too long. The slightly heightened color across his cheek-bones had receded, his lips tightened. She shook herself mentally.

"I'm sorry. I didn't mean to leave you hanging. I got lost in thought for a moment there." She slid into her chair and indicated the other chair again. "Please. Sit down." She added a smile.

Instead of taking the chair across from her, Jax went around the table to sit in the chair adjacent to hers. One that placed his back to the wall and gave a view of both doors. She wished he hadn't. Though not an unusually large man, there was something about him seemed to take up a great deal of space, so that her awareness constantly prickled with how close he was.

His brown forearms with their straight, black hair rested on the golden oak. The hair grew in a slant down the long fingered hands that lightly caged his coffee cup. The hair looked so silky, gleaming softly in the watery light Picket wondered what it would feel like to run a finger across it, feeling the slide of the hair, the warm skin underneath. The alternating play of muscle and tendon.

What was she doing thinking about body hair? Pickett jerked her mind's eye away from the picture that had appeared unbidden, the fly of his shorts unzipped, black curling hair...Embarrassed heat rose in her cheeks, even as she squashed the thought. Sheesh. What was the matter with her?

What were they talking about? Parenting skills. Yes. She was a professional. She could do this. She covered with a little laugh.

"I probably seem a little distracted to you. Actually I am. I'm a marriage and family counselor, right? You'd think people would ask me every day how they could learn to be better parents. But they don't."

"What do they ask?"

"They want to know how to make their child stop being a problem, how to make their child behave, get better grades, not be defiant."

Jax looked at her from under lowered eyebrows. "Is that what I should have asked?"

"No. In fact, they should ask what you asked. Just as you said, the child is paying the price for their ignorance. Sometimes it seems like the major part of what I do is get the parents ready to learn."

Pickett took a sip of her coffee. "Your question made me leap over about ten steps."

Jax shifted in his chair, as if he was getting ready to speak. "Wait," she held up a hand, "there's more. I was also thinking that a counseling relationship would be inappropriate in the context of our living together—in the same house, I mean."

Goodness, she was rattled again, and now she sounded like she was babbling. "That's a long way of saying that I'm impressed that you would ask and I will be happy to help you, in a context of friendship," she finished in a rush.

Something that looked like irritation flickered across Jax's face. Then he nodded as if he had made a decision.

Pickett pressed on. "What you're wanting isn't easy, you know. Being a good parent is a long, arduous, scary, occasionally heart-rending process, and at each stage it's like you need to learn how all over again."

Jax' eyes crinkled in a way he had of smiling without moving his lips. It was the same expression he'd worn when she told him the generator wouldn't work.

He pointed to the motto on his shirt. "SEALs have a saying. 'The only easy day was yesterday.' How do we start?"

ELEVEN

H ere," Pickett handed Jax the heavy book, pulled from one of several cartons in the otherwise empty upstairs bedroom. The rain sounded much louder up here as it pelted the long windows unsheltered by the porch. Earlier Jax had accessed weather satellite pictures on the internet using his laptop which showed that the area was only getting a glancing blow from the hurricane. The eye had come ashore 60 miles or more to the north. Winds, except for gusts, had never reached hurricane force, and already were diminishing.

Crumbling plaster and chipped paint revealed what the downstairs must have looked like before Pickett started renovation. She had apologized on the way up the stairs for its condition, saying that she'd run out of money before running out of rooms to be renovated. So, in spite of the antiques and oriental carpets, she didn't have as much money as it appeared. It explained the few clothes in the closet, the out-dated kitchen and bath.

Pickett was bent over a carton that was bigger than she was sorting through books, her running shorts pulled tight across her delectable bottom. Jax had read recently that the base of the spine was a little-appreciated erogenous zone for women. The tightening in his groin said it was working for him. He could stroke that little indented place, then slide his hands lower, opening…Jax forced his thoughts back to what Pickett was saying.

"Most of my parenting skills books are in my office at the base. These are on child development. The one I just gave you, the Braselton, is the best one to start with."

Jax turned the book in his hand. It looked to be about 500 pages and there were pictures of children on almost every page. "You learned what you know from this book?"

"Some of it. It's about the stages of child development. Every child is different, but all children grow through fairly predictable sequences. You can avoid a lot of head-banging—yours and theirs—by knowing what to expect. Braselton is actually a good beginning place. You'll understand other books on parenting better for having read it."

The spat of rubber soled sneakers sounded on the stairs seconds before Tyler appeared in the open doorway. "Watcha doing, Pickett?" As usual his son showed no signs of noticing him. He ran, untied shoelaces flapping, to the windows where he pressed his nose against the glass, attempting to see through the raindrops.

"I'm showing your daddy some books. What are you doing?"

"I came upstairs to find you." He turned and looked slowly around the room. "Hey! You know, this is a great room!"

The pine floor was bright and gleaming from recent refinishing, but otherwise Jax thought the room was bare and dreary. He slanted a puzzled glance at Pickett who shrugged her eyebrows. She had the most expressive face.

"This can be my room. I can sleep up here and you and him can sleep downstairs."

Now it was Pickett who sought Jax's eyes and he who shrugged, but he couldn't hide the satisfaction of the picture that rose in his mind. Pickett tucked against him in her bed while Tyler slept in a room above. Deeper peach tinged Pickett's cheeks as if she had read his mind or had similar thoughts of her own.

Clearly rattled and trying to cover it, Pickett swiveled smoothly on her toes while maintaining her deep knee bend. Holding out her arm she called Tyler to her. "Come here," she patted her knee. "Let's tie those shoes."

"I don't like my shoes tied. I like my shoes untied." Despite the verbal protest, he sidled closer to Pickett and leaned an arm on her shoulder while setting a sneakered foot on her knee, as if he was perfectly willing. It was the kind of thing he did that made Jax feel crazy and off-balance.

"I know." Pickett sounded calm, cheerful even, as she snugged up the laces. "And you can untie them as soon as you're downstairs. But they need to be tied when you're on the stairs."

"Why?" That was the other thing. The "why" questions that went on and on when he was acknowledging his father's existence.

"Because they could make you fall on the stairs, and you would mash your nose, and then you would cry, and then I would cry."

"But why?"

"Why would I cry? Because I would be sad if you got hurt. And so would you, so we have to tie your shoes." Pickett was looking at the shoe she was tying. She didn't see Tyler's startled head jerk, as if it was almost unbelievable to him that someone might care if he got hurt. Jax had been close to throwing up with relief when he'd snatched Tyler from the path of the car. And he'd gone eyeball-to-eyeball to let him know how furious he was. And scared the kid into wetting his pants, instead of letting him know how important his safety was. Shit.

Pickett finished double-knotting the sneaker. "Other foot."

Tyler planted a tiny hand on each of Pickett's cheeks and turned her face toward his. "Would you be sad Pickett? Really?"

Sad didn't come close to how Jax would have felt if he'd found Tyler's perfect little body lying in the street, bleeding, and too still. But it was probably the word Tyler would have understood.

Suddenly conscious of how seriously Tyler was taking their exchange, Pickett met his eyes solemnly, while her fingers looped the laces of the second shoe together.

"Yes, Tyler," she met his eyes solemnly. "I would. Really."

"Okay," Tyler inclined his head like a king conferring royal favor, "you can tie my shoes."

Pickett's shoulders shook as she double-knotted the second sneaker. Tyler apparently didn't realize that both his shoes were now neatly bowed. "Thank you," said Pickett, as humbly as barely-suppressed mirth would allow. "All done."

Wide grey eyes studied blue ones that sparkled like the ocean on a sunny day. Then Tyler gave a childish giggle, high and free, and flung himself against Pickett. She caught him to her, hugging him close.

Longing that started deep in his gut shot all through Jax. He blinked away wetness. Right that minute he couldn't have said exactly what he was longing for. Maybe he wanted Tyler to hug him, or Pickett to hug him, or maybe he wanted to hug them both.

When Tyler was a baby he had been so easy to hold, to hug. The chubby little arms would wrap around his neck and the soft little body mold to his chest.

When Tyler was two he loved to yell "Catch me!" and launch himself. Jax would catch him, then throw him squealing into the air, while Danielle fussed that he would get hurt or Jax would make him upchuck.

The baby was gone now. Lost. Thin golden arms grasped Pickett, and a lengthening torso relaxed against her as they swayed together, giggling. Would he lose the little boy too? Jax's fingers tightened on the heavy book. The only easy day was yesterday.

"Are you hungry?" Pickett included Jax in her question. She held out her free hand to Jax while keeping the other around Tyler. "Let's go downstairs and get some lunch."

Jax stood, then reached out a hand to pull Pickett to her feet. She was perfectly capable of getting up alone. He had never seen such a combination of grace, strength and agility. It felt like a milestone. He'd touched her before but it was the fist time she'd offered herself to be touched.

He wanted to touch her. Oh yes he did. But it startled him how much he also wanted to be inside the circle of easy affection she threw around Tyler so effortlessly.

And he wanted her to help him regain his son.

Altogether, he was beginning to want entirely too much from this woman with the laughing ocean eyes.

After lunch Jax disappeared into Pickett's office with the textbook. He reappeared a half hour later to ask if he could borrow a note pad, only to disappear immediately. Since she couldn't do housework and couldn't access her case notes, Pickett gave herself permission to read her new Jennifer Cruisie novel.

Tyler and Lucy, with Patterson refereeing, had started a noisy game of hide and seek in the hall that involved much running up and down the stairs with accompanying squeals, barks, banging of doors, clatter of boy feet and clicking of dog toenails.

Jax came into the living room one finger marking the place in the Brazelton text. He gestured with his head toward the stairs. "Are you supposed to let him make that much noise in the house?"

"Are you asking whether I'm supposed to or whether you're supposed to?"

"Whether one is supposed to."

"I don't mind it. I kind of like it, really. It's happy sounding and there's not much trouble they can get into. Let them be free to run and play and make noise."

"Isn't it necessary to teach children to be quiet?"

"When appropriate, yes. But when a child's too quiet, it's not a healthy sign."

Jax digested that for a moment, then took a seat at the other end of the couch, spreading out the book and his notes. "I have some questions."

Pickett pointed to the book opened to a page about three-quarters through. "You've already read that much?"

"Finished it. Now I'm going back and reading for detail."

Pickett knew her amazement showed on her face. His quick grasp of things had been obvious from the start, delighting her with his ability to keep up mentally with her. But somehow she hadn't expected a man so obviously physical to be willing to really study.

"Why are you surprised? You gave me the book to read. I read it."

Pickett didn't feel inclined to tell him that she'd imagined he would leaf through the book at most, then set it aside. It wasn't the kind of book that anybody who wasn't interested in child development would read all the way through.

She also thought he wouldn't be flattered to know she expected him to turn Tyler's care over to her, as soon as he found out what was in the book.

"What are your questions?" she asked.

"Check me out to see if I'm understanding this and getting the most important points."

He quickly summarized his study, then moved on to discussion of the sections of the book which described children of Tyler's age group. In moments they were deep into discussion of height/weight charts, sleep and nutritional requirements, developmental milestones.

Once again Pickett was amazed that he had acquired so much information and understood its significance to Tyler in so short a period, and said so.

"SEALs never stop training. You have to be able to learn fast and thoroughly to keep up." It was said with such simplicity that Pickett wondered if he really thought it was no big deal. No. He knew it was a big deal. He glanced at his notes. "I have some more questions."

The room was stuffy. Heavy gusts of wind and downpours still accompanied fast moving squall lines, but the roaring center of the storm was well past. Even with the windows closed, moisture-laden tropical air had seeped into the house, and Pickett wished it was possible to at least turn on a fan. She could feel a film of perspiration coating her arms and legs, sticking her bra and panties to her skin. She shifted on the sofa, trying to find a position that was both ladylike and didn't require any part of her skin to touch to any other part.

She settled for propping her feet on the chest that passed for a coffee table. She tried folding her hands over her middle but sweated through her shorts in a matter of minutes, so she just let her arms dangle loosely at her sides.

Jax had no such constraints. He sat in a loose-limbed sprawl, one arm along the back of the couch. He was gleaming with sweat, and yet it made him more attractive, defining the contours of his arms and thighs, the strong column of his neck, even emphasizing the almost ascetic quality of his features that took his face from good looking to compelling. He didn't look uncomfortable. He didn't even look like he noticed that the room was uncomfortable.

A surge of pure resentment tightened the back of Pickett's throat. It was so unfair. Being sweaty made him gorgeous. She probably looked like—

she didn't want to think about what she looked like. She pushed at tendrils of hair that kept escaping the clip to cling damply to her neck. What had he asked? Did she think Tyler was typical in development for his age.

His focus seemed to be absolute but to keep hers Pickett found herself slipping into an old trick she had used in college of dividing her mind into a part that was paying attention and another that was observing.

Did he really have to be smart, single minded, built, and good looking? Some remnant of fairness forced her to acknowledge that it really wasn't his fault that he had it all, while she still felt like fat, nerdy Pickett, perpetual disappointment to her family. On the outside she had changed, but it seemed like the old feelings were there to trip her up anytime she let herself be tempted to wish, or dream.

Pickett recognized the slippery slope from resentment to self-pity and jerked herself up short. That was the past. If she was attracted to this man, she should let him know that his attentions would not be unwelcome.

Being attracted was the problem. He affected her with a sensual blast the likes of which she had never before experienced. Finding out he was brilliant had ratcheted up the sex quotient by a factor of ten. Just when she was sure he was a shallow jerk—he had married Danielle for no better reason than that she was beautiful, for goodness sake, and when that didn't work out—

surprise!—abandoned his son. It didn't matter what Jax's excuses were; that's what Tyler would believe had happened. And then he would do something that showed he really cared for his son, and was trying to be a good father, however belatedly. Like reading a reference work on child development from cover to cover.

From one moment to the next Pickett couldn't decide whether she should kick his butt, or throw him on the sofa and have her way with him (after reading a book to find out how.)

Pickett could hear herself answering questions. Yes, she agreed Tyler was more like a five-year-old than a four in language skill. Motor development seemed on track. He was possibly a little immature for his age in emotional/social development but children commonly regressed under stress.

"Stress?" Jax seized the word. "You think Tyler is under stress?"

"Aren't you under stress? Why wouldn't he be?"

"I thought he was unhappy to be with me, maybe that he didn't like me."

"That may be true, but I would guess he's seriously worried about what is going to happen to him. His mother abandoned him, his grandmother left him with you, and he probably thinks you will do what you've always done: show up for a short while and then leave again. And then he'll be alone. Absolutely alone."

"His mother didn't abandon him. She died."

"I doubt if the difference means much to a someone who is not quite five."

Jax was silent for a moment, gazing sightlessly out the window where a momentary break in the clouds bathed the dripping yard in sunshine.

When he looked back his grey eyes were dark with pain. "Does he really think I would abandon him—just go off and leave him behind to fend for himself?"

A lesser person might have turned away from the look of tragic horror on his face, or tried to paper over the moment with platitudes and reassurances.

Pickett felt her own eyes grow moist, yet she did neither.

Her great gift was her willingness to stay with someone, not shielding either herself or them, while they went through the sometimes harrowing process of uncovering their own inner knowledge about the deep truths of their life.

Suddenly a loud thump, followed by a wail, sounded from the room above.

TWELVE

Before Pickett could shift her legs from the chest, Jax had vaulted over the sofa and was out of the room. Pickett got to the door in time to see his powerful legs cover the stairs in no more than four easy-looking strides.

Knowing she couldn't hope to match his speed, Pickett stayed where she was. In moments Lucy and Patterson raced down the stairs clattering and jingling, followed much more slowly by Jax carrying a red-faced Tyler.

He pushed out his lower lip and turned accusing eyes on Pickett. "Patterson made me fall down."

"He did? That wasn't very nice, was it?"

"No. And I bumped my head." He rubbed a tiny red spot on his forehead, then tucked his face into the crook of Jax's neck.

A look passed between Pickett and Jax. An odd sense that he was sharing with her his fright, his relief, his vulnerability to his child's pain.

"So, I guess you're just going to let Daddy hold you, until it feels better."

Tyler stiffened in momentary surprise, then

nodded while snuggling his face deeper against his father's shoulder. A tiny starfish hand came up to rest against the other side of his father's neck.

Jax shifted his precious burden to allow the child to settle more comfortably against him.

The sun chose that moment to come out again, spilling the golden light of late afternoon through the high window on the landing. Like a benediction it gilded the two heads so close together, the tiny body that lay with boneless trust against the broad chest, and illuminated the man's tender expression.

This was their moment. Pickett quietly excused herself to go to the kitchen to make snacks.

Pickett's one loaf of bread was running low so she fixed apple slices and peanut butter crackers. Tyler didn't like the rice crackers, which was all Pickett had, so he licked the peanut butter off them, alternating with bites of apple. Jax pronounced the extremely crunchy texture of the crackers to be interesting, but Pickett thought he didn't much like them either.

He asked if they had fewer calories than regular crackers and looked surprised when Pickett said she didn't know. Having found her knowledgeable about child development, she wondered if he now expected her to know everything about everything.

It wasn't worth pursuing however, so she pointed

out that they should take advantage of the break in the rain to walk around outside for a few minutes.

The sun was warm, the air soft with moisture. Unpredictable puffs of breeze blew glittering showers from the trees and swift-moving grey tatters of cloud chased across the pale blue sky.

Silver sheets of water covered much of the lawn, green bristles of grass breaking the surface here and there. Leaves plastered the walk and even the sides of the porch pillars. Though twigs and some larger limbs littered the ground, there was little evidence of serious damage from the storm.

Patterson and Lucy, reveling in freedom from the confinement of the house galloped madly from bush to tree, and Hobo Joe appeared from underneath the porch, stretching and opening his mouth in a wide pink yawn. Even Quackers waddled out squawking with excitement at earthworms washed up everywhere.

Lucy found an acceptable spot and squatted almost immediately. Patterson, more contemplative by nature, sniffed the bases of several bushes, before lifting his leg.

"Pickett." Tyler pulled at her shorts leg. "Pickett look! Patterson is peeing on the bush!"

"Yes, he is," she replied calmly. Children his age were extremely interested in anything having to do with elimination. "That's what boy dogs do."

"Oh," Tyler looked thoughtful, then walked over to examine the spot Patterson had favored. He studied it for a minute then pulled down his elasticized shorts in the front while digging for his own equipment.

Jax, who had been examining the roof for signs of damage, caught sight of the boy just as his intention became clear. Protest mingled with confusion on his face as Tyler balanced carefully on one foot while lifting the other.

It said much for Tyler's coordination that he was able to balance at all on one foot with both hands occupied, however, the lowered shorts restricted his movement. Nor had he reckoned that lifting his leg would cause the shorts to snap back to his waist, clipping everything between. He gave a little yip, dancing to stay upright.

Jax winced.

Pickett lost it. Not wanting Tyler to see her laughing she turned her face against the closest thing, which happened to be Jax's arm. As the top of her head came just to his shoulder, he made an effective shield.

"It's not funny," hissed Jax, while automatically curving a hand around her shaking shoulders. "That could have hurt."

"That's not why I'm laughing. He was trying to do like Patterson. Like dogs." She lifted one foot. "You know."

Jax looked at his son who was now the soul of nonchalance. His hard belly heaved. He carefully turned their backs to Tyler, then buried his head against her hair, pulling her tighter to muffle both their chuckles.

They broke apart just in time to dash to the

porch, calling Tyler and the dogs, before the wind picked up and another rain band swept across the sound.

THIRTEEN

ours later in the bedroom, Jax watched his son sleep. In the combined glow from the bathroom nightlight and the almost full moon, he could see the cowlick in the right temple so like his own. Tyler lay, arms above his head, one knee cocked as if he had flung himself to sleep.

He hadn't known this was how Tyler slept. Had he ever sat and watched his son sleep before? He couldn't remember. It seemed unlikely.

There was so much he didn't know. Take bedtime for instance. Tyler might look like he had flung himself to sleep, but nothing could be farther from the truth. What on earth had made him think he could say, "It's bedtime Tyler," and Tyler would go to bed?

"I'm not sleepy. I don't have to. Gan-gan doesn't make me." Then tears. "I want a drink of water. I want Lucy to sleep with me. I don't want to sleep with you. I want my own bed."

The book, and being his only guide at present, it was rapidly assuming the status of The Book, mentioned that four-year-olds could be difficult about bedtime. It also gave specific guidelines about how much sleep a child required at each stage.

It would have been easier to allow Tyler to fall asleep wherever he was, as he had done the night before. Jax gave a snort of wry humor. The easy day really was yesterday. Okay. He could live with that. Tyler would get 14 hours of sleep. And he would learn that rules were rules.

If he was honest, though, he wasn't sure if Tyler would be asleep yet if Pickett hadn't intervened with one of her directions that were orders, without ever sounding like an order.

She had produced a children's book, from the store that she kept for her nieces and nephews, and agreed with Tyler that he wasn't sleepy, and didn't need to go to sleep. In fact, it was something he really shouldn't try. Best that he just get comfortable on the bed so he could listen to a story, that his father would read, and rest his eyes for a few minutes. His father would probably have to read the book two or three times, because he didn't know it. But Tyler did, so he could just rest his eyes.

Shivering, Pickett turned off the shower in the bath connected to the therapy room, and reached for a towel. Thanks to Jax the generator was working so that they had water, even if it was cold. A day of humidity and no air conditioning had left her so sticky she couldn't bear to go to bed without rinsing off.

Drat! Her lotions were in the master bathroom. She could forego her nightly ritual. But wait, she didn't have to go through her bedroom where Jax and Tyler were sleeping. A quick dash through the kitchen, across the back hall, and she could nip in through the hall access to the master bathroom with no one the wiser.

Quickly she slipped on her thin sherbet green cotton gown and adjusted its tiny straps.

Pickett peeped into the hall. A wedge of light was showing under the living room door. Good. Jax hadn't gone to bed yet. He was still in the living room reading. She could be in and out without being afraid to make a sound.

He ought to turn off the light in the living room, Jax thought. He wasn't going to read anymore. Maybe he'd take a shower before crawling in beside Tyler.

Tyler did an amazing back-to-front flip. Sleeping with Tyler did not make for a restful night. Something else he hadn't known about his son. He had been in countries where the whole family slept in one bed, but this was the first time he had ever slept with his son. The list just kept growing.

The room was growing cooler now that the windows were open. A brisk breeze brought the scents of pine trees and ocean air into the house. Tomorrow, he and Tyler would return to the beach cottage. He hoped Tyler's willingness to smile would survive the transition. It would be nice if they didn't have to leave.

It would be nice if he was sharing Pickett's bed with Pickett.

Sometimes he saw her looking at him with the female interest he was used to, though she usually tried to hide it.

Sometimes he got inside her physical space just to watch her try to cover up her reaction.

But sometimes those changeable eyes studied him to see how he would handle the next challenge Tyler threw.

She could make him feel like he was back in BUD/S training. Knowing that every exercise was both a lesson and a test. That he was being evaluated at every moment. That he was being watched to see how he would measure up.

A nightlight burned in the master bath, so Pickett didn't turn on a light. The door to the bedroom was open, but knowing how badly it squealed she didn't try to close it, lest she wake Tyler.

She had only intended to apply her face lotion, but hearing no sound from the bedroom, she uncapped the body lotion as well. She loved its silky feel, the way it smelled of wind and rain and green leaves.

Until the past year, Pickett had never appreci-
ated the feminine dedication to grooming rituals,
nor understood how much self-rejection her lack
of attention to her body represented. Now she
reveled in the cool feel of the lotion against her
skin, the soothing massage. She propped a foot on
the counter in order to reach her legs. She enjoyed
the feel of her calves, smooth and firm and supple
under her massaging fingers.

Pulling the nightgown higher she considered
her thigh. Still too soft but you can't fight
genetics. She stroked the lotion higher.

Jax heard a drawer slide open in the bathroom.
She must have come in through the hall. He didn't
hear her go out again. A drawer slide again. Faint
clinking sounds. But she hadn't closed the
bedroom door.

His mouth stretched in a grin. She had the
funniest little habit of talking to all kinds of
things, animate and inanimate. Right now, she was
talking to...her legs? He moved so that he could
see past the partly open door.

Taking advantage of concealment was second
nature. If he remained in the shadow cast by the
door she wouldn't see him, but he could see her in
the mirror. She had one leg up on the lavatory
counter, stroking the smooth curve of the calf. The
movements were slow, sensuous. His own palms
tingled at the thought of touching silky skin, of

letting his hand slide up. Then she pulled the gown to the top of her leg. Now she was stroking her thigh. His eyes followed the path of the hand. Oh yes. In the mirror he could see the shadow of curls, darker than her hair, where her womanly secrets were hid.

His groin tightened with a speed unmatched since he was seventeen.

"Still too soft," she said, smoothing the lotion across the gleaming skin, "but you can't fight genetics."

He shouldn't be spying on her. He should let her have her privacy.

She thought she was alone; he should leave her alone.

He wasn't going to.

He stepped soundlessly into the bathroom. "I like your thighs."

"I like your thighs." The warm, dark voice pitched just above a whisper came from the open doorway.

Pickett jerked the gown down, hastily standing up. My god! How long had he been standing there? Had she spoken aloud? With only the dogs for company, it was a habit she had gotten into.

"Um. They jiggle. A little."

"A little jiggle is nice on a woman." He took a lazy step into thc bathroom.

Pickett snapped the cap onto the tube of lotion. "I'll get out of your way. I just ran in here to grab…"

He took the tube from her nerveless fingers. "I like how this smells." He snapped it open, squeezed a little unto his fingertips, and lifted it to his nose.

"You missed a spot here," he touched the lotion to her neck, "and here," he smoothed his hand across her shoulder. The feel of his slightly rough, warm fingers under the cool silk of the lotion was unbearably erotic.

Unable to move through the sudden wave of pleasure, Pickett watched with almost detached fascination as he put more lotion on his fingers and smoothed it onto the other side of her neck and shoulder.

A soft heavy feeling of heat began to gather at the juncture of her thighs when his hand slid across her chest and dipped beneath the neckline of the gown to brush the tops of her breasts.

He felt the hitch in her breath, and his smile grew even more lazy-lidded. "You like this don't you?" He stepped a little closer, angling his head to bring his lips to her neck. "I like it too. I've wanted to touch you all day. Like this."

Tyler cried out in his sleep, babbling something indistinguishable, then was quiet again. The sound broke Pickett's sensual trance.

"I shouldn't be in here. We shouldn't be doing this."

Jax capped the lotion with slow deliberation and handed it to Pickett. "You're right, this isn't the time or place to make love, but we should be doing this." His lips barely brushed hers before she backed away.

He'd spooked her. But he hadn't imagined it. Her lips had clung to his for a second. He smiled almost grimly as she backed through the door into the hall, lotion clutched between her breasts.

He'd let her run away, for now. But he wanted her, and he would get what he wanted.

FOURTEEN

The next morning Pickett eyed her face in the guest bathroom mirror with disfavor. Too tired to stay awake last night and then too revved up to sleep.

She was an idiot. Hopeless. There she was with absolutely the sexiest, most virile, not the handsomest but still to her eyes the best looking man she had ever been within six feet of, and he was coming on to her, it wasn't her imagination, he definitely was, and she ran away.

Was this what she always did? Run away? Freeze up?

And not only was he sexy, he was likable. He kept surprising her with what a decent man he was. She was impressed with his brains, and she respected his willingness to learn from her but then to work to master the information for himself.. Not once had he acted as if, since she was available and female, he expected her to take over Tyler's care.

She whipped the nightgown over her head and reached for yesterday's clothes. She hadn't remembered to get out clean clothes last night and no way was she going back in the bedroom until she was sure he was out of it.

She looked at her thighs. Thighs that jiggled a little, no matter how much she exercised. Thighs he liked.

She looked at herself, naked, in the mirror. For once she wasn't trying to decide if her stomach looked a lot fat today, or only a little fat, or if her butt looked too wide or her breasts too droopy. She wasn't even looking with satisfaction at definite improvement. She was looking at thighs that he liked. At a body that was desirable the way it was.

He didn't have an ulterior motive.

The generator on the porch outside chugged. Lucy gave her an enquiring look from the doorway. Her heart lurched into another gear.

She could almost laugh. Generations of women had been taught men only wanted one thing. And yet, even with a degree in counseling, she had decided any attractive man coming on to her had an ulterior motive. She'd convinced herself that sex wasn't very important, and that she had far more important things to offer a man. The thought that she had been limiting her acquaintance to men who didn't attract her very much, and, okay, thereby protecting herself from her own fears of inadequacy, staggered her.

She forced a breath through the tightness in her diaphragm. Jax had said something the night of the storm, that she knew was important even at the time, but she hadn't realized why.

Now she did. You had sex with a jerk. Doug was a jerk. Doug was a jerk! At the age of 21 she had been so crushed to learn Doug's real opinion of her, to find out that he would manipulate sexually without finding her desirable, to learn that others in the fraternity knew, and figured they would do the same. She never stopped to consider that Doug was not a representative of a class of beings. Instead, he was a jerk.

She had believed the opinion of a jerk.

The room suddenly seemed to be revolving, as every area of her internal life shifted and reordered itself. Pickett clutched the counter to steady herself, then slowly pulled on yesterday's shorts and tee shirt. She couldn't bring herself to put on yesterday's panties, so she dragged the shorts over her bare bottom, sucking in her breath at the feel of the cold zipper against her skin.

For a moment she considered going braless, but knew she didn't have what it took. Not yet, said a little voice in her head. But she would go into the bedroom to get some clean clothes whether Jax was in there or not. And if he thought, well, whatever he thought, well…Pickett tossed her under things into the hamper next to the washer and dryer in the mudroom, smiling at the sun streaming in the windows, and headed through the kitchen to the bedroom before she could change her mind.

So focused was she on seeing Jax in the bedroom that she didn't know whether to be disappointed or relieved when she entered the kitchen and found him pouring a cup of coffee.

Jax looked up from the cup of coffee he was pouring. It was so early he hadn't expected to see her yet. He hadn't planned to have to do this sweaty from running and unshaven. He rubbed his hand across the morning stubble that darkened his jaw.

She was wearing yesterday's clothes but she looked clean and wholesome, without makeup, her golden curls tumbling as if they hadn't been brushed yet. She halted in mid-stride when she saw him. He took another cup from the cabinet. "I made coffee before I went out to run. Want some?"

Pickett nodded. "You've already been out? How do things look? Is there much damage?"

"Limbs are down. I stopped to help one of your neighbors move a tree that had come down in the road." He poured coffee and held it out to her. "Water is standing in low spots and the ditches are full, but I didn't see much real damage."

When she came forward to take the dark brew from his hand, he could smell the lotion that she used, mingling softly with the aroma of coffee. It brought back memories of the night before, of the feel of her soft shoulder under his hand.

He clamped down on his lower body's instant response. That was the problem. He kept reacting to this woman without thought. Which made the mess he had to clean up now.

"I am glad you're up early. I needed to talk to you without Tyler underfoot."

Her ocean eyes looked a question but she didn't step away from him immediately as she usually did.

"I," he pushed one hand through his sweat damp hair and wished again he had cleaned up. "I need to apologize for last night—"

"Stop."

"Why? I was wrong. I shouldn't have—"

"Stop!" she interrupted again. "I don't want an apology."

"I realize my behavior was unacceptable—I'm a guest in your house for chrissake—but I do think you should let me—"

"Stop!" Pickett pushed her hand flat against his chest, blinked as if surprised by her own actions, and quickly withdrew it. The space between his pecs felt branded where she had touched him. Wait a minute. Something was different. He was definitely inside her space and she wasn't backing away, in fact, she had touched him.

"Pickett, what's going on here?" he asked, softening his voice.

"I don't know." She sneaked a peak at his face. "Okay, I do know, but I don't want to tell you."

She looked so brave and so doubtful, a peach blush tingeing her high cheekbones. Jax smiled. "Tell me."

"I don't want you to say you didn't mean it, when you said you liked my thighs."

Whoa. Nothing in this conversation was going the way he'd thought it would. Thighs. Unbidden, the image came of Pickett pulling the gown higher, smoothing lotion on her thigh, the image in the mirror.

That's what he needed to apologize for, but he hadn't intended to say it, exactly. More talk in a general way about invasion of privacy.

No, wait a minute, between the surge of lust to his groin and embarrassment to his face, all the blood must have left his brain. Were those tears standing in her eyes? Desperately, he scrambled to find the thread of the conversation.

"Do you want me to say I do like your thighs, or I don't like your thighs?"

"You already said you do like my thighs," she said in the voice of one goaded past endurance, "and I don't want you to take it back, okay?"

Had he said that? He had. Last night. And apparently, it was very important to her. Head held as proudly as always, but utterly vulnerable to his opinion, she blotted the corner of her eyes with the tip of one finger.

Something melted in the center of his chest. He didn't dare ask why it was so important, but if it mattered to her, it mattered to him.

"I did say that. I do like your thighs," God knows that was the truth, "and I am not going to apologize for it."

Dark stormy-ocean eyes searched his face. He let her look deep into his own eyes so she could judge his sincerity. "Okay?"

She thought it over. He liked it that he could tell by her face when she was thinking intently, even when her next remark proved he didn't know what she was thinking.

"Are you sure there was enough light for you to get a good look?"

He felt heat flood his face again. "I got a good look."

"I'm embarrassing you. I didn't mean to cross-examine you." Picket reached for a sponge to dab at a drop of coffee.

"Pickett, can we start this conversation over again?"

Pickett tossed the sponge in the sink. She chuckled. "Okay,"

"The reason I wanted to apologize," he pre-empted her protest with a raised hand, "Which I am not going to do, was that I wanted to ask you something." Pickett waited for him to go on. "I wanted to ask you to go to dinner with me. I thought I'd find a sitter for Tyler, and we could go out, just the two of us."

The queen look was back. Pickett inclined her head regally, while keeping her eyes fixed on his. "I would like that."

The queen look did it. His heart was beating like a teenager's. "Pickett."

"Hmm?"

"There's something else I wanted to ask you. I really want to kiss you." That was so lame. Now he sounded like a teenager. Fortunately, for his teenage alter ego, she lifted her face. She looked at his mouth. That was a yes.

Slowly, giving her all the time in the world to pull back, he lowered his lips to hers.

Jax kissed one corner of her mouth, the other corner, felt the moist exhale against his lips as she let her mouth soften and open slightly. He slid his tongue just to the silky inside of her lower lip. She tasted of toothpaste and coffee and newness. When he felt her tongue shyly stroke his, he knew he must either have more, or pull back right now. He broke the kiss.

"That's it?"

"I need a shower. I'm sweaty."

Pickett leaned forward until her straight little nose was inches from his chest and sniffed delicately. 'You're sweaty, all right," then she looked up at him through her lashes and smiled a purely sensual smile. "I like it."

For a second Jax contemplated taking her right there sweaty clothes and all on the kitchen counter. He didn't know what, but something had turned Her Highness from cool to hot.

Part of what stopped him was the knowledge that Tyler could come in at any second. The other part was that she deserved more finesse than a caveman routine. "I'm going to hit the shower," he said, with real regret. "Tyler will be up soon."

"I'll go with you." His face must have registered the picture those words made in his mind, because she added hastily, "I mean, I need to get clothes from the bedroom closet. That's where I'll go. To the bedroom. With you." She squeezed her eyes shut, rubbed her forehead and began to laugh. "Everything I say just makes it worse, doesn't it?"

FIFTEEN

A few hours later Jax with Tyler in the back seat, approached the gleaming white bridge that curved across the inlet to access Topsail Island, only to see the road blocked by the distinctive grey and black cruiser of the Highway Patrol. The young patrolman waved him to a stop.

"The beaches were closed, sir. No one except property owners are allowed on the island."

This whole trip was beginning to feel like war games for SEALs designed by the Army. Nothing had gone according to the plan yet. He turned the Cherokee around, wondering where he would head now.

Tyler stopped kicking, at last, when he realized the car was turning around.

"We're not going to the beach?"

"No. The beach is closed."

"Good. I didn't want to go to Gan-gan's beach house." No news there. Tyler had fussed and whined from the moment Jax had buckled him into his car seat.

It had been an unwelcome change from the child who had waked up sunny and full of chatter about everything. He had lit with joy when Jax told him he could dress himself in anything he wanted to. The results were a far cry from the matching outfits his grandmother insisted on dressing him in.

Pickett had taken one look at the orange bear-printed shirt with blue plaid shorts and exclaimed, "You dressed yourself! What a big boy you are!"

Thinking about how pleased Tyler had been to have a choice in his clothes, Jax realized that Tyler was offered few choices about anything.

"Do you want to go to your grandmother's house in Raleigh?" An hour and a half, down I40 and Tyler could be happy and Jax could get his life back on track.

"No! I hate Gan-gan's house."

Was that fussiness talking or was Tyler telling the truth? "Why do you hate Gan-gan's house?"

Words apparently failed Tyler. In the rear view mirror, Jax could see him looking confused and rubbing his ear.

"Is she mean to you?"

Tyler shook his head uncertainly. "No, not mean...ezackly."

Jax grabbed for his patience. He would have to pull the answers out of Tyler one sentence at a time. He fought the urge to say just spit it out. Pickett would point out four-year-olds would not say I don't know even when they were out of their depth, and they tended to interpret words literally.

What would Pickett ask? "Your grandmother's not mean, exactly. Is she sort-of mean?"

"Ye-es," Tyler answered in the affirmative but in a high, uncertain voice. "Well, see?" he hesitated, searching for words. "She doesn't like little boys very much," he finished, as if that explained everything.

"She doesn't like little boys—did she say that?"

"Yes," Tyler sounded more definite, "that's what she says. She says boys get dirty," he went on, warming to his theme, "and make messes, and I give her a headache. I give her a headache lots," he added matter-of-factly. "So I have to be quiet, so it won't hurt her head in the morning."

With the part of his brain that was ever assessing, Jax noted that although Tyler strung most of his sentences together with and, typical of a four-year-old, occasionally he used other conjunctions, and even dependent clauses like the five-year-old he would be in a couple of months. A tender burst of pride warmed his chest.

"At night she drinks her drink, and she talks and cries and talks, and I have to be quiet and listen. She says she always wanted a little girl and she never wanted a little boy. Sometimes she lets me go to my room, but sometimes she makes me be quiet and listen, and that's what I hate."

Jax had experienced Lauren's harangues in which she made it clear that she found him beneath contempt. They disgusted him, but he'd had no idea that Lauren's hostility extended to Tyler.

"You hate the things she says to you?"

"No. I don't really listen. I just p'etend." Jax thought he detected a note of wily self-satisfaction in his son's voice. "But she won't let me play with my toys while she talks. That's what I hate."

Jax pulled into a service station and punched the automatic dial on the cell phone. Maybe Pickett could help him sort out what he had just learned from his son. A recording said the phone was temporarily out of order. He was thinking about driving to Wilmington where they could find a hotel when Tyler spoke up again.

"I want to go to Pickett's house. I think she likes little boys."

Jax started to explain why they shouldn't take advantage of Pickett's hospitality, then stopped himself. What the hell. He wanted to go to Pickett's house too.

Pickett was picking up fallen branches from the yard when the big green SUV pulled into the drive. She heard the tires in the gravel and crossed quickly to the drive when Jax brought the car to a stop.

Jax slid open the window. "Hey."

"Hey." Pickett smiled. She looked glad to see them. Jax felt something in his diaphragm relax.

"The beach is closed. Nobody but property owners can go on the island."

"I heard on the radio. I didn't think the storm was that severe."

"There was a washover in a couple of places. The highway patrolman said the biggest problem was sand blocking the road." Now that he was here, he couldn't think of how to ask her. "I tried to call you."

"Yes. The electricity came back on, but now the phone is out." Pickett moved her slender shoulders on one of her humorous shrugs. With him sitting in the high-off-the-ground SUV and her standing, their height difference was cancelled and their eyes were for once completely level. Her eyes were sunny sky blue right now. "So what are you going to do? Are you going back to Raleigh?"

"No!" Tyler spoke up from the back seat. "We're going to stay here!"

Pickett's eyes flew wide with surprise, and sought Jax's. When their eyes met, he felt some kind of jolt go through him, as if her surprise had transferred to him. Jax felt his cheeks grow warm. "I was going to think of a nice way to ask you."

It was as if the sun went behind the clouds in her eyes. "Jax, I don't know..."

Damn. That cloudy, wary look was back in her eyes. Even last night in the bathroom when he had rushed her, she hadn't looked like that. He hated that he had put it there. But he wanted to stay here, and it wasn't just that he dreaded the thought of trying to keep a four-year-old amused in a hotel. A hotel would have a pool and they'd be okay. Only, there was something about being here that was right.

No amount of training and planning could cover every contingency. SEALs looked for leaders who had good instincts. Oddly, just for an instant Jax felt like that was what he was doing: taking his team in a new direction because it was right.

"Pickett, don't say no. I know we've already imposed on you enough. We'll try not to get in your way, and we'll figure out the sleeping arrangements for me and Tyler so you don't have to give up your bed."

"I know!" piped Tyler. "I can sleep in my room upstairs and you can sleep in Pickett's bed with Pickett."

The sensual image of that innocent statement jolted through Jax, compelling in its hunger and also confirming the sense of rightness. Jax struggled not to let the blast of sensual heat show in his face.

Jax shook his head ruefully. "You never know at what moment he's going to start listening. But seriously we'll come up with arrangements you'll be happy with."

"I can't say yes right this minute. I need to think it over, and we need to talk away from—" Pickett nodded toward the back seat.

"Daddy! Get me out of here. I need to go find Patterson and Lucy and Hobo Joe."

Jax was out of the driver's seat and reaching for his son in one smooth motion. As he worked the straps, he met Pickett's eyes. "I'm not going to pressure you. We'll talk. But I want you to know that that's the first time he's called me Daddy since his mother died."

Drat and blast that man anyway! Pickett pulled the wet sheets from the washer with uncharacteristic, unnecessary force. When he left this morning she thought they had things on some kind of reasonable footing. He was interested, she was interested, he would call her. They would try things out sans child.

Now what was she supposed to do? How was she supposed to act? She hadn't missed that hot look in his eyes when Tyler suggested, okay innocently, they share a bed. Even now her stomach got on a fast elevator, when she imagined lying on her bed his dark face intent with sensual promise above her.

Pickett had never regretted her nerdy teenage years, or the cum laude on her diploma more. All those years reading and studying, but she didn't know what she needed to know right now. Every woman in her group at the base was better equipped to handle a situation like this than she was.

Suppose they went to bed together and it was a disaster? She would have to face him all the next day, and act normal around Tyler.

Pickett stuffed a towel in the dryer. It had smelled like him when she got it from the bathroom. So had the sheets.

He said he wouldn't pressure her, and she believed him, but that wasn't the problem. Actually it was the problem. Because if he didn't come on to her again, how would she know if he was still interested?

What would happen if she made a move? This morning Pickett had faced the truth that her sexless state hadn't been caused by disinterest. There had been guys, and a couple of professors, who had looked past her overweight, or maybe liked a bit of cushion. And she had several male friends. The truth was she put out strong do not touch vibes any time a man showed more than friendly interest.

She was attracted to him in a way that she hadn't allowed herself to feel about a man in years, maybe ever. The trouble was she had no experience with flirty looks and come hither glances. A bush league player trying to start out in the major leagues.

Some part of Pickett was aghast at herself. Was she really thinking that the complication of a man staying at her house was whether, or more precisely, how to go about seducing him? A man she had only known for four days? She, who was always telling clients to go slow, get to know the person. In order to develop a long term, meaningful relationship that was important.

Two factors were different here. One: she probably knew more about Jax in four days than if they had dated once a week for four weeks. Two: she wasn't looking for a long term relationship. Not with a man who was a SEAL. Every day she counseled families in crisis. In truth, many of the problems they presented with, they'd probably have had in any circumstances. But every problem was made worse by the corroding effects of stress, long separations, rootlessness. That was the crux of it. Military families faced all the challenges ordinary families faced, but lived under conditions that made the challenges even harder.

Looking at her situation logically, though, although she certainly wouldn't marry a SEAL, she would like to marry the right man and have children. For all her knowledge about relationships, however, she lacked experience. She needed a couple of practice relationships, before she tried to make so serious a choice.

Pickett didn't like to think of herself as using a man, but Jax was perfect to practice on, really. The big reason he wanted to stay here was that he wanted her help with his child, and if he got a little sex on the side, that would be okay. He wasn't likely to get his heart broken.

She felt better now that she'd put the decision on a rational footing.

"Pickett," Jax stood silhouetted in the doorway. "What are you doing?" With his features obscured the sense of his physical presence was made even stronger. It wasn't that he was a great deal larger than most men; it was that he was so very there.

Pickett gave an involuntary gasp "I'm loading the dryer."

"It looked like you were in a wrestling match without a referee. Take it easy on those sheets and towels."

Pickett blinked at the accuracy of Jax's observation. She had been wrestling with her thoughts
and taking it out on the laundry. The heavy, wet
sheets and towels, all twisted and tangled, were a
pretty good metaphor for the state of her feelings.

"They're all tangled."

"Let me." Jax reached in the washer and lifted
the heavy, wet mass with ease, separating sheets
and towels. Pickett placed them in the dryer as he
handed them to her. "What's the matter?"

"Louie asks me what's the matter," Jan had said in
Group the other day. "Why does he ask? He ought
to know. I just thought to myself if you don't
already know there's no point in me telling you."

"Hon," Faye, the earth mother spoke up, "the
thing you gotta understand about men is that they
are clueless most of the time. Even the good ones.
Isn't that so, Pickett?"

Pickett nodded to Faye while keeping her eyes
on Jan. "Men and women think very differently. It
is hard for a man to guess what a woman is
thinking, and why."

"Yeah," Kim, who rarely spoke up, shifted in
her corner chair. "the problem is they've got two
heads, and half the time they're trying to think
with the one that doesn't have any brains."

Wild raucous laughter greeted the dryly
expressed witticism. Pickett thought it was time to
redirect the discussion.

"Jan, what do you tell Louie when he asks what's the matter?"

"I said 'nothing.'"

"Was that the truth? Was nothing the matter?"

"I was mad, and it made me even madder that he had to ask. That's why I said 'nothing.'"

"Every woman in this room understands, but it's the kind of thing that just makes a man crazy. Because he didn't know what was going on, but he could tell it wasn't the truth.

"So, he was clueless before, but now he's clueless and confused." Pickett moved to a different point of view. "Let me ask you this: did you get anything you wanted by saying 'nothing' when there really was something?"

"No, he just picked up the remote." As one, every woman in the room sighed. "So you think I shoulda told him?"

"Relationships that grow despite lies and misunderstandings only work inside the covers of romance novels. In real life it's like trying to make a chocolate cake by substituting coffee grounds for chocolate. It won't matter if you do everything else right. It will still taste terrible."

"Pickett?" Jax's voice pulled her back. "Where did you go? I asked you what was the matter."

"I was thinking about something that was said in an all-women therapy group the other day. We were talking about what to say when a man asks you what's the matter."

"You mean you had to discuss that? Women make everything so complicated sometimes."

"Yes, and I guess that was what I was doing. Making everything complicated."

"Let's start over. I say what's the matter and you just tell me."

Pickett was having a hard time squeezing any air past the thundering of her heart. Suddenly the underlying reason for all her wrestling with her thoughts was clear. She was scared.

"Okay. The matter is: this morning everything was clear. You had your life, I had mine. We were attracted to each other. We would try seeing one another to see if we wanted to go any further." Pickett closed the dryer and set the controls. "Now, we're all mixed up together again. We're living together. Except not. We skipped over all the steps. And I don't know how to deal with it."

"You're attracted to me, hmm?" Trust a man to hear that part out of all she had said.

"You know I am. The problem is I won't know whether you're really attracted to me or if I'm just a convenience."

"And you want 'steps?' What steps do you want?"

"I want you to take me to dinner. Or dancing. Or both. And I want you to ask me."

"Okay. I already did ask you to dinner this morning but I will again. Will you have dinner with me, Ms Sessoms? If I can find a sitter?"

"Yes. And we'll ask the White's oldest girl, Virginia, to babysit."

"You already had that part figured out, didn't you?"

"Yes." Pickett caught a glimpse of the clock. "Oops! My client will be here in 20 minutes. I'd better get moving."

Quickly, she gave Jax directions for using the front door. She was grateful for his ready comprehension of her client's privacy needs. Fortunately, the arrangement of the rooms made keeping the therapy suite and living quarters separate easy.

"I think I'll take Tyler and go into Hampstead. If he's going to sleep upstairs, he'll need an air mattress and a sleeping bag."

Pickett nodded in agreement. "That probably would be best. I've had my eye on an antique bed for that room. Unfortunately, right now, I'm not ready to buy it." Her eyes strayed to the clock again. 18 minutes.

"When will you be finished with your clients?"

"I have a private client now, then I have to go to Camp LeJeune. I work with a group for young mothers there. I'll be back around 4.00."

"We'll be back then." Jax placed one finger under her chin and tilted her face toward him. He searched her face for a minute as if looking for something. He gave a tiny nod and dropped a kiss, light and quick on her lips. Then he was gone.

Pickett stood in the mudroom, the dryer rumbling and thumping behind her, touching the lips he had kissed. What did a kiss like that mean?

It hadn't felt sensual exactly, though the sensual promise was never far away. But, on the other hand, it hadn't felt friendly, exactly.

For what probably wouldn't be the last time she wished she was more experienced, not so far out of her league. She stood there until the timer in the kitchen gave the 15 minute warning.

Jax could have told her what the kiss meant, as he headed the Cherokee south on Hwy.17, Tyler strapped in the back seat. It was sheer masculine possessiveness. Territoriality. Jax's brow creased in consternation. Pickett constantly surprised him. She was such a perpetually shifting mix of cool, intellectual precision and warm, humorous caring. Undeniably sensual yet unawakened. But what gave him pause was that around her, he constantly surprised himself.

He wanted her, sure. That was one sweet package she had put together. She wasn't exactly pretty, but watching thoughts chase themselves across her intelligent face, and humor sparkle in her ocean eyes made looking at her face something he just liked to do.

Jax liked women. He liked their soft bodies, and the way they smelled. After a day around men, he liked their lighter, softer voices, and the way they laughed. And Pickett was all woman, pure feminine essence from her tumbling curls, to her soft round pink toes. It was no surprise she turned him on.

But being a SEAL had been his life. Women were a convenience for him, a truth that hadn't changed even when he was married to Danielle. He had never been physically unfaithful to her in their brief 12 months together, but neither had she ever been more than punctuation in the meaning of his life. He had learned his lesson and he made sure he picked women for whom he was equally a convenience. Someone to see and enjoy occasionally but not wanting or expecting him to be part of their lives. So the surge of sheer masculine possessiveness had come out of the blue, surprising him so much that he had acted on his feeling without thinking, something he showed an alarming tendency to do around Pickett.

It was that focus thing. She had a way of focusing on what you were saying, or just on the fact you were there, and you knew you had her complete attention. Most people, even when they were really engaged, had some part of their mind on other things, what they were going to have for dinner, a report that needed to be written, whether their wife would find out where they were last night. Others were busily trying to figure out how they could use whatever you were saying, what it meant to them or about them. Pickett's attention was so simple and pure, so uncomplicated, it had the spaciousness of a Zen temple. At the same time it was so focused that it could hit you like a force.

When she was with you, Pickett gave one hundred percent. He couldn't help but wonder what making love would be like with someone who had that intensity of awareness. How would she kiss him, what would he feel when she took him in her hands? His body tightened at the thought of those soft hands, touching and exploring. Then, when she had looked at the clock and said she had a client coming, and the focus was gone. And he wanted it back! The kiss was about making sure she didn't lose her awareness of him. Of making sure she knew, no matter who she was with, that her attention was his.

"Where are we going?" Tyler's voice piped from the backseat. Okay. He had his own focusing to do. This was not about getting something started with Pickett. It was about living up to his responsibility to his son.

"We're going to buy you a sleeping bag and an air mattress."

"Why are we going to do that?"

"So you can sleep upstairs like you want to."

"Why are we going to buy an air mattress?"

"I just told you." Jax hoped this wouldn't be one of those 'why' sessions. Learning that they were typical behavior for a child Tyler's age had helped his patience, but he still found them exhausting.

"No. I mean why do I need an air mattress?"

"So you'll have something to sleep on."

"Is an air mattress the same as a bed?"

Jax was forcibly reminded just how much a four-year-old—even one who was almost five— didn't know. "Not exactly. You put air in it to make it soft, and you put it on the floor to sleep on it. It's like camping out."

Tyler took a moment to think this over. "It's not a bed?"

"No."

"I want a bed."

"An air mattress will work fine."

"I want a bed."

What was he supposed to say? It was the oddest sensation, this pull of knowing his child wanted something. "Why do you want a bed?"

"Because it's not a bedroom if it doesn't have a bed," replied Tyler with awful patience.

"But we can't just put a bed in Pickett's house."

"Why?"

"Because it's Pickett's house."

"She wouldn't like it?"

"No. You can't just go putting furniture into people's houses."

"But she needs a bed. I know! We can get a bed Pickett likes."

Jax just shook his head. He didn't feel up to explaining subtleties of respecting people's space.

But wait! What was it she had said about an antique bed she wanted?

"That's a great idea, Tyler." Jax was a generous man. He enjoyed buying presents and, since he had a fondness for fancy lingerie, often showed up at his current lady's house with a little something. But this was different. Tyler would be satisfied, and Jax liked the thought of giving Pickett something that she wanted, too.

"You mean we can buy a bed? Yippee!"

Uh-oh. What if Pickett didn't agree?

"Slow down Tyler. We have to talk to Pickett first. She might not want a bed."

"She wants a bed. I know she does." Pause. "She does! She really, really does!"

"We'll see." Like cogs slipping into a different gear, Jax felt himself grow older between one second and the next. Now he knew why adults said that to children.

SIXTEEN

Pickett was almost late to her brain child and pet project, her at-risk-mothers' group, something she had never allowed to happen before.

Women, identified by the base social workers as at risk either to be abused or to abuse, were referred to the group to overcome the social isolation that was the most common characteristic of abusive families.

Research had shown there was something about being in a group with other women that was specifically healing and life-enhancing to women. And yet, tragically, women with a history of abuse were frequently suspicious of other women, and ignorant of how to bond appropriately. Pickett liked to be present when the women arrived to make sure they were greeted by a friendly face.

It wasn't as important now as it had been before the group jelled, of course. Many of the women were making friends with each other. But still there were those who needed to be reassured of their welcome every time. And those who were looking for an opportunity to speak with her privately. Often they needed reassurance it would be okay to bring up a certain topic.

Today she entered the conference room at two minutes to the hour. The room was as gray and utilitarian as ever. For the thousandth time Pickett wished there was something she could do to improve the ambience of the room, to make it a more welcoming, nurturing space that spoke of safety. However, the women there had already arranged the chairs and made the coffee. Regardless of the room's appointments they were making their own welcome.

"Come on in Pickett," called the irrepressible Faye. "We've got everything ready." Several other women smiled and called out greetings as well.

"Thank you." They were welcoming her. Pickett smiled around the lump in her throat at the sudden reversal of roles. It was important that the women take ownership of the group, but Pickett had never considered what she would feel when they did.

It awed and humbled her to suddenly be the recipient of the group's energy. The analytical portion of Pickett's mind also noted a new sensitivity in herself that caused her to feel their welcome, and the affection it implied, more deeply. She'd been opening a lot of old wounds lately, allowing them to drain and begin the process of healing from within. This new keenness of perception was the result. Or was it the relationship (did she have a relationship?) with Jax?

The group spent most of the hour trading hurricane stories. As always, they were stories of women coping alone. Several of the women lived in mobile homes and so had moved to shelters for the duration of the storm. They had used the group-making skills that they had learned to turn the experience from one of fear and hardship into one of bonding and sharing. They had all gone to the same shelter and turned the night of the hurricane into a giant camping trip and sleepover for themselves and their children.

"Were you alone during the hurricane, Pickett?" asked Maribeth in her shy voice.

The picture of Jax, sitting on the other end of the sofa, his broad chest burnished by the candlelight, rose unbidden. And with it a blush. The women had a lot of barely concealed curiosity about Pickett's love life. Pickett had gently discouraged questions since anything she revealed would become fodder for the gossip mill of the base. Even having been raised in a small town had not prepared Pickett for the intense scrutiny and gossip of a military base. Her position as a part time consultant was anomalous enough without adding gossip.

"Um, no. A friend came over." Maybe they would leave it at that.

Fat chance. Faye was as irrepressible as she was sharp-eyed. "A friend, hum? Have we heard about this friend?"

"No," Pickett attempted to soften the negative with a smile, "and there's nothing to tell. Just someone who needed a place to wait out the storm."

That was the truth wasn't it? Except that she had thought about sex from the moment he sat down on the sofa. And he had been about to kiss her in her bathroom. And had kissed her the next morning. And maybe she should count the kiss as they spied on the sleeping Tyler, though she wasn't sure then or now what that had meant.

"Really," drawled Faye. "Girl, you are a terrible liar."

Pickett had a lifetime of experience listening to women talk about relationships but no idea how to talk about her own, even if it had been appropriate. And yet she didn't wish to lie, even by indirection. These women trusted her, and were fond of her. They deserved the truth, or as much of it as she could tell.

"Faye, don't ask me, please. It isn't appropriate for me to talk about. And there's not really much to say."

Faye's face took on a wise look. "Is it someone from the base here?"

At last something she could answer with perfect truth. "No."

"But he's military, right?"

How in the world did she guess that? Or was it just a shot in the dark? "Yes."

"You be careful, you hear?" The caring was evident despite the aggressive tone. "We all know you don't mess around. You don't have much experience with this kind of thing. Half these guys can't tell hungry from horny from lonely. But you can bet on one thing. They might come, but they don't stay."

Several of the group snickered at the double entendre.

"You got protection?"

Pickett wondered how things had gotten so out of hand that a member of her group was giving her, the leader, the safe sex talk. The look on her face must have been answer enough, because Faye went right on. "You don't, do you? You don't have anything in the house. And I'll bet you don't carry anything on you." Pickett shook her head. "Well, pretending like you don't know it's gonna happen is the stupidest form of contraception there is."

"Yeah, that's how I got Samantha." Everybody laughed.

"And remember condoms have an expiration date." Maribeth, who rarely spoke up, chimed in.

"God yes! And no going down on him without a condom, either. You can get the clap in your mouth," opined Jan, who would say anything.

That did it. Suddenly everyone was speaking at once.

"That is so gross!"

"It's the truth!"

"Did it happen to you?"

"No, but it did to a girl I knew. And the dog said she was his only girl friend."

"Okay, okay," Pickett let her voice rise over the clamor. "I get the point. Safe sex it is—in the unlikely event I have any sex at all."

SEVENTEEN

J ax was hosing down all three dogs when Pickett
pulled into the drive. Apparently even Hobo Joe
had insisted on joining Tyler's swimming
lesson in the warm shallow water of the sound.

Late afternoon sun striped the lawn with deep
green and gold. A man, brown and strong, in blue
swim trunks performing a simple domestic task. A
child romping and dashing through the spray.
Bright arcs of water flying from the dogs' coats. A
large white duck flipping water from his wings
then folding them back with a self-important air.
The simple rightness of the scene settled warm
and solid in Pickett's heart. It filled a space she
hadn't known was empty until this moment. It felt
like—it felt like coming home.

They weren't going to stay of course, and there
would be a price to be paid later, but in this
moment Pickett was glad Jax and Tyler had come
and glad they would be staying for a while.

Tyler danced across the grass to the stopped car,
hair standing in wet spikes, goose bumps dotting
his skinny ribs.

"Aren't you going to get out of the car, Pickett?"

"Not until the dogs finish shaking." Just then Hobo gave a mighty shimmy, flinging droplets all over Tyler.

Tyler laughed with delight. "Hobo gave me a shower, Daddy."

"Well, come over here and I'll give you another one. I should have realized that I needed to rinse the dogs first." Jax ran the hose over his squealing son, turned off the water and scooped him up in a beach towel.

He carried the boy over to the car and smiled at Pickett through the open window. "All clear. It's safe to get out now."

Tyler suddenly flung himself through the open window to wrap Pickett in a wet hug. Jax balanced the little body, reveling in the implicit trust, then pulled Tyler back.

Pickett was dressed in one of her tailored slacks outfits, which though expensive and well cut, seemed designed to conceal rather than enhance her attractiveness. For once he didn't feel a skitter of annoyance. Considering where she worked maybe it wasn't a bad idea. He knew what that randy bunch of Marines were thinking, and suddenly he didn't like the idea of other men seeing her delicious curves.

Jax pointed to a wet hand print on the silk shirt. "Sorry about that."

Pickett waved away his apology with a laugh, and opened the car door. "How did the swimming lesson go in the sound? Did he like it better than the ocean?"

"I think we made some progress, but he still trusts me to hold him up more than he trusts the water."

"At least he's trusting you. That's a beginning." Her eyes, as warm as the Gulf Stream and as blue, sparkled with understanding. The turquoise of her shirt doubled the impact of her changeable eyes. "I know you want to share the water with him, but that will come."

How did she do that? How did she know it had almost killed him when he realized his son, his, didn't love to swim? He had just assumed Danielle was teaching him. There was a lot that he had just assumed about Tyler without really thinking about it. Too much. A sudden thought struck him. "Pickett, can you swim?"

Pickett opened the car door, "Sure. Not like you can, but I managed to pass swimming in college."

"Hey, Pickett!" Tyler hopped up and down, clutching the towel around himself. "Can we go get my bed now?"

Pickett looked a question at Jax.

"Um," Jax covered his sudden nervousness with what he hoped was a charming grin, "I was going to lead up to that gradually. Tyler convinced me that buying the bed you want is better than buying an air mattress."

Pickett gave him a long, thoughtful look then pulled her purse and a bulging plastic bag from the car and started for the back door. Jax closed the car's door behind her.

Damn. Why didn't she say something? Jax moved around her to open the screen door to the back porch. "It's what Tyler wants, Pickett. For some reason he doesn't want an air mattress."

Pickett smiled kindly at his son who had followed them, the ends of his towel dragging the floor. "Tyler, can you find some dry clothes and put them on all by yourself?" For answer, the boy raced toward the bedroom he shared with his father.

Pickett put the bag with a drugstore logo on the kitchen counter and turned her ocean eyes directly on Jax. "Are we talking about the antique bed I mentioned?"

At last she was talking but she didn't look as happy as he thought she would. She looked worried and a little angry. "That's it. I thought you would like it."

"I would. But I can't afford it. I had to cancel clients for two days because of the hurricane. I don't have a salaried job. If I don't work, I don't get paid."

"I'm going to pay for the bed."

"No."

This was not going at all the way Jax had envisaged. Danielle would have jumped at the chance to get an item of decoration she couldn't afford. In fact Jax wasn't used to getting a flat no from any woman of his acquaintance. He found himself getting a little angry at having his offer of a gift summarily refused.

"So what's the problem? You want the bed. Tyler wants a bed. I can buy the bed. Everybody wins." She looked so closed. So contained. He unconsciously took a step closer.

"It's not appropriate, that's why."

Not appropriate? He wasn't trying to get her to accept something in her house that she didn't want. He took another step closer.

Pickett thrust out a hand in the universal stop gesture. "And don't you dare try to physically dominate me! This conversation is over." Pickett swiped the drugstore package from the counter and started toward the door.

"I wasn't trying to dominate—"

Pickett hadn't gotten a good grip on the bag, and overfull to begin with, its contents tumbled to the floor. There on the wide pine boards lay a bottle of shampoo, some lotion, a box of tampons, and a box of condoms.

They both froze.

The top had come loose on the lotion and a creamy puddle slowly formed.

Jax recognized the scent that had filled the bathroom the night before. The image of Pickett in her thin green gown stroking her legs, innocently erotic, and then so sweetly vulnerable tangled in his mind with the tough, closed woman who dared him to approach her even as she knelt to pick up the scattered items.

Maybe things were looking up. Jax grabbed a handful of paper towels and went down on one knee beside her.

He handed her the paper towels and picked up the condoms. "Are you planning on going to bed with somebody?"

The mean-eyed squint she attempted to give

him was somewhat spoiled in its effect by her flaming cheeks. She gave the lotion cap a twist so vicious Jax almost laughed aloud. Damn she was cute. And the urge to tease her when she was on her prissy high horse was overwhelming.

Jax feigned innocence. "It was a reasonable guess. It was either that or you were planning to drop water balloons on me in my sleep."

Though she kept her attention on wiping the lotion from the pine boards, her shoulders shook with unwilling laughter. "I hadn't thought of that, but now that you mention it, the idea has merit."

"So sleeping with someone was plan A."

Pickett sat back on her heels, her expression wry. "Actually, my group convinced me that not being prepared for what might happen, and I emphasize might, is irresponsible."

"You talked about us to your group?" Jax worked to keep his voice level, but the thought made his skin crawl.

"No, of course not. But I sometimes forget that they're as busy watching me as I am watching them. They could see something, I'm not sure what. They guessed." Pickett took a last swipe at the floor and stood.

With an abstracted nod, she acknowledged the bag of replaced toiletries Jax handed her. Obviously still deep in thought, she leaned against the kitchen counter.

"It was pretty funny really. I didn't admit to a thing," she smiled philosophically, "but the next thing I knew I was being lectured about the dangers of unprotected sex."

"A reversal of roles, huh?"

"Yes, and fairly humbling, when I realized just how much I needed to hear it."

So Pickett was thinking about sex with him, and the vibes were strong enough for her group to pick up. He didn't want to mess that up, but felt compelled to follow the glimmer of connection he suddenly saw. He tossed the box of condoms in one hand. "So. Do these have anything to do with why you don't want me to buy the bed?"

"I don't know." Her curls were making a bolt for freedom from the restraint of the clasp. She swiped at them, mussing them further. "The boundaries in this situation are getting so blurred I don't think I could find them with global positioning. I'm lost and I'm getting more lost by the second."

"Boundaries, huh? Is that therapist talk?"

"Don't insult your own intelligence," she snapped. "You're an officer in a group using a team model within a strongly hierarchical organization. You must deal with boundary issues, and probably extremely subtle ones at that, all day long. You know what I'm talking about."

"You're right. Let me ask the question so that it is perfectly clear to both of us. Do you think that if I buy the bed, I will expect sex in return?"

"The thought crosses my mind."

What the hell did she think of him? It made him mad, insulted him that she looked for ulterior motives. He had been so proud to think he was offering her something that would please her. He didn't give women gifts to get sex. He didn't need to.

He thought briefly of scraps of silk and lace. That didn't count. He already knew what was going to happen before he bought them.

No, he had only thought that she was sweet, and gentle and kind and very generous, and he had liked to think she would get some pleasure from the gift. It galled him to have it thrown in his face with his motives impugned.

If she couldn't accept it because there might be strings, then he'd make sure she understood that there weren't any strings.

"Okay, let's set a boundary and agree on it. It's important to Tyler to have a bed. That's why I want to get it and that's the only reason. When we leave here the bed is yours to keep or get rid of. But either way the bed is for my son. Get it? Since it's going in your house it might as well be one you like. But you don't owe me a damn thing."

Something that might have been pain shadowed her eyes briefly, but was gone instantly, replaced by her calm, direct gaze. She had a way of looking at him, just looking, that made him feel like they were the only two people in the universe. It gave him the oddest feeling of peace. It made something go quiet inside him.

"Getting this bed for Tyler is deeply important to you, isn't it?"

Yeah it was important, but Jax had learned early not to expect that things that were important to him would mean something to anybody else. When Corey died the brief period during which others had cared to learn his wishes was over. The only thing he had ever wanted as an adult was to be a SEAL.

Danielle had seemed to want so many things: beds and chairs, clothes and cars, dinners and dancing. He had felt suffocated by the sheer meaningless profusion of her unending desires. Whether she had them or not was immaterial to him. She could spend days looking for the exactly right shade for a lamp, or the perfect pair of shoes.

At first he had tried to feign an interest, but if he expressed a preference Danielle could usually explain why this chair or that color wouldn't work. After a while he didn't pretend to care. He only asked how much would it cost, and then they argued about money.

This whole argument confused the hell out of him. Danielle would have leaped at his offer. Now Pickett had shifted what they were talking about again. He wondered if his chances were better if he admitted the bed was important or denied it.

Pickett had a way of seeing into what was going on. She already knew. He went with admitting it, though he felt a tiny clutch as he did so. "Yeah. It's important."

"Okay."

"Okay, what?"

"You can buy the bed. For Tyler." Pickett glanced at the clock. "And if we're going to get to Isabel's shop before she closes, we'd better hurry."

EIGHTEEN

The sign out front not withstanding, Pickett knew that only the most generous assess- ment would call the dim and crowded junk shop an antique store. Rusted bicycles were piled beside bedpans. Dusty dolls with patchy hair sat amidst cracked saucers, and ragged books, and broken implements. The air was thick with the mustiness of items that had arrived dirty, and gone downhill from there, as well as the smoke from the omnipresent cigarettes of Isabel, the owner.

The dismantled bed was in a small back room. Isabel, squinty-eyed against the smoke from her dangling cigarette, used a broom to dispatch the cobwebs that tethered it to the wall, displacing a large amount of dust in the process.

Jax's face, impassive since Pickett had directed him to pull the Cherokee into the sagging building that proclaimed itself Topsail Treasures, Antiques and Stuff, had taken on the appearance of stone. Pickett suspected that he was horrified at the bargain he had made. Looked at through his eyes, the bed was not impressive.

The bed, while certainly not Stickley but a machine made copy, nevertheless had the honest lines and sturdy simplicity of the arts and crafts movement. It was solid oak, darkened with age, and battered. None of the slats of the headboard or footboard were missing though, and the rails were intact.

"Where's my bed, Pickett?" Tyler, who had been happily unearthing treasures from underneath tables, had already acquired a layer of grime.

"This is the bed." Since he was looking right at it Pickett realized he didn't know how to see it. "It's in pieces, see? We'll put it together when we get home."

"Like Leggos?" Tyler leaned against her leg, circling her knee with one grubby hand.

Pickett absently stroked his silken head. "Sort of. You know what? The first time I saw this bed, I thought it was the perfect bed for a boy."

"But you didn't have a little boy so you didn't get it."

"Well, that's part of the reason." Buying a bed for a child she might never have would have been unbearably poignant, even had it been in her budget.

"But now you do have a little boy so everything is just right." Tyler gave a sigh of satisfaction at the story's happy ending.

She didn't have the heart to set him straight. And the bed was being bought now because of a little boy, so the facts were correct even if as an adult she understood them a little differently.

Besides, Tyler and his father wouldn't be staying long enough for Tyler to get deeply attached to her. The thought was not as comforting as she wished it was. Quickly, she moved on. "You know what we need to do now? We have to go buy a mattress and springs."

While they waited for Isabel's extremely slow dial up connection to process the transaction, Pickett had to retrieve Tyler twice from the back of the store where he kept discovering more treasures. The second time she returned him to the counter, he suddenly stopped.

"Look, Pickett," he pointed, jumping up and down. "Fireworks!"

Pickett followed his pointing finger to the front of the counter which was covered with posters and announcements, many tattered and yellow with age. A newer-looking poster advertised fireworks sponsored by Surf City to kick off the fall fishing festival, but she didn't see a picture of fireworks anywhere.

She knelt beside Tyler. "Where do you see fireworks, precious?"

Tyler put a grimy hand on the poster.

Pickett inhaled, then let the breath out slowly. Tyler was four years, ten months. Was he already reading? Keeping her voice casual she asked, "Can you read what it says?"

Tyler looked at the poster, then pushed a fist at his hairline in a gesture just like Jax's when he was frustrated. "Not all of it." Then he brightened as if he'd suddenly made a discovery.

"I can read words I like," he explained with great dignity. "I like fireworks."

Jax signed the charge slip and handed it back to Isabel. Nothing in his demeanor indicated he'd heard Tyler, but in case he had, Pickett wished she could catch his eye to signal that he should play it casual. If he rapped out a demand for more information the way he sometimes did, Tyler would freeze up. Holding her breath, fists clenched in her pockets, she willed Jax to look at her.

But then one side of his mouth kicked up. He knuckled the top of Tyler's head gently. "I guess we have to get you some books that have words you like."

A look of complete understanding passed between father and son. The little shoulders, so often braced when his father spoke to him, relaxed infinitesimally.

It was only a tiny moment out of time, but when, at last, Jax looked at Pickett with grey eyes that shone, she knew he had felt the change in Tyler as sure as she had. She pulled her fist from her pocket and raised the thumb.

Jax grinned like someone who's just been sent to the head of the class. "Okay! Let's load up."

Refusing assistance, with his usual competence and economy of motion Jax carried the solid oak furniture out to the car. When he hoisted the heavy bedstead into the cargo bed of the Cherokee, Pickett gave an involuntary gasp at the masculine beauty with which he performed an action for which male bodies are so suited.

Isabel managed to smile without dislodging her cigarette and gave a hoarse chuckle. "You been looking at that bed a long time, Pickett. Looks like you finally found a man to go with it."

First her group, now Isabel. Did everyone in Onslow County think of nothing but her sex life? Pickett thought of trying to correct Isabel's impression but let it drop. Anything she said would only add to the story that would be all over Snead's Ferry by tomorrow. Though its population swelled during the summer months, Snead's Ferry was really a very small town, if you counted only the permanent residents. When it came to gossip, only the permanent residents counted. Most of the gossip was friendly interest in the doings of neighbors, but a malicious word or two could conceivably harm her fledgling business.

"Don't worry, honey," Isabel said correctly interpreting Pickett's silence. "I don't tell everything I know. Not that I know anything. A man with Virginia tags bought that bed. That's all I know."

Pickett threw her arms around Isabel's bony shoulders in a hug redolent of smoke and dust. Behind her smudged glasses Isabel's eyes watered suspiciously. She pushed at Pickett with the heel of one hand. "Oh go along with you! And don't you ever tell anyone how much I sold that bed for."

By the time a mattress had been purchased, delivery arranged and paid extra for, Tyler was cranky with hunger and a surfeit of shopping.

Without asking, Jax pulled into a fast food chain. Truth to tell, he was a trifle cranky himself. He'd had a surfeit of shopping and of cranky four-year-olds.

"Why didn't you order a decent meal?" Jax challenged Pickett, his voice sharp with irritation. "You don't have to diet all time. You're slender enough."

Another time, another subject and Pickett would have responded with a request for him to mind his own business. But now Pickett felt the too familiar slide of distance forming between them. Here it came. She avoided eating at fast food places not only because her choices were limited, but also because in the land of sandwiches the strangeness of her choices really stood out.

She put down the hamburger with lettuce and tomato wrapped in paper instead of a bun. The low carb craze was a godsend to people like her, but for different reasons.

It shouldn't be a big deal.

It wasn't a big deal.

And yet when she told people, especially vigorous, physical people like Jax, she could feel the withdrawal. Suddenly they were on one side of world, and she was on the other. They were the strong, she was the weak. Pickett knew what would happen now. The masculine interest she had felt, that warm awareness of herself as desirable that sped up her heartbeat at the same time it made her muscles go loose, would disappear.

Jax could be pretty blunt, but he wasn't unkind. He wouldn't say, "You're history, kid." But that's how it would be. The taste of disappointment was sharp on her tongue as she met his narrowed granite grey gaze.

"I have celiac disease. I can't eat any food made from wheat."

Celiac disease. She was the picture of radiant health. Could something deadly be stalking her from the inside? Suddenly Jax's heart was thudding so hard he could feel the pulse in his fingertips.

"Are you sick? Are you going to die?" Trust Tyler to zero in on the question. Tyler's face was white. Jax wondered if his own face was equally colorless.

"No sweetie." With a tender stroke Pickett pushed back the lock of dark hair that fell over Tyler's brow. "I'm not going to die. As long as I don't eat certain things—like sandwiches—I'm fine."

Jax found he could breathe again. She wasn't going to die. But now he felt like an ass. "I'm sorry, Pickett. I was out of line."

Pickett smiled sadly. "It's okay. I probably should have said something before. I know my eating habits look weird," Pickett laughed in self-deprecation, "or very high maintenance."

Jax felt himself coloring. That's exactly what he had thought. That she was rich, bossy, prissy, and high maintenance.

Now he knew she was independent, hard-working and the prissy came off with the business clothes.

She definitely had a tendency to be bossy, but he now thought of it more as ballsy. She didn't so much order people around as simply take over.

"What will happen if you do eat sand-wiches?" Go for it kid, Jax silently urged Tyler on. Tyler's endless questioning was coming in handy for once.

"It would make me feel bad."

"Why?"

"Well," Pickett glanced apologetically at Jax, "it's really not suitable for dinner table conversation."

"Go ahead. He's a kid and I'm a SEAL. Neither one of us has delicacy issues."

Pickett turned back to Tyler. "There is stuff in bread, called gluten, that destroys my intestines. Do you know about intestines?"

Tyler nodded vigorously. "Guts. I saw some guts one time. It was yucky." Tyler appeared to think for a moment, then laid a small hand on Pickett's arm. "Are your guts going to come out?"

Pickett repressed a smile. "No. My guts are fine, now."

"And you'll get all better and then you can eat sandwiches."

"No. I can never eat sandwiches, or cookies, or cakes or anything that has wheat flour in it, ever again."

"Never ever?"

"Never ever."

"Is wheat the only thing you can't eat?" Jax asked.

"I can't eat anything made from any grain that has gluten in it. Rye, barley, malt, oats all have gluten. So, no beer, no whiskey, etc." Pickett shrugged. "Fortunately, I never cared for them anyway."

Jax rapidly reviewed the items he had seen in her cabinets and refrigerator. That explained the tasteless crackers, the weird snacks like taro chips. "But wait, there's beer in the fridge and you have bread."

"The beer has been in the refrigerator for six months. My brother-in-law likes it. And I keep a loaf of bread in the freezer to make sandwiches for guests." She kept food that she couldn't eat so that other people wouldn't be deprived in her house.

With chagrin, Jax remembered that she had served him and Tyler toast, and if he had noticed she didn't eat any herself he only thought she was picky and as absorbed about perfecting her body as Danielle.

He looked at the shining eyes and glowing skin with new respect suddenly mingled with the desire that always simmered.

She took a bite from her hamburger and looked up to find his eyes on her. "What?"

Jax made no effort to disguise the heat of his wanting, and in a moment had the satisfaction of watching the coral-rose tint of her cheeks deepen. Her eyes widened. She drew in a sudden breath. The dimple at the corner of her mouth appeared. "Oh."

Bored with adult talk, Tyler shoved his half eaten burger away. "I want to play on the slides."

Did that kid have timing or what? "Go on outside then." Jax turned to Pickett.

She however glanced at her watch, then smiled apologetically.

"Jax we need to leave if we're going to get to the house before the mattress does."

"Right." Jax swung Tyler up in his arms. "No swings for you pal. We've got a bed to put together."

Pickett had just finished dusting the bed then wiping it with a damp cloth which she insisted on doing on the porch, when the lights from the mattress delivery truck pierced the gathering dusk.

Tyler was shrill with excitement, racing upstairs to his room and back in an attempt to be part of every bit of the action. From a vantage point in the wide hall, Pickett listened to her house ringing with deep male voices, and heavy male treads. Her house or not, at some point Jax had become in charge.

In minutes boxes were moved and the bed and mattress set up, the delivery men sent on their way with tips and thanks.

Tyler was almost beside himself with joy. If, to Pickett's eye, the room looked bare with no curtains, no rugs and no pictures, and only one piece of furniture in it, Tyler found no fault with that, but proclaimed this to be the best bedroom in the world.

At last the bed was made and Tyler tucked into it, a tiny lump in its vast expanse. His eyes were drooping long before Pickett had reached the end of Monster Trucks. Pickett and Jax turned out the light, and leaving the door open, tiptoed away.

Twenty minutes later the strangeness of having Tyler both silent and away had gotten to both of them. Exchanging sheepish smiles they crept back up the dark stairs to peek in on the sleeping child.

The rising moon spilled its light through the uncurtained windows illuminating the tiny out-flung arms and legs. Completely abandoned to sleep, Tyler had no awareness of the two adults watching him from the doorway.

There was a hint of a tender smile playing around Pickett's eyes. She had the most smiling eyes of any one he had ever seen. At the fast food place tonight he had seen demonstrated that for all her frankness and openness, there were parts of Pickett that she withheld. Suddenly he wanted to know what called that smile to her eyes. Careful to move slowly, he touched the tiny crinkles. "What are you thinking about?"

"Having a bed really was important to Tyler."

"Yeah."

"I'm sorry I argued with you about it. Forgive me?"

"For what? You weren't in the wrong."

"No, I wasn't. But I didn't understand—I misinterpreted what was going on. And by arguing I blighted some of your happiness and excitement. I'm sorry for that."

Jax pondered what she had said. What was she saying? Happiness and excitement blighted? Having his motives questioned had hurt. More than he would have thought. He could see her point of view, but he thought she had a better opinion of him than that. And he had wanted to do something nice for her. She had already been so generous to him and Tyler.

Nobody had ever apologized to him before for blighting his happiness. His eyes were suddenly hot and stinging.

He had to clear his throat before he could speak. "Um, it's okay."

"No, it's not okay. Moments like that are precious and fragile, and I stomped all over it." She pressed her lips together. "I'm not saying I think I could have handled it better, just that I wish I had."

The honesty of that got to him. He slid his arm around her resting his hand just below the curve of her waist.

"You know what really bothered me? I wanted to do something nice for you. I wanted to do something that would add to your life. You've been so kind to Tyler, so generous. We've invaded your home, and here we were taking the invasion even deeper. And before you say I don't owe you, it wasn't about owing. I just wanted to give you something."

"Oh boy. Now I'm really sorry." She drew in a deep breath. She turned her face up to his. In the soft glow of the nightlight he could see that her eyes were full of unshed tears. "Thank you for the bed. It is beautiful and it is exactly what I wanted." A tear spilled down the curve of her cheek. "I hope my thank you is not too little, too late."

Jax pulled her closer. "It won't be if you give me a kiss." Even in the dim light he was standing too close to miss the sudden widening of her eyes, the slight stiffening. Oh damn. That wary look again. Suddenly he was tired of it. Tired of what it said about him. Tired of having her slide away.

Gently but letting her feel his superior strength and his determination, he inexorably drew her closer. "Look, you can either trust me to be straight with you or you can't. Decide which it is now."

Slowly he lowered his mouth, never letting his eyes leave hers. He could feel her breath on his face, see the gold flecks in her eyes, but he didn't close the distance until he felt the tiny softening of her body against him.

He smiled. "You're welcome," he murmured and settled his lips to hers.

NINETEEN

Keep it slow. You got her to come this far, don't spook her. To keep himself from grabbing her, from crushing her against him to feel her breasts and fill his hands with the roundness of her buttocks, Jax brought one hand up to cup the side of Pickett's face.

It was a sweet kiss, a kiss that tested, and teased with nibbles, the corners of her mouth. He wanted her. God knows he wanted her, and yet right this minute he wanted this...soft thing more. When her pliant lips slowly opened of their own accord, he slowly swept his tongue just inside her bottom lip exploring the silken softness, and was rewarded when her tongue darted forth in a shy game of tag. How many women had he kissed, never for one minute caring if he was inside their defenses?

When the clamor from his lower body to pull her closer would have overwhelmed his desire for this simple peace, he pulled back, keeping his hand at her waist.

He indicated the bed with a tip of his head. "So, it really is what you wanted, huh?"

"Yes. It looks exactly the way I hoped it would—just right for this room. By the time I give it several coats of polish and find the right spread for it, you'll never know it came from a junk shop." Pickett gave a little gurgle of laughter. "You should have seen your face when we pulled up to Isabel's store."

"I thought you were pulling my leg. I couldn't see you wanting something from a junk store."

They turned toward the stairs. "To tell you the truth I was tempted to tease you a little. You looked so serious."

Jax got a beer from the refrigerator and Pickett got a handful of grapes. They returned to the living room to sit side by side on the big outrageously flowered sofa. Shadows gathered in the corners of the high-ceilinged room. Pickett turned on the end table lamp and Jax reached over her to turn it off.

He picked up her hand and played with the soft fingers. "So why didn't you tease me? It was a perfect set up."

Pickett shook her head. "It would have been unkind. I could tell buying the bed meant a lot to you whether I understood what was going on or not." She squirmed into the cushions, tucking her legs underneath her, and allowed her weight to lean against his arm. "What was going on with you? You never talk about your parents or your home. Didn't you have a bed when you were a little boy?"

"Of course I had a bed. The house we moved into when I was six had six bedrooms."

"Big house. Did you have a big family?"

"Just my mom and dad and me," Jax turned up the long necked beer bottle, taking several swallows. "My mom left shortly after we moved there. Then it was just my father and me." Jax was silent a long time looking sightlessly into the distance. The breeze coming in the open window rattled the plantation blinds. His arm moved to the back of the couch and one hand toyed with Pickett's hair. "I was a little shit."

"That sounds a tad harsh," Pickett murmured with deliberate understatement.

"It's the truth."

"You're not one now. What changed?"

"Corey Blanchard. You might say he saved me from myself."

"Sounds like there's a story there." Pickett finished her grapes and put her napkin on the end table. She settled deeper against Jax. "How did he do that?"

"Corey showed me what a hero was. It was one of those epiphanies." Jax's voice was a dark rumble.

"Epiphany?" Pickett tried to pull away so that she could see his face better in the dim light from the lamp on the secretaire. "How old were you?"

"Ten." Jax pulled her back with ridiculous ease, efficiently arranging her so that she was tucked under his arm. "I'll tell this story my way. My way is holding you."

"We were both ten," he continued. "We had the same birthday and were in the same class. He was a scholarship student at the private school we attended.

"Like I told you, I was a shit. Two guys and me, we were hassling a first grader. We were telling him he was a mama's boy and his mother wasn't going to come for him today. Stuff like that to make him cry."

"Why?"

"Because I was a shit, okay?"

"Uhn-unh. Why did you choose him to pick on?"

"His mother was always there after school to pick him up. She would look so glad to see him, and he would run to her and they would hug and laugh and kiss. It was disgusting. You know how ten year old boys are."

"Who picked you up from school when you were six?"

"The housekeeper. Sometimes my mom sent a cab."

"Why didn't she come herself?"

"She had tennis lessons. She had been on the circuit before she married my dad. She wanted to go back to professional tennis." Jax shook his head. "That's not what this story is about. Stop interrupting me."

"I'm just trying to understand what was happening and why."

"No, this is about Corey, not me. Where was I? We were hassling this little kid and making him cry and Corey walked up and told us to leave him alone."

Jax shook his head in disbelief. "Here was this weedy looking kid. He was taller than me, but skinny, and he had these glasses that sat sideways on his face, and he was new, and a scholarship kid, and he was telling three guys, all of them bigger, what to do."

"What did you think?"

"I thought he was going to get creamed, that's what. I thought he was too stupid too know it, when he knelt down beside the little kid, and kind of hugged him, and told him 'your mother's going to come for you.' Then he stepped between us and the kid and he told him to 'run to Mrs. Wilson. Run as fast as you can.' He was looking at me when he said it and I realized he did know he was going to get stomped. He was going to take us on so that the little kid would have time to get away.

"It was—I don't know how to describe it. I was suddenly so confused. Like when you get turned around in the dark and you think you're going through the door and you walk into a wall instead. I yelled at him 'what the hell do you think you're doing, shithead?'

"And he said 'What the hell do you think you're doing, asshole?' and suddenly I could see myself through his eyes. I mean that literally. I could see myself from the outside. I could see three big guys, we were all big for our age, being faced off by one skinny kid with lopsided glasses. And then I could see us before. Three big guys making a little guy cry. I was ashamed, disgusted, appalled. It hit me like a punch in the stomach."

"Wow. What did you do?"

"I threw up. All over Burt-the-Butt's new Converses."

Pickett smiled. "I guess that ended the fight."

"Yeah." Jax gave a little snort. "Burt and Connor just oozed away, and I was left spewing my guts in front of Corey."

"Corey didn't run away?"

"No." Jax's smile was sweetly reminiscent. "I learned after a while that Corey didn't run away from anything."

"I'm beginning to see what you mean about Corey being a hero."

"Wait until you hear the rest of it."

"Okay," Pickett said agreeably. "Then what happened?"

"His dad came to give him a ride home. His dad was the Presbyterian minister. And I'm thinking 'oh shit, can this get any worse? Now he's going to tell his father,' and Corey says 'Can we give Jackson a ride, Dad? He doesn't feel so good. He's been throwing up.'

"When they found out there wasn't anybody home at my house, they took me home with them, and Corey's dad gave me some ginger ale to settle my stomach."

Pickett quietly noted the significance of the detail. The picture of Jax's growing up was becoming clear. A lonely, angry little boy, not a mean bully, but a child overcome with jealousy, and then shame, encountering simple kindness would remember being given a glass of ginger ale.

"Then Corey's dad took a bag of blood out of the refrigerator and started Corey's infusion. Corey had hemophilia." Jax correctly interpreted Pickett's shocked intake of breath. "Yeah, that's right. If I had hit Corey he could have been hurt, he could've even died of internal injuries. Yet he had faced us off to protect somebody littler. I was always getting into fights. I would have hit him. I felt like throwing up all over again.

"Corey had done something I wouldn't do. I was in fights all the time, but I wouldn't have gone one on three. At first I had thought he was doing it because he was stupid. He knew he could get badly hurt even though we didn't. Corey had more courage than I did. After I really got to know him, I learned that he had more courage than anybody I've ever met."

"You talk about Corey in the past tense. What happened to him?"

"He died when he was, when we were, nineteen. Of AIDs. He got infected from transfusions."

"Oh Jax, I'm so sorry. I can tell you loved him very much. That must have been a terrible time for you."

Terrible? Yeah that just about summed it up. The stunned rage that had sat in his gut for three days since the phone call from Aline, Corey's older sister, was like an overcoat by the time of the funeral. It wrapped him up and weighed him down and kept him from feeling much of anything else.

All the undertaker's arts had not been able to disguise the truth of what lay in that satin lined coffin: a cadaver. All the wit and intelligence, courage and love was reduced to this shrunken, yellowish absolutely dead thing. There was no trace of Corey to be discerned.

Had Corey looked this starved when he'd seen him at spring break? Honesty compelled Jax to remember that he had. While his friend had been near death, he had talked about training for baseball and girls and preparing for final exams. If he had seen he would have kept death at bay with his bare hands. But he had not. He had failed his friend and now that friend was utterly gone, every part of him.

Corey's family had insisted he sit with them under the funeral home canopy at the interment. A sharp April wind was playing rough with the tulips and dogwood blossoms. Jax thought he should be listening to what the minister, some high muck-a-muck in the Presbyterian hierarchy was saying, but all he could focus his attention on was two red tulips that seemed to swing in the wind in perfect alternation.

At some point he saw his father in the crowd standing in the sunshine. Trust his father to be scrupulous in observation of social obligations. His secretary had retained a service that sent cards, gifts and flowers for all appropriate occasions. The service did a pretty good job. Jax knew. He smiled cynically. Poor Father. Attendance at a funeral just couldn't be delegated.

"The distance that obscured details of retreating hairline and lines of maturity enabled Jax to see what he had never seen before. He looked like his old man. His build was from his mother, whipcord lean with intense energy, but his face had the same longish blade of a nose, grey eyes and straight black hair.

Beside him, Corey's mother shivered in a blast of chilly spring that swept across the cemetery. Jax and Corey's father simultaneously put their arms across the back of her chair. Jax withdrew his arm but angled his body to shield her from the wind as much as possible.

"Tell me about it." Pickett's soft voice and softer hand interrupted his reverie.

So he told her things he had never told anybody. How he and Corey had become best friends. It was Corey who gave Jax his nickname saying a name like Jackson made him sound like a pompous ass. He told her how he had spent more and more nights at Corey's house sleeping in a sleeping bag on the floor of Corey's room, his dirty clothes piling up in a corner until Corey's mom demanded that he turn them over for washing.

When Aline went off to college, Corey's stuff was moved into her room which was larger and a set of twin beds appeared. After that Jax went home only on weekends.

Corey was no match for Jax physically but he was so honestly thrilled by Jax's athletic accomplishments that it never seemed to matter. Corey and his father and often his mother attended every game Jax played in through high school.

With Corey's parents to oversee homework, Jax's grades improved, and the number of his fights tapered off. If he was no match physically, Corey was more than able to challenge Jax intellectually and it was Corey who dreamed up many of the elaborate practical jokes that instead of fights now necessitated trips to the headmaster's office.

"After Corey's funeral it was like I could hear people talking from a long way off and they kept telling me things like what a great guy Corey was. And I'm thinking what the hell am I supposed to say? He's dead, don't you get it, he's dead!"

"You were shattered by his death. That's kind of hard to work into funeral chitchat."

"No kidding. Shattered, yeah that's a good word for it. Nothing made any sense, like the meaning of everything had been broken into a million pieces." He was silent for a minute, looking into a past only he could see. "My dad took me to the country club for dinner. That's where we would meet, you know. Until I went to college we had the same address. I started to say we lived in the same house but I didn't live there, and I don't think he did either. There was a dining room in that house, and a breakfast room, but I can't ever remember having a meal with him except at the club or some restaurant.

"I wasn't really listening, he was just disapproving of the courses I had taken, and then he was talking about how transferring my college credits wouldn't be any problem, and I started paying attention.

"He had this plan that I would transfer to an Ivy League school. He said he was sure Corey's death bothered me, but it was just as well that he had died because our relationship had gone on long enough. It was time to put 'all that' behind me and start being a man. Corey, he said, had been holding me back.

"He talked, and I know this is stupid, but I realized for the first time he thought I should be like him. And I already looked like him. I made up my mind right then I would never be like him. I made up my mind to get as far away as I could from his definitions of importance and success.

"I went out the next morning and joined the Navy."

"That's when you became a SEAL?"

"That's not exactly how it works. Qualifying for SEAL training is a long process, but yes, Corey and I had talked about being SEALs. He always knew there wasn't a chance in hell for him. As long as he was alive…" Jax let the sentence die away. "But he was gone. The day I joined the

Navy I knew I was damn well going to do it. I was going to be a SEAL, no matter what I had to go through to do it."

"Because your father wouldn't approve."

"Nah. That was icing on the cake. It was because it was what I wanted to do more than anything in the world. In fact it was the only thing I wanted to do."

Patterson lumbered up from his favorite place in the hall, sneezed, stretched and padded over to press his snout under Pickett's hand.

Pickett fondled the yellow velvet ears. "You're ready for us to go to bed aren't you? You're right. It's late." She craned her head around. "Where's Lucy?"

"I heard her go upstairs." Jax grinned. "I think she's in bed with Tyler."

Jax might be amused by Lucy's choice of bed partner but Pickett wasn't. It wouldn't do to give Tyler a false sense of permanence. Already he was showing signs of attaching himself to living in this house. God knew he probably needed something to cling to, but if he were allowed to become attached to her house and dogs he would just feel doubly betrayed and bereft when he had to leave.

Jax's hand slid, warm and hard, under the hair at her nape. His fingers pressed against her skull to turn her face toward him. His eyes usually cool and distant were glittering with heat. "Go to bed with me."

It was not quite a command, but not a question either. Something aching with emptiness, yet warm with promise of being filled shot from her throat to the juncture of her thighs. Her mouth opened involuntarily as she found herself leaning toward him.

This was desire. This melting in which her whole body screamed "yes!" without a single thought. In that moment she knew that part of her inexperience was due to never having wanted a man before, not like this. Saying no was cool and easy and automatic when she was only mildly tempted.

But the very strength of the pull she felt toward Jax was its own braking mechanism. She worried about Tyler getting attached, but she knew if she went to bed with Jax letting him go would be terribly hard.

And go, he would. Even if he offered her undying love, and he had not, he was a SEAL. Go was what he did.

The caressing fingers on the back of her neck became more insistent.

"I want you. You want me."

Was he really pulling her closer or did she just feel as if the distance between them was disappearing? There was a reason not to do this but she couldn't think of what it was. She said the first thing that popped into her mind. "I haven't had my dinner date yet."

The heat did not disappear from his eyes but she was beginning to recognize the cool look of assessment. "You want me."

There wasn't any point in denying it. Pickett nodded.

"But the dinner is important to you. Why." Funny how he could make a request for information sound like a command.

"I don't know exactly. I guess I'm not willing to be just a convenience to you. A quick stop at a service station along the road of life."

Jax's eyes suddenly gleamed with humor. "That metaphor needs some work in terms of who puts what where."

Pickett thought about it and giggled. Lord, she loved his quick grasp of things. She even liked how he pushed her, didn't make it easy for her. So his next words surprised her.

"If it's important to you, then it's important. What's the name of the fanciest restaurant in Wilmington? I'll make reservations for tomorrow night." He stood with the fluid movement so characteristic of him and pulled her to her feet and into his arms in one movement. "Now I am going to kiss you."

And he did. Just how much he had been holding back was suddenly abundantly clear. He held her so that she was pressed full length against him. One hand cradled and controlled her head while the other scooped up her bottom to press her mound hotly against his erection. The difference in their strengths was never so apparent as he held her off the floor with one hand while moving with blatant intent against her.

He covered her face with kisses, biting at her lips then thrusting his tongue into her mouth in time with the movement of his hips.

He tasted like beer and hot dark man and determination.

Pickett used her arms to pull herself closer, to ease the sudden need to rub her breasts against the solid wall of his chest.

The fingers of the hand cupping her bottom slid along the cleft increasing both sensation and need with a jolt that stiffened Pickett with surprise. A second later she would have pressed herself more deeply against the hand, but he was already ending the kiss, sliding her body down his, letting her go while putting off letting her go till the last possible second.

He steadied her with one hand on either hip until she found her balance, then rested his cheek against her hair, as he fought to bring his ragged breathing under control. Abruptly he stepped away and rubbed his hair in a short, sharp gesture. "There. Now you know how I've felt for the last four damn days."

Inexperienced or not, Pickett knew that seconds more of that searing kiss and she would have been in bed, on the couch, on the floor whatever it took to answer the need that flowed between them like a living entity with a will of its own. He had started the kiss and he had ended it. It was with a poignant sense of loss that she acknowledged that he had done what she said she wanted.

If she took him in her arms now what would happen? No, the same doubts were there. She took refuge, as she often did, in arranging everyone's needs.

"When you go upstairs to take Tyler to the bathroom, make sure you send Lucy to me."

"I'm going to get him up to go to the bathroom?" She tasted like grapes and smelled like violets and aroused woman, and her lips were swollen and red from his kisses, but there was no doubt, Bossy was back. She retreated into bossiness to set her world back in order after he rocked it. The sudden insight made him smile and kick up one straight eyebrow.

"Yes." She gave him a stern look belied by the dimple that appeared at the corner of her mouth. "That is your job and not mine. No really, think how bad he would feel if he wet his new bed the first night he slept in it. And I'm afraid if he did wake up he wouldn't know where he was and it would scare him. So go get him."

Jax pulled up the pajama bottoms of his sleepy son and flushed the toilet. Sure enough when stood at the toilet he had obligingly used it even though he hadn't really waked up. He lifted the soft little body to his shoulder and climbed the stairs.

He'd read about needing to get children up in the night in that book, but he'd forgotten. There seemed to be a lot to this fatherhood business. But Picket knew Tyler would need to go. And she remembered because she thought about how Tyler would feel, not because she was worried about the sheets.

He shifted the limp weight of his son higher up his chest and felt Tyler nestle into him. Tyler would nestle like this when he was a baby, so trusting as if his father's arms were the most right place to be in the world.

With a pang, Jax realized he couldn't remember carrying a sleeping Tyler since he was a baby. Once it was time for Tyler to sleep, it had been time for Jax to leave, or to take him back to his mother's.

Being with Tyler all day and all night without the hovering nervous presence of his mother, or that bitch of a grandmother was a revelation. His kid was funny, bright, inquisitive, and once he could forget about the designer clothes, all boy.

He placed Tyler in the center of the wide bed and drew up the sheet. It was still amazingly warm for the middle of October but at least it had been possible to turn off the air conditioning and open the windows. A breeze was coming in and the room would be cool by morning. He pulled up the soft blanket and tucked it around his son as well.

As he turned toward the door Pickett's voice floated up the stairs. "No, Lucy. You cannot sleep with Tyler. I know you want to, but the answer is no." She was talking to the dogs. He smiled to himself. Just like she thought they would understand every word.

He went to the top of the stairs. "Would it be all right for Lucy to sleep with Tyler? I was thinking about what you said. He might be afraid if he woke up in the night. Having Lucy would help."

A little vertical crease appeared between her brows. Had he transgressed into Boss territory?

"Tyler looks so little lying in that big bed," Jax added.

Her expression was serious but she let go of the straining dog's collar. "Okay, Lucy. Go to Tyler."

Toes scrabbling for purchase, ears flying, the small mixed breed raced up the stairs.

"Thank you."

Pickett nodded in acknowledgement. "Good night."

TWENTY

Pickett bent to turn off the one lamp they had turned on earlier, plunging the room into darkness.

Through the connecting door Jax could see the flood of moonlight spilling into Pickett's bedroom.

In a minute he would go in there alone and she would go to the daybed in the therapy room.

Every instinct he had said that would be wrong.

He had come here knowing he was attracted to her and knowing he wouldn't act on the attraction. Every reason was still valid. He needed to stay focused on Tyler. His place in the SEALs depended on his getting Tyler squared away and doing it right. And it wasn't going to be as easy as he had thought. Tyler's grandmother might have physical custody, but he knew now he would insist on new agreements about visitation. That meant calls to his lawyer and maybe trips to Raleigh to negotiate with Lauren. It was more important than ever that he stay focused on his objectives.

Even if he could afford a to get involved with a woman right now, he should stay away from

Pickett. Damn it, that wary look she had when he got too close to her said she wasn't the kind of woman who would take sex lightly. She would have expectations and a whole list of demands. Taking her to dinner would just be the start of what she would want from him.

He wanted her. He was still half-aroused from their kisses earlier. He shouldn't get distracted by his dick. But God, he wanted her.

He wouldn't be able to sleep in that room tantalized by her womanly scent, a ghost of her in the bed with him when he wanted the flesh. He would spend the night prowling the house like a lion whose prey stays just out of reach.

"Pickett."

Pickett. Just the one word, her name, almost whispered, gravelly with desire, harsh with entreaty.

Pickett halted. She'd never heard a man's voice sound like that before, nevertheless, every cell in her body recognized it's meaning.

She turned around. The plantation blinds in her bedroom had been left open and she could see the half moon just clearing the trees. Jax was a dark figure silhouetted in the doorway, one hand outstretched. Every line of his body spoke of focused intent.

Pickett's heart kicked over at the thought of that much potent masculinity calling to her. Wondered if she could do this. Knew she was going to.

She hadn't left. She turned around. He crossed to her in two long-legged strides. He wanted to crush her to him, to plunder her mouth, rouse her until she longed for the mating of their flesh as much as he did. But the stillness of her figure warned him he couldn't be sure of her yet.

Though his night vision was better than most, he couldn't see the expression in her eyes. Was it her wary look? He hated for her to be wary of him. He wanted her yielded, soft with desire. He wanted her to look at him hopeful of ecstasy, not warily.

He took her hand. "Come to bed with me." Damn. His voice sounded more like a croak than a croon. Where was the low, seductive tone that always worked so well in the past?

He kissed her knuckles and tried again. "I want you so much. I said I'd take you to dinner, and I will, I promise." He rubbed her soft, slightly cool fingers against his cheek, across his brow, "but let me have you tonight."

Jax stopped rubbing her hand across his hair then felt her fingers continue the caress. Had she said yes?

"Did you say yes?"

"Yes."

The feeling of relief and exaltation was dizzying, followed instantly as it was by the cold duty he had to do. He was getting ready to break the 24 hour rule: never hang around a woman's place more than 24 hours after making love. If you do, she'll believe you're there to stay. He had to make sure Pickett understood.

Over the voice in his head clamoring for him to shut up, don't do it, don't mess up now, she said yes you idiot, don't try to change her mind, he said, "You know this doesn't, won't mean…anything, don't you?"

Oh shit he had said it. And now she had stopped stroking his hair and was resting that hand on his chest. Was she going to push him away? Quickly he circled her with his arms. Now that he'd made her hesitate, what did he say to get her back?

The thing was, it wasn't about the 24 hour rule. He wanted to avoid scenes and tearful recriminations as much as the next man, but even more, he didn't want Pickett to get hurt. She hadn't been anything but generous to him and kind to Tyler. She didn't deserve for him to be careless with her feelings.

"You're special. You're not a convenience store on the roadside of life or whatever you said. But, you know I won't be staying, don't you? Not more than a couple more days."

That wouldn't be long enough.

"Or a week."

But it might take longer to get a new agreement finalized. He firmly pushed away the hopefulness of that thought.

"Two weeks at the absolute outside, and that's all there is. Do you understand?"

"I understand."

"And you'll be all right with that?"

For an answer she pulled his mouth down to hers.

That cold tight thing that had been twisting in his gut since the moment she reached for the lamp switch, let go. Warmth spread where it had been.

Just before she reached for him, her heart pounding with the enormity of what she was getting ready to do, Pickett thought of telling Jax that the only thing that made this possible was the fact that it was temporary.

He was offering her the perfect compromise between casual sex and meaningful relationship.

But if they kept talking, they might not ever get started, and she knew her willingness to seize the moment would only last so long.

He scooped her into his arms. He actually did! And it really was as thrilling and romantic as it seemed between the covers of a romance novel. She buried her head in the crook of his neck, nosing aside the collar of the blue polo shirt to inhale the rich enticement of his warm masculine scent.

Still with her in his arms he closed the blinds and turned on a bedside lamp. Only then did he let her slide down his body to her feet.

Her body hugging t-shirt had mostly pulled free of her jeans when he carried her and in only a couple of tugs his hands were molding the silky skin of her midriff. When he tried to pull the shirt over her head she resisted however, burying her nose against his breastbone.

"Shy?"

There was a jerky nod against his chest. He chuckled softly. She moved with such confidence most of the time. A tender amusement filled him.

"Is it the light? Do you want it off?"

Another little jerky nod.

"I'll turn it off if you want me to." He folded her in his arms and rocked her gently. "but I really want to see you. Won't you let me see you, sweetheart?"

A soft shoulder moved in a diffident shrug.

"Don't you know I'm going to like what I see?"

The shoulder moved in another shrug that said 'tell me more.'

Jax almost laughed aloud. He would have, except for the rush of protectiveness that suddenly made his eyes a little wet. "I've wanted to see you, every single inch of you since you stood on the cottage deck and watched me and Tyler."

"I wasn't sure you knew that was me." She hadn't raised her head but her hands were tracing the long muscles of his back.

"Oh yeah. You were a marked woman from that moment on." Her ribcage shook in a soundless giggle. He stroked up her back and used the motion to flip the catch of her bra. He wanted her with an intensity he couldn't remember having felt in years, and in that moment he knew nothing would satisfy him but having her give herself to him.

If he could sit motionless under camouflage for hours, ignoring ants crawling over him, letting his quarry come to him, he could hold off his cravings long enough to let her come to him.

"You make me think of a peach, all golden pink. And ripe and fragrant. I want to see all your colors, and bite into the places that are blushing red, and fill my mouth with your juices." He nibbled kisses down her neck then nipped the junction between neck and shoulder. A shiver ran through her.

Pickett raised her eyes to him, as if searching his face for clues about his sincerity.

"And your eyes. Your eyes change color like the ocean. I want to look in your eyes when I'm inside you and watch you when I make you come."

He insinuated a hand between their bodies and covered her breast, feeling fierce triumph as the nipple beaded against his hand. He stroked the little bud and felt it tighten further. In a moment she raised both arms to his shoulders and he drew the shirt over her head, pulling the bra with it.

He tossed the shirt across the room with one hand while the other sought the button at her waist.

Pickett felt his rough hands brush her jeans from her hips. His frank sensuality was both arousing and a little shocking. She guessed a little disorientation was to be expected when a wildest dream sort of fantasy started turning into reality. She remembered with perfect clarity watching him on the beach and being transfixed by his masculine beauty. How impossible it had seemed that he might even look at her, much less find her desirable. And yet he had fantasized about her too.

His hands found the cleft of her buttocks, one long finger stoking, barely touching back to front, front to back. It wasn't nearly enough, and yet waiting for the moment when his touch would whisper across her most sensitive flesh was riveting.

She felt his fingers encounter moisture and begin spreading it. She wished the wetness weren't necessary. It seemed to add to the general untidiness of the whole process. And she could smell her arousal too.

He made a small sound of satisfaction. "You're already getting wet for me. Do you know what a turn on that is?"

He liked it. Pickett knew a lot about sex from a clinical standpoint, but she had never considered that a man might enjoy the experience of arousing her. That he might find her wetness thrilling. Not something to be put up with, got through. There was that disorientation again. As if she could feel his pleasure in her pleasure.

Would she be able to feel him receive pleasure? She had been wanting to run her hands across his chest maybe forever. Quickly she slid her hands under the soft knit of his shirt to the warm, smooth skin beneath. Suddenly, it wouldn't do—wouldn't do at all—that his skin, all his skin was not accessible to her. She had to rub her breasts against him. Feel his buttocks in her hands.

She pulled at his shirt. "Off! Get this off now!"

He obliged one-handed while somehow hardly stopping that wonderful thing he was doing with the other hand between her legs.

She found the waistband of his shorts. Where was the damn button? Everything felt backwards. She gave a grunt of frustration and jerked hard at the resisting material. "Do something! I want to feel you."

Jax lifted her face to his. His crystal grey eyes with their short spiky lashes were narrowed in a smile that touched only his eyes, and seemed to come from his soul. For a long, timeless moment he searched her face and, seeming to have found something, lowered his mouth to hers.

Jax tried to tell himself he had to take it slow. He was no longer afraid he would spook her, but he still had to make sure he gave her plenty of time. He hadn't been with a woman this inexperienced since he'd had very little experience himself. He liked his sex hot, hard and physical. In another woman her tentative touches and shy fumbling would have spoiled the fun of the hearty game of forgetfulness that he sought.

Instead it was like she gave him her newness, and made sex something new for him too. And somehow that made him hungrier than ever.

It was a kiss of hunger and of claiming. It was a kiss that said now. Now we begin.

He dropped his shorts to the floor and stepped out of them, then pushed Pickett's jeans, together with her panties, down her legs. He spared only a moment's regret that he wouldn't get to see her in the filmy scraps. Oh well, another time, and he already knew there would be other times.

Jax picked up and placed Pickett in the high bed against the pillows piled up against the headboard. He had imagined her here all peach and gold, against the sensual excess of pillows so many times. Triumph, hot and bright, throbbed through him, merging with the insistence of his arousal.

Yes. This was right. All the excellent reasons for resisting the attraction vanished as if they had never existed.

He wanted her. He wanted all of her. He would have her.

Her eyes, almost indigo with arousal, flared as she read his intent.

His skin gleamed in the lamplight. He leaned across her, his weight supported on one arm, muscles bunched. The brown forearm next to her hip was lightly covered with straight silky black hair. She wanted to sleek her hand across it as you would a cat feeling the ripples of sinew and muscle flex beneath.

"You are so beautiful."

Heat flared in his fog colored eyes, but one corner of his mouth kicked up, slightly. "I was supposed to say that."

"And so big."

"You know I won't hurt you, don't you? I won't do anything to you that you don't want." His touch as light as sunshine he stroked across her breast down her belly and came to rest on the golden curls that covered her mound. "I know how to be careful."

"You are a dangerous man."

"But not to you," he acknowledged, stroking both hands back up her torso, cupping her breasts, kneading them with firm strokes. "Never to you." He bent his head to take the nipple into his mouth.

He suckled strongly while continuing to knead the underside.

The sudden surge of pleasure that radiated from his mouth across her body to the juncture of her thighs brought Pickett arching off the bed, digging her fingers into his shoulders to keep the contact.

"Oh. You like that?" He treated her other breast to the same attentions until Pickett could feel funny little sounds coming through her throat. Sounds that cried of the exquisite sense of building fullness that paradoxically longed to be filled.

"Tell me what else you like, Pickett." Jax nibbled kisses across her ribcage, down the roundness of her belly. "Tell me."

"I like that."

"What else?"

"I don't know."

"You don't know?"

"What I did before wasn't...this. If that was sex, this isn't. If you know what I mean."

Jax sat back on his heels and contemplated the woman stretched before him on the mounded pillows. Her lips were swollen and scarlet from his kisses. Her round breasts with their large golden brown aureoles, now coral tipped, heaved with her arousal. Her eyes were the deep blue of the ocean at 35 feet.

Jax had always been a generous lover. He liked sex too much not to enjoy his partner's participation as well as his own. That's what he meant when he asked the question. But just like Pickett could, she managed with one sentence to make him reevaluate all his plans.

She was, as he suspected, deeply sensually aware, and easy to arouse. They could just go on and she would be satisfied, he'd see to it. But for him that wouldn't be enough.

When they were done he wanted her to know what she liked.

He wanted her to know that what she liked was him. His imprint on every inch of her body. No matter who came after him she was always going to define her experience by his lovemaking.

The thought of anyone else seeing her like this, touching her the way he was going to touch her, annoyed him. He dismissed the idea before it could distract him. They weren't here now. He was. For now she was his.

"Does it matter so much, what I like?" That wary look was creeping back, shadowing her brow. "Am I doing things wrong?"

He had been looking at her, thinking, too long. She never stopped thinking, and damn if she wasn't making him do it too.

"No, sweetheart, you're not doing anything wrong, and it does matter what you like. I want to please you." That was the palest possible interpretation of what he wanted but he didn't know the words to tell her. "I want to make it wonderful for you and I want to learn you, so that the next time we make love, it will be ten times better."

Pickett tilted her golden head. "We're going to do this again?"

"Oh yeah."

She sat up and began shoving pillows right and left, pushing them aside and to the floor. On all fours, the delicious, pale globes of her bottom in the air, she tugged back the covers. Then she lay back down and with a smile as old as Eve held out her arms. "Come here."

He rose over her caging her with arms like tree limbs, white teeth gleaming through a feral smile.

"Oh, Lady. You are so going to find out what you like."

And she did.

Sex with Jax was nothing like she'd thought it would be. It was hotter, and raunchier. He pushed her past every inhibition, allowed no stopping for reluctance. When she would have pushed his head away as he nosed the curls between her legs, he held her thighs open wider. "We have to find out if you like this enough to do it again." She did. When she felt the hot slide of his tongue enter her, she almost screamed.

And that was another thing. He demanded she squirm, and make noise.

"Scream," he said. "I love the sounds you make. Let me hear you. Let me know."

And maybe that was what she liked best. The way he relished every proof of her response. He liked the slick slide of sweaty bodies and the slurping sound that happened when they stuck together. Still joined he effortlessly held her to him with one arm while he turned them over and piled pillows against the headboard with the other. He showed her how to rock in rhythm with him.

He inhaled deeply. "Smell that," his voice more a vibration she could feel from the seat of their connection than a sound. "That's us, together."

She wasn't experienced enough to know how to stay on the edge. He had rolled them over and pulled her legs around his hips so that he could better control her motions and give time to savor their joining, but as soon as he spoke he felt her inner muscles clench, and shudders overtake her.

At the screaming edge himself, he supported her with hands spread across her shoulder blades as she gave in to wave after wave. Then he pulled her limp form against his chest and came and came and came.

TWENTY ONE

Jax lay with Pickett tucked beside him, her head on his shoulder one leg thrown across his legs. His fingers idly stroked her upper arm lying across his chest. Under the rose petal skin, he could trace the well-defined shape of biceps and triceps, but with only a little more pressure he could feel the bone, hardly larger than the bones of Tyler's arms. She was so vivid, so maximally present; he rarely thought about how little she was, until he measured her with his hands. Then her delicacy made something catch in his chest and him want to surround her, putting his arms, his body between her and everything.

What she'd revealed at the fast food place came back to him. "Are you okay?" he asked.

Pickett chuckled, and slid her legs against his. "I'm a whole lot better than okay."

"No, I meant what you told Tyler about celiac disease. Is it more dangerous than you told him?"

"I'm healthy, and as long as I watch my diet, I'm likely to stay that way." A clinical chill crept into her voice. "There is a slightly increased risk of cancer, but it's slight. Why?"

"But is it dangerous?" She hadn't really answered his question, and she was smart enough to know what he meant.

"You sound like Tyler."

Jax shook her shoulder gently to let her know he was serious.

"If I didn't watch my diet, it would be devastating."

Devastating. Strong word. Jax's belly tightened, but he resumed his slow stroking of her arm.

"But I do," Pickett went on, "and I will for the rest of my life, and since my diet is so good, I'm probably healthier than most people."

"So why didn't you tell me that you had celiac disease?"

Under his stroking hand he felt her shoulder muscles tighten.

After a long pause she said, "It's hard to talk about."

"Why? And don't tell me I sound like Tyler," he forestalled her. "I'm serious. And I'm going to keep asking until you talk to me."

"You are like a dog with a bone!" Pickett pulled away and rolled to the edge of the bed.

Unh-uhn, she was not going to do her sliding away thing. He snaked an arm and pulled her back, deftly turning her and tucking her against him. "Yep, I am."

Her soft body was still and stiff against him, but she didn't fight to get away. He hated the loss of the warm contentment, and thought briefly of loving her and stroking her until she was warm and pliant in his arms again. It would be easy. She was so responsive to his every touch, and there were ways he wanted to touch her, places to kiss, that he hadn't even started on. He felt himself stir, which was amazing considering what they had done a short time ago.

But somehow that wasn't good enough. He wanted something from her that was more than giving him her body, exciting as that was. It irritated him a little that she didn't want him to know something this important. She didn't go for shallow relationships. Hell, he might, but she didn't. What did she think was going on here?

He wasn't going to give it up. Pickett could feel the strength of the arms that gently caged her. With no hint of roughness, he had grabbed her and tucked her back against him so efficiently, so quickly, she was almost disoriented for a moment. The potent demonstration made her aware on previously unacknowledged level of what his training and strength meant. It was a little scary to realize he could have hurt her with the same efficiency. But he hadn't. Hurt her. At all. One second she was rolling over to get out of the bed, and the next she was tucked back against him exactly as before.

If she protested, even slightly, he would let her go. She let her head relax against the solid wall of his shoulder instead, knowing that it was a kind of acquiescence.

He fingered her hair. Traced the shell of her ear with one fingertip.

"You said 'potentially devastating.' This is not a mild case of the flu we're talking about here. Didn't you know something like that would be important to me?" His voice rumbled against her cheek. His words said barely-contained-patience, but the finger that traced patterns on her neck, her shoulder, down her arm said something else. She'd figured he'd lose interest in her once he knew. "How long have you had it?"

Pickett took a deep breath. She didn't know what to make of his suddenly wanting to know more, but she could tell him the facts. "It's genetic. In some people it shows up in early child-hood. Looking back, I think I started having symptoms when I was 12 or 13 but I wasn't diag-nosed until a couple of years ago."

Jax was silent, slowly stroking her shoulder, down her waist and across her hip, then back up again. "What else?" he asked, at last. "What made you not want to tell me?"

"I don't know." She wasn't going to tell him she'd imagined he would be disgusted if he knew. She started to move toward the edge of the bed again.

"No sliding away. You do that a lot. Are you ashamed of having a disease?"

Ashamed? No, it wasn't anything to be ashamed of. Pickett started to shake her head, then stopped, stunned at the accuracy of his insight.

She was ashamed, not of having celiac disease, but of how she had been before. Fat, unattractive, underachiever, depressed, weakling, and all the character defects she had assigned herself, lazy, undisciplined, passive, helpless, hopeless. She had felt so ashamed of herself for years. Compassion for her younger self made her eyes well up.

"You know what? I was ashamed. I was fat and there wasn't anything I could do about it. Everybody thought I didn't have enough will power or self-respect to stick to a diet. And after a while that's what I thought too. When I was lethargic, I thought I was lazy. I had colds and sore throats and belly aches so often, my sisters thought I was goldbricking."

"The celiac disease was causing all that?"

"In effect, I was starving. I ate nutritious food but my body couldn't absorb it."

"How could you be fat if you were starving?" He sounded like he really wanted to know.

"Doesn't make sense does it? And a lot of people with celiac are too thin, but sometimes they're not. In the early stages of celiac the symptoms are very confusing. Most people have it for years before they're diagnosed."

"What the hell is the matter with doctors?"

"American doctors don't find it as often as they should. But to be fair I'm not sure I ever told a doctor everything. I didn't know that everybody's guts didn't hurt after they ate. I thought it only counted if it hurt bad enough to double you over. Not just how I felt but what I felt turned into something I had to hide. I learned to suck it up and keep going."

Pickett tried to shrug as if it meant nothing, but it didn't mean nothing. Tears welled again as she thought of all the times she had whipped herself with hatred just to find the energy to do the simplest things. Now that she knew what it was to feel well, she saw what Herculean tasks she had performed.

"Hey, are you crying?" Jax rolled to his side to put both arms around her. "I'm sorry. I didn't mean to push you. No that's a lie. I did mean to push you, but I didn't know it would hurt you."

Pickett tried to swallow back her sobs, but the tears once started wouldn't stop. "I'm not hurt" she managed to choke out.

"The hell you're not. Something has hurt you bad."

"Not you."

"Okay." Jax whispered and pressed her face into the hollow of his neck "Okay."

Like many men Jax was uncomfortable with tears, his own or anyone else's. A part of him wondered what the hell he was doing here, holding this sobbing woman. Another, a much more important part, knew that if she had to cry, he wanted her doing it here, in his arms. Where he could protect her.

Whoa! Where had that come from?

He didn't need anyone else to complicate his life right now. His head already reeled with the complexities of trying to figure out how he would balance the demands of a career with Tyler's needs. So why did being here feel so right?

He had pushed past her wariness again and again, when he knew damned well he had other choices, but he had done it anyway. But dammit, he didn't like it when she seemed to hold him away. He wanted…sex, but he'd had sex. His body stirred as he remembered the delicate greed with which she tasted him. It was great. And it wasn't enough.

He stroked the damp silky curls back from her face. The sobs had been replaced by long shuddering sighs, then silence. He had some more questions, but when he turned toward her to ask them, her hand flopped bonelessly against his chest. She had fallen asleep, worn out by the weeping and all that had passed before.

He felt his lips curve in a smile. He liked that almost childlike directness and honesty with which she responded when she lost her wariness. She had approached sex the same way. He wanted her again, but he should let her sleep.

He pulled a pillow into place for her head and turned them both on their sides, her bottom tucked into his groin. His hand found a soft breast and cupped it, marveling again at how perfectly it fit his hand. Absently, he captured the silky nipple between two fingers while his other fingers stroked the underside. He'd already discovered she liked that. His mind drifted. His unruly member, already stirred by the closeness of that enticing cleft, hardened.

Had she ever done it this way? Probably not. Would she be shocked?

Soft buttocks rubbed against him, then rocked with slow experimentation.

"Are you awake?" he asked softly, not wanting to wake her if she was still asleep.

"If I'm not," she sounded half-sleepy, half-amused, "this is a very good dream."

"Would you like to try it this way?"

"You'd have to show me how."

Jax had always looked for bedmates in women who were experienced, who knew the score and were looking for the same raunchy, no strings, no holds barred sex he was. Who knew Pickett's combination of enthusiasm and innocence would be such a turn on? Or maybe it was just the novelty. Maybe once that wore off, he would be no more interested in sticking around than he ever was.

For right now the simple trust and generosity with which she gave herself blew him away, and made the fumbling oddly sweet.

"Put your leg here." He lifted her upper leg to rest it on the outside of his thigh, then slid one hand into the already dampening curls.

"Um. I like that, but I thought we were going to do it this way."

"We are."

"So do it."

Until this minute, Jax hadn't known you could feel a smile all over your body. "Patience, little one. We have to get you ready."

"I'm ready."

"There's not as much stimulation for a woman in this position. You need to be very, very ready."

Jax could almost hear the wheels turning in her active brain as she considered his reply.

"Is there enough stimulation for a man then? I can't touch you very much."

Jax almost groaned with the effort he was making to hold back, not to plunge himself into her warmth.

"Trust me. I am stimulated plenty." He kissed the nape of her neck, then ran his tongue in the shallow groove there. He felt almost ridiculous satisfaction when she shivered and pushed closer, making one of her soft sounds. "That's it," he encouraged. "Enjoy this just for what it is."

"You're enjoying it, aren't you?"

Jax almost gave a sarcastic 'duh,' but he'd caught the wonder in her voice. "I mean," she added, "you're not just going through the steps. You really like it."

Jax swept his hands over her in wordless reply, making evident the pleasure he derived from touching her, feeling her, pleasuring her.

The knowledge set something free in Pickett. Suddenly the sensation gathering between her legs seemed to burst over her entire body in a wave of heat, sensitizing every nerve ending. Sounds, unbidden and unchecked were pulled from her throat with every swirling touch of his magic fingers. Her hips made their own demands, pushing her mound against his hand.

Pickett felt Jax reach across her to the night stand for one of the foil packets then pull away for a second while he readied himself. When he reached under her buttocks to open the swollen petals there, she could not control a fine trembling that swept over her.

Jax paused just at her entrance. "Are you all right? You're not scared, are you?"

"Now." Pickett pushed her hips at him. "I need you now."

He filled her with a slowness that made her want to scream. And then an intensity of pure pleasure jolted through her. "Oh my God!"

Jax stilled abruptly. "Have I hurt you?"

"No. It's so good. It's—um—when you move like that, yes just like that, it is so good."

"Like that?" he repeated the movement.

"Yes. I've never—"

"This must be a good position for your G-spot. You know about them don't you?"

Pickett couldn't help but laugh, an amazingly sultry sound even to her own ears. "I know about g-spots in theory. This is my first acquaintance with my own."

Jax's answering laugh was full of masculine triumph. "Now we know another thing you like."

TWENTY TWO

"Y ou are going to do WHAT?" Pickett's body, seconds before so sweetly nestled into the curve of his, stiffened.

Jax rapidly reviewed what he had just been saying. They had been lying in bed, talking over their plans for the day in sleepy, relaxed murmurs. He'd been idly wondering if the slow stroking of Pickett's breasts would give her the same idea he was getting. With her bare bottom pressed against his arousal there wasn't much way she didn't know what was on his mind.

Jax liked sex in the morning, and it wasn't something he got much of. If his schedule didn't make it impossible to linger in bed, the twenty-four hour rule did. What the hell had he said? Whatever it was, they didn't have to talk about it right now.

Jax pulled her back against him stroking her soft belly. "It's not important, sweetheart. Just a phone call to my lawyer. I can do it later."

"You said you were going to change the custody agreement to make sure you got more visitation with Tyler." Her tone was accusatory. What was the matter with her? She ought to think that was a good thing.

He smoothed a circle around the velvety areole of one plump breast. She really liked that last night. It might work.

Pickett pushed his hand away. "Do you mean Lauren—your mother-in-law—the one that treated me to a diatribe about your deficiencies— that Lauren is going to have custody of Tyler?"

He could try a kiss behind her ear. He moved his lips over the velvety skin. He liked the way she smelled there. Shampoo and soap and warm, sleepy smell.

Pickett shoved a remarkably sharp elbow into his midriff and squirmed away.

No morning sex this morning. Jax flopped onto his back. He covered his eyes with his arm. "This isn't news Pickett." He sounded a lot more patient than he felt. "She's had custody since his mother died. You know that."

Pickett sat up and swung her legs over the side reaching for the first article of clothing that came to hand. Her back to him, she pulled on the blue knit shirt Jax had worn last night, then stood up.

"I knew he was staying with her until you could come for him. It never occurred to me you would give her permanent custody."

"Did you think I would keep him?"

"Yes!"

Jax blinked at her vehemence. "Why are you so offended?"

"I'm not offended. I'm appalled!"

"Pay attention, Pickett. I am a SEAL. I'm away 200 or more days a year. Even when I'm at the base, most of our training takes place at night. I'm gone twelve to fourteen hours at a time. That's reality. Tyler's too young to stay by himself. How am I supposed to take care of him?"

"200 days a year?"

"Yes. Lauren isn't perfect, but she does care about Tyler and I trust her more than hired help I wouldn't be present to supervise. So I'm doing what's best for Tyler, okay?"

After a long pause Pickett spoke. "Have you asked yourself what being deserted by you again is going to do to Tyler?" she asked quietly.

The question burned him. SEALs never abandoned one or their own. "I'm not deserting him," he said through clenched teeth, "I just told you. I'm going to change the visitation agreement. I'm going to make sure I see more of him and I want him to visit me as often as possible."

Pickett was silent. She picked up a brush and began to pull it through the tossed golden curls. The motion pulled up the shirt revealing creamy expanse of thigh.

She seemed to live to show him things that were just outside his reach. To hell with trying to defend himself. Jax stood up disregarding his nudity and half-aroused state. He caught Pickett's eyes watching him in the mirror.

"I'm already on notice that I will have to justify every arrangement I make to Commander

Kohn, but frankly, I don't see how it's any of your business."

Pickett's eyes prickled but she found if she breathed shallowly she could bear the blow he'd dealt to her heart. She met his crystal grey gaze in the mirror. His dark brows were low across his eyes and absolutely straight. This was the man, the warrior, she'd warned herself about repeatedly. Just one of those implacable looks, and no man under him would ever forget his position in the scheme of things again. Nor would she.

It was ironic. Making recommendations about custody was her business. Her job at any rate. Not many times, thank God, but she had been called as an expert witness in custody trials. But he hadn't asked for her opinion.

She was not his therapist.

She wasn't his anything.

She felt her face grow hot. She knew, she knew that an invitation to a man's bed was not an invitation to his life, and yet at the first opportunity, it seemed, she had stepped over the line. It was a good thing—eventually, it would be a good thing—he was so willing to set her straight.

She set the brush on the dresser with great care and slowly turned to face him. "You're right, of course, it isn't my business," she said, and she was very proud of how cool and steady her voice sounded. "I apologize." She turned back to the dresser and began to extract lingerie and clean clothes. "If you want to use the shower in the master bath, I'll use the one off my office."

He had been dismissed by admirals, and wing commanders, once, by a two star general, he reflected, drinking his coffee on the porch as he watched the sun clear the pines. But he had never been more effectively dismissed than by a one hundred pound woman with a mop of golden curls dressed in his faded navy shirt. It was soft and thin from many washings and clung to the slope of her breasts. It had hung down to her forearms and almost to her rosy knees. She should have looked ridiculous, like a child dressed in her father's clothing. Instead she did that queen thing with her head and proceeded to hunt through her underwear as if his presence was not significant enough to be an irritation.

It had turned him on so completely he had to bend over to scoop up his discarded shorts and turn his back to put them on.

He was right. She said so. So why did he feel like he had lost out on something—besides the obvious of course. Damn, she turned him on. But it wasn't just that a pleasant interlude had gotten de-railed. It was…what?

I was a shit.

You're not one now. What happened?

She'd sure changed her opinion of him since last night. Today she thought he was a shit and worse. That remark about him deserting Tyler still burned with an acid sting.

But what if she was right? About Tyler, he meant. He brushed away the fear that she was right about him. She had a way of anticipating what Tyler felt that he couldn't match. In the past several days he had gotten used to sharing the responsibility for Tyler with someone. Someone whose opinion he respected. Not that Tyler was her responsibility. But somehow they shared him in a way that he and Danielle never had. He was going to hate to give that up when he left, but Tyler would be with his grandmother. There wouldn't be much point to continuing. For right now though he would need to do stuff to make sure Tyler knew he wasn't deserted. And the person who could help him most was Pickett.

He shouldn't have said it was none of her business. He wondered how mad she still was.

He tracked her footprints through the dew-wet grass to the garage to find her wrestling a sack of corn into the 30 gallon garbage can she stored the duck's food in.

"I'm glad you're here," she smiled at him and pushed an errant lock of hair from her forehead. "I keep Quacker's food in this can so it won't attract raccoons and rats, but I dumped it in upside down and now I can't get to the tape to open it."

She was doing the same thing she had been doing ever since they argued. Not pouting, perfectly friendly in fact, and yet...

Jax pulled up the large sack of feed, reversed it and dropped it back in the can, then dexterously pulled the string that released the tape.

He replaced the metal lid and turned to face her. "Can we talk?"

"Sure." She started toward the door, angling her body to go wide around him, "is Tyler up yet?"

"He was still sound asleep when I looked." Jax planted himself in front of Pickett. "Look, about this morning. Can we get back to where we were?"

"Where we were." She appeared to think it over. "Having sex, you mean?" She smiled brightly. "Sure. Why not?"

She was still doing it. That thing. Smiling, even meeting his eyes, but not really. She was deliberately misunderstanding him, but still, it ticked him off for her to act like the sex didn't mean anything. Like it meant no more than pouring a cup of coffee or passing the toast.

He grabbed for his patience. "Don't be dismissive. But since you brought it up, that wasn't just sex. It was—you know—amazing. Wasn't it? Tell me you know it was more."

"Well, we already agreed you're the one with experience…" She shrugged but he could tell she was thinking about it. Remembering.

At last Pickett's ocean eyes met his, really met his, and softened.

"Okay," she said. Yeah, that was it, the soft eyes, soft smile. "Okay, it was amazing. I didn't know it could be like that."

He pressed for more. "And it wasn't just physical. It was talking and just being together. Can we get that back?"

Pickett let out a big breath.

"Listen," Jax stepped closer. "I'm a SEAL. There are some harsh realities that go with that. And they're not going to change. I know you don't like what I'm doing with Tyler," he lifted a hand, dropped it back to his thigh, "but can you accept that I'm doing the best I can?"

"I've already apologized," she pointed out firmly.

"I know. And I'm apologizing now, I think."

Pickett's eyes gleamed. "You think?"

Jax grinned in acquiescence. "All right. I am apologizing. I won't tell you to butt out again."

"But you were in the right. I stepped over the line. Where Tyler will live is not my decision to make."

"I wasn't right. We had something good going. We still can. For as long as I'm here, I need and want you to talk to me about Tyler. I want to do the best I can, even if it's not up to your standards. Can you deal with that?"

Pickett was silent a long time. Jax remained silent too. He had said everything he could think of to say. Sometimes you just had to let people make up their own minds.

At last her mobile features settled, and she sighed as if she had come to a conclusion. She didn't look especially happy.

"Pickett?"

She lifted eyes that were both wise and sad. "There's a whole world full of children that are not being raised according to my standards," she said slowly. Then in one of her agile shifts, she smiled with self-deprecating humor, "and when I have children of my own, they will probably be among that number. So, even if you're not absolutely perfect, I guess I can deal with it,"

He wanted to crush her to him. He wanted to pull her down on the cracked concrete and ravish her completely. He wanted to shout in triumph, but the thoughtful little smile that played around her mouth made him tip her chin up very, very gently. She was back with him, on his side again, but not all the way. He couldn't push it.

Until she smiled into his eyes.

Then he kissed her with the hunger that had gnawed at him for over an hour. Gnawed at him a long, long time. Maybe forever.

She tasted of coffee and mint toothpaste and some kind of certainty in an uncertain world.

TWENTY THREE

U h-oh.
      As soon as the kitchen phone rang, she
      knew it was her mother.

Pickett was in the laundry sorting yet another
load of clothes, amazed at how many outfits Tyler
dirtied in a day, not to mention how towels piled
up, and now, sheets.

Pickett was supposed to call as soon as the
hurricane was over, but she hadn't even thought of
it until this minute. She slammed down the lid of
the washer, and dashed for the phone but Jax
answered it before Pickett could stop him.

"Lt. Graham," he growled in that indescribably
military way.

Pickett's mind squirreled frantically for how
she was going to explain Jax's presence to her
mom. Just tell her the truth and let her deal with it.
Yeah, like that was going to happen. Pickett would
never hear the last of it. It would be one more
proof of her flawed judgment, one more instance
of Pickett's eccentric lifestyle.

"No ma'am," Jax was saying. "Nothing's wrong.

We came through the hurricane just fine…No ma'am, no damage to the house…You didn't have to worry, Pickett wasn't alone, I was here…Yes ma'am, the whole time…Sure, I'll get her."

Pickett allowed her knees to give way and laid her burning cheek on the cool metal of the washing machine lid. That's how Jax found her.

"Um, Pickett? Are you okay?"

Pickett nodded, rubbing her face against the coolness. She started to rise up then slumped back.

"Your mother is on the phone."

"I know." Disgusted at her own cowardice Pickett pushed herself upright and swiped her hair out of her eyes. "I wish you hadn't answered it."

"Sorry, I didn't know it would be a problem. She seems like a nice lady. She's real concerned about you."

Pickett smiled wearily. She toyed with asking Jax to tell her mother she would call back, but it really wouldn't help to put it off. She'd might as well face the music.

Jax eavesdropped with unabashed curiosity to Pickett's side of the conversation. This was a side of her he'd never seen.

At last Pickett hung up the phone and turned to face him.

"Okay, this is the plan," she sounded like a general. "You vacuum the downstairs and I'll clean the bathrooms. Then I'll mop the kitchen floor while you get all your stuff out of the bedroom. Make sure that you empty all trash. Do you take my meaning?"

"We're getting rid of the evidence?" Jax hazarded a guess. "But why?"

"Because my mother and as many of my sisters as she can collect will be here in two hours." Pickett said grimly.

TWENTY FOUR

Pickett had often observed that hugs were metaphors. Her mother's hug was cool silk and Jean Naté, a quick tightening, a quicker release, efficient. Pickett hardly had time to bring her arms up to return the embrace before her mother held out her hand to Jax.

"You're Lt. Graham," she said, not waiting to be introduced. "I'm Mary Cole Sessoms, Pickett's mother. Pickett's sisters—except for Lyle, she lives in New York—will be here in a minute. We're so glad you could join our little impromptu family party."

Impromptu party. Pickett nearly choked trying to stifle her snort. Jax would be as thoroughly grilled as the hamburgers, by the time her mother and sisters left.

Not by a flicker of an eyelash would her mother reveal that she was avidly curious about the first man, ever, to stay with Pickett overnight. A steel magnolia if there ever was one, Mary Cole Sessoms had honed her people skills pulling the insurance agency back from bankruptcy after the death of her husband, then going on the make it a million dollar producer annually.

Without appearing to question him, by the end of the day Mary Cole would know everything about Jax, from the date of his last tetanus shot, to his bank balance.

Jax smiled at her mother with just the right mix of masculine appreciation and charming deference. The knit of his deep yellow polo shirt molded to his powerful shoulders and set off his tan. He exuded a confidence so powerful it was clear he saw no need to prove himself. Pickett relaxed a little. He could handle her mother.

Pickett was sure her mother had arrived a few minutes before the others so she could size up Jax without distractions.

Jax now called Tyler over and introduced him, prompting him through the greeting ritual. Her mother's face flickered with surprise then approval at the evidence that he took his fatherly responsibilities to mentor his son seriously.

When they went into the house, Mary Cole excused herself to freshen up and Pickett moved around the living room, straightening pillows that were already straight and making infinitesimal adjustments to the clock and brass candlesticks on the mantel.

If her mother approved of Jax she'd have the wedding guest list made out by the end of the day. It would really be easier if she didn't approve. Then there wouldn't be so much explaining to do when he left. And yet she couldn't bring herself to hope her mother wouldn't like Jax, even if she was in for a big disappointment.

And there wasn't a thing she could say that wouldn't make the whole thing worse, either now or later. She sighed as she made a minute adjustment to the walnut framed mirror over the mantel.

She felt Jax's heat behind her even before he fingered the fine, silky curls at the nape of her neck that had already escaped the tortoiseshell clasp.

"Is having your family come such an ordeal for you?" he asked softly.

Pickett shook her head, a motion that made the warm finger trail back and forth on the sensitive skin.

"I love my family. They're really good to me. But I'm the baby, and no matter what I do, I can't ever seem to grow up in their eyes. They don't think I can do anything right. Not exactly right, if you know what I mean."

"Pickett darling," Pickett jumped away from Jax. Good thing her mother had a habit of beginning to talk before she entered a room. "Don't you want to go fix your hair before Gracie and Jensen get here? You don't want Jensen to see your hair like that," she added kindly.

Why did her mother always do that? Why didn't she say I don't like the way you fixed your hair? If she did, it would be possible to argue with her. Well, duh, her mother wasn't going to let an argument, for God's sake, get started. Oh no. Deflect the opinion onto someone absent. Then Pickett could know she didn't have her mother's approval and wonder if the brother-in-law she loved was secretly disapproving at the same time.

So what was new? It was just another of her mother's little confidence destroying ploys. Okay. The important thing was not to get hooked into defending herself.

"You don't like my hair, Mother?"

"It's not that I don't like it. And you can't help it if this salt air makes hair as curly as yours just go wild."

Mary Cole patted her own discretely tinted waves. The short, sophisticated style suited her perfectly, and every hair was always in place. A good cut was all it needed to be perfectly obedient.

Did her hair look as bad as her mother said? Pickett stole a glance in the mantel mirror. In it she could see Jax leaning against the door jamb, arms crossed over his broad chest. He caught her eye in the mirror and sent her a look so heated, so full of sexual innuendo that Pickett felt the back of her neck grow warm.

With a wicked grin he tilted his head and canted one eyebrow. "Wild thing" he mouthed.

Pickett stifled a giggle. She pulled the clasp from her hair and finger-combed it until her curls flew in gold exuberance. She laughed aloud.

"You know Mom, you are absolutely right. My hair is wild looking. I've decided that's a Good Thing."

Mary Cole's lips tightened fractionally. "Well, of course dear, if that's how you really want to look."

Pickett should have known that asserting her own preference wouldn't make her mother back off. In fact, she would probably start a discussion of Pickett's hair at the dinner table. Her sisters would give lots of kindly advice about how to subdue her impossible hair. Her brothers-in-law would look embarrassed or bored. And Pickett would sit there feeling unkempt and inept.

Her confidence was already sinking like a balloon losing helium. She could hear the rest of the party coming in the back door. Once again she reminded herself that all she had to do was get through the afternoon.

"Pickett," Pickett was enveloped in her oldest sister Gracie's hug. "You look so well! But you've lost more weight." Pickett's weight had been stable for two years. "You're not letting yourself get too thin are you?"

Without responding, Pickett turned to welcome Gracie's husband, Jensen. He hugged her, then bent his 6'4" frame to kiss her cheek. "Hey Little Bit. You look great," he whispered, "and don't let anybody tell you different." He flicked a golden curl and winked. "Cute curls," he added loudly enough for everyone to hear.

Pickett gave Jensen an extra squeeze. What would she do without his steady encouragement? It was he who had silenced her family's objections to her taking over the Snead's Ferry property. Without his support she would never have heard the last of why her moving to Snead's Ferry was a bad idea. Though to be fair, once the decision was made, every one had contributed some sweat to restoring the Victorian era farmhouse.

"Looking go-ood!" Pickett's other brother-in-law, Bobby, hugged her a little closer than was strictly necessary. He didn't mean anything by it, and Pickett had perfected getting an arm caught between their bodies years ago, nevertheless she was always glad when it was over. His wife, Sarah Bea, eyed Pickett's figure-hugging scoop neck coral tee and shell pink jeans. A tomato red belt drew attention to her tiny waist. Her expression made it clear that whatever she thought, she wasn't going to say anything…now.

Jax didn't like the over–hearty tone with it's crude innuendo of the guy who had just come in. He also didn't like the way he grabbed Pickett. She wasn't liking it much either. Jax didn't know what to make of some of Pickett's reactions to her family, but he was sure of his opinion of this joker trying to cop a feel.

Jax eyed the new arrivals. Pickett's sisters strongly resembled their mother and each other. All three women were several inches taller than Pickett, slender and long limbed. Both sisters had an elegant refinement they clearly got from their mother. Sarah Bea's hair was dark blond, streaked with highlights, Gracie's was lighter. All had the family bluc eyes.

Somehow, to Jax's eyes, even though Pickett was shorter than her sisters, almost tiny, she was more. Her coloring was more vivid with the bright gold hair, sparkling ocean blue eyes, pure peaches and cream skin. Her shape was curvier, more intensely feminine. Her voice was warmer.

"I brought soft drinks," announced Sarah Bea gaily. "I knew Pickett wouldn't have any, and I also brought hamburger buns everybody could eat."

Jax idly picked up the package Sarah Bea placed on the kitchen counter and read the ingredients. Wheat flour. Hamburger buns everybody but Pickett could eat. He gave the second oldest sister a long considering look. Had she meant to make the point that 'everybody' didn't include Pickett?

Sarah Bea intercepted his look and colored. "I meant, enough hamburger buns for everyone to eat." Not good enough. He hardened his gaze. "Well, what with us descending on her with no warning, I knew she wouldn't have enough." So, she at least acknowledged that they had come uninvited. Jax was considering whether to let up on her when she added, "that's what I meant about the soft drinks, too. My goodness, who keeps enough food on hand for ten people?"

"Nobody, that's who." Gracie efficiently swept up the conversation and began to organize contents of plastic bags. "That's why we all brought stuff.

"I also brought paper plates and napkins, since Pickett doesn't have a dishwasher." She put a head of lettuce in the refrigerator. "How can you stand this refrigerator, Pickett? It was old when I was young. When are you going to remodel this kitchen?"

"When I have the money." Pickett's voice was carefully expressionless.

"I've offered Pickett the money for new appliances several times," said Mary Cole coming in time to hear Gracie's question. "I hate to see her having to live like this."

"You never offered to buy me new appliances." The arch tone Sarah Bea tried for didn't really disguise the edge in her voice.

"You have a husband."

Jax had heard enough. He struggled to keep his rising ire from showing in his voice. "I think I'll start the grill and check on Tyler." He put a hand on Pickett's stiff shoulder. There was a tiny flinch under his hand that told him just how much her calm demeanor was a façade. He slid his arm around her and pulled her to him. None of the group assembled in the kitchen missed the gesture. Good. "Come out to the garage with me. You can show me where everything is."

"You know where everything is. Why did you really get me out here?" Pickett's eyes sparkled with a rogue-ish invitation, as Jax pulled open the door of the shed on the back of the garage. Jax wasn't fooled. Even with him she was pretending she could ignore her family's harping.

Still, he wasn't going to let slip an opportunity to kiss her. Jax leaned against the work bench, widened his stance and pulled Pickett between his legs. "So I could do this." He nibbled her bottom lip.

"That's exactly what they think we're doing," she said against his mouth.

"Um hum." He angled his head to deepen the kiss.

After a few moments she broke the kiss and tucked her head under his chin with a sigh. The weariness of the gesture made Jax's arms tighten around her. "Why do you let your family treat you like that? You let them put down and criticize you with every sentence. You wouldn't put up with that from me."

Pickett shoved at his shoulders. Though he loosened his hold, Jax refused to let her go.

Pickett leaned back so she could meet his eyes. "So now you've joined the millions who know better than I do how to live my life?"

Her snapping with so little provocation was a sign of how upset she was, but it made his point for him. "That's what I mean. If I step out of line, you let me know it in a heartbeat. You don't allow me, or other people not to treat you with respect."

"So what am I supposed to do? No matter what I say in reply to their little digs, I'm wrong. And then I'm wrong for not knowing how wrong I am. The best thing I can do is just ignore it."

Jax tightened his hold again, nestling her head against his chest. She was so little, so soft. He was furious all over again at how her family wounded this gentle, sweet, kind woman with tiny cuts and sly slights. He couldn't recall that he had ever felt so protective of anyone. He'd like to throw the lot of them bodily off the property.

He'd like to keep her next to him and never let any of them near her.

Unfortunately that wasn't going to happen. This wasn't his property and he wouldn't be staying. He absently rubbed the small of her back in little circles, dropping kisses on her hair.

"That's the trouble, love. Ignoring it isn't the best thing. If you let them get away with it, they'll just do it again, and again."

Pickett pushed out of his arms. This time he let her go. She pulled the grill from its corner and began to brush cobwebs away with a cloth from the workbench. "So what am I supposed to do? Defending myself doesn't work. You say ignoring doesn't work—and I admit you're right. What do I do?" She lifted the cover of the grill exposing a network of clinging webs and several daddy-longlegs spiders. "Yeeech!"

Jax took the grill cover away from her. He knocked the spiders away then ran the cloth around the dome. "Demand respect. Do that Queen Pickett thing."

"Queen Pickett thing?"

"Yeah, that thing you do with your head. Then give them that look that says 'I am going to think over what you just said," he lowered his voice in solemn portent, "and then I am going to grade it.'"

Pickett gurgled with surprised laughter. "Am I that intimidating?"

"You are, and you demand respect for your expertise. It's time you used a little intimidation on your sisters."

Pickett pulled a can of lighter fluid and a bag of charcoal from the shoulder-high shelf. "Do you think this charcoal has absorbed too much moisture to light?"

"Pickett, are you thinking over what I said?"

"Yes, it's just…they do love me, you know."

"Only you can put a stop to it. I'll back you up. You won't be alone." He smiled and winked with charming menace. "One SEAL constitutes a majority."

Pickett pulled the plastic wrap from Gracie's contribution of beautiful paper plates printed with autumn leaves and matching napkins, and chuckled inwardly. That was Gracie. If she had to out off paper plates, they would be paper plates with style.

There wasn't enough room to spread everything out on the ancient Formica countertop, so she unplugged the coffee maker and moved it to a lower cabinet.

"Don't put away the coffee maker," Gracie directed from the sink where she was washing lettuce. "We'll need it for later."

"Then I'll just have to get it out later, because right now I need the counter space."

To make room in the cabinet for the coffee maker Pickett nested two pots, put their lids on a lower shelf. In this kitchen you never moved just one thing.

Gracie shut off the water and turned, holding her dripping hands well away from her oatmeal colored silk slacks and matching silk sweater combination. A tiny pleat formed above her light blue eyes as she considered the problem. She sighed.

"This house is impossible to entertain in. If you had a dining room table we could make it work, but no, you had to make the dining room into an office."

Pickett needed a dining room table so that she could entertain graciously about as much as a pig needed roller skates. She was pulling her head out of the cabinet to say so when Jax bumped against her. When she grabbed for the cabinet door to steady herself, he bumped her again, almost knocking her over. What was with him? Jax was never clumsy. Underscoring the thought he placed two hands on her waist and smoothly lifted her to her feet. "Now," the word hardly more than a moist puff against her ear. "Sorry," he said aloud.

Now? Huh? Pickett replayed all that had just happened. Oh. He thought it was time to demand respect. Her heart executed a triple axel. He had taken his hands away, but she could still feel him there. Okay she could do this.

"Gracie, this is my house. Don't criticize it. I don't criticize your house." Not bad. Her voice was a little softer than she would have liked for maximum effect, but still.

"Oh, I wasn't criticizing. You're just too sensitive."

Damn. That's what always happened. No matter what she said they found a way to make her wrong.

Jax's hand covered her shoulder. Pickett wondered if he could feel how hard her heart was beating. Maybe he could because he added a little squeeze.

"It sounded like criticism to me," he told Gracie.

Gracie's eyes, wide with surprise, flew between Jax's and Pickett's. Would she back off, or fire another round? The moment lengthened. The phone rang once then abruptly stopped when it was picked up in the other room. Everyone was watching them now.

Pickett's heart beat in great body-shaking thuds, but she could feel the warmth of Jax's body along her back. It was strength she literally could draw on. She felt her neck lengthen and her head come up. Oh, that must be the gesture Jax called her 'queen thing.' In that moment she determined that if they had to stare at each other the rest of the night, Gracie would be the first one to blink.

Flustered spots of color appeared in Gracie's cheeks as it dawned on her she had, indeed, been rude. "Well, I'm sorry," she stammered. "I didn't mean...what I meant was..." Gracie saw there was no way to save her remark, so she went back on the offensive. "But if you're going to take that as criticism, I really don't know what it's okay to say, anymore."

The wish to let it go, to smooth things over pulled at Pickett like a down comforter on a cold night. Gracie had apologized—sort of. Their mother would say making a guest uncomfortable was just as bad as being a rude guest. Pickett felt Jax shift infinitesimally closer. No. The tiny nips at her autonomy would never stop if she let Gracie make her own embarrassment Pickett's fault.

"I'm sure, after a while," Pickett's measured tone underlined the words, "you'll figure it out."

She held Gracie's gaze another beat until she felt Gracie's wordless acknowledgement that the rules had changed for good.

Pickett's kind heart made her offer a salve for Gracie's ego. "You're so elegant and stylish, Gracie, that any compliment you give me is treasured."

"Now that's the truth!" Sarah Bea rushed to pick up the conversational ball. "She's such a perfectionist, if Gracie says something is okay, you know anybody else would call it fabulous."

Sarah Bea counted the hamburgers she had patted out. "How many will you and Tyler eat, Jax?"

"Hey Jax," Sarah Bea's husband, Bobby, stuck his head around the kitchen door, "the phone's for you. You might want to take it in another room." His grin came down just this side of malicious. "It's a woman. I couldn't catch everything she said 'cause she sounds like she's been drinking. But she wants to speak to 'the sonovabitch who's stolen my grandson.'"

The leathery leaves of the huge old live oak that reigned over the back of the property were bronzed by the setting sun by the time the caravan containing Pickett's family pulled out of the drive.

Jax stood, brown arm draped with casual possessiveness across Pickett's shoulders, his hand almost touching her breast. Tyler was on her other side leaning against her leg, one arm encircling her thigh. Patterson and Lucy sat at their feet, while Hobo Joe stood off to one side where he could keep the whole party in view.

Pickett tried not to think about the effect of the happily domestic picture they presented to the people in the departing cars, but the misty smile on her mother's face as she turned around to wave said it all. Pure Norman Rockwell.

Well, when no marriage was forthcoming, her mother and sisters would just have to deal with it, whether they approved or not. Pickett's choices, and even her mistakes, were her own to make. Today she had drawn some new boundary lines and from now on, she would enforce them.

"Wave goodbye, Tyler," Pickett coaxed, as the last car pulled onto the blacktop.

Tyler rubbed his face against her leg in a negative motion. "Don't want to," he whined.

"I think somebody hasn't quite given up naps, and had a long afternoon." Pickett touched the sweaty dark hair. "I also think somebody needs a bath."

"Uh-uhn. 'M hungry."

In one fluid motion Jax swept the youngster up onto his shoulders. In just a couple of days Jax had come so far in knowing how to read Tyler, and how to encourage cooperation rather than demanding obedience. "Come on big guy. Let's hit the showers. I need to get cleaned up, too. Maybe Pickett," he threw a hopeful look Pickett's way, "will fix us something to eat if we're nice and clean."

Pickett followed them across the porch, where she held open the screen door for them. "Okay. What would you like?"

"Hot dogs and ice cream," said Tyler, riding his father's shoulder. Jax called out duck and he jerked his head down.

"That's what you had for lunch."

"Yep. That's what I like."

"There are plenty of hot dogs left over, but we've got to make a deal. You have to eat some vegetables before you get ice cream." Pickett spoke to their backs as they moved into the deeper shadows of the back hall.

Jax paused at the door to the bathroom. "Whaddya say, bud?"

"Maybe I won't eat 'em," Tyler's tone was judicious, "but maybe I'll taste 'em."

In fact, Tyler hardly ate more than a taste of anything, and head in hand, eyes drooping, he just stirred the tablespoon of chocolate ice cream Pickett put into his bowl round and round. And when, after exchanging a glance with Pickett, Jax said, "Come on, Ty, let's go read Monster Trucks,"

the little boy merely lifted his arms to be carried.

Tyler would be asleep in minutes, which didn't give Pickett much time. She made quick work of cleaning the kitchen, then dashed to the bedroom to study the contents of her closet. The jeans she'd had on all day wouldn't do.

Her cheeks burned and her stomach flipped every time she thought about what she was thinking of.

Her turquoise camisole was a little dated but it would go with the wraparound skirt of cream chiffon. In a wardrobe comprised by only the most basic and businesslike apparel, it was the most flowing thing she owned. She'd bought it unable to resist its ultra feminine appeal, but the filmy material lifted with the slightest breeze exposing her thighs and as a result she'd never worn it. Flowing was called for tonight, though, and thighs...well, she stifled a nervous giggle, thighs were no longer a problem.

She left the jeans she'd worn all day in a pile on the bathroom floor. She grabbed a two-minute shower, and hardly taking time to towel off, scrambled into the clean clothes.

Now to set the scene. Heart racing, Pickett nervously patted her hot cheeks to stimulate thought— Jax could come downstairs any moment.

She couldn't face the questions he would ask if he saw her cheeks glowing red as a stoplight. However, it was only logical to sit in the porch glider in the dark. Her bare feet made no sound on the smooth painted boards of the porch, as she practically leaped for the glider.

She tugged the silky stuff of her skirt over her knees tried to persuade her heart to beat more regularly. She hoped she wasn't going to lose her nerve. She was very afraid she probably would.

In seconds she heard him calling to her.

"I'm out here," she tried to make her voice light, casual. "It's amazingly warm for October, and the mosquitoes aren't bad."

And then he was there. In the doorway silhouetted against the light. He stood, barefoot as usual, feet apart, hands relaxed. She couldn't say later what made it happen right that moment. Broad shoulders, yes, narrow hips, sculpted arms and legs, the proud carriage of his head, all limned with gold—but she'd recognized his extraordinary masculine beauty before.

It was just that he looked so exactly, absolutely right. As inevitable as a waterfall. As indisputable as a mathematical proof.

She was in love with him.

Her heart turned over in her chest.

Some part of her noted the wrenching, twisting sensation with almost clinical detachment. She'd thought it was a metaphor. She'd had no idea it actually happened.

She felt like a tree that has been sawed through, yet still stands, just waiting for the nudge, the errant breeze that will topple it.

Pickett completely forgot all her plans. For now all she could do was act normal while trying to assimilate the shock.

With a calm manner she was far from feeling Pickett, scooted over and patted the seat next to her. "Did Tyler get to sleep okay?"

Jax sat down, the glider creaking under his weight, and slid an arm around Pickett. "He was out like a light in two and half readings." As always Pickett stiffened slightly, then allowed herself to sink against his chest. It was progress. At least he hadn't needed to insist she let him hold her. He'd been afraid he'd ruined everything this morning. While her family was there, with her typical generosity she'd calmly included him and Tyler in the circle of warmth she threw around her, but during supper she'd seemed nervous and distracted.

He smoothed his hand over her bare shoulder, and fingered the tiny satin strap of the stretchy top she wore. "You changed clothes. Nice."

He rubbed his cheek against her soft curls, and drew her feminine scent deep into his lungs. After a moment Pickett nestled into him more fully and allowed her hand to rest on his thigh.

The heat of her palm seemed to sink deep into his leg, then travel straight to his groin. He set the glider in motion, so that he could feel her soft fingers ride the flex of his muscles.

This was good. A cricket near the porch chirped in counterpoint to the creak of the glider, and he idly noticed that the tide must be out, because the damp fecund smell of the salt marsh was stronger.

"Jax?" Pickett sounded a little shy or uncertain of herself. But maybe like him she was just unwinding.

"Hmm?"

"I'm really curious about the phone call from Linda. I know it's none of my business—"

Jax stopped her by laying a finger over her lips then lingered to trace their shape. "I didn't mean that the way you took it."

Pickett raised her head to look at him in the glow from the light hall light. "Oh?"

Pickett could pack more doubt into one syllable than some people could say in a paragraph. Jax shifted so that he was wedged in the corner of the glider and rearranged Pickett so she lay against his chest.

"I meant it then, but I don't mean it now, okay? After talking to Lauren today I'm not sure how this business of sharing custody is going to work out."

"What did she want?"

"She's totally pissed because I didn't return to the beach house, but stayed here instead. She wants me to return Tyler to her, immediately."

"But you're not going to?"

"I've got fourteen days and eighteen hours left of this leave. I don't intend to let her have Tyler one minute before I have to."

"So you're planning to stay here?"

"Sure."

He sounded so easy, no doubts that here he was and here he would stay. Hope that he meant what she wanted him to mean fluttered but she flattened it before it could take wing.

Oh, it was dangerous, this fantasy that they could become the family she wanted, and every day he stayed, the fantasy would grow more real feeling and more dangerous. She couldn't kid herself any longer that she was happy their relationship would never mature. She'd fallen in love with Tyler almost immediately, and now she knew she'd fallen for Jax, too.

If only he was the man he seemed to be, considerate, dependable, tender with Tyler and with her, full of lightning quick intelligence and earthy sense of humor.

Seeking comfort, she rubbed her cheek against the soft weave of his yellow golf shirt. She inhaled his comforting Jax smell, and let the breath out with a sigh.

He was all those things, but only part-time. Where was the consideration in leaving without notice? And what did dependability mean if she couldn't depend on him to be there when she needed him? So what, if he had a lot of insight and humor if he wasn't there to talk things over and laugh with. He wasn't the man she wanted him to be.

The image of the mythical selkie popped into her mind again. The man holding her was the selkie in his human form. But she must never forget that he was a selkie, and would soon become a seal again, drawn to a wild world where she could not live.

Jax felt the deep sigh that shuddered through the soft, sweet-smelling woman in his arms. She was soft, inside and out, but, by God, she had guts. He'd never been so proud as when she demanded her sisters start respecting her choices. She gave whole-heartedly, and he had a feeling that now her family would start valuing the love she gave them. Which reminded him of something he needed to say.

He squeezed her lightly. "Pickett, I want you to know how grateful I am for all you've done for Tyler and me." She squirmed as if she meant to interrupt. "No, don't dismiss what I'm saying. I know how generous you are, so you're probably thinking it's nothing special. But sometimes I feel like I drove into a magical kingdom, the day I pulled into your drive. No," he corrected himself, "it was before that. Everything started changing the moment you walked up to us on the beach. You're one heck of a lady."

It wasn't a declaration of undying love, but the husky wonder in his voice told Pickett how much he meant it. Apparently even selkies were susceptible to magic. She stroked the silky hair on his forearm, and with the tips of her fingers traced a raised vein. She took another deep breath, this time drinking in the knowledge that some moments are worth savoring for what they are, not what they will lead to. Her dream of a wonderful, secure marriage and family might never come about, but how many women ever got to make love to a selkie?

A buoyant sense of freedom exploded in her chest, scary and compelling and hot with life.

Being around Jax was changing her. She never would have dreamed she would look one of her sisters in the eye and tell her to stop criticizing. The power she had felt in that moment, though her knees had been shaking, still vibrated through her. Suddenly the daring plan she'd had earlier, seemed like a good idea again. When magic was in the air ordinary didn't happen, but sometimes extraordinary things could.

"Thank you," she slid her fingers into the cool hair at the back of his head and touched his lips with hers, "and for whatever you think I've done—you're welcome."

The breeze kicked up a little, ruffling Pickett's skirt across Jax's thighs. He wished it could always be like this between them. The stiffness he'd caused by speaking without thinking this morning was finally gone.

He clasped his arms loosely around her while she traced lazy patterns with her nails down his neck. Confident that he would hold her, she leaned back against his encircling arms, a secret smile playing around her lips.

He had no idea what she was smiling about but he felt amazingly indulgent. "What is it?"

She looked deep into his eyes. "There's something I've been meaning to tell you." She bit her lip prettily, then swept her eyelids down, as demure as a nun. The dimple in the corner of her mouth peeked. If he didn't know better, he'd swear she was flirting with him.

She gave him a wide-eyed, innocent look. "I don't have any underwear on."

Oh God. He almost swallowed his tongue. She had been flirting and now she looked shyly proud of herself. How could she look utterly innocent and say things like that?

Surprise, sensual anticipation, and amusement in equal measures surged through him on a wave of tenderness. She was a darling.

"Come with me," she whispered, and got to her feet, tugging on his hand.

He resisted and used the tug to pull her back against him. "Where are we going?" he murmured against the bend in her neck.

She pulled away again. "Just follow me." She skipped quickly down the short flight of steps, and dashed around the side of the house. The breeze fluttered the filmy skirt offering tantalizing glimpses of bare legs and feet, in the pool of light cast by the kitchen window.

"Come on!"

He couldn't see the point of racing around the yard when they were both ready to get it on, but the devilish light in her piquant face promised fulfillment as well as tease. Anyway, wherever she wanted to be, he wanted to be. Oh man, he was letting her lead him around and loving it.

Quickly he followed her across the drive where she skirted the border of ancient azaleas, solid and six feet high.

It was darker here away from the security lights, but the pale gleam of her skirt showed her to him as she ducked under the spreading branches of the huge live oak.

In the deeper-still darkness under the oak she was no more than a pale smudge, but as his eyes adjusted he could see her feeling around for something.

"Here it is," she called. "Can you see me?"

"I can see you," he almost growled, his voice laced with sensual threat. She was standing beside a swing that had been hung with heavy ropes from a massive branch overhead.

"Good. Because I can't see you. Come over here. Oh!" He gripped her hips and pulled her to him.

She placed her hands over his cheeks and tugged his head down, eager, endearingly awkward, seeking his lips, his tongue.

Warm, soft hands pushed through his hair, tested the resilience of his shoulders, traveled down his back, then fumbled at his shorts button. A flick and the zipper hissed softly.

Never taking his mouth from hers, he used the moment to gather the skirts of her dress until he could slide his fingers against her moist, warm cleft. She was aroused and ready. His cock swelled hot and urgent. A man with a little imagination could do it anywhere. One handed, he stripped the polo shirt over his head. The ground underfoot was soft with the mast of one hundred years of decomposing leaves and the shirt would protect Pickett's bare shoulders.

Pickett groaned her approval and the heat of her hands kneading his back shot straight to his groin. But in a surprise move she pulled away.

"Now, sit down. Here," she bumped the wooden seat of the swing against his shins and pushed the rope into his hand. "Sit in the swing."

The swing seat was a wide plank, clearly planned for the adult derriere or perhaps to allow two children to swing side by side.

"Okay," she approved once he was seated. The moonlight that penetrated the thick foliage stripped her face of all color but her teeth gleamed in a smile of intelligent mischief. "I'm not really sure how to do this."

God, he hated to interrupt this, but he had to ask. "I don't know what you're doing but aren't you forgetting something?"

"Oh. Right." Her hand dived into the pocket of the skirt and dropped a foil packet into his lap. She placed one bare foot beside his hip, and grabbing the rope, stood up on the seat, legs spread to straddle him.

"This is good," he said as he lifted her skirt to nuzzle the inside of her thigh now tantalizingly close to his mouth. The scent of her arousal mixed with the smell of the humid night. He pressed wet licking kisses along the satin skin.

Her "oh!" was more of an inhalation than a word. "Yes. But this is not why we came out here."

He tipped his head back to look up at her face. "Oh baby, you are wrong!" he chuckled. "It's definitely why I'm out here."

She swung her hips out, bending until her face was level with his. "There is more," she assured him, "and you are going to be grateful to the goddess of love that I practice yoga."

Slowly, holding the ropes she lowered herself into his lap. She released her right hand from the rope. "Okay, balance me." She said as she gently took his throbbing erection to her entrance.

His strong hands clasped her ribcage, lifting her up slightly so that she could get her feet out from under her and let them dangle behind.

They groaned in unison with pleasure as he lowered her to surround him and to be filled.

"Um," she said, after a lingering kiss, "I have always wanted to try this."

"What gave you the idea?" Could it possibly be that, lodged hot and tight in a woman's body, he was interested in her mind? God, this woman was fun.

"I saw a Japanese woodcut once in an art history book. I never forgot it. A man and a woman swinging together, their kimonos flowing around them. It was so very beautiful and lyrical…It took me a minute to understand what they were doing."

The honest consternation in her tone made his belly ripple with amusement. Her gasp told him she felt the movement at the center of her body. He felt her answering chuckle massage him with the same delicious effects. "Gives a whole new dimension to the concept of 'swinging', doesn't it?"

"So what do we do now?"

"Well, I hold on to you with my legs, and we both hold on to the ropes and you swing us."

Gently he pushed off with his feet, felt her slide away, then as the swing ascended through its forward arc, slide toward him.

"Don't you slip off my lap," he fought the urge to grab her to him, knowing that releasing a hand on one rope would make the swing lurch. "Don't you dare fall!" It took several passes for him to become confident that she was secure. The gentle rocking, the slow stroking, tantalized yet withstood all his efforts to be in charge of it. Gradually though, he gave in to the motion of the swing, allowing the slippery friction where they were joined to just happen, no one in control. By imperceptible degrees there crept over him an awareness, not just of mutual pleasure, but of sharing, mingled pleasure that was unlike anything he had ever known. His heart swelled, even as his cock grew harder.

"More," she demanded in a breathy whisper, "higher!"

"I'm not going to last long," he said with genuine regret. If he could, he would never let go of this sense of being joined in this timeless moment. But even as he said it, he could feel the walls of her slick passage tightening around him. His powerful arms pumped against the ropes to carry them higher and higher, airborne in the soft, dark night. At the instant of freefall he felt the rippling squeeze of her climax, heard her cries of release. He realized he had lost all control and hooked his elbows around the ropes forming a protective cage around her while his body pumped and shuddered.

Long moments later, once the swing had come to rest, he pressed a kiss to her damp hairline. "Come on, we've got to move."

Limp, she slumped against him. "Unh-unh. Stay like this."

"It's not safe, sweetheart. The condom could slip." He was surprised at how much, right that minute, he wished he didn't care if it did. He wished this moment of joy, this sense of completion shared could result in a baby. He jiggled her gently. "Lock you legs around me. I'm going to stand up."

Using the old school yard trick of walking the swing back until his legs were straight, balancing her weight while getting his feet under him was easy, however, when Pickett's feet touched the ground she lurched and wobbled against him. Jax dealt with the condom with one hand while steadying her with the other.

"Whoa!" she gasped with a shaky laugh, "knee failure! I'm not sure I can walk."

"Are you all right? Do you want me to carry you?" Not waiting for an answer he swept her up into his arms. Surprised, she clutched at his shoulders.

"Can you? Carry me, I mean? All the way to the house?"

He thought about the 30 yards or so to the door, her 110 pounds. "Yes, ma'am," he said with wry understatement. "I, a Navy SEAL, can do this."

"Merciful heavens!" Jax bit the inside of his cheek at Pickett's idea of a swearword. She dropped her arms and let her head fall back in a mock faint. "This is sooo romantic!"

A laugh rang out in the night. Rich, full-throated, masculine, deep.

He was still chuckling as he carried her, all soft and warm and sleepy, into the bedroom.

TWENTY FIVE

A week later, when Jax pulled the Cherokee into the parking spot near the back door, his heart gave a little kick of gladness. It was good to be home.

Oh man. He almost physically recoiled. He'd better think over what was going down here. This wasn't home, not his home anyway. Getting attached to somebody else's home was the stupidest thing he could do. He knew. He'd done that before and paid the price.

Corey's home, not the house Jax's father owned, was the first home he'd ever known. When Corey was gone, it was too.

And the little house he'd shared with Danielle. Danielle had put so much of herself into it, fixing it up for the baby, it really seemed to be hers. Her home that he shared.

"Are we going to stay here tonight, Daddy?" Jax had Tyler unbuckled, and now he scooped him up to swing him to the ground. Since it made Tyler squeal with glee, Jax added a much larger swing than strictly necessary, then pulled the giggling child close for a hug. He nuzzled the little boy-scented neck and added a kiss.

Jax smiled to himself. He could hear Pickett saying "Did you kiss him? You don't want him to grow up thinking men don't kiss men, do you?" Goodness me, no, he thought with soft sarcasm. Wouldn't want that. But it turned out kissing Tyler was it's own reward.

Pickett was always pointing out what he was teaching Tyler by his actions, but it seemed to him that Tyler was doing most of the teaching. For instance how much he liked hugging and kissing the little kid.

He was going to miss this. His heart contracted at the bleak knowledge that somebody else was going to get Tyler's hugs and kisses. Oh well, no use dwelling on that.

"Huh? Daddy? Are we going to stay here tonight?"

"Yes," Jax would have thought it was obvious, but Tyler seemed to have a lot of questions about what was going to happen. The thought of how much Tyler was at the mercy of the whim or the careful consideration of the adults around him struck Jax with such force that he halted in mid-stride.

Did Tyler want to live with his grandmother? What would Jax do if Tyler said he didn't?

"Do we live at Pickett's house now?" Tyler's question was an eerie echo of his own thoughts. "I like living at Pickett's house. Can we stay here forever?"

"Don't you want to live with your grandmother?"

"No." With that single word it was as if a switch had been thrown and the Tyler of two weeks ago appeared. He stiffened, then wiggled to be let down.

Jax set Tyler down, but his arms felt...bereft. Tyler walked away without a backward glance. In a minute Jax heard him at the screen door calling for Pickett and Lucy.

Hobo Joe come racing around the house as fast as a three-legged dog could go, his tongue lolling in a pink doggy-smile. The old reprobate looked glad to see them. Glad to see Tyler anyway. Hobo Joe had accepted Tyler right off, but still kept his distance from Jax.

Jax started for the door himself, but more slowly. Hobo Joe moved to stand in his way. The big old dog must be getting used to him. He never came this close. True, he was still outside arm's each, but still closer than ever before.

"Hello, Hobo Joe. How're you doing, fella?" The absurdity of asking a dog how he felt almost didn't register. Pickett did stuff like that all the time, but he didn't.

Being around Pickett was changing him. Changes he wasn't sure he wanted to make. Like asking a dog a question. Like worrying about what he was teaching Tyler by his actions. Some of what Pickett said seemed pretty silly to him, men kissing men for example, but still he found himself thinking about it.

Hobo Joe took a step closer, yellow eyes fixed on Jax's face. It felt like the dog wanted something.

Hobo took another step, almost in arm's reach now.

"What do you want old boy?" He was doing it again, talking to the dog, but it felt right. "You want to come to me, but you're scared?"

Taking care to move slowly, Jax knelt in front of the dog and stretched out a hand palm up. The same way Pickett said he should approach Tyler. "You look huge to him. You'll be easier to come to if you make yourself smaller." It worked with Tyler. Maybe it would work with the dog.

Hobo took another hesitant step, backed up, then came forward again.

"You want to, don't you? But it's pretty scary to even let yourself want it, isn't it?" Jax continued to kneel talking softly to the dog. "Everybody gets hugs and kisses and petting but you. You get plenty of food and a place to sleep. And it's not enough anymore, is it? You let Pickett pet you but you never ask for petting. Is that what you're asking for now? Well come on. You can trust me."

Jax knelt in the sandy driveway, hand outstretched with the absolute command of stillness. Though he didn't do it consciously, he talked in the slow, almost uninflected rumble that gave his men confidence in tight situations. His senses took on the same heightened alertness. He was aware of the coolness of the breeze that barely touched his cheek, whir of a late cicada, the salty, muddy smell of marsh and the smell of the dog's rough coat.

And he was aware of an odd resonance to his words, as if he was talking to something more than the dog. As if he was talking about something more than how the dog felt.

"Come on, old fellow. You can do it. One step at a time. You can do it."

You can do it. There was another voice speaking to him in his head, saying the same thing he was saying to the dog.

Corey. It had happened so many times that Jax no longer questioned how or why he sometimes seemed to hear his dead friend talking to him. Though he knew if he told anyone they would question his sanity, he had learned when the voice spoke to pay attention. Usually it was just a word, or a short sentence: Stop. Look behind you. The meaning was usually crystal clear in context. But what did Corey mean now?

Do what? What can I do?

Keep Tylor with you.

I can't keep Tyler. I don't have any way to care for him. He has to go to his grandmother.

You can do it.

He wanted to. God knows, he wanted to. From the very first he had dreaded the moment of turning Tyler over to Lauren, even before he knew she drank, but until now he hadn't acknowledged how troubled he was. Until he came to North Carolina, no, until he came to Pickett's house, the distance between them had seemed, not desirable, but somehow normal.

The logistics would be a nightmare to work out with his erratic schedule and frequent absences but to have Tyler right there to kiss goodnight, to teach to swim and play baseball. The kid needed a lot of work on his catch.

But Tyler was so little. He needed somebody twenty-four/seven. Maybe when he was older… Unh-uh. Tyler didn't want to live with Lauren.

You can do it.

The big, black and tan animal was almost within the reach of Jax's fingers now. With aching slowness, yellow eyes never leaving Jax, he slid his grey muzzle under Jax's outstretched fingers. Keeping all his movements slow and smooth Jax stroked the Hobo Joe's head, fondled his ears and as he crept closer, ran a hand across his back and down his flank. At last, he settled onto his haunches, laid his head on Jax's knee and heaved a huge sigh.

Pickett finished entering her case notes, and hit save, just as the screen door banged. She heard the quick spat of Tyler's sneakers on the heart pine of the entry accompanied by the dogs' clicking toenails. She just had time to swivel the desk chair before a compact little body flung itself against her lap.

"Pickett, Pickett, Pickett!"

"What, what, what?" Pickett helped him scramble onto her lap, straddling her knees. She gazed into the shining grey eyes and felt the connection zoom straight into her heart. She had an affectionate nature. She loved all the children she worked with, but not like this. The love she felt for this child filled her entire chest with warm, soft pressure, then overflowed into her throat and filled her eyes. She couldn't bear to contemplate how empty at her core her life had been before he came. She would keep him forever if she could.

"We're going to the fireworks!"

"Not today. Not for a couple of days."

"Tomorrow?" He anticipated the fireworks display with excitement usually reserved for Christmas. They'd had this conversation every day since Jax had bought tickets so they could watch the display from the pier. Pickett had even made him a little calendar so he could mark off the days. Yesterday, today and tomorrow were the only time constructs he could really grasp though.

"No, sweetie, not tomorrow either. But when the day comes, we will go."

"Promise?" He bounced on her knees for emphasis.

She kissed the top of his head. "I promise, promise, promise!"

With the lightning changes of childhood, he pushed himself off her lap in a sort of backwards leapfrog. "Gotta go!" He stuck the landing as well as any gymnast and raced for the bathroom.

Pickett missed his weight across her thighs even as she admired the superb coordination he was beginning to show. Daily swimming lessons were paying off in physical confidence. It was like watching the real child emerge from a brittle shell.

He'd never talked about his mother again since that first morning however. She'd waited for him to bring the subject up, but he never had. He didn't act like a troubled child, but Pickett knew he still had feelings that would have to be dealt with someday. Pickett heard Jax's footsteps on the porch and went into the hall to greet him, resolved to ask if Tyler ever talked about his mother to him.

Through the screen she saw Jax bend down to give Hobo Joe a slap of rough affection. Hobo Joe gave a long tongued doggy-laugh and looked at Jax with shining eyes. So, the two roamers had found each other, had they?

A wise little smile played around Pickett's lips when Jax, carrying a hot pink Victoria's Secret bag, opened the screen door, Hobo Joe at his heels.

"Looks like you've acquired both some lingerie and a dog."

Jax handed her the bag while pressing a kiss to the top of her head. "I can't have a dog. I haven't figured out how I'm going to care for my kid."

The smile took on a hint of sadness, but Pickett only raised her eyebrows in reply.

"Anyway," Jax went on, "he wants to come in the house. Can he come in?"

"Sure. He's always been allowed to come in the house. He just never wanted to before."

"Are you saying he only wants to come in because I'm in?"

Pickett's slender shoulders moved as if to say "what do you think?"

Jax scrubbed his fists across his hairline. "Damn. Come on you big doofus. I've got to make a phone call."

TWETY SIX

Jax flipped his cell phone open, closed it, flipped it open again. He frowned at Hobo Joe stretched at his feet, closed the phone and returned to the kitchen, Hobo at his heels.

Pickett was rinsing snow peas for a stir fry with rice noodles, a dish that compromised between her dietary restrictions, a four-year-old's whims, and an active man's appetite. Though her kitchen was far cry from the elegant waterfront restaurant Jax had taken her to in Wilmington, she was just as glad to be at home tonight. Talking about the fireworks with Tyler had reminded her he and Jax would both be gone all too soon.

She shook the excess water from the colander and dumped the green pods onto a paper towel. Selecting a red bell pepper and a paring knife she cored it, and lifted out the little white seeds, then began to cut it into strips.

"Pickett, can Tyler and I stay here?"

Stay here? He was talking about staying? Pickett's mind scrambled to contain the hope that wanted to burst free within her heart.

"I'm not sure what you're asking," she clarified cautiously. "You and Tyler are staying here."

"Just until I take him back to his grandmother's. But that's the thing, he doesn't want to go to his grandmother's and I don't want him to go. So I'm asking can we stay here until I figure out something?"

Pickett sneaked a look at Jax under her lashes. "Has something happened to change your mind?"

"Not one thing—a lot of things. I used to think anybody would do a better job with Tyler than me. When Danielle was alive and he was a baby, maybe that was true. I'm not so sure now. I've tried to deny it, but since her drunken phone call, I've gotta tell you, Lauren's drinking has me worried." Jax snagged a stool and dragged it to where Pickett was working.

"And I'm not willing," he went on, "to see him once every few months at best. I let Danielle set the terms for how much I would see Tyler. She couldn't handle it that I would make plans to come and have to break them, but call out of the blue and say I had free time." He leaned more than sat on a kitchen stool, legs stretched straight. "Now that I know all I've missed, I don't want to miss any more than I have to."

Pickett's hands stopped in mid slice. Her mind ran ahead of what he was saying. "You mean you're going to leave the SEALs?" Her hope, so long denied, was almost painful. "You'll look for another job?"

"No," Jax waved an impatient hand. "Being a SEAL is who I am. It's what I do. But there's got to be a way to have Tyler with me when I'm in the country."

Disappointment, bitter and black, cold as day-old coffee, filled her mouth. If she could, she would shake herself.

She had known, from the start, anything they had would be temporary, and any love, one-sided. She had known she'd probably fall in love with him anyway, and God help her, she had. But she had always known how it was going to turn out.

Nevertheless, just for a moment there, she had allowed herself to believe he might decide to leave the Navy. To hope he wanted to stay. Forever.

"You don't approve?" Jax cut into her thoughts.

"What makes you think that?"

Jax smiled crookedly. "You have a face that telegraphs every thought that goes through your busy, busy mind."

Pickett focused on making absolutely perfect slices of pepper while she schooled her features into what she hoped was a neutral expression. "I don't have a right to approve or disapprove."

"That never stopped you from having an opinion before," Jax drawled dryly.

Pickett laughed ruefully, and hoped the laugh didn't sound as forced as it felt. "It's true I have an opinion about practically everything. But I'm not the one who will have to live with the results of whatever you decide."

"So what do you think?"

Pickett didn't have one iota of objectivity to bring to this discussion, but Jax would keep on until he got an answer. She carved two more slices before she answered. "I think it will be very hard to provide Tyler with any sort of stability."

"So you think he should go to Lauren's?" He seemed determined to pin her down.

"I didn't say that." Pickett pushed a curl out of her eyes with the back of her hand, then leveled a look at Jax. "I can't say what you should do."

Jax took a step closer, crowding her toward the counter. "Are you being a therapist, now? Is this some of that non-directive bullshit?"

Pickett met his eyes with a don't-mess-with-me glare. "I can't separate who I am from what I do any better than you can." She took a calming breath, made her shoulders relax. "But no, I can't say what you should do, because I honestly don't know."

Jax took a turn about the room, looking out the window, hefting a knife, testing its balance. He pointed with the knife to Pickett's cutting board.

"Tyler's not going to eat the red pepper, you know. He doesn't eat red food today. I had to take the tomato off his burger at lunch."

Pickett shrugged. "More for me."

"See, that's what I like about you. Lauren—harangues—Tyler for things like that, and a week ago I would have tried to make him eat it. You never fuss."

Jax looked at the floor then turned worried eyes back to Pickett. "And I'll tell you what else: Lauren seems to ignore Tyler, almost forgets about him, until he does something she doesn't like. But it's like you're paying attention to him all the time. I'll bet you know where he is and what he's doing right this minute."

Pickett glanced out the window. "He's still under the magnolia. I think he pretends the roots are highways for his cars."

"That's what I mean. It's like your mind has put a tracking device on him. No matter where you are or what else you're thinking about, you are also aware of him."

Pickett tipped her head in a considering look. "You notice that?"

"I notice everything about you."

Shoot. Just when she had him figured, the relationship, or lack of same, firmly settled in her mind, he said something like that. How was she supposed to keep herself from wanting him to stay with her forever?

The kitchen suddenly felt 10 degrees hotter, driven up undoubtedly by the look in his eyes. She hadn't seen him move and yet now they were touching thigh to thigh and his hard, warm palm cradling her jaw.

"I want you." He voice was little more than a growl. "I want you so much. Right now."

He feels lust. Do not read anything else into it. But even as she issued firm instructions to herself, she felt herself growing moist, her body preparing to receive him.

Pickett reached a hand to smooth Jax's hair— okay, to give herself the pleasure of touching its silky thickness. She could feel his erection pressing against her belly.

She chuckled ruefully. "I think you've got me caught between a rock and a," she brushed back and forth across the hard bulge, "hard place."

Jax clamped her bottom in strong fingers to hold her tighter against him and repeated the motion. His pale eyes in his brown face glittered with equal parts amusement and sexual intent. "Okay, what's the rock?"

"Think small boy. Hungry, tired, fussy. Coming in here any minute."

The deep breath Jax took pushed his chest tighter against her breasts, making Pickett nearly groan. He dropped a kiss on the top of her head, and stretched a brown arm to pull forward the other chopping board. "Okay. But don't think I'm going to forget where we were. Do you want me to start cutting up the chicken?"

In a few minutes Pickett visually measured the pile of broccoli, onion, pepper and snow peas and pronounced it sufficient. She brought the conversation back to how Jax could arrange for Tyler to live with him.

"How do you plan to make a home for Tyler in Little Creek?" Pickett studied the arrested expression on Jax's face. "What?"

"Make a home. I hadn't thought of it as making a home."

"What would you call it?"

"I don't know. Living where I live maybe."

"So where do you live?"

"I have an apartment. I don't exactly think of it as home, it's just the place I go."

"Hmm." Pickett set the pan on the heat.

"Up to now, all my thinking has been around finding someone to care for him when I'm gone. When I'm at the base, it's no biggie, he can go to day care, but SEALs have to be ready to go 'wheels up' in four hours."

"Wheels up?" She took oil from the cabinet and added it to the pan. "Like in a plane?"

"Or a helo—helicopter. SEALs constantly train, and our operations, well, they're not exactly scheduled a year in advance."

"How long are you gone?"

"A few days. A few weeks. Every two years there's a six months deployment."

Pickett swirled the oil around the pan. "Hmm."

Jax leaned against the counter arms crossed over his massive chest, one brown bare foot crossed over the other. "You know what? You scare the shit out of me when you go 'Hmm'. I wish you'd just say what you're thinking."

"I was imagining what it would be like for Tyler. You wake him up in the middle of the night and tell him you're leaving but you can't tell him where you're going or how long you'll be gone. Who's going to reassure him that everything's going to be okay?"

"I will. I always have a cell phone. I'll call him and talk to him."

"So you don't see yourself just going off and leaving him?"

"No, that's what I want to stop doing."

"Hmm." Pickett raked the onions and peppers into the pan. "Wait. I didn't mean hmm. I was processing."

"What were you processing?"

"That this is such a big change for you…," she turned to face him. "Why does it scare you when I say 'hmm,'" she twinkled a little grin, "hmm?"

He gave her a sexy, sharkish grin in reply, but not before she caught sight of a look she couldn't define. Vulnerability? Loneliness? The timer for the noodles dinged before she could pursue it. "Dinner's ready. Call Tyler in."

Jax considered the woman sitting across from him. The setting sun filled the kitchen with a pinkish glow. A bar of gold light touched the gold of Pickett's hair with fire, emphasizing even further her vivid peach and blue and gold coloring. As always, she responded with animated interest to Tyler's prattling, and he responded to her by talking a blue streak.

Well he knew how that was. Jax found himself telling her things, and thinking over things she said more and more. Sometimes he thought it was like she had an extra set of senses that brought her information about the world, that made her notice things he'd completely over-looked. He had no idea where her mind was going next most of the time.

"Think of it as Chinese spaghetti," she told Tyler when he asked what was on his plate. Chinese spaghetti. He would have told the kid it was food. Jax forked up another bite. Fresh ginger and a little tang of lemon.

She listened, really listened, to everything he or Tyler said, and then she thought about it. He should have known she'd come back on his remark about being scared when she said "hmm." He should have kept his mouth shut. But that was what happened around her. Things came out of his mouth that he didn't know he was going to say. Hell, that he didn't know he thought.

So why had he said it? It wasn't that he was intimidated by her intelligence. He liked smart women. Sex was a lot sexier when his mind was as engaged as his body.

No, that wasn't it. It was—the truth when it hit made his stomach do a back flip—he cared what she thought. Really cared. Pickett was the most non-judgmental person he'd ever met. She never imposed her values on others, but she still had extremely high standards, and damn if he hadn't started caring about whether he was living up to those standards. Dammit, he knew the first time he saw her, Pickett was high maintenance. Turns out he was wrong about what made her high maintenance, but his gut hadn't lied.

It wasn't that she pouted or cried, or wanted him to show interest in things he wasn't interested in. She didn't demand that he account for his time, or show up with just the right present. He'd figured she was the kind who would fall in love and then have an endless list of demands that he change into someone different from who he was.

That's why he'd made sure she knew what she was getting with him.

But now, he wasn't even sure she was in love with him. She cared about him, sure, but she seemed to give her generous heart to everyone she met.

Nope. Turns out this lady was high maintenance because she'd somehow gotten inside his skin. Things that made a difference to her were beginning to make a difference to him. It was like he was carrying her around with him all the time, and that was changing him, making him think and do and say things he didn't mean to do.

It was going to take a couple of weeks to make all the arrangements for Tyler. He might even have to ask for extended leave. During that time he really needed someone Tyler trusted—someone like Pickett—to leave Tyler with while he got his plans shaped up.

But once he had things set up, he had to get Tyler and himself out of here, pronto. Things were getting out of hand.

Tyler was telling Pickett about his swimming lesson. His cheeks glowed with health now underneath his tan, and the little ribs were not so visible, the bones of his little shoulders not so pointy. His account of his prowess owed a lot to imagination but he was learning. He trusted the water now and his favorite part of every lesson was when Jax would swim breaststroke, the workhorse stroke for SEALs, with Tyler on his back.

Pickett was right about one thing. Everything about where and how he lived would have to change when Tyler came to live with him.

For starters, he'd need full-time live-in child care. And his two bedroom apartment wouldn't be large enough. He had to find a new place to live, a nanny/housekeeper, a school for Tyler and who knew what else.

He began to mentally assemble his team, sorting through whose skills made the best fit with the task to be accomplished.

Chief Petty Officer Lonnie Swales had a genius with logistics that would come in useful. Jess 'Do-Lord' Dulaude had a way of knowing where apartments were available. Jax didn't doubt he could ask Do-Lord and Lon to help him with a personal problem. SEALs were closer than brothers. If he needed their help, they would help him.

They would come from the ends of the earth if they needed to, but fortunately, they were right here, on a training exercise that Jax had been scheduled to participate in.

"Pickett," he spoke across the table, "some of my platoon are at the Marine base on a training exercise. Do you mind if I ask them to come over?"

"Not at all. How long have they been in the area? You could have invited them anytime."

"Unfortunately when you're training, you have weekends off but that's about it."

"You mean you're training twenty-four/seven?"

"You have time to sleep, but that's about it."

"Well tomorrow's Friday so ask them. If you want to we can grill hamburgers or something. I believe I would like to meet some more specimens of the genus: Navy SEALs." The light of intellectual challenge suddenly brought a sunny sparkle to the ocean of her eyes. "I could find out if you are the way you are, because you're the same," she raised a gold eyebrow, "or because you're different."

Jax ignored her deliberate provocation, then slyly raised the ante. "Don't you mean phylum, not genus?"

Pickett rolled her eyes, then huffed out a breath. "Why did you have to say that? Now I'm not going to be able to go to sleep until I look it up."

TWENTY SEVEN

Jax's heart rate doubled before he had the bedroom door fully closed.

In the golden radiance of the bedside lamp, the high-posted bed glowed like an island of light floating in an intimate darkness. Pickett sat on the bed cross-legged, even sexier than he had hoped for in white lace camisole and matching lace panties. It was all he could do not to pant. White lace did it for him every time.

Pickett didn't look up from the large book in her lap, although he sensed she knew he was there.

"What are you doing?" Jax pulled his t-shirt over his head one-handed, never taking his eyes off her.

"I've looked up genus and phylum, and now I'm looking up species." Pickett shot him a sultry glance that said she enjoyed what he was thinking, but was determined to play her little game. "I need to get them straight if I'm going to properly classify you," she added in an erudite tone.

Jax lifted the heavy dictionary from her hands, closed it and set it on the floor. Then he carefully pulled off her little round reading glasses. "I'll tell you how to classify me. Put me in the horny category."

"Ah!" Pickett's eyes sparkled like the ocean in bright sunlight, even though she tried to maintain a scholarly expression. "I shall name the species The Eastern Seaboard Broad-chested Horny-SEAL! Then I can present a learned paper on his mating habits."

Jax seized her under her arms and flipped both of them so that he was lying down and she was straddling him.

As always Pickett was amazed at how absolutely secure she felt in the face of his vastly superior strength. It was as if instead of his strength being a threat to her, he always offered it in her service.

"Don't move." She pressed her palms into the hollows of his shoulders. "If you struggle, you will only hurt yourself." The lazy lidded amusement in his eyes told her Jax enjoyed her pretense that she could pin him as much as she did. "Now that I have such an excellent specimen of the Horny-SEAL in my possession, I must examine him."

The way the lacy white camisole snugged around her pretty breasts had him salivating from the moment he stepped into the bedroom. Her nipples were just barely visible as slightly darker smudges, but already the tips were pushing against the white flowers. He could smell her growing arousal.

Trust Pickett to be turned on with brainy sex games.

"I think you should remove your specimen's shorts. Strictly in the interests of science, you understand."

Her hand stopped its careful measuring of the bulge under his zipper. Her eyes widened. "Are you saying I may have discovered a Horny-SEAL Erectus? This is too wonderful. I can be published in Scientific American." She flopped back to lie on top of his legs. "I am overcome with the thrill."

Jax sat up and began to draw the tiny bikini panties over her hips, letting his fingers tangle in the dark gold curls as he did so. "Let me tell you what else you're going to be overcome by..."

He dropped the panties on the floor, stood briefly to divest himself of his shorts and came back down on top of her. He whispered in raunchy detail exactly what he had in mind.

"Oh no!" Pickett wailed. "This is a Dark Day for Science!"

Jax stopped swirling his tongue around the velvety aureole of her breast to look into her eyes. They glittered with fun even as the lids lowered in sensual anticipation.

"I'm almost afraid to ask, but, why?"

"After extensive research, I'm going to write the world's most learned paper, and now, because of you, it's going to be unprintable!"

Once his breathing had returned to normal and he could move again, Jax reached across Pickett to turn out the lamp, then drew her next to him again.

He liked the time after love making with Pickett as he never had with anyone before. Maybe it was because it never seemed completely over. Even when he had just had her, he still wanted to touch her. His hand, almost of its own volition traveled over her breasts, down her belly, to let his fingers comb lazily through the still damp curls at the apex of her thighs.

He gave a soft tug and was rewarded with one of Pickett's sexy little humming sounds.

"You like that?"

"Um."

"Do you like it better here or here?"

"There. If you keep doing that you're going to get me turned on again."

"And that would be a problem, how?"

Pickett chuckled, a lazy, sated, totally sensual sound. "I've been thinking about something you said tonight. You said your apartment isn't what you think of as home."

"It isn't. It's just someplace to leave my things. I'm not there much."

"Then where is home? Do you still think of your father's house as home?"

"No. It wasn't ever home."

"So where is it? Home, I mean."

"I don't know." She was getting a little too close to what he was thinking about in the driveway earlier. "Do I have to have a home?"

"Most people do. Tyler's going to need one."

"Well, I don't have one, all right?" Uh-oh. He sounded a little testy. Maybe if he answered her she'd get off it. He made his voice sleepy, almost bored sounding. "I guess the last place I really felt like I was home was Corey's parents' house."

"Oh yeah. They bought you a bed and checked your homework. They were your real family." Pickett yawned. "Do you visit them much?"

"No. I joined the Navy the day after Corey's funeral."

"They just let you go?"

She sounded incredulous. What was with her? This was old, old stuff.

"They wrote a couple of times. I couldn't think of what to say so I didn't write back." I couldn't give them Corey back.

"So when Corey died you lost everything?"

"Huh?" Time to give her thoughts another direction. He rolled her on top of him so that he could stroke that downy place at the base of her spine. That always made her melt.

Big mistake. Her eyes were colorless in the moonlight that was just beginning to come through the window but they were darkly troubled.

She pulled up on her elbows to look more fully into his face. "You lost your best friend who was closer than a brother, and you also lost the only parents you knew, and you lost the only place you called home? Whoa!"

It was like she had taken her dainty little foot and with one well-placed kick broken the lock on the door between that time and this one. He sucked in his breath as all the pain, the yawning nothingness came flooding through. He couldn't let her see, and in a second, being Pickett, she would. Then she would want him to talk about it. And if he talked about it right now, he'd probably start to cry. Besides, he didn't want her sympathy. He wanted her. He took her mouth in a deep, plundering kiss.

After a moment her tongue sought his with equal greed. "Are you trying to distract me?" she murmured against his lips.

He slid tickling touches along her cheek, then bit into her soft earlobe, instantly soothing the sting with his tongue. "Um-hum."

Pickett pulled back as if she was trying to read his face in the dark. "Well, if you're trying to keep me from pointing out the connection between losing everything at once and a job that keeps you too busy to notice you don't have a home and makes you turn a relationship with your son into a job description," she offered him the side of her neck, "it's working."

Jax woke suddenly and completely. Moonlight lay in silvery patches across the easy chair and foot of the bed. He could hear the ticking of the Seth Thomas clock on the mantel, Pickett's slow deep breathing. His body felt heavy and relaxed. It would feel good to pull Pickett's soft warmth against himself, but he was too relaxed to do even that.

The moonlight at the foot of the bed seemed to shimmer, as if it was floating on the slight breeze coming in the window. After a while it looked like a man leaning against the tall bed post.

"Corey?"

Moonlight gleamed on white smile. "Yeah."

He looked great. Healthy. He had filled out and even looked as if he had grown. Jax's eyes quickly scanned the vulnerable joints. The swelling of elbows and knees was gone. Corey had strong, straight limbs that flexed with ease. Even in the moonlight, Jax could see that color tinted the cheeks, rounded once again as they had been intended to be.

"You're well."

Corey nodded, smiling like a mischievous elf.

Jax's mind was still trying to sort the possible from the impossible "I don't understand. If you got well, why did you die? Wait a minute. You're dead, I mean, you did die, didn't you?"

"Funniest thing about that" Corey's eyebrows lifted and his eyes grew wide behind his glasses, just as they always did when he got to the payoff of a practical joke. "It turns out after you die, you're not dead."

"That might be funny to you, you shit, but it wasn't a joke to me. I didn't believe you were really going to die. I knew how sick you were but you'd always pulled out before. You said, we always said we would stick together. I needed you! How could you die?"

"I didn't want to die, but it was…" Corey shook his head, "I can't explain. But man, I've never left you."

Images flashed through Jax's memory. The quiet voice that said, Look behind you. Get out. Now. "That was you. You really were there?"

"Yeah. I've always been with you."

"And you're here now?" Jax had a sudden thought. "Am I awake?"

"You're awake. Your mind is awake," he clarified. "Your body is asleep."

"Then am I dreaming, or is this really happening?"

"This is really happening. I needed to talk to you. Pickett's the one, Jax. She's perfect for you."

"Glad you approve." It was true, Jax was glad to know that Corey had seen Pickett. That Corey could see her value and agreed with Jax. It made something complete. "I wish she could meet you."

Corey smiled wistfully. "I know. There's someone…she's…here"

An image formed in Jax's mind. Laughing elfish face surrounded by soft silvery brown curls. "I like her."

Corey's face turned serious. "Jax, I don't have long. I came to tell you that I'll be leaving now. It's time for me to move on. You'll be all right now."

"Move on? You mean you've been staying for me? Why?"

"You needed someone to love you."

Jax could see Corey at 12, skinny, too pale, with swollen joints. Oddly gentle smile saying he wasn't hurt. Corey sitting on the bench, basketball, football, baseball saying "Win one for the gimper." As the years had passed the contrast between Jax's healthy, superbly athletic body and Corey's steadily weaker one grew more marked. There were times, though Jax cringed to remember, when Jax would sense how others viewed his friendship with such a nerd, a wimp, a loser, and with a teenager's sensitivity to appearances he wished he had a better best friend. But Corey was the one pushing him to find his limits and then exceed them, teaching him the meaning of friendship, and loyalty, and courage. Corey had loved him.

"Corey, I loved you."

Corey smiled a wickedly crooked, rakish, pure Han Solo smile. "I know."

Jax laughed. It felt so good to see and talk to Corey again. "Corey, don't go."

"I have to. And you're ready. But I'll never be so far away that I won't know how you are."

"But I won't know how you are."

"I'm well. I'm happy. I love you."

Jax opened his eyes with a small gasp. Silvery patches of moonlight lay across the foot of the bed. Though there was no more sensation of being awake than before, he knew he was awake, now.

Corey. Corey was here. He had seen him and talked to him. Laughed with him. Called him a shit.

Soft joy bubbled through him.

Even after he let himself slide back to sleep a tiny smile smoothed the contours of his mouth.

TWENTY EIGHT

E ven when she knew they'd be cut down by the frost soon, Pickett always hated to pull up still-blooming plants. Nevertheless, while Jax and Tyler made a trip to Wal-Mart this morning, the job got her out of the too-silent house. Pickett blinked back the hot rush of tears. That they were leaving in two days had to be faced, but she wouldn't cry until it actually happened. In the meantime this ever-rising desire to beg Jax not to go could be worked through— literally. Pickett loaded her little wagon with pansies and potting soil and trundled it creaking and squeaking to the urns of fading petunias flanking the steps.

Steeling herself, she fumbled through the mass of flowers till she felt a stem and jerked up the plant, roots and all. The faint sweet-musty scent of the petunias was instantly overlaid by the dark loamy smell of the soil.

She'd brought this heartache on herself. She'd thought she could interfere in Jax's life and not get involved. She'd thought she'd be able to fall only a little in love with him. She thought knowing he was the kind of man she'd never marry would keep her heart safe. She laughed without humor. Sheesh, she'd thought when she met them that first time that Jax was arrogant! Pickett winced at her own hubris and tore another petunia from the soil, cringing at the feel of roots breaking.

In the bright autumn sun the petunias she'd pulled up were already wilting. The same petunias Jax had insisted on saving before the hurricane.

She'd known then the flowers would die, just as she'd known any relationship with Jax was doomed. What she and Jax had was an idyll, like summer annuals, bringing color and joy for a season, but incapable of standing the hardships and cold of winter.

She couldn't regret letting Jax and Tyler into her heart though. Anymore than she could regret planting annuals, knowing they would have to be pulled up. Everything had its season but when it was over, it was over.

With all the petunias piled on the wagon to be taken to the compost pile, Pickett hacked with her trowel at the mat of broken-off roots until she'd loosened the soil. She tapped a pansy from it's tiny plastic pot.

She would not replace him and Tyler as easily as she replaced these flowers. It would be a long time, maybe never, before anything grew in the empty space they would leave.

Pickett pulled off one glove and blotted a tear with a fingertip, before it could fall. She would not cry. For today Jax and Tyler were still here. Surviving was a matter of taking one day at a time.

Pickett felt better having worked everything out in her head. At least, she would feel better if only she knew how to ease the pain of her heart.

She didn't know what else to do, so she added some fresh soil, and planted the pansies.

Lucy, stretched out in the grass beside the wagon, suddenly woke and sat up, ears at alert. Scrambling to her feet, she woke Patterson, who raised his head and uttered a woof of agreement. Hobo Joe, who had not been asleep, since he considered himself on duty any time Jax was absent, slowly turned to face the driveway, the white tip of his tail swinging with dignified restraint.

Jax and Tyler would be here in a minute or two. Though it was possibly as much as a mile away, the dogs had picked up the sound of Jax's car. How quickly their canine ears had learned to isolate his car from all the other traffic sounds.

Pickett slipped the last of the pansies into place in the large urn and began adding fresh potting soil around them. She tamped them in then added water from the hose. The dogs barked in welcome as the Cherokee crunched the gravel and seashells of the driveway.

"Whatcha doing Pickett?" Tyler came flying to where Pickett knelt as soon as he was released from his car seat, while his father retrieved parcels from the cargo hatch. He flung himself into Pickett's arms, almost tipping her over.

"Easy, Tyler," called Jax, "you know I've told you we have to be gentle with Pickett." He ambled over to assist Pickett to her feet, then as she rose, pulled her closer. A tiny, tender smile lit his crystal grey eyes with their thick short lashes and played around the corners of his lips.

"Hi, honey," Jax dropped a kiss on her upturned lips, "I'm home."

He didn't mean that the way it sounded, Pickett cautioned herself, though her good sense warred with the tiny spurt of joy at his soft words.

Whenever Jax was around she battled futile hope. An outsider seeing him announce his home-coming and kiss her in the blue and gold of a perfect autumn day would believe they were a perfect family, when the truth was that they would never be a family at all.

Pickett pushed the thought away. She had made her decision at the outset to be happy no matter how short their time together, and by golly, she would be.

She wrestled the corners of her mouth into a smile that welcomed, she hoped, then pointed with a pink-gloved hand to the large bag he carried. "It looks like the shopping trip was successful."

Jax slanted her a glance filled with sardonic humor. "I'm alive, he's alive."

Pickett chuckled. "That bad, huh?"

"We did manage to get some jeans and a jacket, before we'd had all we could take, so he won't have to wear your sweatshirt if it's cool tonight. But I swear, if I let go of him for a minute, he'd disappear to the toy section. He said he'd never been in a Wal-Mart."

"Maybe he hasn't. The clothes he's been wearing didn't come from a discount store, I can tell you that." That made Pickett think of something that had been bothering her.

"Jax, does Tyler ever talk about his mother to you? It worries me that he hardly talks about his mother or his life in Raleigh at all."

"Why? He looks happy." Jax pointed to Tyler running around the yard chasing and being chased by dogs.

Now wasn't the moment to try to explain her concerns about all the upheavals in Tyler's short life. Pickett began picking up the emptied flats and her trowels, and piling them on the wagon. Jax set his packages down on the steps and came back to help her.

"Pickett," Tyler came running up surrounded by panting dogs. "Is it time to go to the fireworks at the pier, yet?"

"No, darling. We won't do that until it's dark. That won't be for a long time."

"But we're going today, right?"

"Tonight." Pickett could tell Tyler still wasn't satisfied. "First we have to eat lunch. And then I have to go in to work for a while, and then I'll come back and we'll have supper, and then it will be dark and we'll go. How's that?"

"Can't we go before then?"

"I can't make it get dark sweetie, and the fire-works won't happen until it's nighttime."

They watched Tyler race away again. Jax put a companionable arm around Pickett. "He's only asked me that about five hundred times."

Pulling off her gardening gloves, she twined her arm around Jax's waist. "He's probably going to ask five hundred more times so brace yourself."

She's the one. The words from the dream reverber-ated again as they had all morning. While Jax didn't believe in ghosts, he'd felt Corey's presence too many times to doubt that in some way Corey still existed, if only as part of his subconscious. But last night, even though he knew it was a dream, Corey seemed so real. And this morning the joy of re-uniting at last with someone he'd missed for so long, remained. Best not to question the how's and why's. Jax had seen and talked with him. It was enough.

Jax tightened his arm around Pickett, feeling the strength in the slender shoulders, feeling how she adjusted her stance to snuggle in closer. Strong, resilient, adaptable, able to see the humor in most situations, patient. And sexy? His body tightened with need at the thought. If ever there was a woman who could be the one, it was Pickett.

Suddenly, between one heartbeat and the next, he knew. He trusted her with his life and with

Tyler's life. He wanted what they had together and he wanted it forever.

He had no idea how she felt. She wanted him in her bed, and it was clear she had affection for him. But, heck, she treated everyone with affection. She hadn't hinted that she wanted anything permanent and most women would have by now.

Jax's cell phone beeped and he unclipped it from his belt with his free hand while keeping his arm around Pickett. He glanced at the caller ID.

"Hey Mancini. What's up?"

"Lauren's lawyer just called me. She's rejected your new proposal that she keep Tyler only when you're deployed for long periods. She wants Tyler to live with her, permanently."

It should have been bad news. Instead, relief washed through Jax like a cool breeze clearing a stuffy room. Thank God. Until this feeling of relief flooded over him, Jax hadn't known how much he did not want Tyler to live with his grandmother. Tyler was a different child, the child he should be, around Pickett and he loved Pickett as much Jax did. Nope, he wanted Pickett for Tyler, and for himself.

"No way," Jax said to Mancini. "No more visiting. Anytime I can be with Tyler, he's going to be with me."

Jax's eyes narrowed as a Pender County sheriff's car turned into the drive. A woman emerged from the patrol car, her torso rendered shapeless by body armor under the tan uniform. She carried the sheaf of papers in her left hand—

to keep her right hand free to go for her gun, he noted with absent approval.

"I called to give you a head's up," Mancini was saying. "Lauren is going to let you tell it to the judge. She's suing to get custody of Tyler. You'll receive the complaint and summons shortly."

"Looks like it's already happened," Jax told Mancini. "The sheriff's deputy is here with the papers now. I'll call you back."

"Okay, Mancini. How bad is this?" The house was quiet. Pickett had gone to the base to see a client who had an emergency. She was going to drop Tyler off at his playgroup at the church, and pick him up on her way back.

"Bad. She's alleging that you can't be a good custodial parent because of the demands of your job. She also alleges that you have had very little interest in Tyler before now, and that you don't know the child well, or understand his needs."

The irony of the situation killed him. It wasn't true that he hadn't cared about Tyler before, but some of her arguments were the reasons he'd thought she should have custody in the first place. If it hadn't been for Commander Kohn, he'd have turned Tyler over to Lauren, and let lawyers handle the paper work. Now he'd be damned if that was going to happen.

"I'm not going to give Tyler up. How do we fight this?"

"The court is going to look at the best interests of the child, not what you or Lauren wants. She doesn't work. She can offer him a stable home, a home he's always known. Even without child support, she can supply him material advantages." Mancini's deep voice measured the seriousness of his words. "She's not asking for termination of parental rights so she doesn't have to prove you're an unfit parent, just that she'll be a better custodial one. You'll still have the same visitation rights as before. And something else. She's dropped the stipulation about living allowance."

"Hell, Mancini, what are you trying to say? You sound like you're arguing her case."

"I'm going to give it to you straight, good buddy. As long as you're a SEAL, in constant danger and with crazy hours, frequently forced to leave Tyler in someone else's care, she's probably going to win. And even if you're awarded custody," a snowball's chance in hell, Mancini's tone said, "the judge may make it contingent on resigning your commission."

"So my choices are give up Tyler or give up the SEALs? Hell no, to both."

"Well, there's only one other possibility," Mancini offered with a skeptical laugh, "You don't, by any chance, know someone you want to marry, do you?"

Jax's heart suddenly felt too big for his chest. "As matter of fact, I do."

Mancini gasped on a sudden upsurge of hope. "If you were married you'd be giving Tyler everything Lauren can give him, plus a father. Is this for real?"

"Yeah, I've been thinking of asking Pickett to marry me. The woman we've been staying with."

"Then I'd say do it. Marry her as soon as you can."

TWENTY NINE

Two hours later Pickett came into the office and flopped into a chair in a pretend swoon. "I finally convinced Tyler to at least fake a nap, if he wants to go to the fireworks."

Jax gave thanks for her inexhaustible flow of patience with Tyler, and felt the tension in his face ease. It was going to be okay. Corey was so right. Pickett was the one. She hadn't changed out of the prissy slacks and blazer she'd put on to go to the base, but it didn't seem to matter what she wore, the hum of desire was always there.

She was going to think his decision was sudden, but when he looked back, he could see that this moment had been inevitable from the start. All he had to do was find the right words to ask her to marry him.

Pickett rolled her eyes. "Tyler may stay down twenty minutes, so talk fast. What did Mancini say when you called him back?"

"Lauren can sue me for custody, and as things stand now, she'll probably win." Jax raised a hand to prevent Pickett's angry protest. "A judge would see that Tyler has spent a lot more time with her than me, and she can provide a more stable home."

Jax scrubbed at his hairline. "It won't matter that I think she's more than a little screwy, or that I believe she drinks too much to be trusted with a small child. She knows a lot of important people in Raleigh and they'll give her glowing character references."

"So your only option is to leave the SEALs." Jax didn't know what to make of Pickett's extremely neutral tone, but he was grateful for the perfect opening her incisive intelligence offered.

"There's another option. I could get married." He waited for her to pick up on the implications with her usual speed. His heart began to thud as she studied him silently.

"To whom?" she kept the same neutrality in her voice as before.

"To you." Pickett's eyes widened. Her jaw dropped. She blinked slowly. Three times. He knew it was sudden, but she didn't have to look like he just suggested the impossible. The gentle reasoning, the coaxing he had planned, evaporated. "For godssake, what's so hard about that? You love Tyler. I would always know he was safe with you. And we're good together. Good? We're great. And not just in bed. We're a good team. Everything is better when I'm with you. Come on, Pickett, what do you say?"

"But you don't want to get married. You made it perfectly clear from the very first I wasn't to have any expectations."

"Don't tell me you didn't have any. You're not the kind of woman who has casual sex. The longer I've known you the more clear that has been."

"Not casual, no. But I never expected this to turn out to be real. It was like an interlude. I never thought someone like you would look at me. It was a fantasy come true."

"A fantasy. You went to bed with me to satisfy a fantasy?" Jax refused to ask himself why that hurt so much.

"It seemed like too perfect an opportunity to pass up. Anyway, I needed some experience. The thought that I might be desirable to you was pretty heady stuff."

He was damned if he'd let her see how that made him feel. He narrowed his eyes. Made his voice scathing. "So you needed a stud to bolster your confidence? And who better than a SEAL? You're no different from the groupies that hang around bars. I'm not even real to you."

"That is low. And unnecessary. And untrue." Pickett fought back her ire. Both of them being angry wouldn't help. Though he was too far away to touch, she reached out a hand. "And you are real to me. You were right the first time about me. I would never have gone to bed with you in the first place if I hadn't liked you and respected and trusted you. I even knew I'd probably fall a little bit in love with you." She didn't try to disguise her wistfulness. "But as long as I knew you were leaving, soon, it was safe."

"Have you fallen in love with me?"

"Yes. God help me. But I can't marry you."

"Why the hell not?"

How could she tell him when she wasn't sure she could explain it to herself? She wanted Jax and Tyler to be hers forever the way a drowning man wants air. She'd seen almost from the first that she could save him from losing Tyler—something he would regret for the rest of his life. She'd pulled herself back from the wish to manipulate the situation a thousand times.

But as much as she wanted to help Jax, as much as her heart broke for Jax and Tyler, she would be rescuing them. Sooner or later, her love would become a burden to Jax and she would resent him because marrying him would prevent her from ever having the kind of marriage and family she wanted.

And still she was tempted. He hadn't said anything about loving her, but he desired her. And he was right, even if all he wanted was a mother for Tyler, they made a good team. If he were the laughing man she saw throwing Tyler up in the air, companionably making a meal with her, pulling her to him in the middle of the night, providing in a thousand ways for her comfort and security…What-might-have-been made a lump too thick to swallow.

But that was only part of who he was. He was also a SEAL and he'd made it clear he didn't want to change.

Pickett drew a deep breath.

SEALed with A Kiss 345

"First of all because I don't believe that you really want to commit to building a marriage. But mostly, because you're a SEAL."

"You're wrong about commitment. But just for the sake of argument, are you saying if I'd walked up to you, said hey, I'm a SEAL and I'm looking for a permanent relationship, you would have turned me down? Well, duh, stupid question. That's exactly what's happening right now, isn't it?"

"Jax, please. I've hurt your feelings and I truly didn't mean to. Try to understand. I know more than is good for anybody to know about the problems facing military marriages. Marriage is hard. Being in the military makes it harder. But take the separations, the emotional isolation, the fact that there will always be secrets, the fear of injury or death, and then multiply it by 100 and you've got marriage to a SEAL.

"As long as you're a SEAL everything comes in second – a distant second. That's just the way it is."

Picket dropped her head into her hands. "There's too much to overcome. Just too much. I can't do it."

"There are Navy marriages, even SEAL marriages that work."

"I know that."

"No guts, huh?"

Pickett's head came up. "That's the way it seems to you?"

"Yeah. You tell other people how to make a marriage work that you would never take a chance at. You keep your love life limited so that you will never have to try anything you might fail at. You look into the world and real problems through your patients, but you make sure you never face any real problems." Jax made a disgusted sound. "Even a lover has got to go, if he's not a fantasy any more." Jax's face was stark, his crystalline eyes clouded, his mouth twisted in a bitter line. He went to the window and leaned against it, arms braced on the frame.

His inner struggle could be measured in the taut delineation of muscle and tendon and the heaving of his chest. At length he shook his head and straightened but did not turn around.

Pickett reached for him, wanting to touch his too-solid back before it became a wall, before he closed himself off to her utterly. "Jax, I'm so sorry. I know you're feeling—"

Jax whirled with a chopping movement so fast and so violent Pickett took an involuntary step back. "Don't say it. Don't try to tell me you know how I feel. You don't have a goddamned clue how I feel."

THIRTY

Pickett watched Jax's retreating back as he cut across the neighbor's property toward the sound. A sick feeling pressed upward in her chest.

Of all the consequences she had considered when she started the affair with Jax, the one she hadn't allowed for was that he might get hurt.

If only she hadn't been so surprised when he mentioned marriage, she might have handled it better. Even if he only wanted to marry her so he could keep Tyler, he had still felt rejected.

And as for the accusations he had thrown at her, maybe he was right. She didn't live through her clients but she did lack courage. The people who served their country made immense, heroic sacrifices, but so did those who loved them. It would take a hero to go into marriage with a SEAL knowing what she did, and she was no hero.

She wished she could cry, but the unutterable loss she felt—a loss she couldn't name—prevented even that.

When the phone rang, Pickett considered

letting the answering machine pick up but at the last moment answered it.

"Is the stud still there?" Pickett's sister Lyle asked without preamble. Lyle's offbeat, irreverent style had been carefully honed in her role as the family rebel. Though they were closest in age, the three years that separated them had been unbridgeable while Lyle was a teenager, trying to come to terms with her sexual preference, and her artistic temperament. With adulthood, they had each discovered in the other an excellent sounding board. Alike enough to understand without needing long explanations, they were different enough to be objective.

"Don't call him that."

"Why not? Is he a stud?"

Pickett couldn't believe how hearing Lyle's voice lifted her. She mentally compared Jax with every other man she had met, remembered her visceral reaction to his overwhelming masculinity. She giggled. "Yes, he is." Then she sobered, "but he doesn't like it."

"He doesn't like to be a stud? What is the matter with that man?"

"We had an argument. He said I thought of him as studly."

"So what were you arguing about?"

"He asked me to marry him."

"That's awful! The nerve. That's terrible. If that isn't just like a heterosexual man! I hope you told him where to go. Nobody can say things like that to my baby sister and get away with it."

"Lyle, stop it." Pickett was torn between laughing and crying.

"Well, you know you can't marry a man who is studly but doesn't want to be. If it was the other way around maybe…"

Pickett's giggle turned into a sob. "I can't marry him at all. And Lyle, I hurt his feelings…I handled it so badly."

Lyle listened to Pickett cry for a minute, then interrupted. "Pickett, stop crying."

Pickett felt in her pockets for a tissue, gave it up and wiped her nose with the back of her hand. She swallowed a hiccough. "Don't you know you're not supposed to say things like that? That is such bad counseling technique."

"You're the counselor, not me. But if you want to cry long distance, you call me up and pay for it. Besides, I'm an artist and artists can say anything—especially to a younger sister who is acting like an idiot."

"I'm not acting like an idiot!" Pickett hated how peevish she sounded. She hoped she only sounded that way because she had been crying. But maybe she was an idiot to expect any sympathy from Lyle.

"Yes you are. I think any woman who doesn't want to marry is showing extraordinary intelligence, but you're crying because you're in love with him but you're not going to marry him. You're an idiot."

"Who said I was in love with him?"

"Mother." Lyle let that sink in. "I called her after Sarah Bea called me. Sarah Bea said you had taken in another one of your strays, this time a man with a little boy. But she also said you always get the best of everything, so I thought I'd better call Mother. Mother said she thought y'all might be serious about each other, so she was telling everybody, including me, to leave the two of you alone." Lyle huffed. "I don't try to run your business like Sarah Bea and Grace do."

"In that case, why are you calling me now?"

"Because Grace called me and she said he was a stud."

"Grace? Our up-tight perfectionistic, exquisitely restrained sister? She said the word 'stud?'"

"Boggles the mind, doesn't it? What's going on Pickett? Start talking."

It felt good to unburden. Pickett found herself going into detail about how far beyond her wildest dreams being desired by a man like Jax had been. About how gentle he was with her and Tyler despite his great strength. His intelligence, her respect for him. Only to Lyle would she have said what she thought about sex before Jax and what she thought now.

As she talked, Pickett came to see that Jax had given her his respect at every turn, treating her like his equal, a very different equal, true, but still someone on his own level. Now she could put a name to the loss she felt. She had lost his respect. Nevertheless she knew she had to be sensible. She loved him now, but how long would that love survive her resenting him because he would never be the man she wanted him to be? She had saved him and herself, not to mention Tyler, from a world of pain.

"It would never be the kind of stable, dependable life I've always wanted," she concluded.

Lyle made a rude sound. "Since when did stability mean that much to you? If you had wanted stable you could have stayed in Goldsboro and gone to work for Mental Health. Instead you go off to a house that is just barely habitable, and you work at two jobs, either of which could blow away tomorrow."

"Lyle, marriage is different. If coming to Snead's Ferry didn't work out, I could always do something else. You know how much I hate the attitude some people have that if the marriage doesn't work out they can always get a divorce. When I get married I intend it to be forever." Pickett pulled the clip from her hair and ran her fingers through it. "How can I enter into a marriage with a SEAL, knowing that the odds are overwhelmingly against it succeeding? They have a ninety-five percent divorce rate. Ninety-five percent! I'd have to be either a fool or a hero to take on something like that—and I'm neither."

Lyle let out a huge sigh. "Mother would swear she didn't put any pressure on her children to achieve, but we've all got issues around making the grade, and succeeding. In your own way you're as much a perfectionist as Grace is. You believe you know all the rules for making a marriage, and now nothing will do for you but a perfect one." Lyle was silent a minute while she gathered her thoughts. "Pickett, I think you're asking the wrong question. If you don't love him, that's one thing. But if you do love him, if you love that little boy and want to be his mother, then is it really about succeeding or failing?"

"What is the right question?"

"Is this marriage something you can put your heart into."

After talking a while about the gallery in Southport that had shown some interest in Lyle's paintings, Pickett heard Tyler getting up from his nap, and racing to the bathroom downstairs as he always did upon waking up, Lucy clattering behind him. She said goodbye, and was hanging up when she caught sight of Jax coming around the house, a wet Hobo Joe beside him. From the looks of Jax's wet shorts, they had both been swimming. He rinsed the big dog, then allowed him to play at biting the water as it came from the nozzle for a few minutes before turning the hose on himself.

The weather had finally begun to feel like autumn in the last few days, and although it was still warm in the middle of the day, by sunset it was getting chilly. Pickett felt sympathetic shivers chase over her, when Jax, having rinsed his hair, shook the water out of his eyes and stuck the hose down the front of his shorts.

Didn't he experience discomfort or did he feel it and ignore it? He felt pleasure, that was for sure. He was such an intensely physical man and approached sex with an exuberant carnality, making explicit the delight he drew from her body's every texture and taste and smell. And he always gave her his body for her pleasure with the same generosity.

Pickett' face grew warm at the thought of some of the things that he could get her to do.

The questions Lyle had raised rumbled through her mind like wheels on cobblestones. Was she looking for a marriage that fit all the right criteria so that she wouldn't have to put her heart into it? How much had she focused on the fact that it couldn't last because she was simply afraid of failure?

THIRTY ONE

Pickett was watching him. Jax didn't need to look for her face at the kitchen window to be sure, but he did look—just for the extra pleasure of finding her. Who would have thought the awareness that had been trained into him would pay off in this feeling of connection so intense he always knew where she was and sometimes, like now, what she was thinking.

He grinned. He knew that intent, almost studious look. She was thinking about sex. But something else too.

Well if she was thinking about sex maybe he hadn't messed up too bad. He had sure gone about asking her to marry him in the most half-assed kind of way. The swim in the sound had helped him get his head back together.

The tide had been out and he'd had to wade through the warm shallow water almost 100 yards to find water deep enough to swim in. He moved the hose deeper down his shorts. He'd stumbled into quicksand in a couple of places and the slurry of fine sand and water guaranteed grit would make it into every fold and crevice.

It had bothered him some, okay, a lot, to find out Pickett thought he was such a bad risk she never would have looked at him if she'd thought he was serious. But hey, Corey was the only person who had ever wanted him just because he was himself. It didn't matter. He wanted her for Tyler.

And for himself.

He liked the way she touched him. He liked sleeping on sheets that smelled like her. He even liked that she was always thinking of things for him to fix, and she didn't hesitate to keep him in line.

When she was all tidy in her prim little professional outfits, he liked planning how he would mess her up as soon as she got home.

He could live with the fact that she gave her love everywhere, impartially. After all, he was benefiting too. But he didn't like the thought of her going on to some other man. Uh-uh. That was not going to happen.

She would want children. More kids would be good. Maybe a little girl. He could picture her round and ripe with his child. The thought was amazingly erotic. And thanks to his dad, he had money. She wouldn't have to live on a lieutenant's salary.

His proposal had been too sudden. Pickett liked to think things over. So he'd give her a little time. Then a romantic dinner, some wine, a little mood music, show her a ring. He could make this work.

THIRTY TWO

Waiting for the fireworks to begin, Pickett stood on the fantail of the pier watching the last lavender glow of daylight fade to bright indigo behind the cottages on the shore.

She'd braced herself for an evening of terse sentences and stiff silences while they fulfilled their promise to Tyler, but Jax was acting remarkably cheerful, for a man whose proposal had been turned down. He didn't act like his heart was broken.

Which meant she'd done the right thing to refuse him. Didn't it? Whether she was in his life or out of it didn't really make much difference to him. He looked at ease as he listened politely to the elderly man who had button-holed him. He stood still without looking stiff. No shifting his weight on his sandaled feet, no random shoving hands in his jeans pockets. He was just absolutely present.

She, on the other hand, was growing more edgy with every passing minute. Like a cut lip she couldn't keep her tongue away from, her mind traced over reasons she couldn't marry him.

With restless fingers she pulled out the scarf she had tucked into her light denim jacket in case the evening grew cool, and folded it into a bandeau to keep her hair from blowing into her eyes.

She wished she could refold her thoughts and tie them up differently, but there was no way to do that. There was only an echoing hollowness she'd have to learn to live with. The bottom line was always the same. She couldn't marry Jax while wanting him to change.

It was the smell that told Pickett something was wrong.

The ocean breeze had died with the setting sun, and a land breeze was just beginning to push little luffs of air almost straight down the pier.

She turned from adjusting Tyler's jacket and raised her head to sniff the land breeze. Sort of sweet, sort of sulfur, slight odor of decay… cooking gas.

Restaurant was too fancy a word for the four orange vinyl booths and lunch counter that took up one wall of the bait shop. She supposed they had cooking gas there, but it seemed unlikely that the smell would carry the nine hundred fifty feet to the end of the pier.

The breeze died, and now she could only smell whiffs of beer, cigarette smoke and the caramel corn the children were sharing. Underneath was the always-present pier-smell of fish bait and treated wood, long pickled in salt air.

It smelled like what it was: a crowd on a pier, but the feeling of cold fingers stroking her spine from the inside got stronger.

Jax with his almost uncanny sense of where she was and what was going on with her reached out a hand and drew her to him without pausing in the conversation he had struck up with an elderly man. The man was ranting to Jax about a logger-head turtle nest near his beach cottage. He was irritated because he had to walk around the yellow tape that the turtle conservation group had placed around it.

Briefly comforted by his Jax smell, Pickett snuggled closer to his warmth as the breeze picked up again, but then there it was again. Gas. It just didn't make sense to smell gas where there wasn't any.

Jax felt her stiffen and cocked an eyebrow at her, but his wry smile said he had misinterpreted the cause of her unease. He knew well her opinion of people who were drawn to the uncrowded simplicity of the Outer Banks' pristine beaches and then complained because they missed all the conveniences of New Jersey. The man showed no signs of winding down. Pickett waited for a break in his monologue and when none appeared, she shoved out a stop hand.

He man stopped his harangue, more in surprise at her temerity than courtesy. Pickett would take what she could get.

"Excuse us." She pulled on Jax's sleeve. "I

want to leave. Something is wrong."

Jax's eyes met hers in a moment's hard assessment. Then—she wouldn't have believed it if she
hadn't been looking right at him—he went from
being a laid back young man, politely letting an
older man bore him, to being someone else.
Someone she'd glimpsed once before when he'd
come in from the hurricane still enrapt with the
wildness of the storm. His shoulders suddenly
looked broader. His weight moved to the balls of
his feet and he scanned the crowd in one swift efficient sweep, noting the position of every single
person. Without seeming to stop scanning, he
swept up Tyler as he ran by chasing another little
boy about his size.

"What's the matter?" Jax asked tersely while
settling Tyler in his arms.

Pickett rubbed the back of her neck. "I don't
know. I just want to get off this pier." She
shrugged helplessly. "It doesn't smell right. I keep
thinking I smell gas."

Jax lifted his head, inhaled sharply. "I don't
smell it."

"I don't either right this minute, but…"

"Okay, let's head out." Though spoken in a
flat calm drawl, there was no doubt the words
were an order.

Was that how he sounded on an operation? Did
he weigh his men's input and come to instant deci-
sions, confident that he was the one who decided,
who told others what to do. Pickett's work gave her
exquisitely developed intuition, but rarely did she

communicate what she intuited, and even more rarely did she expect someone else to act on it.

There was no time to stand in bemusement, however. Even if Jax's tone had not assumed instant obedience to his softly worded command, her feeling of unease was growing stronger. Pickett could see nothing but a wall of people between her and the safety of the beach. Jax's hand warm and firm came down on her shoulder urging her forward.

"Wait, Daddy!" Tyler craned his head around. His perch in his father's arms put his head above Pickett's. "Where're we going? This isn't the way to the fireworks."

They were definitely going against the flow of the crowd, which parted for Jax as they never would have for her. She patted Tyler's leg. "We'll watch from the beach."

"No! I don't wanna go to the beach." Tyler could see for himself that people were streaming toward the far end of the pier to get a good position to view the fireworks.

Grateful for Jax's bulk at her side, Pickett pressed toward the bait shop and the exit just beyond it. Tyler saw the exit sign, one of the many signs he could read, and started pushing at his father's shoulder, twisting to be put down. "No! We can't leave. We didn't see the fireworks yet! Put me down!"

"It's okay, son," Jax's voice was a soothing rumble, but he didn't let up the pressure on Pickett's shoulder. "If everything's all right, we'll come back."

Suddenly there was a sizzling whistle and pressure on her ears as if the noise extended far beyond the audible range. Pickett had the confused thought that the fireworks must have already started when a hand twisted the neck of her windbreaker swinging her around, and into the opposite direction.

"Run!" Jax didn't loosen his hold on her jacket, but instead, pulled her with him as he ran, holding Tyler against his chest, back toward the end of the pier.

It was a sensation between flying and being strangled. Pickett wasn't sure how often her feet actually touched the rough planks. With Jax holding her, pulling her, almost picking her up, she was running faster than she had ever run. Other people were beginning to run now, yelling. Pickett ignored the jacket's zipper cutting into the base of her neck.

There was a loud boom and the hand on her back shoved her roughly down and something, someone heavy, fell on top of her. Under her the pier rippled and heaved like a carpet being shaken in the wind.

The breath knocked out of her by the fall, it took a moment to sort the extreme heaviness of her chest as Tyler lying on her back, sandwiched between her and Jax.

Pickett tried to lift her face away from the splinter digging into her cheek only to feel Jax's arms cross over her head pushing it back down. "Stay down!"

More booms. The pier shook again. There was the unmistakable whoosh as fire roared for oxygen.

Tyler gave a thin scream and began to struggle, digging sharp little knees and elbows into her back and the side of her neck. His rubber soled sneakers were amazingly hard when they connected with the backs of her thighs. Suddenly he was lifted off her, but before Pickett could relish her renewed freedom to breathe she was hauled to her feet with more strength than ceremony.

"Move it!" Jax pushed her relentlessly toward the ocean-end of the pier.

THIRTY THREE

Even if the hand clamped to her collar would have allowed it, there was no need for Pickett to turn around to know that the pier was on fire behind them. The fitful land breeze enveloped them in smoke and sent sparks dancing past them. A lurid orange light competed with the mercury vapor lamps set at twenty foot intervals.

There was no way off the pier. The fire was between them and the beach and once they reached the tip where it widened into the fantail fishing platform, they would be as far as they could get from the blaze. They were trapped.

Frantic yells punctuated the fire's steady crackling, Tyler howled without let up, while unbelievably, the pier's music system continued to blare the Beatles.

"Hey Jude, don't be afraid. Take a sad song and make it be-eh-eh-ter…"

Pickett swallowed back a half-hysterical laugh and concentrated on maintaining her footing on the planks made bouncy by so many running feet.

A child careened into her legs, clipping her behind the knees, instantly followed by a much larger person. Before she could even attempt to recover her balance Jax had clamped her to his side with an iron arm.

Jax guided them toward one of the crude benches built at intervals against the railing. Most of the crowd, in an effort to get as far away as possible from the fire had packed into the fishing platform. Jax pressed her into the bench with Tyler between them.

Not taking his hand off his son, Jax reached with his other hand for his cell phone. Tyler immediately scrambled to Pickett, wrapping his legs around her waist and clutching her neck in a strangle hold. Pickett pressed his wet face into her neck, murmuring reassurances and rocking him.

Flames leapt 40 feet into the air behind Jax. The bait shop was fully ablaze now and spreading toward the walkways that ran on either side. The land breeze had picked up and was blowing steadily from the north east pushing stinging, oily smoke, sparks and flaming bits down the pier.

Under the roar of the fire, loud even this far away, Tyler sobbing, and the Beatles endlessly repeating nah nah nah nahnahnah nah, Pickett heard Jax calling 911.

A fireman had told her once that a pier, baked dry by years of sun, burned incredibly fast. The nearest fire station was fifteen or twenty minutes away. Pickett fought back her rising panic, and focused on Jax's voice. How could he sound so calm? His tone was flat, almost emotionless, as he assessed the situation for the 911 dispatcher.

Tyler squirmed against her arms as if he wanted to get down. When she tightened her hold, not daring to let him get away from her, he began to hit and kick. He twisted a fold of skin on her neck and she gasped in pain.

The sudden intake of breath dragged the chemical-thick smoke deep into her lungs making her cough until her eyes steamed.

Tyler screamed "I want my mommy!" as he kicked. Her heart went out to him but she could do nothing but grimly try to hang on to him as she coughed and gasped.

Jax snapped the cell phone closed. What the hell? He thought Pickett was getting Tyler calmed down. Most of the time she was better at it than he was. Suddenly the kid seemed to be going ballistic. Pickett tried to keep her face from his flailing hands but he noticed she didn't slacken her hold even when she caught a knee to the solar plexus.

Tyler was hurting Pickett. Jax snatched the child off her lap, more furious than he remembered being, maybe ever.

He felt the tiny rib cage shudder and his stomach turned over in self-disgust. He should just put him down right now and walk away until he got a hold of himself. A glance at Pickett wiping her streaming eyes told him she was not recovered enough to keep Tyler safe if he walked away.

What the hell was he thinking? Tyler was his responsibility. Completely. Whatever was going on with Tyler, whatever he needed right this minute was between him and Tyler and nobody else.

Jax had very little idea what he was supposed to do about the shocked white face, streaked with tears, about the child's meltdown, so he dealt with the part he understood with the skills he had. He pulled Tyler to him until he was holding the little boy's face to his face and in a voice more deadly than loud said, "Don't. Hit. Pickett. Ever. Do you understand mister? Never hit Pickett. Ever."

Two icy little hands gripped Jax's ears, sharp little fingernails digging in. Tyler pulled his face even closer to Jax's, grey eyes glaring. "I'M SCARED. I WANT MY MOMMY!" he screamed.

Oh shit. His mother was dead. He knew that. Didn't he? Did he know she was dead and she was never coming back? Little kids were so little. On the other hand, he had guts. He was willing to get right in the face of someone four times his size and tell them what he wanted.

As if to emphasize his father's thoughts Tyler twisted on the ears and dug in his nails a little deeper. "I want my mommy!"

Not near as much as I do, kid! He'd give anything to be able to turn Tyler over to Danielle right now. No, that wasn't true. He wouldn't hand Tyler to her right this minute even if she was here.

Danielle was a good and caring mother but she didn't keep her head in a crisis.

But a sudden pang of grief took him by surprise. Though he was more relieved than anything else, when he and Danielle called it quits, he'd never imagined her beauty and butterfly charm lost from the world. Utterly gone from his life and from Tyler's. He had failed to love her, failed at being married to her, but not because she was unlovable.

Now that situation was forever unfixable and Tyler— Tyler was left loving and wanting someone who was never coming back. He couldn't give Tyler what he wanted. Shit. He knew how Tyler felt. He wished he could hit something, too.

Jax gently dislodged the rough little hands, one ear at a time. "You want your mommy and everything is messed up and it makes you want to hit something. Okay. I understand. You can't hit Pickett, but you can hit me."

Tyler took him at his word and began to flail arms and legs. He was using more energy than science, nevertheless after a sneakered foot connected with the only soft spot below his waist, Jax pulled his son to his chest and wrapped those little feet behind him.

Then it was only natural to rub the skinny back and stroke the silky head, even if it was a little hard to talk through the tightness in his throat.

He stroked and soothed and murmured the same words over and over. "I'm so sorry your Mommy's gone, but I've got you."

Trust me, Tyler.

"I'm not going to let go. You don't have to be scared."

Trust me.

"I've got you."

And I'm not going to let you go.

Over and over as the wails turned to sobs, and the sobs to shudders.

THIRTY FOUR

A window exploded in the burning structure and a woman screamed. The land breeze was blowing steadily now, pushing the smoke their way—inevitably driving the fire toward them as well. Fire departments and the Coast Guard were on their way. Unfortunately, the pier was situated at the farthest possible point from any of the surrounding towns. Fire trucks would be there in twenty to twenty-five minutes, Coast Guard vessels would take longer. How long would it take for the fire to burn the nine hundred fifty feet to the end of the pier?

Even as he calmed the frightened child, Jax reviewed his options. The fire was advancing too quickly to wait for help to arrive. He could organize the people into an orderly evacuation, and he would jump only when the last person was safe. He could take care of himself in any situation.

But having Tyler and Pickett with him changed everything. For some of the people on the pier, waiting as long as possible and giving help time to arrive offered the best chance of survival, but as

372 MARY MARGRET DAUGHTRIDGE

long as they were with him, Tyler and Pickett were safest in the water. And the sooner he got them there, the better. Every minute of delay meant more hazardous debris in the water. Sooner or later some of the crowd would panic. Panicked people, whether on the pier or in the water, could overwhelm Pickett easily.

For a SEAL, no failure could be more shameful than letting people he was tasked to protect come to harm. His need to protect Pickett and Tyler went even deeper than hating to fail. Every element of the love he felt for them, and every part of himself that he loved with, focused into one determination—to see them safe.

For Jax, there was only one imperative. Get Tyler and Pickett into the water as quickly as possible.

Jax slid onto the bench beside Pickett. She was pale and her eye lashes were spikey with tears but she was no longer coughing.

"You okay?"

She rubbed away wetness on her cheeks with the back of her hand, and nodded. "The smoke got to me for a minute." Her voice was a little hoarse but she gave a tender smile that included him and Tyler. "You got Tyler calmed down. He was having a really hard time."

Pickett glanced toward the fire which had advanced in the moments since Jax had taken Tyler.

"What are we going to do? The fire department isn't going to get here in time, is it?"

"Come on." He pulled her to her feet and began walking toward the end of the pier and the fishing platform.

"How well do you swim?"

"I can keep from drowning. I passed swimming in college, but mainly because I'm pretty good at treading water. Why?" Pickett dug in her heels suddenly. "Wait a minute. You're planning to jump, aren't you?" She warded off the idea with one hand, fingers spread wide, "Uhn-uh. I can't jump."

Jax tightened his grip on her arm and put her in motion again. She would walk or be dragged.

"Jax, I mean it. I can't jump. I couldn't walk onto the diving board. I even hated diving off the edge of the pool." Her voice took on a note of pleading. "Please, Jax, there's got to be some other way. Are you listening to me?"

"No."

"No? You're not listening to me?" Pickett's rising panic snagged on her ever-present sense of humor. Maybe it was hysteria, but wasn't it just like a man to choose a moment like this to admit he wasn't listening.

When SEALs get into trouble they always go to water. Jax could swim literally with both arms tied behind him, and his feet tied as well. Swimming Pickett and Tyler safely to shore was a piece of cake, no worries, as long as she did exactly what he said. He had to convince her to do what he said.

But it involved making her sit and wait for him. There would be time for her to panic, to do something stupid.

Jax pushed her, not roughly, but very firmly onto a bench. The smoke was not as intense out here. He squatted in front of her so that they were eye to eye.

Despite her fear-dilated eyes and pale cheeks, a tiny smile played around her lips. God, he loved this woman. He could feel an answering smile in his eyes, even though he had no idea what they were smiling about. He cocked his head in inquiry.

"You admitted you weren't listening to me."

He didn't see what was so funny about that, but let it go. "I've always listened to you about Tyler. Now you listen to me because this time I'm the expert. I'm going to take Tyler to shore then I will swim back for you. When you see me in the water, you are going to jump to me and I'll take you in."

"Can't I just wait and maybe the fire department will get here? And what about the other people?"

"Anything I can do for the others only increases the danger to you and Tyler, and that I will not do. Nothing is more important than you and Tyler. Do you understand me? Nothing."

There was no time to argue. "You will jump, Pickett." He strove to project absolute confidence that anything else was unthinkable. "You know what they always tell SEALs when we have to do stuff we hate?" He locked his gaze with hers. "Remember, you don't have to like it, you just have to do it."

Every color, every sound seemed enveloped in a pellucid clarity and Pickett's mind seemed able to assimilate huge pieces of information. Moments like this sometimes happened in a therapy session. Every word, every gesture took on significance that Pickett understood with wisdom far more profound than mere knowledge.

In the iron grip of his will, Pickett nodded. The slow heavy thudding of her heart told Pickett she was still afraid, and at the same time she felt absolutely safe trapped on a pier that was on fire. Because of Jax.

She trusted him the same way she trusted her wisdom. And with the sudden clarity of that wisdom, his arrogance transmuted to absolute confidence. Whatever this situation required of him he knew he could do, and furthermore he would let no harm come to her or Tyler.

Secure within himself precisely because he was dealing with danger. Secure within himself because being trapped on a burning pier gave him the opportunity to be fully himself.

Nor could she deny that for him part of the appeal of the situation was its violent raw edge. Life was stripped to its essentials. The choices were about living or dying. He was alive, vibrant, magnificent. The molten light of the fire licked and burnished his skin with red and gold, delineating the sinews of his forearms, outlining the power of his thighs.

An icy hand gripped her heart, squeezed. He was more different from her than she had allowed herself to know. He was alien. Not just her natural opposite in that he was a man. He was utterly other.

Just when her mind would have rejected him, her heart broke free of its icy bond and expanded in a surge of warmth that rivaled that of the fire crackling slowly and inexorably closer. Hot, almost burning her chest, her throat, her eyes, it stole her breath, consuming everything in its path.

He was exactly as he was supposed to be, as perfect and as inevitable as a mountain. Changing him, even wishing him different, would be a sin against his soul and her own soul.

This was love. Knowing that the other was other, not some idealized reflection of herself, and finding that perfect.

Pickett swallowed and her head jerked in a short nod. "After I jump in the water. Then what will happen? What will you do?"

Jax's teeth flashed a teasing, sexy grin in the lurid light. He waggled his straight dark brows with comical innuendo. "The breast stroke."

For an infinite instant she cradled his cheek, relishing the tiny prickles of his beard. "Go," she whispered. "Get Tyler to safety."

"Don't move from this spot until you see me in the water."

Pickett looked over the rail at the black water shifting in the fire's glow. "Will I be able to see you?"

Jax looked a little chagrined. "I'm used to making sure I'm not seen. Give me your scarf." He quickly tied the long swath of silk around his head and faced her. "Will this work?"

His head was covered from the forehead back in silk pattered with flowers. The ends of the scarf streamed and fluttered in the wind. He should have looked silly; instead he looked like a merry pirate, swashbuckling, yet stern, the gaiety of the flowers somehow enhancing the implacability of his purpose. His masculinity sprang from some immutable essence that could not be diminished by femininity, only enhanced by it.

Pickett's heart leapt and swelled as in one of her intuitive flashes she saw what she and Jax had to give to one another. Rather than losing or sacrificing any part, by giving themselves in love, they would each become more perfectly, more fully what they already were.

"Pickett, I asked you, will this work?"

The flowers of the scarf appeared almost black in the lurid light of the fire, but the white background glowed. As soon as she said yes he would leave her to face the fire, to face jumping by herself. She was just barely holding herself together with him by her side. What would happen when he was gone? Her jaw tightened against the up-rushing terror. She pulled in deep breaths, demanding her throat relax enough to get a word out. The most important thing was to get Tyler to safety.

"Yes," she said.

Jax straightened and shifted Tyler to his hip. "Okay big guy. We're going to swim just like we did in the sound, you remember? You're going to hold tight to my neck and I'm going to swim you on my back."

"We're going to jump off?" Tyler started to struggle against Jax's encircling arms. "Uhn-uhn. Pickett's 'fraid to jump."

Pickett grasped the child's ankle to get his attention. "Not any more. That was before." She fumbled for an explanation he would accept. "That was when I was little. I didn't have your daddy with me so I was afraid. But now I'm not. You said it was fun to swim like that with your daddy. You get to go first," she twinkled, "and then it will be my turn."

She was amazing. You'd think she was discussing a ride at a fair. Her shoulders were shaking in a telltale quiver but she found courage to give to Tyler. "Lady, you blow me away." Please God, let her find the courage to...he stopped the thought.

Swiftly he brought Tyler tight against his chest, stepped onto the bench and then the wide top of the rail. One handed he let himself down on the other side and slid carefully onto the pilings that jutted from the base of the pier. The further he could get from the pilings the better. Crusted with barnacles and trailing fishing hooks from a thousand casts that went awry, they were a formidable danger to unprotected flesh. Was Pickett watching? He didn't dare risk his balance to look back at the rail.

"Hold tight with your legs, Tyler. You might need to hold your breath a long time, but you can do that, can't you?" He could feel Tyler's nod against his chest. Skinny legs gripped his waist and sharp little fingers dug into his neck.

SEALs referred to people they were tasked to rescue as precious cargo.

This was his own precious cargo, his son, to be carried to safety but not to be relinquished ever. And that was his Lady. His, by God.

He took a firmer grip on his precious cargo, placed one hand on top of the silky head, to counteract the buoyancy that could otherwise squirt Tyler out of his arms like a pea popped from a pod, and jumped.

THIRTY FIVE

B ubbles caressed and stoked him on all sides. Another time he would have relished the sensual delight of jumping into warm water without 100 pounds or more of equipment. Another time he might have let himself relax and sink as far as he would through the caressing bubbles, content to let the ocean bring him to the surface as it would in its own time.

Tonight he pulled up his knees to stop his descent then kicked for the surface almost as soon as the water closed over his head. The powerful muscles of his thighs propelled them to the surface.

They had only been under seconds but Jax knew an unreasonable measure of relief when he heard Tyler suck in a breath. The kid had been through so much tonight, enough to traumatize most adults. Jax wouldn't have chosen to make this his first experience of jumping into water. In the next moment he knew the apple hadn't fallen far from the tree. The little boy shook water from his eyes, cleared his nose the way he had been

shown, threw back his head and crowed in delight.
"Do it again, Daddy!"

With a loud whoosh flames shot up from a new
section of the building. Pickett heard a loud elec-
trical buzzing and popping and the pier went dark.
People screamed. Seen only in its own light the
fire seemed larger and more menacing. From time
to time burning chunks of pier fell into the water.
The railing was eerily outlined by tongues of
flame and flames suddenly leapt up a lamppost.

Was the fire closer? Pickett couldn't tell. The
wind blew smoke in front of it making it hard to
see. Pickett leaned over the rail to watch the two
heads so close together move toward the shore.
There was only the light of the fire to see by now.
Soon they were lost to sight in the thick pall of
smoke. Pickett choked back a sob. They were all
right. They had to be. Even if she couldn't see
them, she reminded herself, Jax would keep Tyler
safe. But she wished she could see him take the
child to shore. Set him down. Give him to one of
the people who was surely there by now. Was that
the sound of fire trucks in the distance or was it
wishful thinking? Maybe they would get here in
time and she wouldn't have to jump.

She shouldn't think about that. Don't think
about jumping. She hadn't been exaggerating to
Jax. She really did almost flunk swimming
because she wouldn't dive even from the lowest

board. And strangely enough, for her, jumping off the side of the pool was just as bad. Truthfully, she thought she had been passed because the teacher didn't want to have to deal with her again.

Don't think about how far away the water looks. Don't think about how much bigger the swells look from the height of the pier when you can see them from trough to trough.

Don't think about it.

Watch for Jax. In a few minutes he would have gotten Tyler to shore. In a few minutes he would turn around. In a few minutes she would be able to see his head through the smoke.

He actually thought she could do this. Pickett choked back a half-hysterical laugh.

Don't think about it.

She hoped anybody in the bait shop and lunch counter had gotten away. She offered up a prayer for their safety and the safety of all the people on the pier.

Oh dear God help me. Just let me do everything Jax said and get it right.

But he didn't know what a hopeless klutz she was.

Oh, dear God, help me not to think about it.

The smoke was thicker now.

She could only see the water directly below and a little ways toward shore. Would she be able to see Jax? Yes she would. He said when you see me I'll be in the water. That meant she would see him.

A man shouted high and panicky "We gotta get out of here. We gotta jump!" A child wailed, there were murmurs and shouts and several people climbed up on the rails.

Two young men—Marines, judging from their "white wall" haircuts—jumped to the rails. They disappeared and what felt like a long time later there were twin splashes and heads appeared.

Other people began to jump. Horrified, Pickett watched a young woman clutching what looked like a baby climb up on the rail. Before Pickett could reach the woman to tell her to wait, Jax would help her, she leaped from the very tip of the fantail.

Pickett didn't see them come up but the water, dark with burning light, was littered with heads, indistinguishable from one another, and with coolers that had been thrown in as floats. She said a prayer for the woman, and then for herself. How was she going to find Jax?

Pickett. Did someone call her name? Was that…yes there he was. Not looking absurd at all with the flower patterned scarf around his head. He was looking for her.

He had come.

Her heart beating so hard that her entire body shook, Pickett climbed onto the bench and threw one leg over the rail. The foot wide platform where fishermen rested their rods made it hard to get her leg over. She feared she would fall before she could jump. It was never going to work. She couldn't touch with her toes until she had both legs over.

She squirmed around until her diaphragm rested on the platform then slowly allowed both legs to drop over. The trouble was the platform was much closer to chest height than waist height and her legs now dangled. Ignoring the splinters scraping into her arms and chest, she lowered herself down, feeling for something solid with her feet.

At last. But now she would have to let go in order to turn around. Her entire body throbbed with the force of her heartbeats. Turn. She could do this.

Now her back was to the pier and all she had to do was crawl into the piling.

There he was, watching her.

Pickett knew for a fact that she could not jump into that dark, oily-looking water, shifting and moving so that you could never tell where it was.

Jax, however, believed she could. At every turn he'd believed she was stronger, truer, and braver than she thought herself to be. She'd faced some truths about herself—that she kept herself sealed off, rarely letting people know how she felt or what she needed. But because of Jax, she had talked more openly with her sister than she ever had, asserting her needs, revealing her shortcomings, and as a result she had a sister today who was also a friend. She'd opened to her clients and been met with compassion and support.

She'd told Jax she couldn't jump and he hadn't said "Oh you poor thing." He'd said, "Jump anyway." If she focused on the water she couldn't do it. If she focused on him, she could. She could choose to listen to her fear—about everything—or listen to him.

She made herself see only Jax, not the water. She made herself know only that she was going to him. The distance between them didn't mean anything. She reviewed his directions. You will jump feet first. Keep your feet tight together, arms across your chest, pinch your nose. We will swim together. I can. You will.

But she couldn't do as he said while crouched in a ball.

Never letting her eyes leave his face, she slowly stood.

THIRTY SIX

There she was. She'd seen him. The fear, too unbearable to think about, that she wouldn't be there on the fantail, that he wouldn't be able to get to her until too late, released its talons from his gut so swiftly as to leave him lightheaded. In seconds he would have her and then she'd be where she belonged.

What the hell was she doing? She was going over the rail. Why didn't she just stand on it to jump? It was wide enough to hold her little feet easily. Stand up! Jump you idiot! Oh shit. Her legs were dangling. He willed her toes forward until they touched the weathered boards.

She looked so little crouched there clutching an upright with one arm while she turned. With the glare of the fire at her back, he could see little more than a dark shape, and yet for a moment, he had the impression she was looking straight into his eyes.

She stayed like that forever. For eons. Until he was sure she had frozen. He had seen it happen. When the fear became overwhelming and people just curled into a ball. And then she began to move, a funny scooting crab-like crawl onto the piling.

Smoke drifted across her but when he could see her again she was a little further along. Come on. You can do it. You want to jump off a piling? That's just as good. A little further and you're ready. Come on. Come on!

Oh damn. She was frozen again. Maybe she didn't intend to jump. Maybe she had panicked and was simply trying to crawl as far as possible from the fire. No. This time he could see the shine of her eyes as she looked straight at him. She rose from her crouch with the swift fluid grace that was so much a part of her, and launched herself into the air. Feet together, arms pulled in tight, pinching her nose, she entered the water with text-book-illustration technique. Hooyah.

Though he wanted to, there was no point in diving down to where she had entered the water. With an almost leisurely crawl he moved to where the swell would bring her up again.

Bubbles, hitting her face, tickling across her skin, loud burbles and gurgles. It went on and on. She just kept going down and there didn't seem to be anything she could do about it. Soon she would start coming up. That was the thing you could depend on. The ocean would always bring you up.

Her descent was slowing finally but her lungs were already burning, and she still had to get all the way back up. Something bumped her, trickling more bubbles across her face. Reflexively she put out a hand to brush it away and felt her fingers tangle in fabric then close around a tiny, soft…it felt like an arm. A baby's arm. Her first thought was to wonder what child had lost her doll. She pulled it closer and felt a tiny hand brush her face then cling to her collar.

A baby. There was a baby in the water with her. Under the water. Babies would reflexively hold their breath, hadn't she read that? But for how long? Her own lungs were beginning to scream for air. How long had the baby been under? She began to kick for the surface, her efforts feeling clumsy and futile with the unaccustomed weight of her slacks.

"Jax," she screamed as soon as her head broke the surface, immediately swallowing a mouthful of water as she tried to lift the baby above the water. Though tiny, its water logged diaper made the infant amazingly heavy and Pickett went under again.

A cool-warm arm circled her and brought her to the surface. "Easy. I've got you now. Just relax."

Pickett coughed, and coughed but continued to hold the baby as high as she could.

"Breathe," came Jax's voice warm in her ear. "You're all right."

"A baby." Pickett gasped. "It was in the water with me. You take it."

Jax suddenly made sense of the bundle Pickett seemed to clutch so senselessly. He quickly turned Pickett to face him so that the baby was supported between them.

"Is it breathing?" Pickett asked. "Is it alive?"

Wide dark eyes looked into Jax's face with a look of indignant inquiry while a rose bud mouth pulled into a serious pout. The mouth opened in a huge shuddering breath and let out a wail.

"I'd say it is."

"Save the baby, then. I'll be all right. I'll—"

Of all the idiotic, lamebrained—! She had been about to drown herself trying to hold a kid out of the water. Leave her! There was no one he would not sacrifice, except Tyler, for her safety. Shit. He didn't have time to deal with this right now.

"Hush." It wasn't reassurance. It was a command. "Here's what we do. You're going to turn on your back, and hold the baby on its back on your chest, arms crossed across it. I'll tow you." Each word was driven with hammer blows.

Where was the man with the glinting grey eyes that sparkled with ready laughter? This man with the hard face, and harder voice was someone she didn't know. This was the man she'd seen in the grocery store—was it only two weeks ago? Dangerous. Implacable. Remote.

Thank God, he was on her side.

Taking care of Tyler was his job, so he would do it. If she married him, she would be his to take care of too, and he would do it the best he could.

She nestled the baby, who seemed to enjoy this novel form of transportation, a little closer, and was almost sure the stinging in her eyes was caused by the salt water.

THIRTY SEVEN

In almost no time she felt Jax touch the bottom and urge her to stand as well. Wordlessly he took the baby and when she stumbled, clumsy in her wet clothes, steadied her with his other arm.

People appeared to pull her from the surf. Someone threw a large beach towel around her. Before she could ask where Tyler was, he was throwing his arms around her knees.

"Did you jump, Pickett? Did you swim on my Daddy's back? Was it fun?"

Jax's hand caressed the back of her neck. "You'll be okay. Stay with Tyler. I'm going back in."

Before Pickett could reply, he was already diving back into the surf. Yards away he reappeared, head bobbing in a lazy-looking breaststroke that nevertheless covered distance easily.

Then, her attention was taken by the hysterically grateful mother of the baby. No matter how Pickett tried to explain that she hadn't saved the baby, it didn't seem to make an impression. As an EMT pulled the woman away to check the infant over, Pickett lost sight of Jax.

She knelt and wrapped Tyler in the beach towel with her, while scanning the water.

Surfers with their boards started appearing in twos and threes as if by magic, and racing into the water. A Hoby Cat had been launched and was being paddled to the end of the pier. Sirens wailing, the fire department arrived, and set up giant stadium type lights and deployed their hoses.

Suddenly Pickett's eyes found Jax. She blessed her flowered scarf. Because he still wore it on his head she could locate him among the bodies in the water.

"See Tyler," she pointed. "There's your daddy. He's helping people onto the surfboards."

Tyler followed Pickett's pointing finger for a few minutes then sagged tiredly against her breasts.

"I wish he was here with us." His voice wobbled a little.

"I wish he was here too, but he has to be there because he has to save people." Pickett rubbed her cheek on Tyler's salt-matted hair.

"Why?"

Pickett smiled tenderly at the whiny question. "'Cause he's a hero, darling. He's just doing what he has to do, 'cause that's who he is."

"Is he coming back?"

"Sure he is."

"My mommy's dead. She's not coming back."

She tightened her arms and rocked Tyler gently.

"I know, baby." She tucked the towel closer around Tyler's neck and rocked him some more. "I know."

Three separate police officers asked her if all her party was accounted for, and someone pushed a cup of hot coffee into her hand.

And Pickett rocked Tyler, and they waited for Jax.

THIRTY EIGHT

Why the hell did you say you could swim?" Jax's words, no less angry for being soft spoken, jerked Pickett from her near doze.

Jax had been tight-lipped and silent since getting behind the wheel, clearly thinking about the pier fire and their narrow escape. That was okay. Pickett had a lot to think about too. During the eternity on the burning pier, waiting for Jax to swim back to her after carrying Tyler to safety, she had not so much watched her life pass before her eyes as seen it totally re-arrange itself.

Pickett sat up straighter. She blinked red feeling eyes at his profile, lit by the glow of the dash. He had on his no-expression expression. She half-laughed at the unfairness of the attack. "I can swim."

"The hell you can. You're pathetic. You were about to drown yourself in front of my eyes. Shit. I could have been teaching you. I would have been teaching you if I'd had any idea a woman who has lived on the fucking Sound for two fucking years, could not fucking swim."

"Language, Jax," Pickett warned. "There are ears in the back seat."

Jax flicked his eyes to the rear view mirror. "He's asleep."

"He's worn out. So am I." Pickett tightened her grip on her patience. "So are you. Can't this wait?"

"Hell, no. You are going to listen to me, and listen to me good. You go through life like some kind of Mary Poppins, passing out advice and spreading good cheer. Well, when the shit hits the fan, training is what will save your ass."

Pickett's patience slipped another notch. "What are you so upset about? I jumped off the pier, just like you told me to. And I didn't die," she added flippantly.

"That's another thing. What the hell did you think you were you doing letting yourself down over the rail? If you'd fallen from that position, you could have broken your back. And then you waited so long to jump, I thought you had frozen and there wasn't a damn thing I could do about it. You scared the hell out of me."

His hands tightened on the steering wheel, then slowly, consciously un-gripped it one finger at a time. "I don't ever want to feel that kind of fear again."

He took one hand off the wheel to massage his face tiredly, stopping to rub the corner of each eye, the way men do when they're trying to erase tears before they can fall. Compassion melted Pickett's impatience. He'd been so calm. So matter-of-fact and confident. And now reaction had set in.

"I'm going to tell you what you did wrong, and you're going to listen," Jax continued in the same soft growl.

Pickett turned her face toward the passenger window so Jax wouldn't see the tender smile she couldn't quite suppress. She'd tell him later. He was in full testosterone mode, and there wasn't much for her to do but ride it out.

She inhaled deeply to keep the giggly bubbles tickling her insides from popping to the surface. His lecture freely mixed technical jargon with profanities she'd never heard before. She couldn't understand most of it, nonetheless, she had to admire a man who could swear so creatively, and in an absolutely level tone.

They were turning onto the short sand and gravel driveway when he finally ran down. Hobo Joe, who was turning into a good watchdog, met them at the road and raced beside the SUV in his rocking, three-legged gait as they circled the house to the back door.

"Are you done with your rant?" Pickett let her dimple peep and added a flutter of eyelashes for good measure.

Jax slanted her an acid look. "You're not scared of me one bit are you?"

"No, but if you're finished dressing me down, I have a question..." Pickett paused for effect.

"What does," she repeated a salty phrase he had used, "mean, exactly?"

"What?" Jax shut off the engine and slumped back in the seat. He scrubbed at his forehead with a fist. "Shit, Pickett. I'm sorry. I shouldn't have used language like that. I really went off on you."

"Hmm." Pickett noticed he was only apologizing for the language, not the rant. One day soon, they'd need to have a talk about that, but there were other things to be discussed first. "Did you get it out of your system?"

He scrubbed at his forehead again. "Some."

Jax turned out the lights, opened the car door and moved to the back door to begin unbuckling Tyler, almost surprised to note how steady his hands were. On the inside he was still shaking.

All three dogs alerted at the smell of smoke and danger. Patterson whined, and Hobo went to the back of the vehicle to stand sentry. Lucy put her forelegs on the running board straining to press her nose to every inch of Tyler. Tyler whimpered but didn't waken.

"Get down, Lucy," Jax scooped up his son's lax little body, gently settling the heavy head on his shoulder. Precious cargo. "He's okay, Lucy. Everything is going to be okay."

But God! His heart started to pound like a pile driver every time he thought of it.

He'd almost lost everything.

Not bothering to turn on a light in the kitchen, Pickett poured a glass of water from the filter pitcher, and drained it almost in one swallow. Immediately, she filled the glass again but this time savored the coolness washing across her smoke scorched throat. Her damp clothes, her hair, her skin reeked of wood smoke and burning chemicals.

She ran cool water at the kitchen sink and washed her hands, then splashed some water on her face only to be rewarded by stinging when smoke, trapped on her lashes, washed into her eyes. Blindly, she reached for a paper towel to blot her face. Scratchy paper pressed to her eyes, she didn't turn around when she heard Jax come through the hall door. "Is Tyler okay?"

"Yeah. I just skinned him out of his clothes and put him in bed. I don't think he even woke up. What are you doing?"

"My eyes are burning."

"Let me see." Jax was beside her in one step. He turned on the light over the sink with one hand while pulling the wet paper towel away gently with the other. "Come on. Let me see."

With exquisite care he peeled back one eyelid and then the other. His breath was warm and moist on her cool, wet face, and smelled of the Mountain Dew he had all but inhaled in the car driving home. "Hum, a little red, but I think you're okay— wait," he turned the side of her face to catch the light, "what happened to your cheek? It looks bruised."

Pickett felt her cheek. "I hit it on something. I don't remember—oh! It was when the gas tanks exploded and you pushed me down. My face connected with the planks."

Pain filled his eyes, as he ran a careful finger across the swelling. "Oh God, I'm so sorry."

"Don't." Pickett stopped his lips with fingers that trembled slightly. "Glass and burning chunks were flying all around us. You covered my body with your own. You could have been hurt much worse." Pickett put her arms around Jax's waist and laid her cheek against his broad chest. She pressed her ear against him to better hear the reassuring thud of his heart, to get closer to his vital heat. "I was so scared."

His arms tightened around her, crushing her to him. Suddenly he was planting hot, frantic kisses on her hair, her eyes her neck. One large hand cupped her bottom to lift her against him. His erection bulged through the damp denim of his jeans.

"Pickett," his voice was strained, winded, "I've got to have you. I've got to have you right now." He pressed wild, rough kisses to the top of her head. "I know I'm doing this all wrong. I should be sensitive, but I can't. If you don't go with me to the bedroom, I'm going to have you right here on the table. Say yes."

With one hand he unsnapped her jeans and plunged his hands inside.

Her body answered before she did. A tightening spiral lunged from breast to her core, igniting nerve endings all the way. The delicate tissues he stroked swelled and grew moist in his fingers.

Suddenly her need was as imperative as his. This was not seduction or even hot desire, but something far more primal. His need called forth her own need to comfort, to reassure, and to affirm. A tiny voice warned her that she was getting ready to give away her whole self to this man, but still she didn't hesitate. She was a woman whose mate called to her and everything within her answered him.

He pushed her jeans and panties down together, at the same time dropping nibbling kisses on her ears, her neck, in the sensitive hollows near her clavicle.

"Tyler." Pickett squeezed the name out between her own hungry searches of his neck, his night-roughened jaw.

"What about Tyler?"

"He could come in here. We've got to go to the bedroom."

"Is that a yes?" With fluid strength Jax picked her up, swung her through the hall door. "I'm going to take that as a yes."

The sensation of being swept up in his powerful arms, clothed yet bare-bottomed shocked Pickett. It was wild and uncivilized. And she liked it.

She tightened her arms to pull her face level with his and opened her mouth on his, tasting his male urgency, aggressively demanding he come to her as she was coming to him.

Jax's tongue met hers with his own fierce demands as they engaged in a love duel. At the bedroom door, he elbowed the light switch. Never taking his mouth from hers, he stood Pickett next to the bed and pushed her onto its old-fashioned high mattress. Two flicks of those capable hands divested her of her shoes and one efficient tug removed the jeans.

Her bottom was just at the edge of the mattress and Pickett scrambled up on her elbows to scoot further back but Jax stopped her by grabbing her knees and pushing them apart, opening her to his gaze.

Jax liked to look. After her first shyness, Pickett had learned to enjoy offering him tantalizing glimpses, extending their love play by getting maximum use of the sexy underwear he'd bought. Waves of excitement would pass between them as they relished turning one another on.

What he wanted now was not play.

She was open, totally ready to receive him, and he was going to make love to her until she knew, now and forever that she was his. He was going to move within her until she couldn't hesitate as she had hesitated on the pier. Until that awful moment when he couldn't reach her, when he could only pray she had the courage to come to him, was dissolved. He opened his jeans and spread her soft folds with one hand, while he positioned himself with the other.

It was better, hotter, wetter, sliding into her tight fit than ever before. It was so good. Too good.

He froze.

"What the hell am I doing?" He pulled out, closing his eyes at the exquisite sensation, even as he denied himself. Unwilling to lose contact, body to body, he covered her, elbows locked to spare her his weight, their bellies touching.

"What's the matter?" Pickett's eyes were wide, blurred with passion and confusion. Where their bodies pressed together he could feel her heart thump in slow heavy beats.

"The condom. I could get you pregnant."

"God help me," she whispered, "I didn't think of it either." But still, she lifted her arms to pull him closer.

Jax slowly lowered his torso allowing her to take his weight. Long shudders ran through him as he waged a war between his need and his self-control. He rubbed his face into the valley between her breasts, then slid both hands underneath the damp sweater that in their haste had never been removed, touching, clinging to the soft mounds.

"I want to have a child with you, Pickett." His voice was ragged and shaking. "Maybe a bunch a kids. But not until we've got things settled between us. Kids need parents who are married and stay together. I mean it. I know being married to a SEAL is not a good deal for a woman. I love being a SEAL but it's not my whole life anymore. If you can't hack my staying in the Navy, there are other things I can do."

Pickett soothed her hands down the dense muscles of his back until she felt his breath—and her own—begin to slow. She smiled a wise-woman smile. It wasn't how she'd pictured bringing it up, but with Jax, things never turned out the way she thought they would, yet they always turned out okay. Now was the time.

"You know when you asked me to marry you?" She fingered the velvety hair at the base of his skull, "I've been thinking about that."

Jax stilled. Devoid of all expression he asked, "Are you going to change your mind?"

Pickett wasn't fooled by the poker face, not anymore. "Maybe…" She was teasing him, a little, but he deserved it. "I need to know some-thing first. Do you love me?"

Jax rose up, stiff-armed, over her. His black brows snapped together. "Good God A'mighty! Of course I love you! I told you I did."

Pickett blinked at his fierceness. "You did not."

Jax stood so abruptly Pickett had to scramble not to slide off the bed. As soon as he stood, his unfastened jeans began to slide down his legs.

"What the hell do you think has been going on?" He toed off one running shoe. His foot came free with a wet sucking noise. "I asked you to marry me!" He toed off the other shoe. "I want to live with you for the rest of my life!" He pushed down the jeans and underwear together but the damp denim clung to his legs, hobbling him. "I want you to be the mother of my kids," he grabbed a bedpost for balance, "Tyler, and all the kids we haven't had yet." He managed at last to kick his legs free. Naked from the waist down, he glared at her, then as an afterthought whipped his tee shirt off over his head.

Pickett felt her eyebrows climb toward her hairline. "That was saying 'I love you'?"

"I don't know!" Jax grabbed his skull with both hands, then eyed her suspiciously. "Is this one of those talks about love that women relish so much? Because I'm not sure I can do that right now. It's been a long hard day. Either you get it that I love you or you don't."

He paced, stalked, around the room for a minute, then turned around, grey eyes bright with cunning. "Wait a minute. If I say 'I love you' will you marry me?"

Pickett took her time lining up the edge of the duvet she'd pulled across her lap. "Maybe." She permitted herself a mysterious smile. "Why not try it and find out?"

Jax grabbed her shoulders so swiftly her head snapped back. "I love you, love you, love you, love you. Now will you marry me?"

"Yes. I love you too."

"Yes to what?"

"I will marry you, SEAL that you are."

"You will marry me?" Jax gave a shout of laughter then instantly sobered. He sat beside

Pickett on the bed, his face so close she could see the crystal flakes in his irises. "What about my being a SEAL? I've made up my mind, if I have to leave the Navy for us to be happy together I will, but you understand officers don't serve hitches. It could take a year or more for my resignation to be accepted. You'll be married to a military man for a while."

Pickett lifted her hand to his face, absorbing the soft prickles of beard, "I don't want you to leave the SEALs. Not for my sake. What makes you a SEAL is something innate to who you are, and I love who you are. I love you the way you are."

Jax nuzzled her hand, but his eyes remained troubled. "What about Navy life? I can't deny that there are hardships. I'll work to minimize the stress on our marriage as much as I can, but there'll be some things I can't change."

"I know." Pickett infused her voice with hushed comfort. She took his face in both hands, willing him to read the certainty in her eyes. "Before, when I told you no, you said I was a coward. And I was. I couldn't give a marriage less than everything I've got, so I wanted everything to be ideal before I took a chance. It broke my heart to turn you down, but I doubted I could succeed, and I couldn't face the possibility of failure.

"I was scared to jump from the pier tonight, too. So scared." Tears clogged her throat as the memory swamped her. She forced them back. "But as long as I focused on the fact that I was going to you, I could do it. Don't you see? I didn't think about jumping into the water. I thought about going to you in the water. It made all the difference." She took a deep breath and continued. "When I jumped off that pier tonight I suddenly knew I could go through anything, as long as I was going through it to be with you."

She touched his lips with hers in a kiss of promise that quickly turned to passion.

"Now," she whispered between nibbles and soft bites, "are you going to get those condoms, or am I?"

Jax liked lying in the dark beside Pickett, arms and legs heavy with satiation, waiting while sweet swells of contentment floated him closer to sleep.

Pickett smacked him across the rib cage.

"Hoy! That stung!" He rubbed his ribs. "What was that for?"

"Take back the crack about Mary Poppins."

Jax opened one eye. Pickett was lying on her back, arms crossed under her breasts, looking at the dark ceiling. It took a moment to remember what she was referring to. "I already apologized."

"You apologized for the bad language. But I didn't mind—you were only swearing because you were upset. The Mary Poppins crack was personal."

"I admire Mary Poppins."

"Yeah, right. Why, I'll bet she's even one of your heroes."

Jax pretended to think it over. "I wouldn't say hero. More of a fantasy." Okay, he was teasing her now. So sue him. Pickett, when she got all righteous, was irresistible.

Pickett made a rude sound. "Give me a break."

"Seriously. Corey and I used to fantasize about what it would be like to—you know—do her."

"Ee-yew." Pickett waved her hand in front of her nose. "I did not want to know that." She was silent for a minute, and Jax could almost hear questions begin to tumble around in her mind. She was so cute when her curiosity got the better of her.

She propped herself on an elbow to look into his face. "How could you?"

Jax moved a shoulder. "What can I say? Teenage boys think about sex pretty much all the time. You go through a lot of fantasy material." Pickett continued to look at him dubiously. "What's the matter? I'm telling you you're a fantasy come true for me."

"Hmm."

"That means you're thinking. Am I forgiven for calling you a Mary Poppins?"

"Are you sorry?"

"No." Jax caught her hand before she smacked him again. He scooped her propping elbow from under her, rendering her flat on her back again. He loomed over her. "Listen carefully because this might be the only speech I'm ever going to make on this subject.

"I love you. I hate that you can't swim, and that is going to change, but I love you anyway." Pickett started to interrupt. "Uh-uh. I'm talking. You're listening. You do remind me of Mary Poppins. You wade into messed up lives and straighten them out, just like she does. Like her, you're magic. Everything's brighter, richer, funnier, every dream is more possible when you're there.

"Some ways you're not like her though." Jax allowed himself a teasing smile. "Mary Poppins, after all, was 'practically perfect in every way.'"

Pickett hmphed.

"On the other hand, you turn me on way more than she ever did." Pickett made a grumbling sound and he relented. "Sweetheart, you're real. I love you so much. I'll do anything I can to make our marriage work, but I can't promise happily-ever-after, and more than most, you know what you're getting into. You have the guts to make hard choices. And no matter how scared you are, you always choose love.

"Mary Poppins isn't a hero to me. But you are."

"Oh."

"Yes, oh." Jax slid an arm under Pickett. Now that she had him awake again, he wasn't as satiated as he thought, but holding, just holding her, was good.

"All right," Pickett conceded at last. "But no more tirades when I don't come up to SEAL standards, okay? Us magical creatures don't like it."

Pickett scooted closer and nestled next to him on her side, one leg curled across his thighs. She stroked his neck for a minute with her soft, warm hand. He'd wondered the first time he met her if she really was that soft all over. She was. She snuggled into a more comfortable position with a sleepy sigh, then tapped his breastbone three times to get his attention.

"One more thing. Making one 'I love you' speech is not going to cut it. You are going to have to say it—in words—every single day for the rest of our lives."

Jax's stomach shook with silent laughter. That was Pickett.

He always knew she was gonna be high maintenance.

ABOUT THE AUTHOR

Mary Margret Daughtridge, a Southerner born and bred, has been a grade school teacher, speech therapist, family educator, biofeedback therapist, and Transpersonal Hypnotherapist.

She is a member since 2002 of Heart of Carolina Romance Writers, Romance Writers of America, and Romancing the Military Soul, an online writing group, and she is a sought-after judge in writing contests.